Also by Cathryn Grant

Cathryn Grant

MADISON KEITH

Ghost Story Collection - Volume 2

STONE COLD
DEADLY STREETS
LONELY GHOSTS

D2C Perspectives

This book is a work of fiction. References to real people, events, establishments, organizations, or locales are intended only to provide a sense of authenticity, and are used fictitiously. All other characters, and incidents and dialogue, are drawn from the author's imagination and are not to be construed as real.

Visit Cathryn online at CathrynGrant.com

Cover photography and design by Lydia Schufreider
Copyright © 2013

ISBN: 978-0-9896410-0-5

ABOUT MADISON KEITH

BOTH THE LIVING and the dead like to reveal their secrets to Madison. As the administrative assistant in the basement office of a suburban church, she gets plenty of opportunity to hear from both. Through it all, Madison offers up a steady stream of opinions on everything from the subject of religion and ghosts, to finding a soul mate.

The Madison Keith series includes:
FATAL CUT (#1)
SHALLOW WATER (#2)
UNHOLY CHILD (#3)
STONE COLD (#4)
DEADLY STREETS (#5)
LONELY GHOSTS (#6)
LAST CHANCE (#7)
EATEN ALIVE (#8)

Cathryn Grant

STONE COLD

A Suburban Noir Ghost Story

Published by D2C Perspectives

One

AT FIRST I DIDN'T realize that what I'd discovered was a human foot. The long bones of a foot can look an awful lot like a hand, if you're not familiar with all the details of skeletons, which I'm not. It sounds creepy, I know, but it really wasn't. At least not until they dug up the area around where I found the bones and there was an entire skeleton. The Sheriff speculated it had been buried there at least a year since all that remained was bone. The dirt was packed solid, as if the ground hadn't ever been disturbed. No one knew what made the foot bone emerge all of a sudden. Most likely an animal dug it up, maybe trying to bury his own bone or a small stack of nuts.

It wasn't how I'd planned to spend the long weekend visiting my best friend Renee and her husband in Oregon. Finding a body made the weekend go differently than we'd imagined. We set out to have a wonderful time in a stone house perched on a cliff overlooking the longest, flattest beach I'd ever seen — miles of sand and the ocean, stretching out forever. When I arrived on Thursday just before dusk, the horizon was shades of gray, water blending into pale sky.

I'd driven all day, which wasn't as difficult as it sounds. I left my San Jose condo at four a.m., so I was out of the Bay Area before commute traffic started. I hit the California-Oregon border just after lunch, and reached the area twenty miles south of Newport by dinnertime. It was a relaxing and beautiful drive because easily a third of that stretch of Highway 101 runs right along the coast. Not that I was spending a lot of time looking out at the water, I was watching the road. But still, I could feel it there, looking spectacular and peaceful. There are quite a few sections of 101 that wind through the redwood forest as well, which has its own kind of beauty. The thick, silent trees make me feel as if the world will survive.

There's nothing like sitting in a car all day with the iPod playing my favorite tunes and my mind wandering wherever it pleases. It wanders much further afield when I'm out of my usual environment, and that's one of about fifteen reasons why I love road trips. The other fourteen are: different food, meeting new people, passing through unfamiliar towns, stopping to hunt through thrift stores to find stuff I never would have found near home, seeing my friends who are usually at the other end of the road trip, getting spoiled by not having to figure out what to make for dinner, eating candy without feeling guilty because it helps me stay awake when I'm driving all day, getting time off work (even though

I love my job), seeing how goofy people can be (like the family that has a giant yellow *South Park* bus in the front yard of their small farm on a two-lane road in Northern California), seeing lots of horses which is something I never see in daily life, and watching the weather change as I go ... That's only eleven, but I'm sure there are more that I've forgotten.

Anyway, the drive was easy. Even though it took about twelve hours of actual behind-the-wheel time, it went fast. I didn't feel at all tired when I arrived.

The house where Renee and Mike were staying is about thirty-five years old, but it looked like it could have been standing around for two hundred years. You don't often see houses that are all stone. Of course, it wasn't constructed of stone like a castle, the stone was a facade. It's three stories tall and sits on a bluff. There are lots of rather small windows, not the massive picture windows you usually see on coastal homes, so it looks somewhat castle-like. The house belongs to Mike's Uncle and Aunt — Bill and May. They used to live there most weekends in the fall and spring. Mike's Aunt May spent entire summers there when her twin daughters were growing up. I guess they weren't fond of the winter storms, although some people visit the Oregon coast in the winter *because* of the storms. Mike also spent a lot of time there when he was a kid. His parents sent him up there for a few weeks every summer, once they'd exhausted the array of summer camps. Once he became a teenager and then went off to college, he didn't visit for about seven or eight years. Aunt May had died about a year ago — killed herself, actually — and Mike's cousins, Leila and Liz, lived there now. Since the cousins were gone for the weekend, Renee and Mike had invited me to visit. Renee and I had only seen each other once since she and Mike got married and moved to Portland, so I was very excited to catch up.

As I said, the house is on a bluff, about forty or fifty feet above the beach. It's surrounded by pine trees to the north, and a tangled garden of ferns and vines and trees, some fallen over as the result of storms, but still hanging on to life. A path leads into the garden and then to a grove of pine trees that has a big open space in the center, covered by clusters of branches so the sky is barely visible. I thought it was like a secret hideout, a place I would have loved when I was a kid. When they first showed it to me, Mike said it gave him the creeps, which I thought was a bit strange.

Once I arrived at the house and saw how dramatic it was in real life, more than had been obvious in the photos, I was filled with curiosity about the place. I wanted to know why such a misfit-looking house had been built on a coast that's lined with modern structures offering multiple layers of wide decks, and massive windows, homes designed to grab as much of that spectacular view as they can.

What is it about a view of the ocean that takes our breath away? Is it just because we don't see it all the time, or something about looking out and not seeing any evidence of human life? Because it's the same in the mountains or desert. Any time you can look out and see nothing but the earth itself, it's soul satisfying. It makes me think we're missing something, living crushed up against each other. Although, we can get pretty excited looking out at night on a city filled with skyscrapers, glittering with lights. So who knows, maybe it's only because we're looking at something so much bigger than ourselves, bigger than the car dashboard and the kitchen sink and office walls and computers and the inside of the grocery store that we stare at every day.

The house was such an oddity, it was almost as if they'd built the house for the ocean to look at them rather than the way it should be. Seeing the house in real life made me even more curious about why Aunt May had killed herself. I wasn't sure if Mike knew, but I was sure that the first chance I got, I would ask him. The very first chance. Not right after saying hello, but while things were still fresh, while they were showing me around.

I rang the bell and Renee opened the door immediately. She's tall with chocolatey brown hair and brown eyes and the longest, most slender fingers I've ever seen. Her feet are long and slender too. In some ways, so is her hair, it's long and thin, and on some people that might look lank, but on her it doesn't, it looks delicate and, like I said, slender.

She lunged at me and hugged me. "Are you hungry? You must be. You always are, and after that long drive!"

I dragged my duffel bag inside. Mike appeared around the corner. He hugged me with one arm and picked up the bag with the other. "I'll take this to your room first, and then we'll give you the tour."

"But dinner. She must be starving."

They looked at each other and smiled.

"How long is the tour?" I said. "I snacked all the way." I pulled my box of red vines out of my messenger bag. There were only three left. "And that's the second box. Not to mention cheese curls."

"I should have known," said Renee. "We'll do the tour first."

The entryway was long, narrow, and windowless. There wasn't even a window next to the front door or in the door itself. The walls were white, and the only artwork is a large, framed black and white photograph of the ocean on the wall to my left.

Mike returned and led me through the house. Renee followed. The ground floor consisted of the kitchen, living room, dining room, a guest bathroom, and a master bedroom suite where Mike and Renee were staying. The living room and dining room were side by side and looked out on the tangled garden and grove of pine trees that I already mentioned because I got ahead of myself.

The second floor had four bedrooms, each pair sharing a bathroom. Leila, one of the twin cousins, lived in one of the bedrooms on the ocean side, and Liz had one of the bedrooms on the side that faced inland. I would be sleeping in the bedroom that shared a bathroom with Leila's room. As Renee and Mike walked me through the house, I began to notice that every room was painted white and most of them had very little decoration on the walls — a large framed photograph here and there. The surfaces of tables and dressers were mostly free of the objects you normally see.

The third floor was the most interesting. It was one large room. There was a cluster of windows on three of the walls, all three feet wide and about four feet tall. It would have been a perfect place for one or two large windows. The side of the room near the stairs had a wood railing and was open to the floor below. There were a few chairs arranged in groups, one with a table and a game of scrabble in progress on top. A red telescope sat in front of the windows that faced directly at the ocean.

"I always wanted a telescope," I said.

Renee laughed.

"That's everyone's first reaction," Mike said. "But we hardly ever use it. Only when guests are here."

I walked to the telescope and put my eye up to the viewfinder. It was pointed at the strip between two of the windows. I moved it slightly and saw tree branches and only a glimpse of the ocean. I moved it again until it looked out over the water. A sailboat appeared close enough to clearly see the three sails and two people standing at the stern. I pushed the telescope gently to the left and saw nothing but water. Now I understood why it wasn't used very often. "There's not much to look at. The view is better just staring at the unmagnified water," I said. I moved away from the viewfinder and glanced at Renee.

"It's kind of the luck of the draw. In the spring, you can sometimes see the whales are migrating north. You just have to stand here a long time. Most people don't have the patience."

I could understand that. But I also thought that I'm the kind of person that does have the patience. "Can you see whales, or dolphins at this time of year?"

"Every so often you'll see a whale, but I've never seen a dolphin," said Mike. "There are quite a few sea lions." He walked over to the telescope. Mike's not super muscular and he's the exact same height as Renee. His hair is a similar color, so they look very good together and give off an air of being equal partners that's reflected in their bodies. Since I'm several inches shorter, Mike had to raise the telescope to peer through it.

"Sea lions are great," I said. "They always look like they're having fun, don't you think?"

"I never thought about it." He was still looking through the scope. I wondered what held his interest on that empty expanse of water.

Renee leaned against the wall. Her dark hair looked darker against the almost white paint, and her face looked dark because the light was behind her so I couldn't see her features very clearly. "I've always thought that," she said. "All they do is play, or climb out of the water and sunbathe."

I knew I'd be back up to this room at some point to spend some time looking through the telescope. It would be great to watch a sea lion swimming by with close up detail so I could see his whiskers and soulful brown eyes — a creature living in the frigid water, but as warm-blooded and full of life as I am. It makes you wonder how they stand it, out there with no bearings whatsoever, just swimming and swimming. I know their fat and fur keep them warm, but it looks so cold and so vast.

As we headed down the two flights of stairs to the ground floor, I said, "It's a strange house. It doesn't look like other beach houses."

"My Aunt liked medieval history. She wanted to live near the ocean, she liked walking on the beach, but she didn't like beach style houses. She called them piles of sticks. It's almost like she'd been influenced by the *Three Little Pigs*," said Mike.

I laughed. I love Mike. Not love as in I'm staking out my best friend's husband, but love as in he's so perfect for her, and he's so much fun, and I'm glad I like her husband because it would be terrible to not like the person your best friend decides to spend the rest of her life with. "The stone walls are cool, but I don't know why you'd want to build a house overlooking this amazing beach and put in all these tiny windows."

"She felt it wasn't safe to have big picture windows, that a storm would blow them out."

"Does that actually happen?"

"I don't think it happens here. Maybe if you live in hurricane country."

"Why did she kill herself? That's so awful."

Mike kept walking down the stairs. He shrugged one shoulder but didn't say anything.

We went into the dining room. Renee said she'd get the dinner. I offered to help, but she said she wanted me to sit down and relax. I reminded her I'd been sitting for twelve hours. She said, "Well you were concentrating, which is stressful. Besides, I want to surprise you with a grand flourish." So I sat.

Dinner was cioppino with sourdough bread. She made the cioppino herself, which was very impressive because I'd have no idea how to do that. She said it was easy.

During dinner I asked them all about Portland, how they liked Oregon, and their jobs. Mike works in high-tech. Since I used to be an administrative assistant for a high-tech company, I know how many hours those people put in, it's like they never get a day off with their smart phones and laptops following them everywhere they go, but he writes computer software and loves it, so he doesn't mind the endless hours. Renee is a pre-school teacher. After she talked about the school where she's teaching now, I told her about the child care center they're opening at *Central Avenue Church*. The childcare center had a rough start, since at first the church voted not to have it, but after a woman called them on their selfish attitude, and then was murdered, their views changed. If nothing else, they realized they should make better use of all that expensive real estate they own.

Before we were half-finished with our second bowls of cioppino, I heard the front door open. Mike got up and left his spoon sitting in his cioppino.

"His cousins," Renee whispered. "We thought we had the house to ourselves. They were supposed to go to Seattle, but they changed their minds. They called right before you got here and announced they were driving back."

"Why are you whispering?" I whispered back.

She smiled but it had an icy look to it. "Because usually I'm talking about them behind their backs, so I'm used to keeping my voice down."

"Why do you talk behind their backs?"

She looked up.

I turned. Two women who looked to be about five or six years older than me stood in the doorway. Seeing the twins made me think of my boyfriend, JD, because he's a twin. And, yes, I call him my boyfriend now. I don't know how many dates you have to have before some officially becomes a boyfriend, but it was easier than calling him, *the guy I'm going out with*, even in my own head. He seems like my boyfriend, although we haven't slept together yet. I didn't want to rush that, it has to be the perfect timing. I don't know if sleeping together is a requirement to call a guy your boyfriend. I don't think it is, but everyone views it differently. In my mind, if you're only going out with one person, then he's your boyfriend. At least if it goes both ways.

"Thanks for waiting for us to eat dinner," said the twin on the left. She wore low cut blue jeans, a shrunken tee shirt which showed her belly, sprinkled with goose bumps. Not surprising, since the sun had set and there was a good wind going along the edge of the bluff. Her short shirt also helped display the bar stabbed through her navel. I have a lot of piercings myself, but they're all in my ears — seven on the right side and four on the left. I also have a few tattoos, so it's not like I'm opposed to body art, but those bars through navels give me the creeps. So do tongue rings, and studs in the nose because I worry the other side is scraping the inside of your nose. I shivered and looked away.

Renee stood. "This is Madison. She drove all the way from California in one day, so I wanted her to get something to eat."

"You should have waited. You knew we were coming. It's rude, isn't it Mike?" Did she think Mike was going to attack his wife? She either didn't know him very well or was too caught up in her own sense of injustice.

Surprisingly, Mike said, "Sorry Leila."

Renee smiled. Ever so slightly she glanced at me and I knew she was saying, *see why I whisper?*

The other twin's name was Liz. Her hair was chopped off short around her neck in one of those styles that looks like it was randomly hacked off, leaving all these sticking out chunks and different lengths, but really is a very expensive haircut and takes time to style. She wore clothes similar to Leila's and their expressions were equally vacant. They were taller than Renee, who's five-nine, and they had the build of fashion models. Every movement was like a pose for the camera. Leila was thin, but Liz was even thinner. She looked like a pale shadow of her sister in several ways — blonder hair, hazel eyes to her sister's dark brown ones, more delicate skin, and a prominent collar bone and wrist bones.

I put my napkin next to my bowl and pushed out my chair.

"No need to get up," said Leila. "Since you drove all the way from California, we don't want to interrupt your dinner."

I smiled and stood anyway, and knew that as soon as Renee and I got a chance to be alone, there would be a lot of whispering going on. I couldn't imagine how she tolerated staying here with these two. Of course, that hadn't been the plan. I couldn't imagine how she managed having them in her life at all. Or at least the one — Leila — I wasn't sure yet about Liz, but if she lived with that twin all her life, she'd either have to be equally poisonous or seriously damaged.

They remained in the doorway and waited for me to walk across the room. As I reached to shake Liz's hand, Leila turned and spoke to Mike. "You'll take our stuff back to our rooms. Right, hon?"

Liz shook my hand, while Leila managed to fumble around and ignore me until the opportunity had passed.

They seated themselves at the table and looked expectantly at Renee. "What are you serving? I'm sure it's something a-*maze*-ing," said Leila. She turned to me, apparently now deciding I was worth some attention, if for nothing else than as an audience to her drama. "Renee is a fant-*tas*-tic cook. Or maybe I should say *chef*. She really should open her own restaurant. She's wasting her talent babysitting all day."

I looked up. Renee had disappeared into the kitchen. I didn't blame her. A moment later, Renee returned with two bowls of cioppino that she placed in front of Leila and Liz. "Why don't you chat with Madison and I'll clean up the kitchen so we can all relax after dinner."

"She's a teacher, not a babysitter," I said.

Leila flicked her hair over her shoulder. "Whatever. She's depriving the world of her talent. I bet she could become a celebrity. Besides, nannies are mean."

"She's not a nanny or a babysitter, and I don't think she wants to be a celebrity. Although she is a great cook."

"Are you arguing with us?" said Leila.

I put a clam in my mouth and chewed slowly. The next morning and a walk alone with Renee on the beach couldn't come fast enough. I thought I could plead out of the evening early — worn out from all that driving. Suddenly I actually did feel a little tired. I decided I could cut the evening shorter by going out on the back patio as soon as I could finish my meal. I'd smoke the third of my three cigarettes that I allow myself per day. Then I would spend enough time in the living room to be friendly, and as soon as I could, I'd escape to my room and send a text to JD to see if he wanted to Skype. I hoped they had a decent internet connection.

Two

THE NEXT MORNING it was drizzling, but while we drank coffee in the kitchen and stared out at all that gray — gray water, grayish sand, gray sky, trees with a gray tinge from all the mist — Renee assured me it was likely to change quickly. "The forecast is partly cloudy, only a slight chance of rain, so once this is past, there probably won't be much wind. Perfect for a long walk."

We both knew what a long walk would include — gossip.

Liz and Leila were still asleep. Or at least still locked up in their bedrooms, but I think Renee wanted to be cautious. It wouldn't be good to get caught with our heads close together, making catty comments about them. Once we were out on that seven-mile stretch of sand, we could talk as loudly and as long as we wanted to, without looking over our shoulders.

Renee pushed back her chair and went to the counter. She pulled the coffee pot off the burner. "I guess I better make another pot for the cousins. Do you want any more?" She lifted the pot to show me what was left.

"Sure."

A few minutes earlier, Mike had taken a few sips from his mug, and then left the room, saying he was going to go catch up via his laptop on what was happening in the world. I'd worried for nothing about the internet connection. It amazed me how good it was in this isolated spot, three miles from a tiny strip of restaurants, shops, and vacation homes interspersed with real homes, and miles from anything that could rightfully be called a city. I suppose the internet is everywhere. We can't live without it. The night before, after we went to our rooms, I'd chatted with JD over Skype. We planned to do the same on Sunday.

I was almost finished with my third cup of coffee, when the cousins came into the room. They were dressed as if they were going to the mall, Leila's long blonde hair blown dry and straightened with a flat iron, and Liz's styled with gel so it stood out from her narrow forehead. Their faces were spectacular with blush sculpting their cheeks and lots of shadow and liner on their eyes. Their high heels clicked on the white tile floor.

They scooted into the chairs at the head and foot of the kitchen table. "You are such an amazing cook, Renee. I can't wait to see what you whipped up for breakfast."

Given their ultra-slender figures, I was surprised they ate breakfast. Maybe it was a weekend thing, or someone-to-cook-for-you thing.

"I don't do breakfast," said Renee. She smiled.

"That's not healthy," said Leila.

Renee carried two mugs to the table and set them near me. She got the coffee pot and filled them but didn't bother to hand them to the sisters. "I seem to be holding my own on the health front. I usually eat a banana later in the morning."

"You really don't have any breakfast?" said Liz. She got up and walked around the table. She picked up one of the mugs and walked over to the counter, peering at the stove as if she suspected Renee was lying and the gas was really lit, ready to take on a pan full of eggs. "I'm starving."

"It's your house, you know where the cereal is. Mike brought some eggs with us and I think he stashed a bag of English muffins somewhere."

Liz and Leila didn't speak.

I pushed back my chair. "I think I'll go look around the garden."

"It's raining," said Leila.

"Just mist. I have a hood."

Leila shivered elaborately. "There's all kinds of vines and everything is overgrown. It's probably filled with spiders. Maybe even mice. Or rats." She smiled. She still hadn't picked up her mug of coffee. I wondered if she was so stubborn, she would rather let it get ice cold, waiting for Renee to put it directly in front of her, rather than lean forward and strain herself, reaching across the table. I suppose it was childish of Renee to not put the coffee in front of them, but I was pretty sure by now that she thought of them as Mike's problem.

I rinsed my mug and put it in the dish drainer.

"Aren't you going to eat?" said Liz.

"I'm in the banana crowd too," I said.

I smiled at their expressionless faces.

THE LIVING AND DINING ROOMS opened onto the back patio, so once I had my hoodie and UGG boots on, I could go outside without having to pass through the kitchen again. I was feeling a little disappointed that these two prickly people would be there all weekend, making me want to escape every meal, hoping that they'd find something else to do in the evenings. They were so dressed up. I hoped they planned to drive up the coast and look for something more exciting than their stone house, half hidden in a thick cluster of pine trees, looking out at the ocean through its narrow windows like someone squinting at the horizon. I didn't understand how they lived here all the time. They didn't seem the type.

The patio was slate. At the edge was a border of beach grass, trimmed so it looked like a normal garden plant, rather than growing wild and unrestrained. Past that, the yard turned to natural ground cover with a dirt path worn through it. The path split near the edge of the yard, one leg leading to the long flight of spindly wooden stairs that went down to the beach, and the other to the cluster of trees.

The path wound into the plants, and I followed it. Huge shrubs and viney, jungley-looking plants grew higher than my head. After about fifteen or twenty feet, it sloped down slightly and I had to duck to get under the low branches of several pine trees that touched each other. Past that was the open area Mike and Renee had shown me the day before. Pine needles covered the ground and the branches formed a natural roof. It was almost a perfect circle and standing in the center of it made me feel like a little kid. I would have loved to have a hideout like that when I was a kid. No one inside the house could possibly see you, and you could sit in that area, listening to the quiet, and never be found.

Not that I had to do a lot of hiding, since I was an only child, and since we lived in a rural area where the closest neighbor was a quarter mile away, and since I was home-schooled. I was actually the opposite, looking to be found most of the time. But there was still something in me, probably in most kids, that made me want to find secret hideouts. It made me drag sheets into the living room and drape them over chairs so that I had my own tent. I have no idea what creates that fascination, and no idea where it disappears to when we're adults. Or maybe it's still there, we just ignore it because we have lots of work and social obligations. Maybe it's the thing that makes people go into their offices and close their doors.

The grove was warm and inviting, like a circle of trees wrapping its arms around you, covering the dirt and exposed tree roots with its warm blanket of pine needles, soft and silky under my feet. It was comforting because the earth wasn't feeding itself with the stench of decay you usually get from other kinds of plant and animal death. Instead, it smelled dry and clean, with a hint of fresh, damp air. It struck me that the ocean didn't have the salt-water smell I was used to at home. Maybe because we weren't in a bay, but right on the coast where there's more wind and strong currents.

The trail started up again on the opposite side, but I decided not to pursue it for now. I hoped Renee was ready for a nice long walk.

As I turned to go back the way I'd come, a delicate breeze brushed across my cheeks, warmer than the breeze I'd felt outside the grove — wind that swept up from the beach, along the edge of the bluff. I put my hand on my cheek. My fingertips were cold and hard. The breeze laced through my fingers and although they remained stiff, I had the sensation of spring weather. The soft touch of rose petals and tulips stroked my cheek. I dropped my hand. The scent of pine needles had faded and I smelled nothing but pure, clean air. I turned to see if a space had opened up in the branches to allow wind to enter the tightly enclosed space. There were no openings. No piece of sky was visible, the branches and closeness of the trees was thick. Beyond that, vines and other plants crowded together as if they all needed each other to keep warm against storms moving in from the ocean.

I closed my eyes to see if the air against my skin grew more intense. It remained the same, but I heard something. The constant roar of waves crashing on the sand had subsided until it was more of a soft swoosh. I heard someone humming. My eyes popped open and I did a complete three-sixty degree turn, to see if anyone had joined me in the grove. I was alone. Still I heard the humming and it seemed to flow in the same rhythm as the breeze that continued to caress my cheeks and now my forehead and the tip of my nose. The humming wasn't a distinct tune, although it was melodic. Finally, I stopped turning and after a few minutes the breeze and the humming evaporated into nothing. All I heard was the increasing roar of the sea and the thud of footsteps on dirt.

Three

"MADISON?"

I PUSHED away the branches, ducked under one particularly large bough, and crept along the narrow path that was really no more than a gully through the vines and other plants covering the ground. When I turned the corner back into the proper garden, Renee stood on the leg of the path that led to the beach stairs.

"There you are. You disappeared," said Renee.

"Were you humming?"

She looked at me, her dark hair barely visible under the hood of her jacket. "Humming?"

"I heard humming. Inside that grove." I gestured behind me. "At least I think I did. Maybe it was the wind?"

"I've heard humming out here before."

"What is it?"

"I don't know. It sounds like someone trying to remember the tune to a song, but it doesn't all come out so it's only a few wandering notes."

I walked along the path. When I reached her side, she started toward the stairs. I followed. We walked down all eighty-five steps without speaking, concentrating, I suppose, on making sure our feet landed securely on each weathered board. The railing was thin and worn, pocked with holes, but the wood was satiny smooth from wind and salt and water. When we reached the beach, we took off our boots and socks and left them by the bottom step. That's one of the things I love about the beach. It's a place where you can leave your things, as long as they aren't super valuable — like a camera — and know that they'll be safe, shoes or a beach towel and chairs, no one will touch them because nearly everyone on the beach has left their own things behind when they go for a walk. At least that's how I assume it is, because I've never had my shoes stolen and I don't know anyone who has. I suppose thieves could walk along the beach the same as they prowl any other place, but maybe they don't. Maybe it's too much trouble. Walking on sand takes more effort than strolling on pavement, and there's really no cover under which a person can slip away unobserved.

We headed south without discussing our planned route. It might have been the wind that pushed us in that direction, although at some point you have to walk both north and south, so choosing to start with the wind at your back doesn't provide any real benefit.

"Can you believe those two?" said Renee.

"Are they always so ... strange?"

Renee nodded. "They're awful, but Mike's close to them — they spent so much time together when they were kids."

Renee hunched her shoulders and walked a bit slower. To our right, the waves crashed, one after another, as if they couldn't stop, tossing up white froth that was so bright, it looked like there was light under the water. We'd crossed the loose, dry sand, and started walking past the water line. The wet sand was firm, almost as hard as concrete. My feet were cold, but it felt good to be walking barefoot. Broken bits of shells, worn smooth by the water, and pebbles and small stones were scattered out all around us. I bent and picked up a red stone with a streak of green through it.

"There are agates on this beach. Up that way." Renee waved her hand in the direction we were walking. "Sometimes you can find them lying out here in the surf, but most of them collect in the area up there where the water pools when it comes out of the tributaries."

"I wouldn't mind finding an agate."

"It's easy. Look for stones that are sort of clear orange with white streaks on them."

I studied the ground, which slowed my pace. "So Leila and Liz are going to keep living here?"

"It looks that way," said Renee. "It has bad memories for Mike's Uncle."

"Because his wife is dead?"

"The house was her dream. The whole medieval thing, you know."

"Doesn't anyone know why she killed herself?" I don't know what's wrong with me that I had to ask that. My asking seemed cold, as if I didn't really care that Mike's Aunt was dead, that my first thought was wanting to know the dirt behind it more than I wanted to think about his feelings, but I was really curious.

"Not really. She'd been a little ... off for quite a few years, since the twins were kids, I think. She talked to herself all the time. Mike thought she was mentally ill, but his Uncle never mentioned it. He acted as if it wasn't happening, as if nothing was wrong."

"I suppose that might explain why Leila and Liz are the way they are. It would be awful to have your mother kill herself."

Renee nodded. "It would. But they were horrible before that."

"Really? How long have you known them?"

"Since the first time I came here — five years ago. They treat like we're their hired help. I don't mind them acting like the house belongs to them, because it sort of does. But Mike grew up coming here and his Uncle always told him he was welcome any time. I hate it that they seem to think I'm here to cook for them and to make sure they're entertained."

"They're almost non-human." I didn't really mean that literally, but I couldn't think of another way to describe it.

Rude or arrogant or self-absorbed or anything else didn't begin to fit.

"I know."

"Does Mike ever call them on it?"

"What's he going to say?"

"I don't know — *quit treating my wife like she's your personal chef?*"

Renee laughed. "I miss you."

"I miss you too."

"You should move to Portland."

"I'd hate all the rain."

"You get used to it."

I was sure I would not get used to it. I like being outside, and I don't like getting wet when I'm out there. Once in a while it's okay. Walking in the rain can be fun, especially if it's warm, but the idea of wrestling with an umbrella every time I stepped out my front door, or having the house or the inside of my office dark from all the clouds did not sound appealing. Although, if I could live in the stone house, or rather, a beachside house with more windows, and look out at the ocean every day, I think I could tolerate it. "So when did she kill herself?"

"Right after Mike and I started living together — about four years ago."

"And *no one* knows why? They think she just lost her mind? How would that happen? Do people lose their minds for no reason?"

"I think they do. But I don't know that she lost her mind, exactly. I think she was unbalanced, maybe … I don't know. I really don't know."

"I can't imagine what that must feel like. To know your mother can't be bothered to take the time to watch the rest of your life play out."

"I know."

"Do the twins ever talk about it?"

"Not to me. Remember, I'm the hired help."

I laughed, then stopped myself quickly. "How did she do it?"

"Hung herself."

"Oh. That sounds painful."

"She did it here, actually."

I paused and looked at Renee. "And you never mentioned that part?"

"It didn't seem important."

I thought it was very important. What if I was a superstitious person, what if the idea of anyone dying here was too upsetting and I couldn't bring myself to sleep under the same roof? Of course, none of those things were true, and I supposed Renee knew me well enough to realize that.

"Does it bother you?" she said.

"No. Not really. Where did she do it?"

"You're morbid," said Renee.

"I don't like to think of it as morbid. I'm curious. Aren't you?"

Renee turned and walked toward the water. The waves were further away as the tide continued to head out. Just ahead of us, four gulls stood on the wet sand, letting the water slide in over their feet, not twitching at all, as if they didn't even notice the cold or the fact that water was creeping up their legs. I wondered how deep it had to get before they would decide to take off. Once it touched their feathers? They looked like statues, staring out at the water. They were so low to the ground, I doubted they could see past the crest of the waves. Were they waiting for food to wash in and land at their feet, or were they enjoying the view? I wanted to think they were gazing at the slowly emerging sun, the beauty of the water, the ability to stand there without having any obligations, to simply bask in the pleasure of living at one of the most beautiful coastlines in the world. And it truly is. It turns out that the town just south of the stone house had been rated in the top ten vacation spots in the world by a famous travel guide series. The town is called Yachats. The first time I said the name, I said Yack-ats. She laughed. The *ch* is pronounced like an *h*, so it's really Yah-hahts, or at least that's how it sounds if you're from California. That might not be phonetically correct if you're from the northeast, or the south, or Chicago.

I followed Renee to the water. We tugged our jeans up to our knees and took a few steps closer. When the water hit my ankles, it wasn't as icy as I'd expected. Maybe because my feet were slightly numb from walking on the cold sand. "So are you going to tell me?"

She looked at me.

"Where she did it."

"In the room with the telescope. You saw how high the ceiling is, and those beams."

"So she nailed a rope to one of the beams? Is that strong enough to hold a hundred and something pounds? Unless it was a huge nail. Or a hook."

"God, Madison. Do you want me to take you to the police station so you can read the autopsy report? Although I doubt they'd give it to you."

"I'm just asking. It's frustrating to know a few details and not all of them."

"There's a space above one of the beams. It makes you think she studied it for a while, planning what she would do. She stood on a step ladder and pushed the rope through the opening so it could loop over the beam."

"Oh."

"Is that enough information?"

We waded further into the waves. They were fairly gentle. We stood for a few minutes. The only sound was the crash of water. Then one of the gulls took off and as it rose in the sky, it shrieked, presumably encouraging the others to follow.

"Hanging herself isn't the worst part of the story," said Renee.

A large wave rose up in front of us, rushing at us. We screeched and danced back, scurrying sideways like crabs across the sand with an uneven gait, trying to outrun the water, which is possible, but you really have to be quick on your feet and watch where you're going. We didn't quite make it, and the wave splashed up our thighs, soaking our jeans. As the wave receded, we slogged through the water, walking at an angle, moving closer to the dry sand.

"The most horrifying part is Leila and Liz."

"Did one of them find her?"

"Liz did."

"Oh. How sad."

"You would think."

"What do you mean?"

"She was completely nonchalant about it. Both of them were."

"Maybe they were in shock?"

Renee shook her head so hard, her hood slipped off. It bunched around the back of her neck but she didn't pull it back on. The sun was out now. The wind was stronger, but it wasn't the cold, biting kind. "They weren't numb and withdrawn or anything like that. They were …"

After we'd walked quite a ways, I started to wonder if Renee had forgotten she was speaking. She stopped and looked up at the houses lining the coast. She put her hand over her brow to block the sun, but it also prevented me from seeing her eyes. "They were giddy."

"Giddy?"

"That's the only word I can come up with."

"That could be nerves, or something. Denial? Are you saying they truly thought it was … exciting?"

"A little. Mostly they seemed wound up about the drama. Immediately, the minute the ambulance took her body away, they went shopping for black clothes."

"Okay …"

"They talked about it incessantly, but never cried, never said they missed her, never even, and this is the most freaky part, never asked why. When someone kills herself, don't people usually want to know why they did it?"

"Did she leave a note?"

"No."

"Maybe they knew why?"

Renee dropped her hand from her forehead and looked at me. She pulled her sunglasses out of her pocket and slid them onto her face. "Not that I know of."

"And her husband didn't know?"

"If he did, he never said anything."

"What did he think of his daughters' reactions?"

"I never really heard. I guess Mike spend lots of time talking to his Uncle. It was one of those things where the kids lived in their own world, separate from the adults. You know what I mean?" Renee reached into her other pocket and pulled out her phone. It vibrated in her hand. "Mike's calling. I forgot I promised him I'd help carry in some of the wood he's chopping." She shoved her phone back in her pocket. "Sorry. I don't know why he thinks he has to do stuff for them. If they can't manage to chop wood, they can hire someone. There's plenty of people around this area who are happy to do odd jobs like that."

"I'm going to keep walking. You don't mind going back alone, do you?"

"Of course not. You can walk forever here. Enjoy yourself, just don't go into the water, since you're alone."

"No worries about that." I grinned. "Well, maybe just my feet."

"You know what they say, never turn your back on the ocean."

"I know that."

"I had to say it." She wiggled her feet into the sand, like she was trying to root herself to the spot.

We said good-bye and I headed off down the beach, looking far out into the distance now that I was alone and not concentrating on what Renee was saying. Even though the sky was almost completely blue, with a few thin, high clouds, a light mist still hovered low over the sand, so it really wasn't possible to see the length of the beach. Renee had said this stretch was seven miles, but the mist made it appear as if it went on forever.

The gulls had moved further up the beach and gathered into a larger group. I passed three people playing Frisbee, and every so often I passed someone jogging, or walking a dog, or a couple holding hands. The sand was so hard that my feet hurt a bit, but there was something about the long expanse, nothing but flat sand, no streets to cross, no buildings, no obstacles whatsoever, that made me want to keep going. Even when I thought about turning back, the next immediate thought would be — *why not go a few more yards?* And there were always a few more yards.

Ahead I saw something lying in the sand, in the wet part, where the occasional wave came up and washed around it. At first I thought it was a boulder, but as I got closer, it looked too smooth for a boulder. I squinted, trying to figure out what it was. It had a pink tint to it. The closer I got, the more I realized how large it was, and I went back to thinking it was a boulder, all the roughness removed by the constant washing of the waves. It was pink and gray, mostly gray.

As I got closer, my heart beat faster. I had a sickening feeling that I knew what it was after all. I wanted to look, but I didn't want to look. It was becoming clear it was not a boulder or any kind of natural thing you'd want to see during a stroll on the beach. It was about two feet high at the thickest part and about six or seven feet long, maybe more, because it was curved around.

When I knew for sure what it was, I stopped walking — a dead sea lion. An odor drifted my way. I pressed my hand over my nose and mouth and tried to breathe through my fingers, although I didn't want air going into my nose at all, it smelled so bad. I also wanted to cry but that would make breathing even more difficult. I'd never seen a sea lion up close. It was enormous.

Out in the water, hundreds of yards from shore, they look sleek and lean and playful. This poor guy looked fat and formless. His eyes were gone. The minute I noticed that I looked away. His whiskers were still there. His flesh was mottled pink and gray with splotches of green.

I turned left and walked up to the dry sand so I could circle around him without getting near, without looking into those empty eye sockets. The body was so exposed, lying there with nothing around, decaying in plain sight. It seemed like such a humiliating way to die. Well, I didn't actually know how he'd died, but to be there after death, your body in all its crudeness, birds picking at it. Surely bugs were inside of it, possibly crabs. The more I thought about it, the more I felt like I couldn't keep walking. I didn't want it to be there, I didn't want it to turn into a pile of spoiled meat, but I supposed it was too late for that.

With my hand over the lower part of my face, wanting to look, but not wanting to look, I kept walking. Every step felt like a huge effort. Strolling along the shore was no longer something that made me feel alive and connected to the earth. Right then, I hated the earth, and the way it wants to get its fingers into every living thing, pulling it down into its arms. There's no escape.

I turned and made a wide circle around it again. Once or twice I glanced to my left, wondering why I felt I had to look when I didn't want to.

All the way back to the spot where the stairs from the

stone house reached the sand, I tried to push that poor sea lion out of my mind, but he kept coming back, as if he wanted someone to think about his fate. I thought there were people who took care of things like that, removed dead creatures from the beach, but maybe this beach was too vast, or maybe they had a backlog.

I climbed the stairs slowly, not wanting to stay on the beach, but not wanting to go back inside the house and face those obnoxious women. Part of me was wishing I hadn't come to Oregon. It was not working out to be the fun-filled trip I'd expected.

Four

DINNER THAT NIGHT WAS salmon with a light, creamy sauce, wild rice, and green salad with the freshest tomatoes I'd had in a long time. Unfortunately, I only ate two chunks of tomato and I could barely look at the salmon because the pink flesh with a thin gray layer looked exactly like the dead sea lion.

Leila wasted no time in asking me why I was such a picky eater. She took a sip of her wine and stared at me, waiting for an answer.

My stomach heaved. I didn't want to explain it. After less than two hours of total time with this woman, I knew she would find a way to twist it into something that was wrong with me. Still, I didn't want to hurt Renee's feelings, since she'd prepared such a perfect meal. And I was absolutely sure the salmon was fantastic. I picked at a few grains of rice, put them in my mouth, and took a tiny sip of water.

"Well?" said Liz. "Leila asked you a question."

"I heard her."

"You look like you're going to puke," said Leila.

"I don't feel that great."

"What's the matter?" said Renee. "If you're sick, you should stay in your room."

Normally I would have thought she was concerned. I knew in my head that she sounded snappish because she was tired of the vitriolic atmosphere that hovered around Leila and Liz. I knew she probably didn't feel that great herself, going to all that trouble to make a delicious dinner while I skipped lunch and napped all afternoon. I hadn't explained to her what was wrong. I don't know why. I think it might have been because I was so sad, and at the same time felt that I might be over-reacting. I couldn't help it. I knew that Leila and Liz would accuse me of being overly sensitive and dramatic and make me feel worse.

My eyes teared up, because even though I knew all of that, Renee sounded harsh and cold and slightly angry with me. "I saw a dead sea lion on the beach. It was decaying, and it upset me. Maybe more than it should have." I bit on my lip before I blurted out a description, comparing it to the salmon that was covered with the delicate sauce that looked similar to the wet sand shifting around the edges of the sea lion's rotting body.

"You're awfully squeamish," said Leila.

"Not really."

"Things die," she said. "People die."

The story Renee had told me that morning came rushing

back as if Leila had spilled her glass of wine across the wood table. I'd forgotten all about it after I saw the sea lion, so obsessed with his degrading experience, exposed to the elements and anything or anyone who wanted to pick at his flesh. "Yes, they do," I said. "And it's upsetting. Especially when you see it up close."

"Why?"

I didn't even know how to answer that. What was wrong with her? With both of them. I wanted to blurt out something about their mother, but I wasn't sure what that would be. Had they lost their minds? They seemed normal enough, except when they started talking. They were beautiful women, with their blonde hair, perfectly cut so it moved like silk, except when Liz put gel in hers. They looked sort of pleasant when they smiled. It wasn't as if their eyes were blank and lifeless, or there was too much white showing around the iris so that they looked mad. Some of their comments could be written off as bitchy, lots of people are like that — bitchy women, men who are jerks. But these two were way at the end of the scale, and in some ways, they scared me.

"Why is it upsetting?" said Leila.

Renee's chair was pushed slightly away from the table, so she didn't have to move it further to stand up. She picked up her wine glass and went into the kitchen. I was glad. If she wasn't looking at me, watching to see if I betrayed her confidence, it would be easier to smack these two down. I wasn't sure if the things she'd told me actually qualified as a confidence, but I try to be careful about repeating what others tell me, if it's something personal. "You don't think it's upsetting to see something dead? That's a normal human reaction."

"You said you over-reacted." Leila smiled at me like I was a two-year-old.

"I said I might have. And what I meant is that it's stuck with me and made me feel sick all day. But I guess I'm more sensitive than average."

"Who are you, Emily Dickenson? A woman with a delicate constitution?" said Leila. She smiled again, a very gentle turn of her lips, as if she wanted to assure me she was complimenting me by likening me to Ms. Emily.

There was no point in saying anything more. She clearly had some goal to upset me, or make me look silly. Or maybe not either of those things. I really couldn't figure out what she was trying to do, but despite my better instincts, I couldn't keep my mouth shut. I usually can't. Maybe we were more alike than I'd realized, because she didn't seem to be able to keep her mouth shut either. Mostly, I kept talking because I really wanted to understand the lack of concern over death, and not really the sea lion's death — their mother's.

I had to figure out a way to turn it around. Maybe lots of women are vicious, blood thirsty, virtual fangs protruding over their lower lips, but if they are, they don't show it quite so easily. "It was very upsetting, that's all." Because Leila dominated the conversation, which was more like an interrogation, I hadn't looked at Liz for a few minutes. I glanced in her direction and saw her lip was shaking and her nostrils were pinched as if she'd sucked in air and hadn't let it out. The edges of her lower eyelids were pink. For a moment I thought she would cry, but she turned her head away.

"Can we talk about something else," said Mike. "I want to enjoy Renee's amazing dinner, not listen to a cat fight."

I think we'd forgotten he was there. He hadn't spoken since well before Renee left the room. He leaned back in his chair. I wondered why either one of them had thought it was a good idea to invite anyone to this house if there was even the remotest chance the twins might be there. Or was there something about me that had set them off? I was fairly sure that wasn't the case, though. Renee had already told me they were horrible, and neither Mike nor Renee seemed surprised by their behavior.

Mike looked past me. I turned. Renee stood in the doorway leading to the kitchen. "Does anyone want dessert? I made brownies." She walked into the room and passed behind my chair. She stopped and put her hand on top of my head. "Do you want to go lie down again? I can wrap this up for you."

I nodded and felt her hand move with my head. She kept it there for a moment longer, then reached around me and picked up my plate. I was grateful for her effort to defuse things, and grateful that she wasn't insulted. But I didn't want the twins to think they'd beaten me down. Even more, I had to know what was wrong with them. I decided to stop the pretense. This wasn't about the sea lion at all. Not that I knew what it was about, but since Leila clearly had no concern for my feelings, why was I being so polite, so hesitant? "I heard from Renee that your mother passed away. I know it's been a while, but I wanted to tell you I'm really sorry for your loss."

Leila, seated across from me, looked directly into my eyes as if she was waiting for me to cross a line by asking why she was so casual about her mother's suicide. But her gaze was full of knowing that despite my desire to match her outrageous attitude, it was my line and I wouldn't cross it. Liz was to my left. I had that self-conscious awareness of the side of my face that you get when someone is staring, as if there's actual heat coming from their optic nerve onto your skin.

"No need to be sorry," said Leila.

"It must be awful, having your mother die like that."

"You can say it. She hung herself."

"Did you have counseling? To help with your feelings?" I said.

"Why would we do that?" said Leila. "And why do you care? You don't even know us. It sounds a little voyeuristic."

I knew I should give up. I wasn't going to win. "I don't mean to be cruel, but it seems like I was more disturbed by that sea lion than you were about your mother."

Leila shrugged. Her hair slid over her shoulders. She put her hand behind her neck and flipped her hair back where it had been. "Why are we talking about this?"

"You didn't understand why I'm so upset about a dead animal and I don't understand why you give the impression you could care less about your mother."

The strange thing was, despite how awful my words sounded, neither of them reacted much. Leila didn't look surprised that I'd crossed that line after all.

Mike pushed his chair away from the table. The legs scraped the wood floor. "I thought you were going to lie down, Madison."

"I am." I stood and walked to the doorway that opened into the hall leading to the stairs. Renee walked in the opposite direction, carrying my plate. Mike followed her. I felt like I was in some kind of surreal stage play, or one of those play-acting games — a murder dinner party where you each take on a role. Nothing seemed solid, most of all Leila and Liz.

Mike closed the kitchen door, and I figured this was my last chance to find out what was going on without really upsetting my friends. "Did your mother hurt you or something? Were you relieved that she killed herself?"

Leila smiled. "You want us to feel like it's our fault. That we were so awful she couldn't stand to be around us any more."

"I didn't say that."

"It's what you think. It's what everyone thinks, you're just the only one who says it out loud."

"How do you know what people think?" I said.

"I can see it on their faces." Leila looked at her sister.

I turned to look at Liz. She was also smiling.

I really didn't know what else to say. It was so confusing my head felt like it was full of soda water, bubbles popping, my view of the room getting slightly dark around the edges. I couldn't understand how Mike and Renee could bear to be around them for five minutes, much less how they'd managed to maintain some kind of weird, phony relationship all these years.

I backed toward the door, searching my brain for something to say, trying to make sense of their smiles. If I hadn't been feeling ill, and now slightly weak from not eating anything since breakfast, I would have considered driving home right then. The best alternative was to go to bed. It was possible my food-deprived state was making me distort the conversation. If it had been as horrible as it sounded to me, wouldn't Mike have done something instead of leaving the room? I wanted to slide under the cool sheets, pull the comforter up to my chin, and drift into oblivion. I was so tired, I wondered how I'd make it up the stairs.

"We hope you feel better," said Liz. "A good night's sleep will help."

Maybe they did know what people were thinking.

Five

THE MINUTE I LEFT the dining room my head stopped spinning and the nausea settled itself, as if the soda water that seemed to fill my head a moment earlier had poured from my brain down into my stomach. Instead of going to my room, I climbed to the third floor.

The observatory was the best part of the house. The white carpet and white walls and pink-tinted beige wicker furniture provided a soothing atmosphere. The glossy red of the telescope stood out against all that white and sand like cherry lipstick on a dead woman.

It was nearly sunset and I was surprised no one had closed the blinds because light poured into the room. Although I suppose when everything is white and beige, there isn't much that can fade. I wanted to use the telescope but thought I should relax for a minute to make sure my stomach was truly getting back to normal. I sat on the sofa and looked at the narrow windows.

There was a bowl of stones and shells on the glass-topped coffee table. Across from me, near the stairs, was a small bookcase half full of books, a few magazines stacked in the empty space on the top shelf. A table at my left had the scrabble board with the same tiles laid out as I'd seen the day before. I wondered how long they'd been there. I couldn't imagine coming up to this room with its view of the ocean, the telescope, and the soothing piano music playing softly from hidden speakers, and wanting to bend your head over a scrabble game.

The sun was moving quickly toward the line where sky meets water. The sky was a deeper blue, the clouds pink, and the light coming into the room was no longer blinding.

I stood and went to the telescope. I tipped it so the eyepiece was at the right level and closed my left eye. Looking through the long tube distorted everything. I was able to move it so the setting sun wasn't even visible, which made the water and the sky look darker. A gull sat on the top of a swell in the water, so magnified that even the small hole in his bright orange beak was sharp and clear. Everything was so close, I had the feeling that I was sitting in a boat nearby.

I moved the telescope to the left, further still from where the sun was now dipping its toes in the ocean. The water seemed to be moving past, and the feeling that I was sitting on top of it increased. I hoped it didn't make my stomach start rippling in time with the tide, but so far so good.

My brow ached from pressing it against hard plastic and

from staring so long with just one eye. I closed my right eye for a few seconds and when I opened it, I saw a woman standing on the water. I jumped back and knocked the telescope. It swung up and bumped my nose. There wasn't any blood that I could feel, but it hurt. There couldn't be a woman out in the middle of the water. Lack of food and my disorienting conversation with those crazy twins was making me hallucinate.

I looked out the window without the aid of the telescope and saw nothing. There were a few clouds that had settled low over the water. The pink had changed a grayish purple tinge, so I figured that's what I'd seen. I put my eye to the scope again and nudged it further to the left so I wouldn't fixate on the same spot. The woman was right there. She wore a large sun hat. She held the hat in place with her left hand as if she was afraid it was going to blow off her head, even though there was no wind blowing at her clothes or tugging at the brim of her hat. Her shoulders were bent forward as she peered through the waves at the ocean floor.

I moved away from the telescope and went to the sofa. I thought about going to get Renee to find out whether she could see the woman, but the possibility of encountering the twin monsters kept me seated. I closed my eyes and leaned my head back. I must be imagining things. I definitely needed food, although I didn't feel all that hungry. For several minutes, maybe more, I sat with my eyes closed. The rest of the house was silent. I wondered where they'd all gone. I supposed Renee and Mike were in the kitchen cleaning up, but then wouldn't I at least hear the occasional sound of water moving through the pipes? For all I knew, Leila and Liz were still at the dining room table, like delicate spiders, waiting for unsuspecting prey to walk into the room so they could attack, fangs out, piercing delicate skin, injecting their poison. I shivered.

Finally I got up and went back to the telescope. I figured it had been enough time that whatever combination of setting sun and clouds I'd seen had moved on. Now I would be able to look out and not imagine a woman walking across the surface of the water as easily as if she was strolling through a meadow filled with short, soft grass.

The telescope seemed slightly unfocused when I first put my eye up to it again. I adjusted it. The woman was still there. The apparition couldn't possibly be a low cloud formation over the water. She wore a long sundress. The hem dragged through the swell of the waves as she walked. I tried not to blink as she moved across the liquid surface. I could see her feet lifting and stepping forward as if they were hitting solid ground. Although the image was quite distinct, I had another flash of doubt, insisting that I was hallucinating.

Time dissolved as I watched her walk back and forth. It wasn't clear whether she was pacing or looking for something, or someone. Each time she changed direction, I had a different impression. When she headed south, she seemed languid, moving with a gentle swaying. Then she'd turn north and lift her head, staring out across the vast, endless sea, straining forward. Then she would look down as if she was trying to peer through the waves for something below the surface.

The bone around my eye started to ache, and my neck was sore from holding it in a steady position for so long, but I didn't want to turn away. When I'd walked away from the telescope a few minutes earlier, I'd hoped to see nothing when I looked again. Now, I worried that if I stopped watching, the woman would disappear. Her trudging back and forth as if she was wearing down the fibers of the living room carpet, or creating a dirt path like the one that led through the wooded area mesmerized me. If she was a ghost, was it her voice I'd heard humming when I stood in the grove?

I decided she probably wasn't going anywhere. I stepped away from the telescope. Once again, I went to the window to see if I could catch a glimpse of her without the assistance of the telescope. There was nothing. Not even the faint shimmer of her straw hat.

When I'd first seen her, I'd assumed I was seeing a ghost. But now that I knew for sure that she was only visible through the telescope, I was confused. It wasn't that the telescope was pointed at a spot impossible to see with the naked eye. I moved closer to the glass until my nose was pressed against it, straining to see across the distance. The windows were clean, except for the part that had now been smudged by my nose. Nothing broke the surface of the ocean.

I backed away from the window and stared at the telescope. Was the ghost only visible through the lens? Was there something even stranger than a ghost — a telescope capable of seeing an event from the past, or the future? That sounded crazy, even in my own head. I ran my fingers through my hair, lifted it off my neck, and let it fall down my back. My reflection appeared on the glass. I looked paler than usual, although that might have been aided by the white and sand tones behind me, soft around the edges.

"Are you feeling better?"

I saw Mike's reflection appear beside mine at the same time I heard his voice. I turned. "I think so. I'm light-headed but I don't feel as nauseous any more." I realized it might be that I felt better because I hadn't thought of the sea lion all this time. But even as that memory skidded back through my mind, the sick feeling didn't follow on its heels.

"Were you using the telescope?"

"How did you know?"

"I can see the height's been adjusted."

I didn't know he was such an observant guy. I waited, hoping he'd keep the conversation rolling, because I didn't want to say anything about the woman. I needed time to digest it. That's somewhat contrary to my usual tendency to blurt out whatever drops out of my brain onto my tongue, but when it's something related to ghosts, I'm learning to be somewhat cautious. Not everyone believes in them, and if you don't approach it the right way, they'll dismiss you as gullible or slightly off balance. And then they'll disregard other things you say because they've pegged you as someone who is disconnected from reality.

Mike stared at me, and I wondered if he'd seen the ghost and was waiting to hear my reaction. Although I'd known Renee for years, I had no idea where she stood on the matter of ghosts, and I couldn't begin to guess what Mike might think of the subject.

It turned out his thoughts were in a completely different place.

"Sorry you had to be here when my cousins are around."

"No problem. It wasn't like I expected to be the guest of honor or something."

"They can be abrasive."

Was he kidding? Those two, especially Leila, were so far beyond abrasive, I couldn't think of how I'd describe them to JD when we Skyped the next day. I'd meant to send him a text just to say hi, but then I saw the sea lion and the whole day went downhill from there.

"I hope they didn't hurt your feelings," said Mike.

"I have thick skin."

"So does Renee, but they get to her."

"What about you?"

"I'm used to them. They were difficult as far back as I can remember."

"Difficult how?" I moved sideways and sat on the couch. I let my flip-flops fall off and put my feet on the glass-topped table. I supposed they would leave smudges, but I really wanted to stretch out. I think I'd been holding myself stiff all evening, trying not to aggravate my nausea, and not being very successful.

Mike sat in the chair facing the couch. He kicked off his athletic shoes and put his feet on the table. "My Aunt could never handle them."

"Do you think that's why she killed herself?"

"I don't think so. But she hired a Nanny when they were pretty small. She spent hardly any time with them."

"What did they do?"

"They refused to talk to anyone but each other. They repeated whatever any adult said. Constantly. Verbatim."

"Don't lots of kids do that?"

"For an afternoon, or on and off for a few months. They did it for nearly a year. Every. Single. Word."

"That sounds beyond annoying."

"They did awful things. They hacked off their mother's hair when she was sleeping. They threw up all the time, as if they were born knowing how to make themselves puke."

"Didn't they get in trouble? Put in time out, or something?"

"Sure. But they just laughed. And then mimicked whatever was said to them. Nothing fazed them. They just didn't care if everyone hated them. They didn't care if their mother plucked out all her eyebrows because she was so upset."

"Renee didn't mention the eyebrows."

"She doesn't know everything."

"Why didn't your Aunt or Uncle do anything?"

"You're not listening to me. Nothing worked."

"Didn't they send them to therapy?"

He folded his arms across his chest. "Not that I know of."

"Renee didn't tell me any of that stuff, just about their bizarre reaction to their mother's suicide."

"Renee hates them. She's angry that they're here while you're visiting."

I stared at him. "Why do you even come here?"

"I love it here. In spite of everything. You can see why." He stood and walked to the window. "It has some kind of hold on me."

It was getting dark and the ocean was hardly visible, but Mike stared out anyway, as if he was seeing something. Maybe he was seeing something from the past. "I think, at first, I was flattered that two older girls wanted to play with me when I was so much younger," he said. "At least that's what I assume was in my mind."

"I can see that."

"Then they got mean. They ganged up on me. We played hide and seek and they left me hiding for hours. I was too stupid, the first few times, to realize what they'd done. And I knew they were good hiders and I wanted to win, so I stayed hidden until my bladder couldn't stand it. Other times, they tied me up and…"

When he hesitated, I wondered why he was telling me this.

He continued talking. The words rushed out, as if he had to say everything at once or it would be too late. "They tied me up and put duct tape over my mouth and left me alone in that grove of trees. I'd be there for hours. They poured milk on me. It soaked into my clothes. My shirt stuck to my skin and it felt like I was covered in slime. They found stray cats and brought them into the grove. They pulled up my shirt and poured the milk in a puddle on my stomach and let the cats lick it off. If I cried or even whimpered or moved, the cats growled. Leila and Liz just laughed. Then they'd leave and the milk would go sour and I'd stink. Sometimes beetles crawled on my skin and I would moan, hoping someone might hear me. It seemed like they knew when I was worn out and couldn't cry any more, or was on the verge of wetting my pants, then they'd finally come back and let me go."

It was the kind of story a person holds inside all his life. But I didn't understand, if it was so easy to talk about now, why he'd never told Renee. I suppose it didn't put him in the best light — that he hadn't fought back. Still, why was he suddenly telling me? I'd spent time with both of them before. Of course, the twins hadn't been there and the subject hadn't come up. I didn't want to hear any more, for two reasons. The first because what he'd told me so far was upsetting enough, and I was already unsteady over the sea lion. And second, I didn't want to know something about Renee's husband that she didn't know. Because then what was I supposed to do? Tell her? Not tell her and feel like I was keeping a secret?

"Why did you put up with it?" I couldn't decide whether he was a loser or a victim of abuse. "And why are you telling me this?"

His back was toward me and I continued to wonder what he saw outside the window in all that darkness. "They're older than me. I was an only child. Who would I tell? My Aunt expected the Nanny to take care of everything. My parents weren't around. To be honest, I don't really remember. Maybe I was just scared that something would happen if I did."

"So why are you telling me?"

He turned. "I don't know why I'm telling you. You're always a good listener. You don't judge people. I can't tell Renee, she'd be even angrier. And maybe because I don't know why I put up with it and I don't know why I put up with it now, and I don't know why I even come back here. It's as if that part of my life is the most significant part. Maybe that's when I felt most alive. Their torture burned it into my DNA or something. Like I said, the place has a hold on me."

I did not want to hear this. "How old were you?"

"Four."

"Liz and Leila?"

"Nine."

"I guess most little kids are intimidated by older kids."

"It wasn't only the age difference. And it wasn't something about a little kid discovering sex, getting excited about older girls over-powering me or something perverted … don't think that." He stepped closer. I could see his eyes, pleading, the pupils dilated from staring into the darkness.

I wasn't so sure I agreed with his conclusion, but I didn't say anything. It was his job to sort out his thoughts and feelings, not mine. I really, really did not want to know anything more. I just hoped that when he did sort it out, he'd talk to Renee about it. Not that I have any experience to draw on, but I don't think a marriage can work all that great, or be that satisfying, if you're keeping secrets from each other. At least if you're hiding something that had a huge effect on you. I know I sure don't want that kind of marriage.

"It was their confidence, I think. Their lack of fear. They weren't, still aren't, afraid of anything or anyone. It's quite powerful."

"I suppose." I didn't think I'd call it powerful. I'd call it scary, almost terrifying, but obviously he had some kind of childhood affection that caused him to see them in a different light than I did. A distorted light.

I stood.

"I'm sorry to be going on and on," he said. "You probably want to go to sleep, since you weren't feeling well."

"I'm fine now. But I'm ready to go to bed."

"Do you need anything to eat? There's bottled water in your room."

"Water's enough. I'm still not hungry. I'm a little woozy … I feel like I'm seeing things."

He narrowed his eyes, like he knew what I was talking about, but he didn't ask what I thought I'd seen. I was sort of glad. I half wanted to talk about it, and half didn't feel like explaining it. He was focused on the here and now, or at least the here and now of his childhood. I didn't need to yank the conversation into supernatural territory.

I walked to the stairs.

"I think I'll stay up here for a while," he said. "Sleep good."

"I plan to." I walked down the stairs. The rest of the house was dark and deathly quiet.

Six

I DIDN'T FALL ASLEEP until about ten-thirty, partially because my brain would not stop inspecting what Mike had told me.

When I first started tossing and turning, I thought about going outside for a cigarette. I'd had one after dinner, but I was below my quota of three for the day. Smoking would calm me, might even help me fall asleep, although supposedly the drug I'm embarrassed to admit that I'm addicted to — nicotine — should have the opposite effect. I wasn't sure if it was the ocean air that had weakened its grip on me, or the sea lion and the resulting nausea. Probably that. But it was cold and quite dark, and I figured it was good practice for quitting to not rush off to have one every single time I thought about it. Especially since it wasn't a genuine craving, or desire, just a thought passing by.

I didn't like it that Mike was keeping a secret from Renee. Not that it was any of my business, I just didn't like knowing something about him that she didn't know. I don't think it was a secret in the sense that he was hiding something from her, or lying, but still, it was there. Why did he have to tell me? What happened that made him suddenly start giving me all that unwanted information? I'd rarely talked to him one on one. When we did have conversations between just the two of us, it was small talk. Was his sudden revelation, his uncharacteristic compulsion to talk to me, also an effect of the ocean air?

After flipping from my back to my side to the other side, I got up and sat in the chair near the narrow window. I wrapped an extra blanket around my legs and drank an entire bottle of water in about eight gulps. I thought about opening my laptop and going online to see if JD was around, but I didn't feel like talking about what I'd seen on the water, or the sea lion, and definitely not about Mike, so there was really no point. Although I missed him.

I wondered whether not wanting to tell JD any of those things about my day was a bad sign. Did it mean I was keeping secrets from him? I would eventually tell him about the sea lion. And definitely about the ghost, at least I was ninety-five percent sure it was a ghost. What else would she be? I didn't know if I'd tell JD about Mike and the weird hold his twin cousins had on him, that those girls tortured him and he never did anything to fight back. Even now.

Eventually my thoughts stopped running and slowed to an easy jog and then a quick walk. I was sliding back under the layer of blankets when I heard Leila's voice on the other side of the wall. I'd had the impression from the silence of the house that the place was well soundproofed, but apparently not. Or maybe she was talking super loud on purpose … because she was talking about me.

"She's a drama queen," said Leila.

"Totally," said Liz.

"Can you believe how she went on about that sea lion?" said Leila. "Oh. Oh, Oh. I can't possibly eat dinner, my poor sensitive tummy," she continued in a high-pitched voice, which was nothing like mine because mine is more of the alto variety. "You'd think she'd never seen a dead animal before."

"Maybe she hasn't."

"She's a little naive. Or at least she pretends to be."

I rolled onto my back to be sure I heard every word clearly. It's not that I make a habit of listening to private conversations, but of course I was curious. If nothing else, I wanted to understand what was wrong with these two. Although why I cared is a good question. I just did. And I wasn't doing anything wrong, I hadn't snuck up on them, and I wasn't someplace where I didn't belong, listening in. I was in my own bed and if it didn't occur to them that I was right on the opposite side of the wall, that was not my problem.

"Why do we think she's pretending?" said Liz.

That was odd. Why would she say *we* instead of *you*, as if she expected her sister to tell her what to think? As if she assumed, before she heard the reason, that she would agree? I wasn't sure if other twins spoke that way, or it was another example of how odd they were. JD didn't talk about his twin brother as if they had a single brain. Quite the opposite.

"She's that kind of person."

I sat up in my bed. How unfair. She knew nothing about me and I am most definitely not the kind of person who pretends to be someone she's not. And why would I pretend to be naive? Maybe I look at things simplistically, or I try to focus on the good side of people, so I might seem naive, but it's not that at all. Naive means you don't get how people really are, how the world really works, and I totally get that. More than a lot of people.

"Then what's she up to?" said Liz.

"We haven't figured that out."

So, they both talked as if they were a single entity. I wondered whether they were aware of it. I hadn't noticed it earlier. Possibly they reserved it for when they were alone. Although they were so unselfconscious about it, the words just flowed as if they weren't listening to what they were saying.

The bed springs squeaked as they moved from where they'd been sitting.

"She doesn't belong here," said Liz.

"Not at all," said Leila

"How can we be rid of her?"

Wow. They went right from not wanting me around to getting rid of me? And why? I hadn't done anything to them.

They seemed sour toward me the minute they walked into the room while I was eating my cioppino that first night.

"She brought her here. She should take her away."

I shivered. I don't like to be melodramatic, but now they sounded downright demonic. I assumed *she* referred to Renee. Thinking about what Mike had said about their childhood games, I wondered if they longed to go back to those days when they had Mike all to themselves.

"She was literally sick about the seal. We could leave something else for her to find."

"That's an idea."

Their voices blended into one. What they said was so vile, my brain couldn't wrap itself around trying to distinguish who was speaking. It seemed as if it didn't matter, since they appeared to view themselves as a single person, and since their attack on me came from a single mind. When someone is planning to deliberately do something to upset you, that gets the upper hand over the finer details of voice inflection.

"But not something too terrible."

"Well of course not."

"But something that will make her really sick."

Someone giggled. Then the other one giggled.

My head ached from listening to the conversation. It was starting to sound like someone talking to herself. There was nothing I could hang on to. For all I knew there was a third person in there with the same voice and I was listening to a whole crowd. My brain felt like it was sliding sideways, trying to find a phrase or inflection to pin to Leila or Liz.

"She was up in the observatory, you know."

"Doing what?"

"Talking to someone."

"Well it wasn't *her* because she was cleaning up the kitchen."

At least that phrase let me know which *her* they were talking about.

"So it must have been him."

"Are you sure?"

"It must be."

"He didn't tell her anything, did he?"

"It's possible. But I don't think he would."

"Do you think she saw her?"

"That's possible too. She's very nosey, and she seems like the type."

Now my skull felt like it was going to split open. I had no idea who was saying what and couldn't make sense of what they were talking about. I wanted them to shut up so I could go to sleep. At first it had been interesting, even though it was upsetting. Now it was like insects crawling around on your bare skin, creeping up your nostrils so you start smacking at your face to make them stop.

As if they'd heard my thoughts through the wall, their voices dropped suddenly. Now I heard nothing but murmurs and an occasional tiny laugh. After a while, they were silent. I didn't know if they'd fallen asleep, if Liz had gone back to her room. I didn't hear the bed creak or the sound of water for teeth and face washing.

The bizarre conversation marched around inside my head for a while, little pieces popping up as if they wanted to step into a spotlight and get some attention so I'd realize how important they were. But I couldn't fit them together and my head was aching even more, the pain spreading across the top of my scalp. Even my hair follicles hurt. Eventually I must have fallen asleep. I know I slept because I had a dream. Not as strange as I would have thought, given the events of the past twenty-four hours.

I dreamt I was walking in the water, just past my ankles. It was much warmer than the ocean, but it was still the ocean. The water clung to the hem of my dress, plastering it to my legs, making it heavy. After a few minutes I looked up at the stone house. The red telescope poked out through the window. At the end, where it should have been a circle of glass, was a huge eye, staring. Watching me. Suddenly, the water became cold. My feet grew numb and I couldn't move. I looked out across the waves, looking for a place to hide from the eye of the telescope. Every time I glanced back up at it, the eye grew more intense, pulsing, making me feel it could read my future, that it knew everything about me. I tried to run, but the water pulled at my dress and dragged me back.

Finally I woke. I got up and went to the window. The moon was out, but it wasn't bright enough to really see the surface of the ocean. I drank half a bottle of water then went back to bed and turned to my left side. The room on the other side of the wall was silent. I stared at the window until the sky started to get light.

Seven

I FINALLY GOT OUT of bed at about five. I took a shower that was longer than normal and cooler than normal because I wanted the swollen feeling in my head to go away. I'd slept well after all, but I still felt those aching knots inside my brain that came from listening to the twins talk to each other, or one twin talk to herself, something I hadn't considered until the shower water hit my hair and slicked it down my back. Then it occurred to me the whole thing could have been staged for my benefit. After all, they'd lived in this house on and off since they were little kids. They must know that voices could be heard through the walls. The outer walls of the house may have been stone, but the interior walls were conventional wood and plaster and perhaps very light on insulation.

I dressed in thick yoga pants, a long top that was almost like a short dress, my UGG boots, and a hoodie because the house was a little cold. Once the sun came up, I planned to walk on the beach, going north, of course.

The hallway outside my room was dim and quiet. All the doors were closed. When I started down the stairs, I glanced at the flight leading up to the observatory. I hadn't been aware the night before that anyone was listening to my conversation with Mike, but apparently at least one of the twins had been standing at the foot of the stairs.

The first floor was dark too, and the door to Renee and Mike's room was shut. I went through the dining room to the kitchen. I pushed open the door. The room was bright, with lights over the table and the cooking area and the sink all turned on. Renee stood in front of the coffee maker, her hip pressed hard against the counter. She held a half-peeled banana that looked like it should have been eaten three days ago, which immediately made me think of the dead sea lion. This time, there was no nausea.

Renee bit the banana. "Hi," she said. "Are you feeling better?"

"Much."

"Want some coffee?"

"Definitely. Why are you up so early?"

"I'm kind of depressed," she said. "I thought we'd get a lot more time together, and today is your second to last day. I thought we could go to Yachats for lunch. Just us. They have a great restaurant with anything you're in the mood for — fish tacos, burgers, crab sandwiches, pizza..."

"Sounds good."

She lifted the pot and filled a pink mug with coffee. She handed it to me. "I guess I shouldn't be talking about food when you didn't eat dinner. Are you sure you're okay?"

"I'm good. I'm starving now."

"What do you want?"

"English muffin is fine. Do you know if there's peanut butter?"

She nodded and took out the bag of muffins. She split one in half and dropped the two slices into the toaster. "Why are you up so early?" she said.

"I had a weird dream." I told her about it while she finished eating the banana.

She dropped the banana peel into the garbage and for a minute, all I could think about was how I'd love to have that peal in my compost bucket at my condo. I wasn't going to ask for rotten food, and I sure wasn't going to drive it back to California. But I couldn't stop thinking about how perfect it would be. "What do you think it means?" It wasn't really a fair question since I left out part of the story — that I'd looked through the telescope and seen a ghost walking on the water right before I went to bed — but I still felt compelled to ask her.

"Someone watching you through the telescope? Maybe nothing."

"Maybe," I said.

"What was last thing you saw before you went to sleep?"

"Um. Well not right before I went to sleep. But I was going

to talk to you about that. Later."

"What?"

I glanced at the door. It was still closed. I didn't really think it was open, but knowing what I heard through my bedroom wall made me wonder if everything I said, or thought, in this house might be picked up by someone else. More specifically, picked up by those very strange women sleeping nearby.

The English muffins popped out of the toaster, as if to emphasize my concern that Leila or Liz or even Mike might burst through the kitchen door at any minute. Renee pulled the muffins out of the slots and put them on a plate. She carried the plate and a jar of peanut butter to the table.

"Aren't you going to eat anything besides that mushy banana?" I said.

She laughed. "I'm fine. What were you going to talk to me about?"

I glanced at the door again. I couldn't shake the sense that someone stood just on the other side, listening. Like I'd listened the night before. "I don't know if I should say, right now."

Renee looked at the door. She remained staring in that direction for almost a minute, maybe more. "Are you up for a walk?"

"As long as we go in the opposite direction of the sea lion," I said.

"Of course. Besides, north is a longer stretch."

I ate my muffin and we agreed to meet at the top of the

beach stairs in ten minutes. Clearly she was as convinced as I was that we'd be overheard, that we had to leave the house to escape those two — mirror images and mirrored brains.

We walked down to the beach, barefoot and silent.

The minute our feet hit the sand, I started talking. "I don't know how to tell you this, I hope you won't think I'm crazy, but I've had a few experiences with ghosts this past year. I think I saw one from the observatory last night, through the telescope. How weird is that? I don't know if you believe in ghosts, and I don't want you to think I've lost my mind since I started working in a church, but I've seen ghosts twice and felt a strange presence another time. Do you? Do you believe spirits come back from the other side of the grave?"

Renee laughed.

"What's so funny?"

"You said you wanted to tell me something and you squished the last eight months of your life into two sentences. I do think ghosts are possible. Why not? And I know what you're saying about the telescope."

"You do?"

"Yes. A few times when I've looked through it, I saw a woman walking across the water."

"Well that's the last thing I saw last night." I stopped. The last thing I'd really seen was Mike, but I still wasn't sure what to tell her about that conversation. I wasn't trying to hide it from her, I just wasn't ready to bring it up quite yet. I had no idea how she'd react, and to be honest, I was a little nervous.

Despite being best friends, I really know very little about their relationship. And people's emotional reactions can be a lot more unnerving than seeing a ghost.

"Who is she?"

"I have no idea."

"Have you asked Mike about it? He must know."

We walked across the wide expanse of sand to the water's edge, then turned north. Mist hung over the beach so it looked deserted, but as we walked forward, people emerged from the vapor as if they were being conjured up out of nothing.

"Mike doesn't believe in ghosts. He thinks they're imagined by people who refuse to accept death."

"Well there's not believing and then there's coming face-to-face with one," I said. Although the telescope wasn't exactly face to face, not like the two I saw in the church garden, or even the Blue Lady — the ghost I'd seen in Half Moon Bay, when I first met JD.

"He doesn't even like me to mention the idea."

"Has he seen her?"

Renee stopped and dug her toes in the sand. "I don't know. Like I said, he won't discuss it."

"Not even to tell you if he's seen her?"

"That's right." She burrowed the toes of her left foot deeper, as if she was trying to root out a pebble or a seashell.

"I suppose Leila and Liz might know who she is. If they've seen her."

"Who would want to ask them, right?" Renee laughed.

We started walking again. Whatever she'd been digging around for remained buried in the sand.

"Have they mentioned it?"

She shook her head. Her hair hardly moved, it was damp from the mist and clung to her cheeks. Wisps of shorter hairs curled out, wet and stiff.

"Is it their mother?"

"No. The first time I saw her was before their mother died."

We walked for quite a ways in silence. First I was thinking about a woman hanging herself and what it would be like to walk into a room and see your mother ... I couldn't even finish the thought. It almost made me want to have some compassion for Leila and Liz. Almost. Then my thoughts drifted back to Mike. He'd never struck me as a closed-minded guy and his adamant refusal to discuss ghosts made me view him in a new light. I had a slight feeling of guilt wrapping around my heart, like the mist hovering around us. The guilt settled down and squeezed gently. It was telling me that the longer I waited to tell Renee about my conversation with him, the more it would appear as if I'd been hiding it from her. Yet the way he was talking to me had made me feel like it was his secret. Maybe I was supposed to keep the secret. When someone tells you something in confidence, that's how it should be, but when that person is married to your best friend, how does that work? I didn't like thinking about where my loyalty belonged.

"I don't like how he is when those two are around," said Renee. "He lets them behave like monsters. They treat me like crap, and he apologizes to me but never says anything to them."

It was the perfect opening for me to tell her about their torture, but I said nothing.

"Sometimes, I think he's buried something in his subconscious," said Renee.

I really wanted to change the subject, but nothing was coming to mind. How had we ended up talking about her husband? I'd much rather be speculating about the ghost, but she seemed strangely uninterested. "Like what?"

"If I knew, it wouldn't be buried."

"True."

"I just don't understand why he lets them treat us so badly."

"I suppose he's used to them being in charge, because they're older."

"I know. But we're adults now."

"It's hard to change how you were as a kid. It's like when you run into one of your high school teachers and they want you to call them by their first name."

"Is it? Because don't you eventually start doing that?" said Renee.

"Not always."

"I think you do. And I think that we're more or less peers

now. They're only five years older, it's not like they were teenagers and he was a little kid."

The conversation drifted into nothing as we kept walking, stepping in and out of the waves that washed up and moved the stones and bits of shell around on the sand. I picked up a smooth white shell, shaped a bit like a boomerang with a streak of orange down the center. The surf washed out and I walked to where the water had covered the sand a moment earlier. I saw a gold-orange stone that was somewhat clear with a thin strip of white. I picked it up and held it on my palm. Renee walked over to my side. She plucked it out of my hand and rubbed it on her jeans. "You found one. That's an agate." She handed it back to me.

I put it in my pocket where it made a satisfying click against the shell. Maybe I'd give it to JD.

Eight

AFTER OUR WALK, Renee decided to go back to bed for a bit. She said she hadn't slept much the night before. I made another pot of coffee. Before it finished brewing, I stuck a mug under the spigot to catch what was still coming out and filled my mug. Then I put the carafe back on the burner. It sizzled from coffee that had dribbled onto the hot plate during my switch, but I figured I'd wipe it up later.

I took my coffee into the living room. The fireplace was dark and full of ashes, which made the room seem cold. I held the mug with both hands to warm my fingers, but the heat got too intense so I set it on a coaster.

I looked out on the patio and the grove of trees. It seemed like a week since I'd crept under the branches, but it had only been a day and a half. My sense of time was distorted. I suppose that comes from being in a different environment, out of a regular routine, so there's nothing to mark the hours. Or it could be the ocean. Or the distracted, disconnected aura that hovered around the twins.

Knowing the vast expanse of the Pacific Ocean was right beyond that grove of trees and tangled flowering shrubs, was difficult to grasp. It felt as if I was standing in the middle of the woods. Once again, I tried to figure out why they hadn't built the house so the living room looked out over the endless beach and the water. Maybe the living room was designed for relaxing in front of the fire after dark. The observatory was the place for soaking in the view, but still...

I sat on a chair that faced one of the long narrow windows and tugged off my boots. I curled my feet to the side and leaned on the left arm of the chair. Despite being all wrapped around myself, I was still cold. I took a sip of coffee, which helped. Outside the window the mist pressed against the glass, drifting along the edge of the patio where the slate ended abruptly. Succulents clung to the ground, sprouting yellow blooms that grew on long knobby stems and lay across the greenery, rather than standing up like normal flowers. Beyond that were the shrubs and small trees that helped create the privacy inside the grove. I decided that as soon as my coffee was gone, I'd go out to explore it further.

The conversation I'd overheard the night before floated back through my mind. Maybe I would tell Renee about it over lunch. Maybe I'd even tell her about Mike. Shouldn't he have told me it was a secret if he didn't want me to say anything? Now that I thought about it, he definitely should have. He knew Renee and I were close, that we'd been friends since high school. He couldn't possibly think I was the best person to tell his deepest secrets to. Maybe he *wanted* me to tell her. I took a long, slow drink of coffee that warmed me all over inside.

When my coffee was gone, the mist had grown thicker and moved closer to the house. I got up, put my boots back on, and went to the kitchen to wash my mug and wipe down the hot plate under the coffee carafe.

Outside, the air felt warmer than it had when Renee and I were walking on the beach. I suppose because there was absolutely no wind. The mist hung there like it wanted to soak permanently into all the shrubs and trees and dirt. I crossed the patio and stepped onto the narrow dirt path that was worn through the ground cover. The shrubs and large leafy plants were taller than me and I felt like I was in another world, walking along, lost from sight. I stopped suddenly, wondering whether the twins might have been looking out from Leila's room, or the observatory. I couldn't remember if the patio and the path were visible from the observatory or if the angle made it impossible to see down to that area. I don't know why I suddenly thought of them, or why I was worried they were watching. Maybe because now I realized I'd felt they were watching me since the moment they walked into the dining room that first night. Maybe it was my dream.

I was more eager than ever to go back into the grove, to recapture that sense of privacy. I knew for sure they couldn't see me in there.

I ducked under the branches that formed the entrance to the grove. The air inside was even warmer. I bent over and ran my palm across the covering of pine needles. They were soft as a cotton quilt, and dry. I sat down and crossed my legs at the ankles. I closed my eyes and breathed in pine and fresh air.

After a few minutes of breathing as slowly as possible, considering I'd just finished a large mug of coffee, I heard the quiet humming. I opened my eyes. The sound was so faint, I wasn't sure whether I was remembering it or actually hearing it. I walked across to where the same path continued on the other side of the grove.

I heard birds chirping and fussing. I ducked under the branches to exit the grove. A few feet ahead of me stood a large cage, five or six feet wide and about four feet high. It was a very substantial cage, with wire that was thicker than you see in a normal birdcage, like the kind I have for my parakeet, Simon. Inside were canaries and a few other birds I couldn't identify. Metal pie pans of seed and a pan filled with fresh-looking water sat on the bottom of the cage. Why was there a cage out here in the woods? I sure hoped they could handle the cold. Maybe, hopefully, someone took them inside during the winter. I stood watching them for several minutes, soothed by their burbling and chirping and fluttering. I listened carefully, trying to decide whether their sounds had caused the humming, but I finally decided it was not at all the same. They fussed over their feathers, picking out bits of dust, and fibers of bark that fell through the top of the cage.

The next section of the path was narrower, less worn, with smashed down plants rather than bare dirt. I walked a few yards, pushing branches and huge leaves out of my way. The effort was making me warm, so I pulled off the hood of my sweatshirt and unzipped it part way. I took a few more steps and as I passed the branch of a flowering tree, my hair got caught in it. I stopped to untangle myself and saw that a few feet ahead the path stopped abruptly with a drop of nine or ten inches.

Poking out of the ground was a cluster of bones. Right away I knew they weren't bird bones, or any kind of animal bones. I broke off the branch that had been caught in my hair and dug at the dirt. The bones appeared to be a hand with no thumb, but after a moment, I realized it must be a foot.

I dug around it a bit more until the whole thing was exposed and then decided I'd better leave it alone. I hoped Renee was taking a very short nap. And I hoped even more that I was not going to have to watch the twins' caustic reactions, but of course, it was highly unlikely I could hide what I'd discovered. I dropped the stick nearby and pulled up my hood. Suddenly, I was cold again.

As I made my way back along the trail, past the birds, still burbling and hopping around, looking completely unfazed by the fact that something human was buried less than twenty feet from their cage, I wondered if Mike, or the twins, had any idea there was a grave in their backyard. Of course, I didn't really know where their property ended, so maybe it had nothing to do with their family or their house.

Inside the grove of trees I paused and tried to bring back the peaceful feeling I'd had when I was there only a few minutes earlier, but it was lost. I waited another minute for the humming, but heard nothing.

I made my way back to the house. I stepped onto the patio and brushed debris off my boots and yoga pants. I was a little sweaty from all the effort of fighting branches and vines. I unzipped my hoodie all the way and went into the house through the kitchen. It was empty and my mug was the only thing standing upside down on the dish drainer. The coffee was still turned on and it smelled stale. I didn't think I'd been gone that long.

I went through the dining room and down the hall to the master bedroom. The door was closed. I knocked, hard.

Mike opened the door after I knocked a second time. "Hi, what's up?"

"I found some bones out in the wooded area. A foot, I think. Is Renee awake?"

He opened the door wider. Renee sat on the window seat that looked out to the north. She was sipping coffee.

"Come on in," said Mike. "*What* did you find?"

I walked into the room. I hadn't meant to blurt it out like that. "I found some bones. I think it's a human foot."

Mike's lips were pale and his neck looked like the trunk of a birch tree, pure white, with rough black spots where his beard was unshaven. His face looked nearly the same color as the white, blank walls of the bedroom.

Renee frowned, as if she wasn't processing the words. "What are you talking about?"

"I was walking through the grove of trees." I waved my arm behind me to indicate, I hoped, the opposite side of the house. "I took the trail that leads out the other side. There's a cage full of birds. Did you know that? Who feeds them?"

"Those belong to Mrs. Harrington. She lives in the house on the opposite side of the pine trees."

"That broken-down cottage?" I said.

Mike nodded.

"Is that her property?"

"No. She wanted them in a protected area, so my Uncle told her to go ahead and have the cage built there."

I wanted to ask more about the birds, why they were outside, whether she brought them in during the winter, but I figured the foot was the more important topic of conversation at this point. "Anyway, I went past the birdcage and there was a small drop-off where the dirt had crumbled away and there were bones sticking out."

"Ew," said Renee.

"What makes you think they're human?" said Mike. "Have you ever seen a human skeleton? Except in high school biology class?"

"No, but I think if you come look, you'll see that's what they are." As I said this, it occurred to me that I'd known immediately they were human. I wasn't sure if it was the size, or there was something about them that made me just *know*. As if there's some subconscious connection where you recognize your own species without having to analyze it. Or it could be that I'm just always looking for the most dramatic and interesting conclusion so I assumed they were human. "Should we call someone? I guess you don't all 9-1-1 for someone that's been dead for quite a while. Or do you?"

Mike walked to the chair at the far corner of the room. He picked up his jacket and handed Renee's to her. "Let's go see." His face was still extremely white. I wondered if he was upset about finding a body on his Uncle's property or if there was something else going on in his head.

We walked down the hall to the kitchen and out to the patio. It was too good to be true that the twins were still asleep. If the police came and carried the bones away before the twins woke up, that would be so much easier, but it probably wasn't going to happen. Maybe the twins would behave like normal human beings around public officials. Or maybe not.

Mike and Renee followed me along the path. Surely Mike knew the way, but I guess they wanted me to lead them to the exact spot. I ducked under the branches. They tugged at my hood like they'd grabbed my hair earlier, as if they didn't want me to keep going, wanted to keep their secret in the tangled vines and trees and thick undergrowth. Mike sucked in his breath and stopped for a moment, but then he followed me into the grove.

The birds chattered with greater intensity as we neared their cage. They stood on their perches, staring out at us, heads turning to follow our progress. I stopped a few feet from the place where the path dropped off. Pointing would have been too dramatic, so I simply stepped to the side and waited for them to see the thing sticking out of the ground.

"Oh." Renee's voice was soft and had a slight tremble.

After a moment, Mike said, "I wonder how long it's been here."

"Who could it be?" said Renee.

"I wonder if the rest of the body is here," I said.

Renee looked at me. Her eyes were watery. She hadn't put on her makeup, and yet her lashes were dark and thick. The benefit of having such dark hair. Although my hair is very dark red, the color of copper, I have pale eyelashes — not at all dramatic. I could use mascara, but it doesn't look that great and it's not worth the trouble. It bothered me that I was thinking about eye makeup right then, but I couldn't help it. Her eyes were exotic, and so teary, that it was hard not to have them consume my attention.

I picked up the branch I'd used earlier and poked at the dirt around the bones. The stick snapped in two.

"We should leave it alone," said Renee. "And call the Sheriff."

I knew she was right, but couldn't stop thinking about whether this was just a foot that an animal had carried here and dropped, or if there was a whole body underneath where we stood. I moved back. The ground looked normal, covered with growth, rough and packed down solid. If there was a whole body, it had been there for a while.

The voice of one of the twins, maybe both of the twins, sharing the quest, cut through the quietness of the grove, shrill and demanding. "Is anyone here? Where did you all go?"

Mike called out, "Over here."

Renee glared at him. She stepped back as if she wanted to disappear among the trees. "Why did you say that?" She spoke in a low whisper.

Mike looked at her, his face slack and almost ashamed. I wasn't sure if I was imagining that, but if I wasn't imagining it, then why would he be ashamed? I suppose because Renee clearly did not want the twins to find us, and she probably didn't want them to know about the bones, the possibility of a body. She didn't want them in any part of her life, and here he was, so eager to respond, as if they were the most important people to consider. He looked down at his feet, he kicked at the dirt, hard. A chunk of earth was dislodged by the toe of his shoe, exposing another piece of white bone.

"Over where?" The voice was even shriller, angry that we weren't easy to find, that we were deliberately hiding ourselves.

"In the..." Mike's voice was rough. He cleared his throat and looked at Renee. He swallowed.

"Tell us where you *are!*"

Renee climbed out of the ivy where she'd been standing, a brave place to be, considering it might have been the hideout for rats or mice, for sure insects and spiders. She walked back the way we'd come, past the birdcage. She turned. "Don't let them come out here. I'm calling the Sheriff."

Mike reached into his pocket. "I have my cell right here."

"I don't want them to see this, and I don't want them involved before it's necessary. If you call now, they'll hear you."

He shoved the phone back in his pocket, but didn't move to follow her. Renee ducked under the branches and disappeared into the grove. The birds were still silent. When I'd passed the cage before they'd warbled and mumbled greetings and chirps about what was on their minds. In fact, they'd been making sounds the whole time we were standing there looking at the foot bones. Their sudden silence made it seem as if we were far from any houses or civilization of any kind, until one of the twins spoke quite loudly. "There you are. Where's Michael?"

There was no response from Renee. At least none that I could hear, but her voice isn't shrill and angry like the twins, so maybe only their strident tones carried through the thick growth of trees and plants.

I walked past the birdcage and turned to look back at Mike. He seemed completely lost and I wondered if he would stay by the bones. But then, the twins would come looking for him, and Renee had made it clear she didn't want to let them know what I'd found. I ducked under the branches into the grove. The birds started warbling softly again. I glanced back and could just make out the gray of Mike's sweatshirt. It was none of my business whatever was going on with him and Renee, but I saw her point of view that letting the twins know about the bones would complicate things. I didn't know how, just that they would figure out a way to create drama out of it. If nothing else, they'd want to take control. For all I knew, with their weirdly dispassionate view of death, they would want to re-bury the foot and forget all about it, not report it, and let it remain where it was forever.

On the other side of the grove, once I got past the taller trees and thick growth of shrubs, I saw that the sky had managed to reveal a few patches of blue. In the distance, the surface of the ocean was flat and calm. It promised to be a beautiful day and the thought of spending it watching a body dug out of the ground, dealing with law enforcement people wandering around, made me sad.

I waited, hoping Mike would follow me. I closed my eyes and felt the sun on my face and willed him to feel that blue sky drawing him out of the overgrown tangle of plants and vines, away from the bones, and back to where Renee wanted him to be — at her side. After a few minutes — minutes filled with one twin or the other calling, whining, demanding — the soft humming started again. A light breeze sprang up with the music. The tune was so faint, I wasn't a hundred percent sure it wasn't in my own head. I opened my eyes, thinking Mike had appeared, that he was humming and his movement had caused a shift in the air around me. I was alone. Before I had time to think it through or notice if the music continued, he emerged from the grove. In his hand was a small branch that had been picked clean of bark and for half a second, I thought he was holding one of the bones.

We walked along the path, out into the open part of the yard. Renee was waiting near the kitchen door. Leila and Liz stood at the center of the patio. Their arms were folded across their ribs and their expressions were identical — the corners of their mouths turned down, their eyes hard as stones.

"Where were you?" said Liz. She wore a thin, lime green blouse with short sleeves and no jacket. Goose bumps covered her arms and ran up her neck.

"Madison found…"

"It's not important," said Renee.

Mike was so eager to jump to whatever they wanted. I know it was a simple question, but he didn't have to give in to their demand for an explanation. Eventually they would find out what we'd discovered, but not yet. Renee turned and went into the house, closing the door behind her.

"It's important that everyone abandoned us," said Leila.

"Are you always so self-absorbed?" I said.

"Ooh," said Leila. "The redhead has some fire in her after all. She's not all about tummy aches and sadness over acts of nature." She was dressed more appropriately for the cool air, with a white turtleneck shirt and a dark brown leather coat. But they still looked an awful lot alike in their dark blue skinny jeans and black boots with high, narrow heels and sharply pointed toes. Leila had her hair pulled up into a ponytail, which highlighted the similarity of their faces. As I'd noticed before, Liz's was a narrower, paler reflection of her sister's.

"We only asked a simple question," said Liz. "There's no need to blow up."

"I didn't blow up."

"You got awfully grouchy," said Leila.

"Where were you?" said Liz.

Mike didn't speak. He walked around me and went into the house.

"What's wrong with him?" said Liz.

It suddenly occurred to me that Mike might have an idea who the bones belonged to. Maybe he didn't want Renee talking to the Sheriff, even on the phone, without him there. Although if that was the case, why had he lingered in the wooded area when she said she was going to call and report what we'd found? I walked across the patio and opened the door to the breakfast room.

"Where are you going?" said Leila.

"Inside."

"Obviously," said Liz.

"What's going on?" said Leila. She walked to where I stood

and blocked me from going through the door.

"Excuse me."

Without me noticing her movement, Liz was suddenly right next to Leila. "We want to know what you were all doing out there and we want to know why you're ignoring our questions. It's insulting."

I skipped over the comment about insulting behavior and said, "Do you always talk as if you're one person?"

"What?" said Leila.

"You say *we*, instead of *I*. When one of you talks, you make it sound like you're both asking the question."

"What?" said Leila and Liz at the same time.

"Never mind."

"What were you doing out there? And don't give us that same BS about it not being important. All three of you wouldn't have disappeared for half an hour if it wasn't important."

Leila's shoulders pressed against her sister's, forming a blockade that prevented me from entering the house. I stepped back and walked to the door that led to the living room. I pressed the handle, opened the door, and went inside. They hurried to the door and pushed their way in before I could close it.

"We want you to answer us."

"You're crazy," I said. "Leave me alone."

"We'll ask Mike, he'll tell us."

"Fine. Do that." I walked across the room, forcing myself

to notice my boots sinking into the soft, thick carpet, determined not to look like I was running away from them, that I was afraid of them. There was no reason to be afraid, but I was.

Near the door into the hallway was a large orange-glazed pot that came up to my waist, the only brightly colored object in the entire house. It was filled with dried branches from trees. Tiny stars dangled from the twigs. I went around it and stepped onto the hardwood floor.

"Why are you such a bitch?" said Liz.

I leaned against the doorframe. "You two act as if everyone should do whatever you want, and you say horrible things to people."

They stared at me as if they were waiting for me to continue.

"I heard you talking about me last night."

"You listen in on other people's conversations?"

"I think you knew I could hear what you were saying." I pulled my hair back off my shoulders and twisted it into a knot on the top of my head. The room was too warm for my hoodie and my UGG boots.

"Whatever," said Leila.

"I know you don't want me here, for whatever reason. But I'm staying until Tuesday morning and you might as well get used to it. Until then, I'd appreciate if you could gossip about me when I'm not right there, and other than that, just stay away from me."

"Aren't you friendly." The strange thing about Leila's tone was that it didn't have that sarcastic lilt you would expect from that comment.

"I don't know what's wrong with you, but something's not right. Maybe because of your mother, maybe something else." My stomach growled and I remembered that Renee and I were going to lunch soon. I turned and went down the hallway and jogged up the stairs to the observatory. I wasn't sure if Renee would think to look for me up there when she finished calling the Sheriff, but I wasn't going to stay in the same room with those two for one minute longer. I hoped the Sheriff would take his or her time and that unearthing bones wouldn't interfere with our lunch plans. My stomach rumbled again. It sounded enormously loud in my ears and in the quiet room, despite the quieting effect of the thick carpeting.

I walked directly to the telescope as if I was compelled by something out on the flat sea, drawing me to look. I stopped, almost afraid to peer into it. I both wanted and didn't want to see anything out there. The feelings were in equal parts and for a moment I froze. Then I heard the humming again. I walked back across the room. A slash of sunlight cut across the carpet, making the furniture look even paler than it was in its normal state. I could hear Leila and Liz whispering in the living room. It was strange that the sound of their whispers carried out into the hallway and up the stairs. The whole house must have paper thin walls, contradicting the solid illusion given by the stone exterior. I stood at the top of the stairs, trying to determine if their whispers were the humming I'd heard, the sound shifting into something musical because it was distorted. The whispering stopped and I went back to the telescope. I wasn't sure if the humming had stopped. Sometimes, you hear something and then it's so faint, you're not sure if you're remembering the sound or still hearing it.

I tilted the telescope down. Someone else must have used it after I'd been up there the night before. It made sense that Mike looked into it after I left, although since he insisted ghosts were a figment of the imagination, I wondered what he would think if he saw the woman walking on the water.

With one eye shut, I pressed the eyepiece close to my brow and looked out. All I saw, filling the entire circle at the end of the scope, was flat, gray-green water. For several minutes, maybe longer, I continued to look, but there was nothing. My neck started to ache and the bone around my eye hurt, so I moved away and walked closer to the window. I put my hands on the sill, which was low, forcing me to bend over slightly.

"What are you looking at?"

I turned. Liz stood near the top of the stairs. I waited for Leila to appear at her side, but Liz was alone. My first thought was that I couldn't believe Leila had let her sister out of her sight, that Liz must have escaped. I had no idea where that thought came from. What gave me the idea that Leila was running the show? She was louder, stronger, more aggressive. It seemed like Liz truly was her reflection, that the single-brain speech style was because Liz had literally been consumed by her dominant sister. A fantastical thought, but it took root and wouldn't let go.

"The ocean," I said. "I could stare at it forever." Before the words were even completely out of my mouth, I regretted that I'd revealed even a sliver of my thoughts. Both of them lashed out so easily, with no warning, and I've found it's better to keep feelings to yourself when you're around combative people. But then my initial thought dug its roots in deeper — that with Liz alone, I didn't need to be as concerned. Liz needed Leila to channel all those poisonous comments through her. Liz looked somewhat empty without her twin standing by her side. Her blonde hair was almost white. With her eyes fully dilated, it felt like she wasn't really focusing on me. The shape of her nipples through her blouse made it obvious she was still cold, even though the house was warm, especially in this room with the sun pouring in through the windows that faced southeast.

"Were you using the telescope?" said Liz.

This was my opening. Was I going to be afraid of a tongue lashing, of ridicule, or was I going to be my usual bold and curious self and not let these two, or this one by herself, get under my skin? "I was. I saw something strange yesterday and I wanted to see if it was still there."

"What did you see?"

I waited. Her eyes remained dark, only the pupils visible from where I stood.

"What did you see?" Her tone was soft, melodic. None of the harsh edge that she displayed when Leila was at her side. I would have expected a lecture, something along the lines of, *I asked you a question.*

"I saw a woman walking across the water. Have you ever seen anything like that?"

"I haven't used the telescope in years. Since I was little."

"Did you ever see a woman?"

Liz moved to the couch and sat down. She stared at me, and then she lowered herself to her side, curled her knees up close to her chest and wrapped her arms around her lower legs. She closed her eyes and a wisp of hair fell across her cheek.

"She looks like our Nanny."

"Did she die?"

"She left us." A tear slid out from under Liz's eyelid.

"I think the figure I saw is a ghost. Did your Nanny die?"

"She left us."

"Are you saying I'm seeing something from the past? Did you ever see a woman through the telescope? After your Nanny left?"

Liz turned her head, dragging her hair across the couch so it generated a bit of static and stood out from her head. "I don't know. I said, I haven't used the telescope in a long time."

"Why are you crying?'"

"I'm not." She sat up and fluffed her hair back into place.

"You looked like you were crying."

"It was from lying down. The fabric irritated my eyes."

I didn't believe her, but I wasn't going to argue. First of all, I was far more interested in whether the woman on the water was revealing herself from some past event, or was dead. I was much more inclined to believe the second idea. I was familiar with ghosts, to some extent. Looking into the past was something completely outside my experience, and an unlikely possibility.

"Where is she now?"

"We don't know."

"Why did she leave?" You seem bothered by it.

"We didn't need a Nanny any more."

"Why would she be appearing in the telescope?" I felt ridiculous even asking the question.

"She was always looking for Leila."

"Is that why she's looking down into the water?"

Liz stood. "I don't know why I'm talking to you. It's an illusion, that's all. Ancient history."

"I'm interested in history."

"Well I'm not."

She walked to the stairs and went down, disappearing from sight without ending the conversation or saying good-bye. I guess she thought it had ended. I went back to the telescope but saw nothing. Just a flat expanse of sea.

Nine

THE HOUSE SEEMED to be deserted when I went downstairs. Neither twin was in the living room. Leila's brown leather jacket was tossed on the pale gray couch. The sleeve hung over the side, touching the floor as if there was a hand inside running its palm across the carpet.

The kitchen was quiet and cool and dark, the coffee pot turned off. I was really hungry, and not only did I want a nice filling lunch with some of those fish tacos or a crab sandwich that Renee had described, I wanted to talk to her. She'd gone to report the bones, but she couldn't possibly still be on the phone, it had been at least twenty minutes. Hopefully, the Sheriff, or whatever official was assigned to investigate death in a rural place like this, was already on the way. Maybe Renee had gone back outside, but there was no one on the patio when I'd walked through the living room, so I decided to check her bedroom first. The door was closed. No sound came through from the other side. After my experience of the thin walls, I figured that meant she wasn't there, or at least she wasn't talking on the phone, or to Mike. I knocked.

"It's open," said Mike.

I turned the knob. Mike was on his back, stretched across the bed with his heels over the edge. His eyes were closed. Renee was on the window seat again, her knees bent, hugging her legs close to her chest. Her face was turned slightly toward the trees outside the window. I felt awkward, as if I'd interrupted them, and yet they obviously hadn't been talking, and it wasn't as if they were making love, with her sitting over there in the window seat. Still, the mood in the room made me feel I'd walked in on something private.

"Should I leave?"

"Of course not," said Renee. She straightened, pressing her spine against the wall, tilting her head back.

"Did you call the Sheriff?"

"Yes. I suppose we'll have to delay lunch until they get here. Unless Mike can handle them." She didn't turn to look at her husband when she said this.

"Madison should talk to them." He didn't look at me, just announced it as if it was a settled plan.

"I don't see why," I said. I supposed they might ask who found the bones, but it didn't make any difference in this case. Usually they would want to know the time, what the person saw, things like that. But what did it matter if I found flesh-free bones at nine in the morning or three in the afternoon or two weeks ago? As far as I could see, I was irrelevant. Not in general, but in this situation.

"Because you found them." Mike pulled his hands from behind his head and crossed his arms over his ribs.

"Do you have any idea who it could be? Now that you've had time to think about it?"

"Nope."

I didn't believe him. He seemed too sure of his answer, too quick, and too something else. It seemed as if he was warning me, or even begging me, not to ask any more questions.

The sun must have moved higher in the sky, but even though most of the clouds had dissolved, the room was getting darker. Outside, the trees grew so close to the house, they didn't allow much sunlight to reach inside the room.

Renee stood and pushed the cushion against the strip of wall under the window to straighten it. I wasn't sure if I should go outside and wait for the Sheriff or stay in the room and force them to go with me once we heard a car pull up, if you could even hear a car from inside their room. The bedroom was around the side and I didn't think the driveway was visible from the window seat.

"They should be here in a minute or two," said Renee. "Let's go wait in the foyer."

I didn't want to wait in the foyer because it would be impossible to talk without risking the twins overhearing us, or showing up to hijack the conversation, but clearly Renee didn't want to stay in the bedroom with Mike sprawled on the bed, brooding.

"Do you want a snack?" she said as she closed the door behind her. "Don't worry about our lunch, the restaurant is open straight through from eleven in the morning until midnight."

"I'll grab a piece of bread and peanut butter. Do you want any?"

She shook her head.

When I returned from the kitchen she was standing with her hand on the doorknob. I'd never seen anyone so eager for the police to arrive. I suppose she wanted to get it over with. Peanut butter gummed up my tongue, but I still managed to ask, "What's wrong with Mike?"

"He's disturbed about the bones."

"Why?"

"I'm not really sure, to be honest."

"Is he worried about who it might be?"

"Not worried, but he loves this place, and I think he's bothered that it's getting an aura of death — his Aunt hanging herself, and now this."

I chewed my bread and waited for her to say more. I would have thought he hated the place, given how his cousins treated him whenever he stayed here.

The tones of church bells filled the hallway, drowning out anything either one of us might have said. Both of us twitched in response to the loud, sudden noise. I think we'd expected to hear something from the front yard, tires on pavement or car doors slamming, footsteps on the front porch. I shoved the corner of my folded piece of bread into my mouth and chewed as fast as I could, grateful that I hadn't smeared peanut butter too thickly near the edge, so the piece I had in my mouth was mostly bread. I swallowed hard and curled my hands inside the pockets of my hoodie.

Renee opened the door. There was a guy in a Sheriff's uniform. I looked past him. The passenger side of his SUV was empty. There were no other vehicles. It looked like they didn't believe we'd found human bones, or they would have sent more than one guy.

He asked our names and who owned the place and basic stuff like that. He introduced himself as Brick Harmon. "I understand you *think* you found a human bone," he said.

His emphasis on *think* was very intense. He might as well have sneered at us. I explained that it was more than one bone, a foot and something else, possibly a lower leg. He didn't respond.

As we led him around the side of the house, along the path, and through the grove, no one spoke. I wanted to ask him why he didn't believe us. If you work in law enforcement, you probably get a lot of crazy calls from people who think they saw something they didn't. But recognizing that fact doesn't make it any less insulting when someone doesn't believe you, doesn't trust that you're a logically minded adult and you're not going to leap to fantastical conclusions.

He poked the toe of his boot at the bones sticking out of the ground, and then scraped around them with his heel. If it turned out these belonged to a Native American, he'd get in trouble for disturbing the area more than necessary. Although I figured that was unlikely, there was something fresh about the bones. That's a strange word to use, but it's the only way to describe it. They looked cleanish and firm, not cracked and decaying like I'd expect of something ancient.

"These are human," said Brick.

"We already told you that," I said. It's not the way you should normally speak to officials, but I didn't like the about-face, one minute saying you *think* you found something, implying we have no idea what we're talking about, and the next minute, acting like the thought of the bones being human had never occurred to anyone until Brick declared it to be true.

My snappish tone didn't prompt him to glance at me, so I guess we were more or less invisible in his eyes. He pulled the stick out of the loop on his belt and poked at the dirt, dragging away clumps of weeds, scraping away rock and loose soil. He straightened and stepped away from where he'd been digging. "I shouldn't mess around here, I'm only checking to see if it's the whole guy or just the foot and leg."

I nodded. Renee stood a few feet back, her hand over her mouth. She definitely did not want to be there. To me, if it was a recently deceased body, like the sea lion, seeing what remained after death was very upsetting, you could still recognize the life in it. But this didn't seem like anything living at all. A pile of sticks, almost.

"I'll call our Coroner and have him out here today or tomorrow. Most likely tomorrow."

"Tomorrow?"

"We're a small group, and we need to have investigators come in from out of the area."

"Do we need to be here, to show them the spot?"

"Someone needs to be available to answer questions, show them the route through the trees. Once the body is removed, I'll need to arrange interviews with all of you."

We walked back through the grove, again, in silence. I had nothing else to say to this guy and he made it clear he didn't think much of us. Renee lagged behind, but I couldn't wait to get out of there. When we reached the open area at the top of the bluff, Brick stood with his back to the gorgeous, fantastic Pacific Ocean — a tired scene to him, I suppose — and looked directly at us for the first time. Mostly at me, which was strange because I was a visitor and Renee would be the more likely candidate for acquiring information. "Any idea who it could be?"

"Of course not."

"That's a very definitive answer."

"I never saw this place until three days ago. How would I know anything about who might have died here? Or been murdered."

"What makes you say murder?"

"You don't usually bury a body in the woods, with no coffin or grave, if they die naturally."

"It could have been accidental," he said.

I looked past him at the water. I wanted him to leave. I wanted to have lunch with Renee, to really talk, which seemed destined not to happen this weekend, because everything was interrupted, or the twins grabbed center stage. I wanted to tell her about JD, and I kind of wanted to tell her more about the ghosts I'd seen back home, to get her perspective. And if the sun stayed out, which it was supposed to do, I wanted to walk on the beach again. It was a horrible waste of a day to be standing here talking to this guy about something I knew nothing about. That doesn't mean I wasn't hugely curious, but talking to him was not going to satisfy my curiosity. The only people who could answer his questions would be Mike and the twins. I smiled at the thought of sicking those two on him. That might be entertaining. Maybe we'd made a mistake, hiding the discovery from them.

He looked at Renee. "Do you know who it is?"

She shook her head.

"Where's your husband? And the women who live here?"

"Sleeping," said Renee.

I wasn't sure it was a good idea to mislead him, but I wasn't going to disrupt that course of action, now that she'd chosen it.

Brick walked to his car, calling back over his shoulder to remind us that someone needed to be there all day for the Coroner to come by — most likely in the morning, but he couldn't guarantee it.

The minute his door slammed shut, I said, "Mike should be here."

"He doesn't want to be involved."

"How can he not be involved?"

"Leila and Liz can be here. It's their responsibility. They live here and they know much more about the place than Mike. Maybe their mother knew who was buried there. Maybe that's why she killed herself."

"Can you imagine those two talking to Sheriff Brick?" Renee smirked.

"I wonder if the twins know who it is. If they don't, I wonder how the Sheriff will figure out who it is."

"They'll search missing persons reports."

"Only for this area. If someone stayed here on vacation, or just for the weekend, how would they ever know? It could be anyone." I ran my fingers across my scalp and lifted my hair away from my skin. The sun was making my head itch. It felt good to massage my head with my fingertips and feel the warmth of my hair across the backs of my hands. I let it fall back down across my shoulders.

"Let's go get lunch," said Renee. "I'll tell Mike what's going on and he can tell his cousins." She went inside the house. I sat down on the front steps to wait for her.

THE DRIFT INN restaurant was in an old wooden building. The entry had a narrow space filled with gift items from local artists — knitted scarves, handmade soaps, jam, photographs, and other odds and ends. It wasn't the kind of shop that said, *we're trying to suck more money out of you*, but had a simple, unpretentious air of, *this is a friendly place and the people who live around here are creative, you might like to buy some of the things they've made*. I know shops don't have a voice that tells you what they're about, but they do have different auras. A quick stop at a gas station, a souvenir shop at a national park, and one on the wharf in San Francisco all say something different.

I looked around while Renee stepped into the restaurant itself to give the host our names. It was only a fifteen-minute wait for a table, and in that time, I managed to pick up three bars of homemade scented soap, one for Pastor Kate, one for Cindee, and one for me. I also bought six jars of jam — three for JD and three for me. The salary of an administrative assistant doesn't provide a lot of extra spending money, but besides everything being handmade, the prices were amazing. The soap was only five dollars for a thick bar that was five inches long and four inches wide. Each bar was wrapped in cellophane with sage green satin ribbon around it — very nice.

The restaurant has rough wood floors and most of the tables are wood booths. There's a bar along one wall, and the window to the kitchen is open into the restaurant area so servers can pick up the food there. The owner has a thing for designer umbrellas, and large, fabric umbrellas, some painted with scenes, others with abstract color designs, all fully open, hang from the ceiling. You can't help but think of Mary

Poppins when you see them, because it looks like they're descending into the restaurant. At least I couldn't help being reminded of Mary.

We sat at a wide booth near the windows that faced the street, so people passing by on the sidewalk looked right at us. The booth was large enough to hold four people very comfortably, which gave us lots of elbowroom. We looked at the menus and I immediately saw what Renee meant. I would never be able to decide because half the meals were favorites. They had pizza with all the toppings I love — artichoke hearts, for example. They even had a pizza with fresh crab. They also had fish tacos with homemade salsa and avocado and black beans, crab salad, crab with melted cheese on sour dough bread, and dishes with tofu. They had burgers, so I suppose that was one thing that isn't a must-have favorite, but I do like them from time to time.

Renee ordered a glass of Oregon-grown Pinot Noir. I ordered an iced latte. We studied the menu without talking. Finally I decided on the crab pizza and hoped I'd have time to come back for lunch the following day so I could try the fish tacos. Renee also ordered pizza with fresh crab. When the server left, I picked up my latte. The glass was already sweating and for a moment it didn't want to let go of the table. There was a big puddle of water where it had been sitting. I wiped it with my napkin. "Who do you think the bones belong to?"

"I don't know."

"Not even a guess? Aren't you dying to know?"

"Not really. Can't we talk about something else? Tell me more about your new guy."

It was funny that she called him my new guy because it wasn't as if there'd been a string of "old" guys. Just the one boyfriend, and it was going on two years since that ended. I was glad she asked. I wanted to tell her all about JD. I didn't have many opportunities to go on about him. I'd been looking forward to gushing a bit, but now, the body in the yard occupied my mind. It was funny that I'd been longing for a chance to talk to her about JD, but now that I had a chance, I couldn't stop obsessing about the bones. "Why don't you want to talk about who might be buried there?"

"It's too upsetting. And why do you care? You should be enjoying the beach, fantasizing about coming back to visit and bringing your boyfriend."

It was startling to hear someone else refer to JD as my boyfriend. Of course I'd told her that I now thought of him in those terms, but the sound of the word, with other voices talking in the background about food and the weather and the beach and family troubles, along with glasses thunking on wood tables, sounded both casual and very official at the same time. She stared down into her wine glass. She'd taken that first sip, but nothing since, and I had the sense she wasn't fully aware she was drinking wine — it could be tea or water for all the attention she was paying to it.

"I care because it bothers me to see someone buried

without a real grave. And it bothers me to know that it probably means that person was either killed accidentally and someone hid their death, or they were murdered. And I can't stop thinking about it until I know what happened."

"We might never know."

"But I have to try. Mike must have some thoughts about it. What was going on with you two when I came into your room? I felt like I interrupted something important. Are you sure he doesn't have any idea about who it could be?"

She continued to peer into her wine glass, still not drinking it. The server brought our food, which was upsetting because I knew most people who didn't want to answer a nosey question would use that interruption to change the subject and then I'd be forced to increase my nosiness. The minute the server left, before I picked up a piece of pizza, I said, "I know it's none of my business, but I wondered why he told me to come in if you were having a serious conversation."

She took a sip of wine and pushed her plate away from her. I pulled a slice of pizza away from the rest. The cheese stretched across the plate, refusing to let go as I lifted it to my mouth.

"That's probably super hot," said Renee. "You might want to wait a minute."

I flicked the tip of my tongue at the pointed end of the pizza. It was burning hot. I put it back on the plate and drank my coffee, letting one of the ice cubes roll across my tongue.

"He said he has no idea who it could be. We weren't even

talking about that, we were talking about Leila and Liz. I don't see why we ever need to see them again. I don't understand why he can't stay away from them. We can find another place on the coast if we want to go to the beach for the weekend."

Something about the quietness of her voice, or maybe that she pushed her plate even further away, made me think that she only told me half of what they'd been talking about. And not the interesting half.

"Were you fighting about it?"

"I forgot how prying you can be." She nudged her plate again. It was starting to creep onto my side of the table.

"Are you not hungry?"

She looked up at me. "What?"

"You're pushing your plate away."

"It's hot."

That made no sense, but I decided not to wander off down that track or I'd never find out what was going on. I really hoped that the part she wasn't telling me was that Mike had finally let her in on the weird relationship he had with his cousins. That I wouldn't have to be in the middle of their marriage any more, knowing a significant secret. But it wasn't like I could come out and ask her, because if that wasn't it, then I'd accidentally betray his confidence. Instead I had to keep living with betraying her, because that's what it felt like. I picked up my pizza and took a bite. The crab was sweet and firm and the cheese was light so it didn't drown the flavor of the crab. "Mmmm."

Renee smiled. "It's good, isn't it."

"Yes." I took another bite.

"He said if he stops coming here, they win."

"What does that mean?"

"I have no idea. That's when you came in. When I asked him later, before we left for lunch, he said he didn't remember saying that."

"Oh. That's kind of frustrating."

"Yes." She pulled her plate back to her side of the table, picked up a slice of pizza, and took a very large bite. It was a small pizza, so the wedges weren't enormous, but her bite consumed a third of it. She chewed slowly, and I could tell the center part where she'd bitten was still on the uncomfortably hot side and she'd taken too much and her cheeks swelled as she tried to chew carefully, not burning her tongue, and not choking, and not letting food fall out of her mouth. To be honest, it was fun to watch. But then she swallowed, not having chewed quite enough, and it looked uncomfortable, watching her throat work around all that cheese and dough and the whole thing still a little too hot. She picked up her glass and drank some. She and kept the glass in her hand, poised for another sip. "Anyway, I'm sorry it hasn't been such a great vacation for you. The dead sea lion, bones in the yard, Leila and Liz."

She shivered when she said that, and I couldn't decide which of those three things made her shiver. Maybe it was all three. "Sometimes I think he's afraid of them," she said.

I could see that.

"Sometimes *I'm* afraid of them." She took a long sip of wine and looked directly at me. Her brown eyes looked darker than ever. "But even though I'm sometimes scared of them…" She sipped more wine, set the glass down, rested her forearms on the table, and leaned toward me. "I don't understand why they have such a hold on him. I think he's hiding something from me, and that's not good for a marriage. And he might know who those bones belong to and he doesn't want to tell me that either." Tears rushed into her eyes and she blinked fast. She tilted her head back to keep them from trickling down her face, but it did no good, some of them spilled over. She took her napkin off her lap and pressed it under first one eye, and then the other. Then she held it to the tip of her nose. "He does anything they say. Anything."

No wonder she wasn't curious. Curiosity was terrifying because she didn't want to know whether he truly would do, had done, anything. "I'm sorry," I whispered. She had no idea how sorry I was.

Ten

LUNCH WITH RENEE HAD BEEN somewhat dissatisfying, except for the food, which was fantastic. I'd brought home two slices of pizza. I hid the box under a bag of lettuce in the fridge because I didn't put it past the twins to eat my food. Clearly they thought everything in the house belonged to them by default. Including Mike, and possibly Renee.

Watching Renee twist her face, trying to stop her tears from flowing, felt like the dull blade of the table knife had wedged itself in my heart. Not a sharp pain like you'd expect if you were stabbed, but an aching pain that wouldn't stop. The pain of her sadness was magnified by the secret I was keeping. I had no idea what I should do. One minute I knew I wasn't a friend if I didn't tell her, the next minute I knew I was a person who couldn't be trusted if I did. I couldn't wait to go to my room and boot up my laptop and launch Skype so I could chat with JD. Of course, after my experience the other night, I wasn't sure how I would do that without the twins overhearing every word, if they happened to be in Leila's room.

As soon as my pizza was secured, I wandered around the house looking for another place where I could talk to JD and not risk having them sneak up to listen. I thought about taking my laptop outside. It would be fun to video chat on the beach. The sky was creamy blue and the breeze was so light, I had to stare at the trees for several seconds before I could tell whether the leaves were fluttering. I doubted the wireless internet reached quite that far. It would be cool if it did, though.

The whole first floor of the house was silent, but the twins' SUV was in the driveway, so they had to be somewhere. I shivered, and glanced behind me at the darkened dining room. For all I knew, they were watching me, trying to figure out what I was looking for. I walked up to the second floor. All the bedroom doors were closed. I started up the steps to the observatory. It was so peaceful up there, but without a door, and with that open side that looked down to the floor below, it was the least private place in the house. At the far end of the hall on the second floor was a door I'd assumed led to a closet, but maybe it was large enough to curl up in. I opened the door. It was a small room, not large enough to function as a bedroom, although there was enough space for a twin bed and a small desk or dresser. Instead of furniture, the room was filled with boxes, stacked floor to ceiling along both sides. There was no window. I figured if I sat near the far end, the boxes would muffle my voice. Hopefully they wouldn't also insulate the internet connection. I scurried back to my room and got my laptop.

I'd left it powered on, so it only took a minute for it to wake up and find the internet. I launched Skype, turned up the volume, and waited to see if the telephone icon near JD's name was green, indicating he was already on line.

He was. The minute he answered and clicked his video on, I felt my shoulders and my whole face relax. His hair was wet but combed into his usual short ponytail. He wore a black t-shirt. He smiled and my heart felt suddenly soft with a tiny pinch of happiness that was almost like someone had squeezed it gently. "Hi," I said.

"Hi."

I felt warm hearing his voice and I wished the tiny room had a window so I could breathe in some fresh air.

"You look great," he said. "I missed your smile, and those wicked green eyes."

"My eyes aren't wicked."

"Are you sure about that?" He grinned.

He looked like himself, but not. When people are on a screen, TV too, I suppose, they have this dull look that's less vibrant. Not exactly 2D, but not their full essence. Maybe it's because you only see part of them, or you don't smell them, or maybe there's some other aspect to human beings that doesn't come across on the screen. The reflection of their aura or their soul, the thing that lingers in ghosts. I thought of the woman walking across the water, visible only through the telescope. She was perfectly formed, not ghostlike at all. That might be why I wondered if I was somehow seeing back in time rather than a spirit in the here and now. How could her aura or her soul be communicated across hundreds or thousands of feet of seawater? And I didn't feel anything when I saw her. With the other ghosts I'd seen, they somehow managed to change my physical sensations.

"You're quiet," said JD.

"I was thinking."

"About?"

"Ghosts."

"What a surprise. Did you see one in Oregon?"

"Actually, I did."

"Really." He leaned back against the headboard of his bed where he was sitting. He put his hands behind his neck and stretched his elbows out so that his arms formed triangles. The plain dark wood, in a solid, undecorated panel behind him, blended with his dark hair, make his face more prominent.

"I still can't quite believe it."

"Why not?"

"It's weird. I only see her when I look through this telescope in the observatory — a big room on the third floor. At least it's supposed to be an observatory, but it only has four small windows on each side. Isn't that odd, that a house looking out over such a beautiful scene only has these narrow windows?"

"That doesn't make sense. But tell me about the ghost, that's a lot more interesting than windows. Who is it?"

"I don't know. And no one here seems to know who she is."

"Have Renee or Mike seen her?"

"Renee did. But we haven't had much chance to talk about it."

"Why not?"

"It's a long story."

"Tell me."

I wanted to tell him about the twins, the dead sea lion, to explain more about the ghost, to try to sort out my thoughts while he listened, but I was suddenly tired. It seemed like too much work. Maybe it was the Skype, it's not the same as curling up together on the couch, or sitting at the table with a cup of coffee. Or going for a walk, or even driving in the car and talking. Video chat has a way of making you feel as if you're on stage, performing instead of talking. "What's going on with you?" I said.

"Hearing about your ghosts, and how you can spend three days with your friend and not get time to talk, are a lot more interesting than mixing drinks and pouring beer."

I lifted my laptop off my crossed legs and set it on the floor.

"All I can see are your knees," said JD.

"I'm stretching, hold on." I put my legs out straight and scooted a few inches until my back was against one of the stacks of boxes. I put the laptop on my lower thighs, balancing part of it on my knees. "Mike's cousins are here — they tend to dominate things. And yesterday I saw a dead sea lion. It made me feel ill, so I slept most of the afternoon, and this morning I found some human bones, so we were busy with the Sheriff."

"Holy crap. That's a lot in two days. *And* a ghost?"

"It didn't seem like a lot, just a bunch of small things."

"I assume the ghost belongs to the bones."

"I suppose." Of course, I already knew that, but I'd been so focused on wanting Renee or Mike telling me who they thought was buried out there, I hadn't given much attention to the connection.

"Did that freak you out, finding bones?"

"No. I only found the foot. And I was more upset about the sea lion."

"Why's that?"

"It was so sad."

"It is sad."

I lifted the laptop off my legs again and set it on the floor again. I put my hands on my face. My palms felt cool on my skin. I didn't want to look at him. I couldn't explain how that sea lion made me feel. It wasn't that I couldn't put it into words. It's hard to talk about something that makes you want to hug the other person when you're telling him.

"Madison? Where'd you go?"

"I'm right here."

"I can't see you. Are you okay?"

That's what's so sweet about JD, or one of the things. He seems to know right away, most of the time, when something's not quite right, even though I haven't known him that long. Of course, it's not hard to figure out. Since I'm constantly talking, when I stop, anyone who knows me even a little will notice I'm strangely quiet. "It's hard to explain how sad that sea lion was. Beyond sad."

"You've seen dead animals before, haven't you?"

I put my legs in the yoga lotus pose and propped the laptop on my knees, wedged against my feet. "You know I've seen more death than I should have. Remember, I found Fred's body. And Lorraine's. And Linda's. But it was sad that it hadn't been buried, that it was decaying."

"Those things are like 800 pounds, aren't they?"

I shrugged.

"It's not like your average beachcomber could bury it."

"I know. It just felt so exposed. That everyone was staring at it, feeling disgusted, when it used to be a beautiful creature."

His lips looked tight and a little turned down at the ends. His sympathetic expression dissolved some of the sadness that had swollen inside my throat until I almost couldn't swallow.

"It doesn't sound like you're having a great vacation."

"The beach is gorgeous." I didn't want to be whining and complaining. I don't know why I'd gone off on the sea lion. I should have stuck to the ghost, or told him more about the bones and how it was making me crazy that Mike claimed that he couldn't even guess who might be buried there.

"Has it rained much?" said JD.

"Hardly at all. We've walked on the beach both days. It goes forever, completely flat. The sand is so hard it almost feels like you're walking on a sidewalk."

"It sounds like lots of catching up time."

"That's the only time, because of Mike's cousins. Renee thought they were going to be out of town this weekend. I don't think she would have invited me if she'd know they'd be here. She probably wouldn't be here either." I lowered my voice, not really trusting the stacks of boxes and the distance from their bedrooms. "They're the most horrible women I've ever met. They treat Renee and Mike like trash. Their behavior is bizarre — their mother killed herself a year or two ago. Renee said they acted like it was no big deal. And they mocked me for being upset about the sea lion."

JD's face turned red so fast it looked like he'd suddenly choked on something. His eyes narrowed. "Mocked you how?"

"They kind of laughed, and said I was over-sensitive."

"Wow. Did you put them in their place?"

"They're not the kind of people who are easily put in their places."

"Did Renee or Mike say anything?"

"Renee tries to ignore them. Mike's sort of afraid of them."

"*Afraid?* What a whuss." JD's voice boomed out of the speakers. I quickly clicked the key to lower the volume.

"It's not like that."

"It sure sounds like that. Do you want me to come up there?"

I laughed. "Mike knew them when he was a kid. I think they have some kind of older kid power over him. You know how that is."

"Sure. Sure. I know how that is. When you're ten. Not when you're thirty years old, or whatever he is."

"Twenty-eight. You don't know how they are."

"I don't have to."

"Anyway, they're really weird. Almost mentally disturbed. They talk like they're one person. Last night I heard them talking about me in their room."

"What did they say?" JD pulled his hands out from behind his head and crossed his arms. He looked pissed off. Or worried. Or disgusted. I really wasn't sure which. Maybe all three.

"That they wanted to get rid of me, that I was over-sensitive, like I said. I don't know. Let's not talk about them."

"I think I should come get you. I could fly up and we could drive back together."

"That's stupid."

"No it's not."

"You're kidding, right?"

"I'm not."

"I can take care of myself. I don't need you to rescue me." He was treating me like a child. Sure, Leila and Liz were horrid, and I did think they were slightly deranged. I hadn't realized I thought they were truly unbalanced until I said it to JD, but I didn't need him to protect me or save me or whatever it was he thought he had to do.

"I'm worried about you."

In one way it felt nice to hear him say that, in another way, it annoyed me. I can take care of myself. I've done it quite well for twenty-seven years, more or less. Okay, maybe only about ten years, but still. I liked his concern, I liked his support, and that he didn't brush off how horrible the twins were, but I didn't like him acting as if I couldn't handle things without his help. And I didn't like him calling Mike a whuss when he didn't understand the situation. Of course, I hadn't really explained the situation, and I couldn't. Back to that secret-keeping again. "Don't worry. I'll be fine. Just don't bring it up again. Okay?"

He looked hurt. Really hurt, but that was too bad. Besides, he'd get over it, just like I'd get over being annoyed and maybe a little defensive that he didn't think I was competent.

"Where did you find the bones?" he said. The change of subject was abrupt, forced, but I think that was the best thing after all that.

"There's a grove of trees, it's really secluded, almost covered by branches crossing over each other so you can't see much sky. It's warm and cozy because there's a thick layer of pine needles on the ground. There's a trail that leads into it and then goes out on the other side. Outside the grove there's this big outdoor birdcage, and when I walked past the birdcage, I saw some small bones sticking out of the ground. I thought it was a hand at first, but it's a foot. We also saw the lower part of a leg. The Sheriff is coming back tomorrow with someone else to dig it up and take it away."

"Why are they waiting until tomorrow?"

"There's only two guys, I guess."

"Mike and Renee don't have any idea who it is?"

"Renee doesn't. At least that's what she told me. If Mike does, he's not saying. Although I haven't seen him much since I found them."

"How long do they think it's been there?"

"I guess we'll find that out when they start digging it up."

"They weren't worried about someone disturbing things?"

"He put that yellow tape around the whole area. And a sign."

"Oooh, a sign. How is that supposed to keep anyone out?"

I smiled. "I guess it won't."

"Especially animals."

"If animals were going to get it, they already would have."

"True."

"I should sign off and go see if I can help Renee with

dinner. Or at least hang out with her."

"Madison?" He leaned forward so his face almost filled the screen.

"Yes?"

"I didn't mean to piss you off. It sounded like they were treating you like crap, and I got upset."

"Okay." His words, and the look on his face made my stomach feel like it was turning to liquid.

"I know you don't need me to come charging in to save the day. It's hard to imagine you putting up with that kind of crap. You're not a whuss, even if Mike is."

"He's not. You'd have to meet his cousins to understand what they're like."

"No thanks."

We both laughed.

"So are we good?" said JD.

I put my hand close to the tiny camera eye, as if I was reaching out to touch his palm. His hand filled the screen as he did the same. It was disorienting, because my instinct was to put my hand on the screen, the same as I would if I was simulating touching his hand through glass, but for him to see it, I had to put it in front of the camera.

"When will I see you?" said JD.

"I should be home by seven or eight on Tuesday." I'd already told him that, but maybe he wanted to hear me say it again, maybe he was still wanting to drive with me, even though he sort of apologized.

"I'm going to try to switch shifts so I can come by your place and take you to dinner. If you want me to."

"Definitely,"

"Okay then. Text me when you leave. And when you stop to eat."

"Sure."

"If you want."

I smiled. "I'd text you every mile, but I might get caught."

He grinned. We said good-bye and I closed the Skype window, which made its usual loud whooshing, sucking sound as if it wanted to pull me out into the virtual atmosphere.

Eleven

THE SHERIFF AND THE CORONER were there at eight on Monday morning. It's a good thing I'm an early riser. Everyone else was asleep. If the bell woke them, they didn't let on.

The night before, all five of us had managed to get through dinner and several argument-free rounds of *UNO*. There were only minor verbal attacks from the twins and no one mentioned the bones. We'd agreed that Mike would tell them in the morning, before the Sheriff started asking questions.

After the card game wound down, I'd gone up to the observatory, but I didn't see the ghost, no matter how many times I pressed my cheekbone against the hard-plastic eyepiece of the telescope. Leila and Liz were so innocuous that evening, I felt like they'd decided to re-group and were biding their time. Maybe they'd been curious about why we were all in the grove and had gone out later and seen the crime scene tape. I could imagine them not being deterred by the sign, digging around, looking for something interesting, something that would give them an inside scoop, or even more power over Mike. Or maybe they didn't need to dig around, maybe they didn't even need to go out there because they knew what we'd found. Maybe they knew whose body it was.

It didn't seem right that I was the one left to greet the Sheriff and the Coroner, lead them out to the grove, and then hang around as they began digging. Sure, I found the bones, but it wasn't my backyard. On the other hand, I was curious, so I wasn't completely annoyed that Mike was asleep, that he still hadn't talked to his cousins. Not that the Coroner or the Sheriff would be able to answer any of my questions right then, and possibly ever. How did you go about discovering who a skeleton belonged to? Where did you even start? I asked that question, but the Coroner was not the chatty type.

Brick told me there were a *variety of ways*.

I asked what ways, and he said, *investigative techniques*. I waited for more information, but when he didn't speak for quite some time, I gave up, which I suppose was his intent.

For a while, I stood back watching, way back, because Brick kept saying, *move back*. Then it started to drizzle. Brick held an umbrella for the other guy while he wiped moist dirt off the bones and put them into bags. Clearly they didn't want me there, and although walking in a light rain can be pleasant, if it's warm out, standing in the rain in the woods on the Oregon coast, with two people who think you're a nuisance, is not my idea of a fun time. So I left.

Inside the house, it appeared that everyone was still asleep. It was 8:45 and the coffee pot was empty and dry and glistening. I made a pot and wandered into the breakfast area, wondering whether Renee was finally done with wanting to spend time at the house. I hoped Mike didn't care so desperately about keeping that part of his life alive that it would put a wedge in their marriage. It seemed as if they loved each other too much for something ordinary like a house to damage it, but this place wasn't quite ordinary. He had a crazy attachment to it that went beyond reason. The house wasn't even that great. It was nice-looking and the inside was beautiful, but the longer I was there, the more confused I became over why someone would build a house that minimized their view of the ocean. It was almost as if they wanted a glimpse of the spectacular coastline, but not let it get too close.

I was sitting on the living room couch, sipping coffee, and looking out the window, wishing all those trees and shrubs weren't blocking my view, when Leila came into the room. She wore skinny jeans and a shimmery blue tunic with equally shimmery ballet flats on her feet. "Why is there a Sheriff's truck in the driveway?"

"Hi," I said. "Did you sleep good?"

"I asked you a question."

I really had hoped Mike or even Renee would get the honor of explaining what I'd found, but there was no dodging her now. "There's a body buried out in the grove of redwood trees."

"Why are they out there?"

I thought that was a rather strange response. Wouldn't most people want to know additional details about the location of the body, or who it belonged to? She wouldn't know it was just a pile of bones, so she'd think it was recognizable. Recent. Wouldn't she? "It's actually a skeleton. They're removing it."

"Did you make enough coffee for us?"

"Yes." If it was anyone else in the world, I would have handed her my mug and asked for a warm-up, but I decided to make do with what I had, since it was still half full and moderately hot.

She returned with a cup of coffee and walked to the window.

"You can't see anything," I said.

"I know that."

It sounded as if bluntness was the only style she knew, so I decided, far too late, to go head to head with her. "Do you know who the bones belong to?"

"How would I know that?"

"It's your parents' house. You've lived her for years. Did anyone ever go missing?"

"This area is very secluded, anyone could dig a grave out there and no one would ever see."

"Possibly."

"What do you mean by that?" She still faced the window so I couldn't read her expression. Not that I'd necessarily be able to do that anyway. As I said, she had a rather blank look to her. Maybe because half of her brain belonged to her twin, so there wasn't much going on in there.

"It's not very likely someone would stop with a dead body, cut across your property, carrying their shovel, and start digging," I said. "They wouldn't even know there was a clearing and a trail through there."

"Our neighbor built her birdcage on our property. Or maybe it's her property. We don't really know where the line is. So the bones probably belong to someone she knew."

"So you had no idea someone was buried out there?"

She turned. She ran her fingers through her hair, arranging it over her right shoulder, which was angled in my direction. She smoothed the strands of hair for several seconds, running her hand from her neck down to the ends like she was stroking a cat's fur. "Why do you care?"

"Why don't you?"

"It has nothing to do with me."

"If someone found a skeleton in my backyard, I'd think it had a lot to do with me."

"Well you're a nut case."

I laughed.

"See what I mean?" said Leila.

I stood. "I really don't need to worry about it. The Sheriff said he'll be asking you questions."

"But it's killing you, isn't it? You're so nosey. In case you haven't figured it out, we don't like having you here."

"Why do you talk like that? Speak for both of you?"

She lifted her eyebrows and went back to stroking her hair. She hadn't taken a single sip of coffee. She looked past me toward the hallway. I turned. Liz stood in the doorway. She wore the same black boots as the day before. Her skirt left lots of skin between the hem and the tops of her boots. Her hair was plastered to her head, completely pulled off her face and drawn into a point that was stiff with gel at the nape of her neck.

I turned back to Leila. "Why do you say *we*, even when your sister isn't in the room?"

"We're close."

"It's confusing."

"Are you easily confused?"

Talking to her was giving me a headache. I drank the rest of my coffee. It was cold. I walked across the room and was headed into the kitchen when Liz spoke. "Why is there an SUV and a van in the driveway?"

I told her exactly what I'd told Leila.

"How did you find her?"

"You know who it is?"

"No."

"You said *her.*"

"We didn't say we know who it is," said Leila.

Liz thudded across the carpet, the heels of her boots

sinking into the fibers. She stopped at Leila's side and put her hand on the coffee cup. "Can I have some?"

"There's more in the kitchen," I said.

She ignored me. I knew I had to talk to Liz alone if I was ever going to satisfy my curiosity. I left her to sip out of Leila's mug and walked out of the room. I set my mug on the kitchen counter and went out through the dining room. I hurried up the two flights of stairs to the observatory and went directly to the telescope.

I didn't know what I thought I was going to find out. It made the most sense that the bones belonged to the woman walking across the water. Obvious, in one way, a bit of a leap in another. And what would seeing her, or not seeing her, help me figure out? She was nothing more than an image. I'd seen her multiple times now, and it didn't seem as if she had anything to tell me. She was just there. Looking for something.

I lowered the telescope. For a moment, I wondered who had been looking through it after I was last here. But then I pushed that thought aside as I became aware of how ridiculous it all was — believing a ghost would show herself through a telescope. Like it was a portal to another world. And as soon as that thought passed through my mind, there she was, walking across the water, peering down, occasionally glancing out across the sea. The clouds and light drizzle did nothing to obscure her form She didn't seem to have any awareness of the rain, as if she existed on a different plane, where the sky was clear.

I watched her for several minutes, longing to know what she was looking for, still unsure whether she was truly a ghost and not some trick of water and light and my active imagination. Her shape was sharp and clear enough that if my mind didn't know otherwise, I could think it was a live human being walking across the water, swells covering her feet and lower legs, but never making it look as if the waves had an effect on her movements.

Without warning, she began to run, racing across the water. She fell suddenly, headlong on her face, as if she'd caught her foot in a trap. All I could see was the back of her, blending with the waves, her clothes wet and clinging to her form, her hat floating over her head and upper back. Then she disappeared.

I cried out and stumbled away from the telescope. It was so vibrant, I felt as if I'd just witnessed a woman's death. I don't know if I was scared or horrified. I ran to the window but all I could see was a vast expanse of water and sky. Still, I pressed myself against the glass, straining to see out, not really sure in which direction I should turn my gaze.

"What are you looking at?" Mike's voice was so quiet, at first I thought I'd imagined it, like I was imagining everything. "Madison?"

I turned. "Who was she?"

"I don't know. Did they already determine it was a woman?"

"Is it your Aunt? Or someone else?"

"Of course not. My Aunt had a proper funeral and all of that."

"I'm not talking about the bones. I'm talking about the woman that can be seen through the telescope. But I guess you don't believe in that sort of thing. So you've never seen her?"

He glanced at the telescope.

"So you have seen her, you just can't admit it."

"I never thought the idea of dead people returning had any validity. I thought they were stories the twins made up to scare me. I thought I was dreaming it, seeing something from the past, but I don't think that any more. She wears the same kind of hat their Nanny wore. I hardly remember their Nanny, but I remember that hat because Leila was always grabbing it off her head. The Nanny would be so angry."

"So she quit? She couldn't handle them either?"

"Everyone said the twins were awful and that no one could control them. But that's not true. The Nanny loved Liz."

"What about Leila?"

"I don't think she liked Leila much. I only have a few scattered memories. How much do you remember from when you were four?"

I actually remember quite a bit, but if he didn't, there was no point in telling him that. "What does it all mean? Did she die? Liz was vague about where she went or why she left. She just said she went away. That's a strange way to put it, don't you think? Is it possible those are her bones?"

"Everything those two say is strange."

The room grew dark as filmy gray clouds moved across the sky, making the off-white carpet and creamy furniture looked stark.

"Do you think the Sheriff will be able to figure out who the bones belong to?"

"Who knows," said Mike.

"I think she's gone now," I said.

"Who's gone?" said Renee. I turned. She stood at the top of the stairs, leaning her hip against the railing.

"The woman in the telescope."

"She's not always there," said Renee.

"I know, but she slipped under the water while I was watching. As if she drowned. Just a few minutes ago."

"Maybe the bones belong to her," said Renee.

"I was wondering that too."

"Now that you found her remains," said Renee, "Now that someone might figure out why she was buried without a grave, she can rest."

"That's a neatly tied up story," said Mike.

"You never know." Renee walked across the room and put her arm around Mike's waist. He leaned into her and she pressed back so it looked as if they were each holding up the other one. Just as it had earlier, it seemed as if I was interrupting something. It also made me want JD by my side. I realized my prickly independence had caused me to make a mistake, telling him to stay away, making sure he left me alone. I still didn't want him flying to Oregon in some misguided attempt to rescue me, but I think I made him feel as if I didn't need him or want him around at all.

After a few minutes of silence, we all sort of turned at once and walked across the room and down the stairs. Renee said she was going to cut up the stir-fry vegetables she was planning for dinner so we could stay outside all afternoon if the sun came out. Mike said he'd help. It had stopped raining and the Sheriff's SUV was still in the driveway, so I decided to go out and see what was going on with digging up the grave. The twins had disappeared. I assumed they'd gone up to their rooms.

I was wrong. When I ducked under the branches and into the grove of trees, I saw Liz on the opposite side. She was hugging herself, looking cold and stiff in the tiny pink t-shirt that topped her black skirt. She stood near the birdcage, watching as they tied up the plastic bags and started shoveling dirt back into the empty grave. Brick was unwinding the yellow tape from around the trees.

I crossed the grove slowly. I paused, waiting to hear the humming. There was nothing but silence. I waited for several more minutes, but no matter how I strained, I didn't even imagine hearing it. I started walking again. My footsteps were soundless on the thick layer of pine needles. The ground was dry because it hadn't rained hard enough to penetrate the covering formed by the layers of branches high above. I stepped out and paused a few feet from the birdcage. Some of the birds murmured quietly but Liz didn't turn to look. She seemed completely unaware of my presence. She was biting her lower lip, staring at the disturbed pile of dirt and stones.

"Is that your Nanny?" I said.

She didn't startle, so I suppose she'd felt my presence after all, had known I was watching her, waiting to pounce with a question she was now suddenly willing to answer. She nodded.

"Did you tell them?"

She shook her head.

"How did she die?"

Liz hunched her shoulders up to her ears. She shivered and rubbed her arms.

"Why didn't you bring your coat? Should we go back to the house?"

"No," said Liz.

She still hadn't looked at me. For a second, I wondered if she knew she was talking to me, she looked so dazed, so disconnected from what was going on. The only evidence that she was even aware of her surroundings was her shivering in the cool, breezy air.

I walked over and stood next to her. The birds got quiet, and after a minute, I couldn't even hear them moving around on the perches or pecking at the metal pan full of seed. "What happened to her?"

"When she was sleeping, Leila tied her up."

"It sounds like Leila liked to tie up a lot of people. Didn't your parents do anything?"

"Nanny was afraid she'd lose her job."

"So she didn't tell them? What was her name?"

As if she hadn't heard me, but was compelled to explain, she went on. "Nanny was afraid to go to sleep. She was so tired. She called Leila the devil. We didn't like that, so we tied her up when she took a nap on the beach. We pulled her into the water."

I felt light-headed. I turned and wrapped my fingers around the wire of the cage. I leaned forward, trying to get the blood back to my head. "Wasn't there anyone else around?"

"Not in the winter. Most people don't stay here in the winter."

"That's so horrible."

"Mother buried her. Mike saw us digging but we didn't tell him what it was."

Her tone, the stiff, disconnected cadence of her speech was cold, sending chills racing up and down my body. "Is that why you tormented Mike? So he wouldn't tell?"

"He would remember that, not the digging."

"You were children. Why would you...?" The question suddenly seemed pointless. "Why are you telling me?"

"You asked. If we didn't tell you, Nanny's ghost would. She came around a lot more when you were here. Every day.

Sometimes more."

I never thought the ghost was trying to speak to me, but apparently Liz did. I could have told her that the ghost disappeared, that finding her bones seemed to be enough, but that also seemed pointless. The Sheriff would talk to them, and I suddenly realized that he would force them to answer questions individually, and that he'd get the whole story from Liz, as long as Leila wasn't there telling her what to think, re-creating her view of the past.

I GOT UP EARLY on Tuesday so I could hit the road by sunrise. Renee had already made coffee and packed me a bag that included brownies, carrot sticks, whole wheat bread with peanut butter and some of that homemade jam — strawberry — that she'd bought at The Drift Inn. She had a second bag with a few bottles of water. We took our mugs of coffee outside and walked down to the beach. The light was soft and the air was still. It looked like it was going to be a beautiful day.

"I'm glad you came up here," Renee said. "Even if it was nothing like we thought it would be."

We walked toward the water's edge. The tide was out. Pebbles and bits of shells littered the wet sand. The waves rose, curled over, and rushed to shore with a steady, soothing rhythm. The foam was as white in the pre-dawn shadows as it was in the middle of the day. "If part of being friends means having lots of memories, I think this weekend will stick with us for most of our lives."

"That's true," said Renee.

We inched closer to the water until we were standing in that perfect spot where the waves come up and spread around your feet, but have lost most of their force so they don't splash up your legs. "Is Mike okay?"

She nodded. "He still doesn't understand why he allowed Leila and Liz to torment him all those years." She laughed softly. "I think he was sort of hoping you would tell me about it so he wouldn't have to. But I guess you were the practice run, and once he'd stopped holding it inside, it wasn't as hard to tell me about it."

"Do you think you'll ever come back here?" I said.

"If they do something to Leila and Liz, lock them up. Mike's planning to visit his Uncle. He wants to look into maybe buying the place, if those two are gone. But I don't know if they send people to prison for something they did when they were kids."

"I hope they at least put them in a mental hospital. Why do you think he loves it here, even with so many bad memories?"

"How can you not?" Renee lifted her coffee mug out over the water. She brought it back and took a sip. "And even with the awful things they did to him, he still spent a lot of his childhood here, and I'm sure there are good feelings mixed in with the bad, even if he can't remember the details. In some ways, he said it seemed like a game. He thought he'd get bigger and eventually get the upper hand."

"It's weird how scary things and cruel things stand out more clearly than good memories. It's kind of sad," I said.

"He absolutely can't remember anything about his Aunt burying the Nanny's body. So not all scary things."

"You kind of have to wonder whether he's scared of the twins because his mind understood what he saw, but then it got locked away in some back corner."

Renee didn't say anything. She looked out over the water, maybe hoping to see the ghost. I don't really know, but that's what I imagined she was looking for. "They were smart girls, knowing that torturing him might make him forget the rest."

"What a waste," said Renee. "They're beautiful, smart, but their brains are …"

"I know."

I walked further into the water. The waves lapped at the hems of my jeans. They'd be stiff with moisture and salt while I drove, but I didn't really care.

Our conversation meandered over Mike and the house and the twins and JD. Part of me wanted to talk more about the ghost, tell her about my previous experiences, but I didn't want to rush through those stories, and there really wasn't time. It would have to wait until we saw each other again. Finally I said I had to get going. The sky was getting light.

ON THE DRIVE home, I thought about all the things that had happened. Every twenty miles or so, my thoughts drifted back to the sea lion. I wondered how long he, or she, would have to lie there exposed, waiting for dignity. I thought about him swimming, so full of life, and then his life was over. I thought about how I'd been keeping JD at arm's length, waiting for some perfect time when it would be the *right* time to make love. Who knew why or when your life was going to end. I should enjoy my life right now, and if I wanted to make love with him, why was I trying to put a schedule or all these rules around it? It made me shiver, thinking about how cold and calculating I'd been.

When I pulled into my parking slot, JD was sitting on the front steps of my condo. His elbows were propped on his knees and his jacket was lying next to him. I wondered what he was thinking about, staring out at the tiny park-like area across the street from my unit. His face looked so familiar, so welcoming, and yet, suddenly different, as if I'd never truly looked at him before. Watching him waiting for me made my insides melt. He stood and smiled. He looked so happy. I wondered how happy he'd been when he found out the evening was going to end differently than he expected.

THE END

Cathryn Grant

DEADLY STREETS

A Suburban Noir Ghost Story

Published by D2C Perspectives

One

SINCE I STARTED working at Central Avenue Church I've encountered five ghosts. I'm recording the experiences in a dark brown leather notebook I bought for that purpose. Later, I'll explain more about why it's so critical to record these things. The notebook isn't a journal where I write about everything that happens, and my feelings, and all of that. It's more of a record book. I write a few sentences about each spirit — the circumstances of how and when they appeared and whether or not they were trying to communicate something to me, or to anyone who might be paying attention. It's not that I'm special and they appear specifically to talk to me. I think they're hoping to find anyone who will listen and I happen to be a better-than-average listener. I'm also an above-average talker.

I write about them in calligraphy with a narrow felt-tipped pen that has a chiseled tip. That way I don't have to mess with bottles of ink and the potential for smearing the words. I'm taking a calligraphy class, and I love the thrill of seeing beautiful script flow across the page. I have horrible handwriting. It's mostly just printing with the letters connected, so it's nice to see something attractive on the pages. Fancy letters somehow manage to highlight the importance of the experiences.

I haven't given up my pottery classes, but I seem to have huge creative urges, and I'm finding pottery is harder than it looks. Much, much harder, as in, I start with a lump of clay the size of my head and end up with a vase large enough to hold three toothpicks. Calligraphy isn't exactly easy, that's not why I took it up, but it doesn't take as long to produce something semi-respectable, and it's satisfying to write in my notebooks and be pleased with the results.

There's a page for each ghost I've encountered. I know those experiences will stay with me, they'll remain vivid even if I don't record them in the notebook, but I like seeing them recorded in beautiful script.

I haven't done anything to invite these beings to appear to me, but there are two ghosts I've longed to see for quite some time and perhaps that's why I'm alert to aspects of life that many people aren't aware of, or sensitive to other realms, whatever you want to call it. The ghosts that I desperately want to see belong to my parents. They died when I was fifteen years old. Murdered, if you want to know the truth.

IT WAS THE first week I was in public high school after

fifteen years of being home schooled. I should explain about why my parents wanted to home school me, but that's for another time. It's more important to tell the story of their deaths, because it affected me more than anyone can imagine, except for those who have experienced something similar. And it does make me very fixated on the idea of spirits returning or lingering around the living, making themselves known, possibly providing little hints as to what they regret, or in the case of murder, how their lives ended.

Not very many people know my parents were murdered. I haven't mentioned it to anyone at work, including Pastor Joe or Pastor Kate. My boyfriend, JD, doesn't know.

Most people might blurt out that information the first time they meet someone, since it's a part of your life that's always close to the forefront of your mind, but I'm the opposite. I used to tell people, but I learned right away that it makes them look at me differently. There's a mixture of pity, a bit of horrid fascination, and that's followed by awkwardness. They start censoring what they say, afraid of offending you, or possibly making you cry. No one wants to make another person cry.

THERE STILL AREN'T any suspects for my parents' murders. It's been over twelve years, and if I mentioned it to people, they'd tell me to stop thinking the killer will be found, but I'll never stop. I know the detectives don't spend much time on it any more, but it's still on their radar, I think. And it will always be on mine.

It's not that I want the spirits of my mother and father to return and tell me what happened. That would be helpful, but it doesn't really work like that. At least it hasn't so far in my experience. The ghosts I've encountered have let me know that something's not right, or communicated feelings that turned my thoughts in a certain direction and helped me get ideas about some details of a murder, but it's not like they appear and give you a rundown on the whole scenario. Maybe that happens to other people, I don't know. The only other person I've met so far who has seen a ghost is JD. That's one reason we hit it off right away.

I don't understand why all these spirits, total strangers, have appeared to me, but my parents have not. It might be that I need to go back to the house where I grew up, or it might be that I want it too badly and that's creating some kind of intense energy that's keeping them away. Until I started writing in my notebook, which I bought during the drive home from visiting my friend, Renee, in Oregon, it never even crossed my mind that my parents' spirits might be lingering, and that possibly I could see them, or be made aware of their presence. That's why it's critical that I record the important details. I might see a pattern if it's all written down. It might help me understand the spirit world and maybe, somehow, I'll find a way to say good-bye to my parents.

Finding their bodies was the worst experience of my life,

and I hope there's never anything else that even comes close. I was pretty messed up for a long time, but my Aunt and Uncle finally sent me to a therapist and that helped. My Aunt, who raised me after my parents died, didn't believe in therapy — she thinks it's a lot of useless finger pointing at the past. She thinks it doesn't do anything but make you self-absorbed and thinking you're better than other people, and maybe a little bit, refusing to do what other people expect of you. But one of the detectives investigating my parents' murders pretty much insisted she'd better take me to a therapist or I'd never recover. The therapist introduced me to meditation and yoga, and encouraged me to take art classes, but those are also stories for another time.

It was the third week of school, a hot September afternoon when the weather feels like it should be mid-summer, and I suppose it is, because summer doesn't technically end until late September. But the way school schedules are organized, and the way stores are always trying to sell you the next thing that's coming up, most people feel like September is autumn. I wonder how much that messes with our minds, behaving as if it's one season when it's really another.

I walked up the long path to our front door, oblivious to anything wrong inside our small, white house. I unlocked the door but my key felt strange in the lock. I remember that because I think it was the last normal thought I had for a very long time. It felt slippery, and I realized later that was because the door wasn't locked. The house was quiet, but there was nothing unusual about that. My mother liked to read or crochet in the afternoons; she did all her cleaning and a lot of dinner preparation in the mornings so she could relax with tea after that. When she was home schooling me, all the learning was done in the morning — we started at seven o'clock and were done by noon. After lunch I read books and worked on art projects. My mother was very big on me learning all kinds of artistic skills. I took piano lessons, painting, ballet, and jazz dancing.

Anyway, I put my backpack on the bench in the front hall and went into the living room where I expected to find her. This whole coming home from school was new for me, but she'd been in the living room every afternoon for my entire life, and she wasn't there. The room felt as if all the sound had been vacuumed out. It was a good-sized room with a big fluffy couch, a rocking chair, and two wing chairs with a table between them. There was a window that was only seven or eight inches from the floor and about eight feet wide. It looked out on the backyard where we had an oak tree and a vegetable garden, a huge flower garden, flowers in pots on the porch, and two pear trees. The walls were white. There was a lot of white in our house, which made it always feel very clean and tranquil. The furniture was pale too, and all of the color came from artwork — paintings, photography, and vases of flowers.

The silence was like nothing I'd ever experienced, as if all the people had been sucked off the earth. I didn't hear any birds or traffic. The only sound was my breath, shallow and suddenly quite loud inside my own head, as if it was echoing between my ears. I took a step toward the window to see if she was outside, and the sole of my sandal scraping on the carpet was rough and scratchy and extremely loud. There was no movement in the backyard, not even a squirrel or a swaying tree branch.

I stepped back into the front hall and waited. I don't know why I hadn't called her name. I think it might have been the silence, because everything I did was so loud, feet stomping, breath slicing in and out of my lungs, that I thought she would hear me and call my name first. Then I realized I'd taken a deep breath and was holding it inside, waiting.

The kitchen was empty, as I'd expected. I glanced into the hall bathroom and walked a few steps farther and turned into my bedroom. It was pristine, as always, slightly dark since the sun was on the opposite side of the house, making the purple chair I'd painted myself look almost black. I went back to the hallway that ran straight from the front door to the back of the house. My father's office was across the hall from my room, but that door was open, so I knew he wasn't working in there. Even though the feeling had been there all along, from the minute I walked into the utter absence of sound, I finally recognized that I was terrified. Tears were pooling in my eyes. My throat felt like a hose that's twisted back on itself and the water is a tiny drip coming out the other end.

If someone walks into an empty house, the first thought

should not be fear; it should be that no one is home. And although my mother, and often my father, were always home, there could have been a logical explanation for them not being there. But instead of considering any possible explanations, I was gripped with panic, shivering as if the walls were coated with ice. Later, my Aunt told me that I felt those things because going to school and coming home like a normal kid was such a new and strange experience, I was over-sensitive. I couldn't possibly have *known* something wasn't right. But I did.

I went to the doorway of my parents' bedroom and there they were. They were lying flat on their backs, on the wrong sides of the bed. My mother always slept on the left side and my father on the right, if you were looking at it from the foot. But they were reversed. My mother wore a dark blue sundress with orange and yellow flowers. Her feet were bare. My father wore his usual jeans and a pale blue shirt. Their eyes were closed. Their skin had a gray tinge. Their lips were unsmiling. They each had a bullet hole in the center of their foreheads. A round, perfect hole, and no blood that I could see at that time. I fainted.

When I woke up, I laid down on the bed between my parents for a short time. I cried for part of that time and tried to breathe, but anything I thought about is lost somewhere inside my brain, wherever memories go. I don't remember calling 9-1-1 or the detectives coming to the house or what I did for a few days. I know I went to live with my Aunt and

Uncle. My Aunt let me stay home from school for one week and then told me it was time to start facing my reality.

It's been a long time, and I've never seen their ghosts, felt their presence, or in any way been aware of them trying to reach out to me. But I have to believe they are. Trying. Even after all these years.

And that's why I'm recording my experiences in a notebook — I'm hoping I'll see a pattern, and understand what kinds of circumstances encourage spirits to make themselves known.

Two

IT WAS A Wednesday morning in mid-summer. I arrived at the office early because the church newsletter was due out that week and I had a lot of work left to do in terms of final editing and finding a few more pieces of clip art to illustrate some of the articles. I have a lot of fun with that part of my job and don't like to rush it, and sometimes it can take quite a while to make a decision.

The sun was just high enough to cast shadows at seven a.m., so at first I didn't see the man lying at the back edge of the parking strip where the property slopes up an ivy-covered incline. The ivy is not really very attractive but it saves time for the gardener, which I suppose saves the church money. Ivy is nice in the right amount and in the right spot, but there's too much, covering the whole area from the sanctuary to the street, and up near the sanctuary running down the slope where the ground is dug out so the basement office area is somewhat exposed. Too much of anything makes it less attractive. Some people might say that about my earrings, since I have so many piercings — seven on one side and four on the other — but as long as I wear smallish earrings, I think it looks good. It's like snails, one or two of them look kind of cute creeping along the sidewalk, but if there were two hundred, it would give me the shivers. Even birds are that way — beautiful in small groups.

I grabbed my messenger bag, water bottle, and lunch bag off the passenger seat, tugged my travel coffee cup out of the holder, opened the door of my Beetle, and climbed out. Since I was juggling all that stuff, and the bag was dangling from my right shoulder, I nudged the door closed with my left hip, which meant I was facing the street. As I turned toward the church the birds paused in their chirping for half a second and I heard something else — a moan, or maybe just a whisper.

The man lay on his side with his knees pulled up to his chest and his arms wrapped around his lower ribs. He had a shaved head with some dark stubble growing back and a huge beard that hadn't been trimmed in a very long time. The beard was covered with dirt. He wore a navy blue down jacket, black jeans, and thick-soled, scuffed up boots that laced up past his ankles.

I took a few steps closer and said, "Are you okay?" A stupid question, I know. Obviously he was not okay, but the tendency for most of us when we're shocked or caught off guard is to ask stupid questions to which we already know the answer, filling the air with our voices because we want the person to know we're concerned or paying attention, but we really have no idea what to say. Maybe I shouldn't assume everyone does this, but I think most people do. That's why people say *watch out* after someone whacks their head on a cabinet door.

There was nowhere to set all my stuff without getting it dirty. The parking strip is gravel and there's all that ivy, but I knew I had to call someone. I turned back to the car, managed to free two fingers and pull on the handle and let all the stuff except my coffee mug slide onto the front seat. I dug my cell phone out of my bag and walked back over until I was about three feet away from him. He smelled like he hadn't showered in a week or more, and there was another odor, a chemical smell, but I wasn't sure if that was coming from him, or was something the gardener had sprayed on the ivy and the redwood trees that grow in that area.

I heard another whisper and was about to turn my attention to my phone when he rolled onto his back. I could tell he was trying to groan but it came out in a whisper. He jerked to his side and threw up. His whole body arched so that half of it wasn't even touching the ground, and then he collapsed onto his back. He convulsed like that two more times. His eyes rolled up so most of the iris was hidden and his eyelids shuddered for a minute or two. His face grew dark as if a huge cloud had moved in front of the sun, but it hadn't. In fact, I could feel its warmth getting more intense as it moved a bit higher.

The darkness slid off his skin like a piece of charcoal gray chiffon had been dragged across him. At first it was like sheer, flowing fabric, then it transformed into something more like smoke, but much thicker. It rose up out of the man. Intense pain, like someone had taken a hammer to my stomach, spread through me. I doubled over and the phone slipped out of my hand and crashed on the gravel. I clutched my stomach and cried out. The dark thing was still hovering over the man's body and all I could think about was the blue sky and singing birds and that in spite of all that, I was cold and my stomach hurt like nothing I'd ever felt, and my throat burned as bile ate away at it.

There was a roaring sound like the ocean in my ears, but underneath it, as if he, or someone, was right inside my head, I heard a whisper, so strained it made my own throat feel more raw and almost bloody. *Help me. Sorry. Sorry. Just wanted someone to talk to me. Sorry. Help me.*

And then the thing that was hovering over his body moved up higher and I realized it was wrapping itself around him and me at the same time. I was even colder and for a minute I wondered if I'd ever get away from it. I felt a deep, endless loneliness, a reflection of the isolation I felt when I found my parents. Then it faded and there was nothing but blue sky and one bird chirping its little heart out.

I realized I hadn't looked at the man for several minutes, or longer. I didn't want to move closer. My stomach no longer hurt and my throat was better, but I was sweating. At first I wasn't sure I'd have the strength to even bend over and pick up my phone, but I did.

I cradled my phone in both hands and then I looked at him. I was pretty sure he was dead. Of course I was sure, I knew that I'd seen his spirit leaving his body and it was not the pleasant, heading-into-the-light kind of thing you hear about. Although what do I know. Maybe he did head into the light and it was only the leaving that was dark and painful and frightening. Or maybe only for me, maybe he felt better. His eyes were wide open and his lips parted slightly, but his face didn't show any particular expression — not peaceful but not agonized either.

Since I couldn't really help him, I decided to go inside and call 9-1-1 from the church office. I went to my car and leaned against the open door for a few seconds. I picked up my cup and took a few sips of coffee, then gathered up all my things and shut the door with my hip again, but I didn't have that déjà vu feeling when I did it. I climbed the stairs from the parking strip, pausing on each step to catch my breath.

WHILE I WAITED for the police to arrive, I made a pot of coffee. Then I went outside and up the stairs. Although I didn't want to look, I had to glance at the street to be sure the man was still there. I doubt he could have gone anywhere, but maybe he wasn't really dead. Maybe I assumed he was dead, but it could have been the after-effects of his seizures or something like that. Part of me thought I shouldn't have left him lying there all alone, like a plastic bag of trash that had fallen out of a passing truck on its way to the dump. I could have called the police from my cell phone. I didn't absolutely have to make a pot of coffee, it was just habit, and I'd had a cup and a half before I left the house, plus what was in my travel mug. It wasn't like I needed more.

To be honest, I was a little scared to stand near a stranger's corpse, although I can't say why. It wasn't just the thing I'd seen come out of his body. It was the fact that I didn't know him. Sure, we were outside, it wasn't like I was locked in a basement morgue, surrounded by death and the chill that comes with a morgue, but I just really didn't want to be there. Maybe I didn't want to be there because I was afraid of the thing I'd seen come out of his body — his spirit leaving, at least I hoped it was leaving.

When I'd found Fred's body after he was murdered in the church garden, I wanted to stay with him. He was my friend — I'd taken my breaks at the same time he took his breaks from gardening. We smoked our cigarettes and talked, or sometimes smoked and simply enjoyed the presence of another person.

I paused at the top of the steps that lead to the path running throughout the property, one leg going to the sanctuary, one to the stairs back down to the front parking strip, one to the garden at the back, and one to the multi-purpose room. The railing was spotted with dew, but I held it for a moment anyway. Then I let go, wiped my palm on my skirt and walked slowly past the rose bushes to the other set of stairs. He was still there, still lying on his side. The shadows of the trees, long and thin at that time of the morning, covered his face and obscured the texture of his beard so it looked like an animal was curled up on his collarbone. I took a few steps closer to reassure myself that wasn't the case.

I let out the breath that I'd been holding tightly inside and hurried over to the multi-purpose room, unlocked the door to the kitchen, and put my lunch in the fridge. It was clear that I should wait with him, no matter how squeamish I felt. A dog could come by, a child walking to school ... and really, how cold of me to leave him lying there all alone, even if he was dead and even if I had no idea who he was. No one deserved that. Tears swam across my eyes for a minute, but I reminded myself I'd had a shock and it was okay if I made a mistake and abandoned him. I could correct it now.

As I started down the stairs, a large white sedan and a black and white police car pulled into the parking strip, trapping my Beetle between them. A male cop got out of the black and white and the same detective who had come to the church when Fred died, Karen Palmer, got out of the white car. The cop was about forty, short and thinnish, his body looking a bit lost inside his uniform that seemed too big in the sleeves. Detective Palmer has blonde and brown streaked hair cut to her shoulders. She had it tied back in a very tight ponytail so it almost looked from the front like she had no hair at all. She wore black slacks a very nice white shirt with long cuffs and a big stiff collar, very stylish for a detective. They both glanced up at me. They looked over at the body at the same time and their car doors slammed one after the other.

We all sort of reached the man's body at the same time.

"Are you Madison Keith?" Detective Palmer said.

I nodded and stuck out my hand. "We met before. When the church gardener was murdered."

She nodded but didn't acknowledge that she recognized me or that she remembered Fred. She stuck out her hand but didn't really shake mine, just sort of grabbed it and let go. It looked like she was in a hurry to get down to business. She knelt by his head. "What time did you find him?"

"About ten after seven."

"Do you always start work this early?"

"I have to get the church newsletter wrapped up today. I get lots of interruptions, so I like to get here early when I can concentrate and get things done."

"And he was lying like this when you found him?"

"He wasn't dead yet."

She stood and put her hands in her pockets. Out of one she pulled a pen and the other a tiny notebook, so thin I wondered how she could write about more than one case at a time. Maybe in suburbia there aren't enough crimes to require a hefty notebook. "How do you know he wasn't dead?"

"He was moaning. He said he was *sorry, help me*, and stuff

like that."

"What other stuff?"

"He said he just wanted to talk to someone."

"At the church?"

"I don't know. He wasn't clear. That's all he said, he wanted to talk to someone. Then he said *sorry* again and *help me*. He said that several times."

"Have you seen him before?"

"No."

"He's around here a lot. We've had complaints. He's a transient."

I noticed people like that word — transient. It helps them think homeless people are happy nomads or something. I guess some homeless people like living on the street, at least that's what Pastor Joe said. He says they don't want to follow the rules for shelters, not consuming alcohol or being required to work on trying to find a job. But that's not the same thing as *wanting* to live on the street. It's not wanting to follow the rules. If you say transient, you don't have to think about how horrible it is that human beings have no money and no food and no place to sleep and we all just walk past them and hope they don't smell too bad, and really hope they don't talk to us, or ask us for money, or do anything else to make us feel guilty. At least that's how it is for me.

"You're sure he never came around?" Detective Palmer said.

"Not him. At least not when I was here. One other guy

has, but not this guy. I'd remember his shaved head and that beard."

The detective smiled. "Yes, you would. What happened after he said *help me*?"

"He looked like he had a seizure that kept going on. And then ..."

"And then, what?"

It wasn't a good idea to tell her about the thing I'd seen. She'd think I was crazy. She'd basically ignored me when I mentioned the appearance of ghosts when she was asking me questions after Fred's death. It wasn't worth mentioning what I'd seen this time. She'd just talk over me. "He died."

"Why did you pause? Did he say anything else?"

"No."

"Then why the hesitation?"

I shrugged. She would give up. Eventually she'd let it go and figure I was upset at seeing someone die right in front of me.

But she didn't give up right away. She stared at me, not speaking. As the silence continued, the uniformed cop moved back, clearly not wanting to be the one to interfere even though it looked like he was a bit uncomfortable with no one talking, just staring at each other. The detective thought if she stared at me and said nothing, I'd start babbling. That's how most people would respond. But I can stay silent as long as anyone, and I wasn't going to mention that dark thing and the feelings I had. No matter how awkward it was with her staring and not speaking, hearing what she had to say about the ghost would be far more awkward.

"Why do you think he said he was sorry?"

"How would I know?" It was a dumb question. I'm pretty sure she asked that question to show she was still in charge, since my stubbornness had won out over hers.

She closed her notebook, pulled out her cell phone, and punched a key. She asked when the coroner was planning to get there, listened for a few minutes, and then ended the call. "Thank you for your help, Ms. Keith. That's all. We'll contact you if there are more questions."

"Why do you think he died?"

"Poison," the cop said, the first word he'd spoken, except for an occasional clearing of his throat.

"We don't know that," the Detective said.

"Looks like it," he said.

"How can you tell?" I moved closer to the cop, trying to get him to look directly at me.

"The convulsions. Maybe strychnine. I saw a guy die from that before and it was just like you described. Someone wanted to get rid of him."

Detective Palmer turned her back toward the cop and crossed her arms. "Let's wait for a thorough examination. By a medical professional. There could be a lot of causes."

"Why would someone poison him?" I said.

"That's enough," the Detective said. "Thank you for your time. You can get back to work now."

"I haven't started work."

She gave me a tight, closed-lip smile. I took a few steps back but I wasn't ready to leave. There was a chill in the air that hadn't been there earlier and I half wondered if the spirit would return. I also wanted to see if I could linger long enough for the coroner to arrive, although I suppose there wasn't going to be an autopsy right here in the street in front of Central Avenue Church, so waiting wouldn't really get me any more information. "Do you need my cell phone number?"

"We can contact you at the church office if we need to. And it's unlikely you can help us any more. Unless there's something you've forgotten to mention."

I got that hint loud and clear, but I still wasn't going to mention the ghost. I'd talk to JD about it, get his take. In some ways, it didn't matter. I'd seen it and now it was gone, so unless it came back, what difference did it make if I'd seen a ghost leaving a man's body, or if it had tried to make me sick, or whatever it wanted? I looked up the hill toward the sanctuary, then smiled at myself as I realized I was checking to see if it was still up there somewhere on the church property, watching us.

Three

THE BODY AND the cops were gone by the time Pastor Kate arrived at eight-thirty. I suppose I should have called Kate and Joe, or at least called Pastor Joe, to report that a man had died right there on Central Avenue. But between wrestling with my mistake in leaving the guy alone, and then the police arriving and talking to me, I honestly didn't think about it.

Now I was in the uncomfortable position of having to explain what happened and telling them about it after the fact and most likely having them be annoyed that I hadn't been more alert to proper protocol. Not that we have a church policy or protocol for what to do when a man dies on the ground four feet from where you're standing, but I know they would tell me that I should have been thinking ahead, rather than just reacting. Apparently, that's my main flaw in my job when something dramatic happens, like someone calling the church, distraught because a loved one died, or a slightly deranged person showing up in the church office. And you would be surprised at how many slightly off-balance people do show up in the church office. Or maybe you wouldn't.

When Joe gave me my performance review, and a little raise, which was very nice, he said I don't think ahead. I'm too focused on what's going on right around me. I thought that was a good thing, being present in the moment. That's what I've learned from yoga, but I suppose there's a balance — focusing on the moment but also thinking about safety issues and handling a crisis with professional demeanor.

When she arrived, Kate walked directly to the coffee pot. She lifted the carafe off the hot plate, popped up the plastic lid with her thumb, and sniffed. "What time did you get here? This smells stale."

"I'll make another pot." I wheeled my chair away from my desk.

"I wasn't complaining, just making a comment." She filled a mug with coffee.

"I'll still make another pot. Now that you mention it, the office smells like old coffee."

"There's no rush. This is fine." She blew on the surface of her coffee. She walked to the chairs that face my desk and sat down. She set her mug on the little table between the two chairs. "How was your weekend?"

Even though it was Tuesday, I hadn't seen Kate since the week before. Since there are quite a lot of church events on the weekends, Joe and Kate work Saturdays. And you can't predict when someone will have a baby or die, plus Joe performs a fair amount of weddings on Saturdays. And of course they work on Sundays, so Monday is their only day off. Because they like having a live person answer the phone, I'm still here on Mondays.

"I had a great weekend," I said. "But I need to tell you what happened this morning."

She picked up her mug and sipped. She lifted her left hand and ran her fingers through her hair. It's so pale it's almost white and I'm always amazed at how silky it looks when she runs her fingers through it like that. It's really beautiful. I think she should consider growing it longer, but she keeps it quite short. "It's only 8:35, what could have happened?"

"I got here early to work on the newsletter, which now I haven't done anything on and I hope it's not going to be late."

She nodded and put her hand over the top of her mug, as if she was warming her palm with the steam.

"There was a man lying in the parking strip."

"What man?"

"A homeless guy. The cops said he comes around this neighborhood a lot…"

"What cops?"

"He died. I called the police."

"He was dead? You made it sound like he was sleeping there."

"He died while I was watching."

"Oh, how awful." She stood. "Why didn't you call?"

"Everything went so fast."

"Was it one of the guys that comes around regularly?"

"I've never seen him. He had a shaved head and a huge beard."

"That's Toby."

"I wonder why I've never seen him before."

"He's usually hanging around on Sundays. Some of the members give him cash. I can't believe he's dead. Are you sure?"

"Of course I'm sure."

"Sorry. It's a shock."

So much for her thinking ahead. Everyone says strange things when they're caught off guard, and maybe I'm just more easily startled, so I don't plan what I'm going to say or do. Apparently Kate didn't always demonstrate the most professional approach either. It's not that I'm being smug about it, just pointing out that it's not a huge character flaw and impediment to doing my job that I don't always think ahead, like the time that guy came in who wanted to sell Central Avenue Church on having a little religious book stand in the entrance to the sanctuary on Sunday mornings. I went upstairs to look for Joe who was at the senior citizen lunch we have every Thursday. Kate wasn't around, so the sales guy was alone in the church office for a few minutes. He walked right into Joe's office and stole two hundred dollars out of Joe's desk drawer.

No one mentioned that Joe wasn't very smart to leave cash

in his desk drawer, they were all about how bold the guy was to start opening drawers when there were over thirty people right upstairs in the multi-purpose room eating homemade beef barley soup and turkey sandwiches. And they nicely pointed out that I shouldn't have left a stranger there, especially someone who thought it was okay to sell stuff during worship services. I didn't know that selling things during church hours was frowned upon, although I can certainly see why. And I guess they thought that should have proved to me he was a shady character, and really, I shouldn't ever leave a stranger alone in the office. Well if the office is that dangerous, what about me? Why is it okay if I'm there alone with them? Joe said it's not like violent people come by the church, but petty thieves are everywhere. He worries about safety because the offices aren't visible from the street. A lot of the time when I'm working there, I'm the only one in the office. He insists I keep the door locked when I'm alone, but if someone knocks, I still have to answer it, so I'm not sure what that accomplishes. Of course, I'm more likely to run into dangerous ghosts than a living person who's a threat to my safety.

"I can't believe he's dead. What happened?" Kate said. "He's was so young, only thirty-two or so."

"Why was he homeless?"

"Why is anyone homeless? Drugs. Alcohol. The downward spiral of losing your job, running out of money, can't pay rent, can't get a new job, getting evicted, living in your car, losing your car."

The room was quiet for a few minutes. I suppose we were both thinking about how inevitable that spiral is, and how scary.

"Was he hit by a car?"

"No. He had convulsions, which made the cop think it might have been poison. But the detective told him to stop speculating when they didn't really know."

"I don't understand why you didn't call us."

"There was too much going on."

She sighed and took a very long drink of her coffee, downing nearly half the mug. She didn't wince, so I guess it had cooled enough, or she has a much tougher esophagus than I do. I like my coffee hot, but not right out of the pot and it had only been two or three minutes.

"Why would anyone poison him? I know people hate it when homeless people wander around the neighborhood, but poison?"

"They don't know for sure."

"I know. But if he wasn't hit by a car, or stabbed ... it's so awful that someone has to die in the street. I can't even think about it, I get so upset. There's something wrong with our culture that we can allow that."

"I guess we don't usually see it."

"True. We should have a memorial service."

"Did he have a family around here?"

"I don't know. Call Joe, he should know about this right away."

I didn't see how calling Joe would make a difference at this point, I could tell him when he came into the office. Sometimes, before he comes to the office, he makes hospital visits for people who had surgery, or delivered babies. He has a very erratic schedule. Being a minister requires a lot of different things — funerals, preaching, eating lunch with seniors, weddings, visiting the elderly in convalescent homes, counseling people, teaching classes. I can see why he likes it. Most jobs don't have that much variety. It would be kind of fun to have a job that had a different schedule every day. Although maybe that can start to feel the same after a while. I'd have to ask him. I could have asked Kate right then, but I was more interested in Joe's perspective. Kate's job doesn't involve as many interesting things, like marriage counseling or memorial services, for example.

Kate and I talked for a bit longer. Twice she told me to call Joe, but I didn't pick up the phone, and she didn't leave the chair, so I didn't get around to it. After twenty minutes or so, she finally got up and poured more coffee and went out into the large, underground room that forms the rest of the basement, and back to her office that's adjacent to the conference room. Her feet tapped on the linoleum, echoing through that large, unused space. When she reached her office, everything was quiet.

By that time I figured Joe would be there any minute, and it wasn't some type of emergency where I needed to interrupt whatever he was doing by calling his cell phone. I got to work on the newsletter layout, which was even farther behind schedule.

Joe didn't show up until ten, so I managed to get all the text arranged with a decent amount of white space, and only two articles flowed onto a second page. I found clip art of a basket stuffed with ears of corn and a chicken leg and a slice of watermelon that was perfect for the announcement of the annual church picnic. I also found an image of a little girl with stubby braids to go alongside the article about the summer activities at the childcare center. I still needed to find one or two more images before I proofed and printed it and started making copies and folding and stapling, which is the time consuming and less interesting part.

When Joe opened the door, he walked directly to my desk to pick up his phone messages. There was only one. "What's new?" He looked at the name on the message and the lengthy note that ran onto the back of the paper — a detailed explanation from a woman who had called to complain about a few ants she'd seen in the church kitchen, insisting that they needed to be eradicated right away or we'd have an infestation. She went on to chastise people for not properly cleaning up after themselves.

I interrupted his reading about the ants. "I probably should have called you right away ... a homeless guy died in the parking strip this morning. Kate said he comes around regularly, but I've never …"

Joe looked at me. "Who died?" He shoved the message in his pocket.

"A homeless guy. He had a shaved head and a big beard. Kate said his name is Toby. The police came, and the coroner, and they removed his body. I didn't think to call you because I was out there with him waiting for the police."

He rubbed his goatee. It's almost like that thing acts as some kind of amulet to help him think because he rubs it every time he hears something he wasn't expecting. It's as dark as his hair with a few streaks of gray. It seems that thirty percent of the guys you see have one of those things growing in one form or another. Maybe men follow fashion trends more than they admit.

"What happened? Was he hit by a car?"

Why did they both assume a car hit him? I guess that's the logical explanation when someone dies on the street, someone young who most likely didn't have a heart attack or a stroke. And people that die from those afflictions don't tend to drop dead in the street. I wonder why that is, now that I think about it. Once or twice in my life I've seen someone lying on the ground with emergency workers and vehicles clustered around, but both times the person got up after ten or fifteen minutes, so I suppose they only fainted. Or they were drunk. "The cop thought it could be poison, because he had such violent convulsions. He said my description reminded him of a guy he saw die from strychnine, but the detective said he shouldn't be speculating."

"Did they know how long he'd been dead? Was he there all night?"

"He died right after I got here."

He took a step away from my desk. He turned and walked to the coffee pot, but didn't pour a cup. He backed up to the chairs and sat down. "Are you okay? Do you want to talk about it?"

Because Joe's so used to counseling upset people, he tends to think everyone wants counseling. But that's not the case, especially for me. I can work through things pretty well on my own. Besides, what I really wanted to talk about was the spirit leaving Toby's body, but Joe has made it quite clear, on several occasions, that he doesn't believe in ghosts and he doesn't want to discuss the idea and he definitely doesn't want me talking about them to anyone who comes by the church office. It's a bit restrictive, but I like my job, so I keep my encounters to myself most of the time. I discuss them with JD, but he's only seen the one ghost — the Blue Lady — so he doesn't have as much experience and I do most of the talking.

"There's not much to talk about," I said.

"Tell me the whole story. From when you got here."

I explained driving up, seeing the man — Toby — the things he said. It felt like I was leaving out a huge part of the story, almost lying, when I skipped over the part about his ghost leaving his body. Luckily Kate came back into the main office right then, so I was able to put it out of my mind.

"I think we should have a memorial service," Kate said.

"Who would come?"

She sat in the chair next to Joe. "Does that matter?"

"Isn't that the point of a service?"

"Not necessarily." Kate looked at me as if she expected me to jump in with a supporting point of view. "Besides, I'd go. Shouldn't at least one person mourn his passing?"

"I mourned."

They both looked at me.

"I'm sure it was difficult," Joe said. "But don't be dramatic."

Joe can be harsh sometimes. He's nice, he's understanding, he's a very good listener, but he's fairly black and white in some of his views. He also tends to be more outspoken around me. I guess he feels forced to hold his tongue around his parishioners so he blurts out even more around me, since I'm not a member of the church. You could call me an outsider. And maybe that's something I've been all my life. Being home schooled definitely made me an outsider when I first showed up at high school. And having my parents murdered makes me feel like I don't fit in. People don't necessarily treat me like an outsider because most don't know they were murdered, but it sure makes me feel like one. It's not like that's something I have in common with ninety-nine percent of the people I meet. Actually, a hundred percent, because I've never met anyone else whose parents were killed.

At one time I did meet some people who had loved ones who had been murdered. The therapist had suggested I join a support group, but after two meetings, I decided it wasn't for me.

The first meeting they let me sit silently, but the second meeting they pushed me to tell them how long it had been, how I'd found my parents, what that felt like. What did they think it felt like? Somehow they all seemed like a bunch of ghouls, not just the two facilitators, but even the other group members, wanting the details, wanting to suck up my sorrow to make themselves feel better, or maybe to think they were helping me, even if they couldn't help themselves.

Joe went on, "A memorial service is to comfort the family members and friends who are left behind. In this case, as far as we know, there isn't anyone."

Kate folded her arms, which always makes her look like one of those nesting Russian dolls, except those dolls have large heads and no neck, and Kate's head is slightly smallish on top of her broad shoulders. "It's also a way to give closure to the person who died."

Joe stood and went to his office door. "The person who died is gone, they don't need closure and they have no idea someone is remembering them. Maybe some churches teach that, but we're not one of them. We don't want to mislead people by acting as if it matters to Toby or has any impact on his ultimate destination. That decision has already been made."

I'd like to say I had no idea what that meant, but I did. Central Avenue Church definitely believes in heaven and hell. Pastor Joe wasn't speculating about where Toby had ended up, not at all, but he was confident Toby made some kind of decision along those lines at some point in his life.

"Don't be so dogmatic," Kate said.

I was glad to hear her say that. Because I knew that Toby hadn't fully gone anywhere. Sure, I'd seen his spirit leave his body, but how did anyone know where it went after that? I had a feeling it hadn't gone far. Joe acted like death came and you shot out at the speed of light, decision made, fate sealed, life over. It's not that simple.

AN HOUR OR so later, Cindee, Joe's wife, came to the church to have lunch with him. She does that sometimes when he has evening meetings or other ministerial events and she's been missing him. She brought leftover meatloaf and scalloped potatoes. They went upstairs and ate in the church kitchen. It was only eleven-thirty, too early for my lunch, but Joe eats breakfast when he gets up at five in the morning, so eleven-thirty is reasonable. Besides, I wouldn't want to interfere with his lunch with his wife, unless they invited me, which they didn't.

I proofread the newsletter. It looked like I was going to be staying a bit late if I was going to get it into the mail that day. Not that it was a matter of life and death that the church newsletter gets mailed the twenty-fifth of every month or hell will freeze over, but it does need to get to people before the first so they can know what's coming the following month.

The final draft was sliding out of the printer when the office door opened and Joe and Cindee walked in. It had only been twenty minutes, so I guessed they'd eaten fast. Maybe they didn't have much to talk about. Although they have four daughters, so you would think there would always be something to talk about. Not to mention a church of over three hundred members on the roster, and over a hundred and fifty who attend regularly, all with their own opinions, anger, happiness, grief, expectations, and needs. Of course, Joe doesn't tell Cindee about the personal things that people bring up in counseling, but still, not everyone is private about all those viewpoints and expectations, so Cindee gets an ear full on a regular basis, as do I.

Joe went into his office and Cindee parked herself on one of the chairs across from my desk. That's the good thing and the bad thing about my job. I'm a sitting duck. People come in to the church office to see Joe, or to drop off something for Kate, or talk to her about an upcoming kids' activity, or complain about one that already occurred, or because they're early for a meeting or an event. They plop in one of those chairs and start talking to me, as if it's my job to listen. And in some ways, it is. It's not like answering the phone and producing the newsletter and the weekly bulletins and double-checking the total for the offerings that come in each Sunday keeps me frantically busy. I'm supposed to be a friendly face, someone to make visitors and members feel welcome, and listening goes along with that. But there are times when I feel slightly trapped. Most people don't ask whether I'm busy, they just start talking.

Of course, I love talking to Cindee. I don't see her much, but ever since we went to the bar in Half Moon Bay after I'd found her friend's drowned body, I've known we could be friends. She's about fifteen years older than me, she has four children, she's a stay-at-home mom, married, and quite religious, so it might seem like we wouldn't have much in common, but there's a connection. I can feel it. It's not that I view her as some kind of substitute mother figure, she's not old enough for that. In some ways, she seems quite close to my age. You'd never know she has a daughter who is ready to become a teenager, and three others after that.

She and Joe look good together — they both have dark hair and fairly light skin which makes them look dramatic. Cindee's hair is long and curly and her eyes are green, but lighter than mine. She dresses quite casually, jeans most of the time, but somehow manages to look dressed up in jeans and a silky shirt and sandals or boots. She doesn't wear any make-up, and maybe that's one thing that hints at me that we're kindred spirits since I don't bother much with make-up either, except mascara once in a while. She's taller than me, but not by much, maybe five-seven, and just as thin as I am, despite those four kids.

She shifted sideways on the chair and tucked one foot up

under her thigh. "That's so sad that Toby died."

"I know."

She set the fabric bag with the lunch containers on the floor and put her purse on top of it. "Are you arranging the memorial service?"

"Joe didn't seem to think there should be one."

She scrunched up her face. "Why not?"

"He said there's no family."

"So?"

"Did you talk to him about it?"

"A little bit. He said Kate wanted a service. And you agreed."

"I didn't think my opinion counted for anything church-related." I smiled and I'm not sure what my expression looked like, but Cindee laughed.

"Your opinion counts far more than you realize."

"That's good to know."

"Are you okay? Joe said he died right in front of you."

"I'm fine."

"It's so awful that he might have been poisoned. I know people hate seeing the homeless wandering around the area, but I can't imagine knowing someone had that much hatred, that they would go that far. It's too hard to believe."

"I wonder how long it will take them to find out for sure."

"It's good you were there. That he wasn't alone when he died, even if he was all alone during his life."

"I don't think it matters that I was there. It's not like I

offered any support. I didn't do anything to make him comfortable."

"But still, another human being. I think that's important."

In some ways, Cindee is far more spiritual than Joe. She looks at the meaning behind their beliefs, while he seems to focus a little too much on words and structure, or something like that. I tried to talk to her about ghosts that one time while she drank her glass of wine and I drank my iced coffee at The Distillery bar. She was very definite that she didn't believe in that sort of thing, but if there was anyone, besides JD, that I could tell what I'd seen when Toby died, it would be Cindee. She's sensitive, she's an artist — a painter. And she sort of admitted people who say they've encountered a ghost *have* actually seen something, since she thinks it's a result of their grief — wanting comfort after someone is gone. But with Joe fifteen feet away, and his office door open, it wasn't a good time. Still, I waited, hoping she'd say something that would give me an obvious opening.

"It would be too awful to think of him slipping away from the earth without anyone even knowing he was gone. As if his departure was invisible. One moment he's there, and then …" She snapped her fingers. It was quite loud and I was impressed with her finger-snapping skill. Not everyone can do that.

"His departure wasn't completely invisible."

"I know. That's why it's good you were there."

"That's not what I meant."

She looked up past my head, as if she'd just noticed the clock on the wall behind me. She leaned over and picked up her purse, pulled it open, and rummaged around for a minute. When her hand emerged, she was holding her sunglasses. She put them on and stood. "What *did* you mean?" She slung her purse over her shoulder and picked up the bag of dishes.

I pushed back my chair and hurried around my desk, "Let me open the door."

Her forehead creased above the top of her sunglasses. "It's only one bag, I think I can open the door."

"I'll walk out to your car with you. I need some fresh air."

Her brow stayed furrowed and I wondered if she was thinking it was odd that someone who goes out and pollutes the air with cigarette smoke a few times a day was suddenly craving fresh air. I had an urge to tell her about Toby's spirit, and I didn't want Joe to interfere. There was every chance she would brush me off, but the last time we'd discussed the subject her friend had just drowned, so maybe now she'd be more interested.

The door to the church office fell closed behind us. The day was getting quite warm, into the eighties, and the sun was beating down on the sidewalk that runs along the side of the office and leads to the stairs. Moisture sprang up on the back of my neck and around my nose as I followed her along the walkway. My feet were damp against the soles of my sandals. That made the climb up the stairs seem treacherous as my feet slid around like I was on wet grass.

"Toby's death wasn't invisible. I saw his spirit leave his body."

Cindee skipped the second to last step and set her foot on the path as if she was suddenly in a hurry to get out of there, but I wasn't going to give up.

"Joe gets frustrated when you talk about ghosts," she said.

I grinned to myself. She did think differently than her husband. She hinted she thought my experiences might be real — she said *Joe* didn't like me to talk about it, not that she didn't like it. "It's hard not to talk about it."

"Why?"

"It's so unusual, and I don't understand it. And nothing like this happened until I started working here."

She stopped and turned to face me. "Really?"

"Besides, I don't see what the problem is."

"It's not what we believe."

"But that doesn't have anything to do with me."

"True. So you never saw a ghost before you started working here?"

"No."

"That's strange. I wonder why?"

"I don't know, but I don't have an over-active imagination. I'm not crazy."

She laughed. "I need to run errands before the girls are out of school. Can you tell me about it another time?"

"Sure."

We set a time to meet for morning coffee the next week.

She continued along the path, pausing to inhale the scent as she passed the rose bushes. When she reached the second set of stairs, she looked over at the spot where I'd found Toby. She stood there for half a minute, and then she went down the stairs. She never looked back to see whether I was watching her.

Four

THE MINUTE WORD of the memorial service got out, which took all of Tuesday afternoon since Kate asked a few people to help organize it and each of them told a few other people, and on it goes, the phone started ringing. Everyone had an opinion about whether or not the church should be having a service for a man some considered dangerous, most considered a huge annoyance, and a few considered someone who needed love and a human connection and was denied that for the last part of his life.

Caroline McCarthy was the most vocal. She felt so strongly about the issue, she didn't bother to call, she showed up in the church office right before lunch on Wednesday. I wondered if she'd just heard about it mid-morning, or if she'd been stewing all night. It would have been interesting to know how long it took the fire of gossip to get going. Judging by the phone calls, the bulk of which came in after I'd left for the day on Tuesday, not long. Twenty-five calls. I suppose compared to the number of active members, that's not much, but it's a lot of messages to write down, and it made quite a stack on the desk. Two stacks, actually, a smallish one for Kate and a pile for Joe that was hard to keep tidy.

Apparently Cindee hadn't even waited for Joe to get home before she guilted him into agreeing it would be a nice gesture to have a service. After all, wasn't the church there to help people like Toby? Weren't they supposed to be showing love to every person, no matter what their situation? She called him on the office line about an hour after I'd talked to her. Joe agreed. And I don't think it was under coercion, from what I could overhear at my desk while he talked to her with his office door wide open. I think he really came to see his first reaction was wrong. I heard him say, *I know you're right, sometimes I think too much about the fallout instead of doing the right thing.*

I wasn't eavesdropping. I was at my desk, doing my job. With his door open, and his voice that's so good at projecting sermons and other public comments, it's impossible not to hear. He needs to close the door if he wants a private conversation.

That pile of pink phone messages would be the fallout. Or at least the start of it.

Caroline McCarthy opened the outer door, stepped inside, and went immediately to Joe's office. She knocked on the door.

"He's not in there. Can I help you?"

She turned and glared at me. She had brown hair in a ponytail with the end tucked into the elastic band. She wore jeans and a cotton shirt with the tails out, which looked kind of uncomfortable for another day of 85-degree weather. Her hands were thin and she had a large diamond on her left hand and a pearl ring on her right ring finger. "When do you expect him?" Her voice was soft, almost difficult to hear, but had a firm edge.

"He's at the community ministers' meeting and they have lunch together, so probably not until about two."

"Probably?"

"He didn't say whether or not he was coming directly back. Usually he's back from the ministers' lunch by two. Do you want me to ask him to call you?"

"I want to talk to him face to face. I'll come back." She opened the door and the minute she stepped through she turned back. "Kate's here, right? At least her car is."

"Yes." I wondered why if she'd noticed Kate's car, she hadn't noticed the absence of Joe's Miata.

After she disappeared into the basement area, I got up and stretched my arms over my head. I walked toward the coffee stand that's right by the door leading to the basement. I switched it off. It was getting too hot for anything but iced coffee and that wouldn't taste very good since it had been sitting in the pot for a few hours by that time.

It's not that I'm nosey, I'm curious. I really wanted to know what she was so wound up about, and I wondered why Kate was just as good as Joe for whatever was on her mind. Usually if someone wants to talk to Joe, they want Joe. They turn to him for spiritual guidance and only talk to Kate if they have kids and want to discuss one of the children's programs.

Actually, I *am* nosey. Curious and nosey are kind of the same thing. And half the fun of working in the church office, if I'm honest, is all the drama. Not that I've liked it when someone was murdered, but it's interesting to watch people when their ordinary routines are disrupted. And good portion of the time, people who show up in the church office have had their ordinary routines disrupted.

It was a risk to hover near the door because if someone else came in, it might be obvious what I was doing. But there was no risk in Caroline or Kate catching me listening to their conversation because I would hear them tromping across that hard linoleum floor long before they were anywhere near the door to the main office.

"Why would you do that?" Caroline said. Her soft voice was no longer soft, so I had no trouble hearing.

When Pastor Kate spoke, I only caught a few words, something about compassion and optional attendance.

"He was a creep. He scared my daughter. He looked like an ex-con."

Kate spoke clearly this time. "He wasn't."

"How do you know that?"

I didn't hear her answer but she spoke for quite some time.

"It was bad enough he kept coming around here, stinking up the garden…"

"He didn't stink up the garden," Kate said.

Caroline kept going as if Kate hadn't interrupted. "… Begging for cash, standing too close to young girls, breathing his foul odor on them, leering at them. Someone should have called the police a long time ago. Why you would honor someone like that, why you would expect *anyone* in this church to attend a service, is beyond me."

Caroline's voice echoed slightly and I guessed she'd moved out of Kate's doorway and into the basement.

Since Kate's voice was easy to distinguish now, she must have gotten up and walked into the basement as well. "Like I said, you don't have to attend."

"You're sending the wrong message. You're telling my daughter you don't value her, that that some guy leering at her is okay because he was hungry and homeless and addled, so he didn't know how he came across, which is a crock, by the way."

"Don't read all that into a simple service. Toby was alone and shoved aside when he was living, and he died on the street. Can't we at least remember his humanity?"

"He was a pervert. I'm glad he's gone."

Caroline's sandals smacked the floor as she stalked across the basement. I returned to my chair before she reached the office. She walked past my desk, her footsteps now silenced by the carpet. She didn't speak to me as she flung open the door. She let it fall closed on its own.

AFTER WORKING AT Central Avenue Church for a year and a half, I'm still amazed at the controversies that flare up. In some ways, a church is like a large extended family with all sorts of tiny histories involving fights and hurt feelings, and in other ways it's like a separate country, with specialized rules and regulations, existing in an entirely different world from the rest of society. Maybe that's how the world works overall — a collection of groups — maybe we're all still tribal after all.

Caroline McCarthy has three children — a fifteen-year-old girl, a thirteen-year-old boy, and a ten-year-old girl. All three of them participate in various groups that Kate's responsible for — the youth group, the religious rock band, and the after-school homework club that meets once a week to help kids learn good study habits. Every good thing Kate had done for Caroline's kids flew out the window as Caroline pursued her mission to make sure the church did not have a memorial service for Toby.

When Joe came into the office that afternoon, he had a fresh stack of messages. There'd been four calls from other parents of teenaged girls. Apparently Caroline had been busy on the phone after she rushed out the door without speaking to me, her wrapped up ponytail twitching like the stubby tail on a Doberman Pinscher.

Joe picked up the stack of messages and stood in front of

my desk reading through them. I tried to stay busy, working
on typing up the prayer requests that would be printed in the
bulletin for next Sunday's service, but I knew Joe was going
to interrupt me any minute. I could feel him getting ready to
make a comment. I guessed he would either regret he'd
agreed to the service, or his stubbornness would kick in and
he'd double-down on his enthusiasm for remembering a man
who was almost a ghost even before he died, lurking around
the church, not speaking much, and scaring people with his
enormous beard and large outdoor backpack filled with
everything he owned in the world.

Joe wore khaki slacks and a pale blue shirt that make his
skin look a bit bluish under the florescent lights. Or maybe
the hint of blue resulted from the controversy, outlined in
twenty-three pink slips of paper and all the phone calls he'd
be required to make that afternoon instead of whatever else
he'd had on his to-do list. "It's good to know most of the
people who called are supportive of the idea," he said.

I nodded.

"I really have no idea how to handle this. It's a nice gesture
to have a service, and I hope some of the other homeless
people who knew him feel comfortable attending. Caroline
McCarthy and Sandy Berger used to complain about him
from time to time, but I always thought he made them
uncomfortable because he was somewhat deranged, that they
felt guilty about his condition. That the complaint about him
staring at their daughters was a bit of smokescreen."

"So you think they made it up?"

He backed toward the armchairs and put his hand on the back of the chair, placing it over the stack of messages as if he didn't want to see what was there, as if he wanted them to slide down onto the seat of the chair. Then he could walk away and not have to deal with them. "I'm not saying they made it up."

"But you think they're exaggerating."

"There's a good possibility."

I opened the bottom drawer of my desk and pulled a hair clip out of my bag. With the office below ground level, it stays cool most of the time so there's no air conditioner, but the temperature outside was creeping up to ninety degrees and it was getting warmish in the office. I pulled my hair up to the top of my head and clipped it. I'm sure it looked messy, a few strands falling out, the rest of my hair lumpy, but it felt instantly cooler and it wasn't exactly a good time to get up and go to the restroom to fix my hair.

"People who aren't healthy mentally, or have addiction issues, can seem like they're looking at you a certain way," Joe said, "when really, it's just an inability to use conventional facial expressions."

"Is that what you think?"

"To be honest, I don't know what I think. Sometimes I get tired of every single thing being a cause for disagreement. We can't change the size of the candles on the altar without someone complaining."

"I don't think being upset about a crazy guy staring at your daughter is the same as not liking the new candles."

"Whose side are you on?"

"Are there sides?" I smiled.

"It seems that there are."

"I think it's sad that he died alone, on the side of the street, that he never got a chance to get his life back on track. And if people don't want to come to the service, they don't have to. I'm sure a lot of them will not want to sit side by side with a bunch of homeless people."

"I'm sure not," Joe said. "But what do you think about the complaints from Caroline and Sandy and the others?"

"You can't control whether someone stares at you. Like you said, there might be a lot of men staring at their daughters, they're just able to hide it, so no one's aware of it."

"Is that what I said?"

I waved my hand in the air, "All that stuff about conventional facial expressions."

"I'm glad you can interpret." He smiled, but still didn't look very happy. It was more of a grudging smile. "I have no idea what to do, though."

It's not like Pastor Joe is indecisive, or that he gets swayed by public opinion. It's more that he's truly baffled when people complain about things they could ignore, or things that are insignificant.

You'd think after being a minister for twenty years, he would know that every decision will generate opposing views, and that he'd have methods for dealing with that.

Sometimes people up and leave the church if they disagree with one policy or another. It can be over extremely petty things, like the time a woman said she was going to look for a new church because she was horrified that Pastor Joe asked the church to pray for a couple's new baby that was born six weeks prematurely. The couple wasn't married and the woman thought those kinds of prayers should not be made public. Joe brushed that one off because he thought she was cruel, and maybe the church would be better off without someone so full of hate that she'd withhold prayers from a struggling child.

This time was different.

"Did he ever bother your daughters?" I said.

He squeezed the stack of notes ever so slightly and I could see his knuckles turn white as he pressed his hand against the chair, either angry at me for voicing something he didn't want to think about, or angry at the thought of Toby leering at his daughters.

"He was drowning in alcohol. In some ways, he wasn't responsible for what he did."

"Did he bother them?"

"Not that I know of."

"What would you do if he had?"

He glanced at the door to the basement and then looked at the wall behind me for so long, I thought about turning to see what had grabbed his attention even though I knew his attention was inside his own head, thinking about what he would do, but not wanting to discuss that angle with me. "So you think Caroline and the others are over-reacting? That their kids were simply uncomfortable with Toby's condition and his lack of sense? Or that the parents were actually the ones who were uncomfortable?"

"I wasn't there, but yes, I can see that."

He stood. "It helps to get your perspective. Thanks."

"Any time."

He went into his office. One of the pink slips had fallen and was stuck between the cushion and the back of the chair. I went over and picked it up. The name was one I didn't recognize, but I remembered the caller. She spoke with a crispness in her voice that sounded like a bird tapping at a pane of glass. I carried the slip of paper to Joe's office.

He had the phone to his ear, either listening or waiting for the call to connect. He's like that. He might seem to waffle over decisions but he doesn't waffle over getting stuff done. If there were calls to be made, no matter how unpleasant the conversations might be, he got down to business. I placed the pink paper on his desk and left, pulling the door closed behind me. It seemed like these were conversations he should have in private, even if he didn't realize that.

Five

THAT NIGHT JD was coming over for dinner, so the minute I got home, I put the recipe I'd printed from AllRecipes.com on the counter and went upstairs. I kicked off my sandals and changed out of my cotton skirt into a white sundress, which made my very pale whisper of a tan look slightly darker. I grabbed my flip-flops with the thin white straps to put on after I made dinner so I wasn't barefoot when JD arrived. Not that he'd mind.

I went back downstairs and into the kitchen to get Simon's cage. He likes to be with me when I'm cooking, but I didn't want him tweeting his head off while we were trying to eat dinner, and the dining area is pretty much just an extension of the kitchen. I carried his cage into the living room and set him on the coffee table. I filled his tube with fresh water, put my finger in the cage and let him climb on. He cocked his head and stared at me with his round, dark eyes, as if he wanted to know why the routine had changed. Like I do nearly every night, I promised him I'd get him a companion — soon. I think he's starting to not believe me since I've been saying it for so long. I'd like to get a larger cage and have five or six parakeets, but I don't know whether they would get each other all wound up and create a huge racket. I like to sleep with my balcony door cracked open and Simon sleeps in my room. I'm sure my neighbors, with their balcony three feet from mine, aren't bothered by his cheerful tweeting in the morning, but six birds might not sound as melodic.

I got out my wok. I was making a Szechwan shrimp recipe, mixing it up a bit by serving risotto on the side. It's an odd combination, but JD and I both like risotto and we love stir-fry, so it sounded good to me.

As I was turning down the gas on the risotto, JD knocked on the door. He prefers knocking to ringing because he thinks doorbells are a stupid invention. His belief is that if your house is too big to hear someone give a good solid knuckle rap on the front door, then your house is too big. Of course, in my condo I can always hear him unless I'm in the shower, and I don't hear the bell when I'm in the shower, so I guess he's right.

I opened the front door and he stepped into the entryway. When he moved to the side to close the door, he bumped the antique bench with an oval mirror in the center of the tall back and hooks on each side where I hang my bag and my jacket and scarf. He turned toward me, put his arms around my waist, and pulled me against him. The day had been hot, but I was cooled down from my shower. I'd been running the air conditioner since I'd arrived home. All the warmth of his arms and his chest pressing against me felt so good I didn't want to go back to finishing up dinner. His stomach growled. "I guess your belly disagrees with me."

"What's that?" he tightened his grip.

He kissed me long and slow and when we finally paused, my voice came out in a whisper. "I was thinking you feel so good I don't want to finish cooking dinner, but then your stomach growled."

He laughed. We walked to the kitchen with our arms around each other.

"Need me to help?" he said.

"You could pour water. And light the candles."

He lit the candles first, flicking the match along the strip of sandpaper so quickly I wondered if it would catch, but it burst into a bright flame. He lit all four candles at the center of the table without having to light a second match.

"Do you have any wine? I could use a glass. I Skyped with my brother before I came over. So much drama. I need to unwind."

He knows I don't drink wine. I don't know why he thought I'd have some, so I didn't answer.

"Madison? Did you hear me?"

"I don't have any wine, you know that."

"No big deal. I thought you might have picked some up for me, since you know I like it."

Was that supposed to mean I didn't care what he liked? I made the whole dinner menu with him in mind, but I didn't do wine. I don't like it. I don't understand the point of drinking it. If I have too much drama, or need to relax, I go for a walk, or meditate, or do yoga, or just about anything that would make me feel better. I don't see how sipping tart liquid and getting groggy makes you feel better. "What's the drama with your brother?" I scooped risotto onto our plates. I covered the pot to keep it warm in case JD wanted seconds, in case I wanted seconds — I could eat risotto for breakfast.

"That smells great." He stood behind me and looked over my shoulder. "What's in it?"

"Be patient, you'll see."

He didn't step back so I nudged him with my shoulder. I scooped shrimp and carrots, green onions and water chestnuts sliced into thin spears onto the risotto. Steam rushed up to my face, but the aroma was so wonderful, I didn't mind.

JD sat down while I grabbed a lime out of the fridge and cut it into wedges. He prefers lime instead of lemon in his water, and I hoped it made up for not having a glass of white wine or a beer. I suppose if I was a good hostess, or a truly devoted girlfriend, I'd make sure to stock what he likes to drink, but it's expensive and I figured being with me should be relaxing enough. Maybe that's a little controlling, I don't know.

After he ate a few forkfuls and raved over the food, he

plucked four grapes off the bunch sitting in a bowl between us and I asked him again about the drama with his twin brother.

"I don't want to think about him right now. I'll tell you later, okay?"

That made me curious, but he gets so wound up about his brother, I decided not to push it. "We have some drama at the church, too."

"Don't you always?"

I laughed. It did seem that way. I'd already told him about Toby, and a bit about the ghost, when we talked on the phone the night before. Although I preferred to talk about the ghost instead of church squabbles, there really wasn't much else to say without repeating all the things I'd already told him — wondering if it still lingered around the church, wondering what Toby needed in order to be at peace, all the usual questions. What I really wondered was whether his spirit would find me again, whether I had some kind of permanent connection, since I'd been there at the moment he died. "There are quite a few people who don't want to have a memorial service for him."

"I can understand that."

"You can?"

"Sure." He put two forkfuls of risotto and shrimp in his mouth, one right after the other.

"Do you like it?"

He nodded and chewed and talked around what was still in

his mouth, "Definitely wanting seconds."

"Why aren't you surprised about people not wanting the memorial service? The guy died right in front of the church, he used to hang around there, and in the neighborhood, it seems like the humane thing to do. Rather than pretending he didn't exist, being glad that he's gone."

"That's just it. I'm sure a lot of people are glad he's gone."

"What a horrible way to think."

"Yes. But it's an upscale area. I'm surprised the police didn't make sure he stayed away. Some people don't want to be reminded that the world isn't fair. Most of them probably think it was his fault he was living on the streets. Alcohol, laziness. And I'm sure the people at church hated him coming around asking for money, making them feel like they weren't following their beliefs if they didn't help him. They probably worried he was dangerous."

I put a piece of shrimp in my mouth. I chewed slowly then took a sip of water. The candles glowed, not even flickering slightly, the air was so still, since I'd turned off the air conditioning and opened the door to the back deck before we sat down. JD's dark blue shirt looked black and his eyes were dark, almost fully dilated since the sun had gone down and the candles were the only light in the room. The framed photograph of Vernal Falls in Yosemite across from the table reflected the candlelight. "Well then if they're glad he's gone, you would think a memorial service wouldn't bother them." I hated saying that, I thought it was horrible that anyone would be glad someone was dead, but maybe he was right.

"Aren't memorial services supposed to be for family and friends?"

"Yes."

"Does he have any?"

"Friends?"

"Or family. Does anyone know if his parents are living, if there's anyone in the area?"

Immediately I thought of my parents. I put down my fork. I took a sip of water. I hadn't mentioned my parents' death to JD yet. Of course I'd told him they were dead, but I hadn't mentioned murder. It's just too huge, and with the few people I've made the mistake of telling, it changed everything. I don't know why. I guess it's so unusual, it makes people uncomfortable, they don't know what to say. I think, I hope, they feel sorry for me. Although I'm not really sure I want them to feel sorry, exactly. I don't know what I want. It just makes me different. Not that my whole goal in life is to be like everyone else. I took another drink of water, trying to drown that train of thought. "I don't know if he has any family. Not that we know of. I'm sure the police will find that out."

"Of course, if he does, who knows if they'll even want to come."

"Anyway, a few women are really upset about the service because they'd complained that he leered at their daughters and made them uncomfortable. That he was a pervert, I guess is what they're saying. They're angry that Pastor Joe didn't do more to get rid of him before, and they sure don't want a service."

"So what's he going to do?"

"Have the service. Do you want to come?" I had no idea why I blurted that out.

"Do you want me to?"

That surprised me as much as my unplanned invitation. Why would he want to come to a service for a guy he'd never even seen? Maybe he guessed right away that I was still unnerved from watching a man die, still thinking about the ghost, not wanting to be alone, even though I knew Kate and Cindee would attend the service, so I wouldn't be there with a bunch of total strangers from the church. "Maybe. If it works out."

"Okay. Sure." He finished his water. "Great dinner. Thanks."

I smiled.

After dinner I made coffee and we sat on the back deck looking at my tiny lemon tree. All we could really see were the three lemons, pale as white onions in the moonlight. It was so warm it felt like mid-day. I love it when it's dark but the air is warm and you want to be outside, feeling the silkiness on your skin. When it's cold, the world seems like a dark and scary place, but when it's warm, everything feels kinder, as if the darkness is comforting you and giving your eyes some rest rather than threatening your life. I mentioned this to JD and he said he'd never thought of it that way, but agreed he didn't much like being outside at night in the winter.

When the conversation wound down, we went upstairs to my bedroom.

AFTER JD AND I made love, we drifted to sleep. When I woke, I got up and put on my fluffy white robe that I've had since I was twelve, but it still fits because it was too big at the time. I pulled a cigarette out of my purse, went out to the balcony, and closed the sliding glass door. It was eleven-forty. The air had cooled down, but it was still nice — the dry warmth of night when the coastal fog hasn't come inland after a hot day.

There's barely room for two plastic chairs on my balcony, but it's still nice to sit out there. In the daytime, a sliver of the foothills is visible and at night, I can see lights from the high-rise buildings that are sprinkled throughout downtown San Jose — hotels and office buildings, condos and apartments.

I put the cigarette in my mouth. Despite my supposed intention to quit, for the past year I haven't managed to reduce my daily cigarette count below three. All three of those occasions, after breakfast, one mid-day, and one in the evening, are such engrained rituals that it's hard to decide which one to let go of. Sometimes I wonder if it's more about the ritual than the actual addiction to nicotine. Although maybe the addiction makes the ritual more of a need. I just know they're calming, focal points of each day. I like smoking. It makes me slow down and stop thinking for a bit, forcing me to pay attention to the world going by. Of course, I couldn't see much of the world in the dark, but I could watch my thoughts in a more leisurely way. Most people would think it's terrible that I admit that I enjoy smoking, and that I don't really want to quit. They'd be horrified that someone like me, young and healthy, educated on the effects of cigarette smoke, would still cling to such a deadly habit. I know I'll quit someday. I want kids, eventually, and I sure wouldn't smoke when I was pregnant, or when I had children around, both for health reasons and to avoid setting a bad example, but that all seems very far away right now. So ninety-percent of the time, I enjoy my cigarette without thinking about my health or the future.

The tip hissed as the flame hit the paper, then settled down. I put my lighter on the balcony rail. The ashtray was under my chair, so I pulled it out a bit where it was within easy reach. I could cram a small table between the chairs, but I don't really need one so it doesn't seem worthwhile to make the space even more crowded.

Smoke wove its way into my mouth and down my throat. There was still no air moving at all, so when I slowly exhaled, the smoke floated gracefully toward the rail and hung there for a beautiful moment before it faded into the darkness.

Instead of my thoughts settling on Toby's ghost, they drifted past that and meandered around to my parents. The problem with not telling anyone my parents were murdered is that when I start getting closer to people, it then starts to swell into a big issue as to when I'm going to mention it. No one at Central Avenue Church knew, and JD didn't know, and suddenly it was feeling like I was withholding a huge part of my life from all these people that I'd become close to, in varying degrees, over the past year or so. I didn't want to think about when or how or who to tell at work, but I definitely needed to tell JD. Soon.

There's no casual way to mention something like that. I don't mean to make that sound cold, as if I don't feel anything about their deaths except the dilemma of how to bring it up. It's just hard. JD had asked me about my family at various times. He knew I didn't have any siblings and he knew my parents were deceased, but he hadn't, like some people might, asked what they'd died of, since they died so young. He'd been very sympathetic that they were gone, but I'd quickly steered the conversation to my aunt, and he didn't pursue it. There was no good way to tell him without it seeming dramatic. Especially since I hadn't mentioned it when it would have been the easiest. Now I was stuck. I'd have to just blurt it out and try to explain why I don't talk about it much.

My cigarette was half gone when the door slid open. I leaned back. JD stood behind me. He put his hand on my head. "Why did you leave?"

I lifted my cigarette to show him, although of course he smelled the smoke and he knew why I left, that wasn't really the question. The question was actually — *I woke up and was startled that you weren't there and it made me feel disoriented for half a minute.*

"Can I join you?"

He stepped onto the balcony and closed the door.

"Aren't you going to put on any clothes?"

"It's dark. A better question is why are you wearing a robe?"

I smiled, but he probably couldn't see me. "It's not quite as warm as you think out here."

He stepped around me and sat down. I handed the cigarette to him. He took a drag and handed it back.

It was almost time to put it out, but I didn't want it to end, didn't want to shift to sitting there in silence, or talking. I didn't want to change anything. That's why I like smoking. Time seems to stop for a few moments, and there's nothing better than feeling like time has disappeared, or at least moved into the background for a while.

"You've never gotten up to smoke in the middle of the night before."

"Sometimes I do."

"Never with me."

"That's true."

I took a final puff and leaned over to stub it out. "I was going to tell you something."

"You sound serious."

I was glad he hadn't turned on the light in the bedroom,

glad it was dark, because that made it a little bit easier. I didn't have to look at him, noticing his face, trying to read his reaction. Or misread. "There's something I never mentioned about my parents."

He was quiet, but I think I felt him shift toward me, turning slightly in his chair.

"They were murdered."

For a minute he was quiet. "Why didn't you tell me that before?"

"I don't like to mention it."

"Why not? How did you ... I don't know what to say ..."

"Which is why I don't usually bring it up. It tends to be a conversation stopper, it changes things."

"How? I don't understand why you didn't tell me."

I had no idea which question to answer first. I wasn't sure I wanted to answer either one. And really, I'd answered the one as much as I could. He just didn't understand the answer. So I took the easiest. "They were shot. In their bed. I found them when I came home from school. It was only a week after I started going to a regular school."

"You poor kid."

And that was exactly why I don't like to mention it. Now I was different in his eyes, a *poor kid*. Someone damaged or traumatized, someone who wasn't normal. Someone who needed sympathy when I don't. I got over it. Sure, it took a very long time. And I'm sure it still affects me, that it's changed who I am. And of course I think about them all the time, think about how I miss them and how I miss the things I would tell them about my life, but I don't need sympathy. Not any more. I'm not a poor kid. I'm twenty-eight years old. They were murdered when I was fifteen.

"Who killed them? Why?"

"I don't know. It's an open case."

"They never arrested anyone? Had any suspects?"

I shook my head. I don't know if he could see that or not in the dark, but I didn't want to talk. Already I regretted bringing it up right then. But when is the right time? *When?* I had to tell him, we're a couple, we're sleeping together, which is supposed to be the closest you can be to a person. But I didn't like what he'd said, calling me a poor kid. Now those words were going to stick in my head and circle around and everything suddenly seemed different between us. "No. There are no suspects."

He reached over and put his hand on my leg. He nudged my robe to the side so his palm was on my skin. It felt warm and comforting, which made me slightly less fixated on *you poor kid*. Slightly.

"Why did you wait so long to tell me?"

"There's no good time."

"I'm ... I don't know what to say. Are you okay?"

"It's been a long time."

"I don't think you get over something like that."

Now I wanted him to stop talking. I'd known this would happen. Nothing he said was going to be right and I didn't want it to turn into this huge thing where he was lumbering around like a man in a tea parlor, over-crowded with small tables and delicate chairs and lots of china teapots and cups and crystal vases that he can't help crashing into.

"I wish you'd told me sooner."

"Why? Does it make a difference?"

"No. But I feel like I didn't know you before. I feel like you're hiding yourself from me."

"I'm not hiding anything. Have you told me every detail of your life?"

"Having your parents murdered isn't quite the same as who was the first girl I kissed or whether I ever shoplifted or committed vandalism."

"Did you?" Even though I was looking out at the glittering lights of the Fairmont Hotel, I could feel him staring at the side of my head, feel the heat of his thoughts coming through his eyes, intensifying his gaze.

"Did I steal or throw rocks into the neighbor's back yard?"

"Yes."

"Does that matter?"

I'd never felt our conversations were so combative, or sparring or whatever you call it, but suddenly it seemed we weren't on the same wavelength. I wasn't sure if it was my parents, that I'd shocked him and he was still recovering, or something else. Maybe it was me. "It doesn't matter, I'm just curious."

"All kids do stuff like that."

"I didn't."

"Okay, most kids. Boys. But you changed the subject. Is it too hard to talk about them?"

"You haven't answered the question," I said.

"Yes. I shoplifted. I took nuts and bolts out of the boxes every time my Dad took me to the hardware store. I had a whole milk carton full of them. Why didn't you tell me and why don't you want to talk about your parents? You keep trying to change the subject."

"It's kind of a big thing. And it feels like I'm throwing a stick of dynamite whenever I mention it. Like right now."

He took his hand away from my thigh and shifted in his chair. He dragged it forward an inch or so. The plastic legs scratched at the concrete floor. He stretched out his legs and propped his feet on the railing.

I wished I had another cigarette. Right then. More than anything in the world, and more than I'd wanted one in a very long time. I felt like I couldn't think or that I absolutely had to have something to do with my hands. The feeling grew stronger the more the minutes ticked past without JD speaking. After another minute, I couldn't take it any more. I stood and went inside.

"Where are you going?" he said.

I pulled two cigarettes out of the box, stuck one between my lips, and went back to the balcony. I handed a cigarette to JD, lit mine, took two quick puffs, and handed the lighter to him. It made me feel better, although deep inside I was angry at myself for going over my limit, and for expecting something of JD that I couldn't put words to. How can I expect something from him when I don't even know what it is?

I smoked the whole cigarette, letting my mind go blank. It felt better and I was calmer and no longer filled with the strange, irrational anger I'd had a few minutes earlier. When I stubbed it out, he put his out at the same time. He took my hand.

"Let's go back to bed. I want to hold you."

I let him lead me inside. He closed the screen and slid into bed. I let my robe fall off my shoulders and got into bed. I made my limbs relax and snuggled into him and let him feel as if he was making everything okay.

Six

JD MADE THE coffee the next morning and I made toast. We ate on the deck. It was warm already — another beastly hot day ahead. We didn't talk about murder or shoplifting or vandalism and I wondered when that conversation would start up again. I had to be in the office at eight-thirty, and even though he didn't start work until three, he left when I did.

The church office was cool and quiet, no one there but me, which was nice because I was still feeling a bit jittery from whatever had passed between JD and me. For all I knew, he thought everything was fine, and maybe he just needed to absorb the fact that my parents were killed and I'd never told him until now. The whole reason was because I didn't want to derail our relationship before it even started, and now I'd done that anyway. Or maybe that was all in my own head. I didn't like how he'd responded, and I'd known I wouldn't like it, so I felt a little bit like I set him up — that he couldn't do anything right. And really, he couldn't. There is no good response, no right response, so no matter how people react, no matter what they say, it's wrong, and I get upset.

Pastor Joe came by, picked up some books from his library, and said he was going to work on his sermon at his home office. The sermon wasn't coming together, and he couldn't be interrupted. Kate called and said she was spending the morning buying stuff for the upcoming church picnic. Of course the kids and teachers at the childcare center are always lurking around upstairs, but they never come down to the office, so if I don't eat in the kitchen at the back of the multi-purpose room, I can go the entire day without seeing any of them, or even hearing them, the basement is so well insulated from the rest of the world.

It's always somewhat creepy down there when I'm by myself. It's fine in the office area, but walking through the dark underground space that's between the main office and Kate's office and the conference room can be unnerving. For some strange reason, the restrooms are on the opposite side of the building and the light switches for the whole area are in the alcove where the restrooms are located. Now that we have the childcare center, I know there are almost always people around, but as I said, they seem far away and it still feels scary. It's worse since I encountered some kind of dark spirit back there when the church members were deep in their controversy over opening a childcare center.

After two cups of coffee, I had to use the restroom, so I

hurried across the basement. When I came out, I turned on the lights so they'd be lit for the rest of the day. Of course when I went home I'd have to turn them out, so I'm not sure I saved myself any scary trips.

Back in the main office, I poured another cup of coffee, turned off the pot, and took the coffee and my cigarettes outside for a smoking break. I hadn't had a smoke after breakfast, which meant I allowed myself two mid-day breaks. I'd smoked a fourth cigarette the night before, but this was a new day.

Now that we have a childcare center, there aren't many outdoor places on the property where I can count on being alone. Since the kids were having an outdoor playtime, I walked down the steps to the parking strip. It probably didn't look that great to have me standing twenty feet from the church sign smoking, but I figured it would only be a few minutes.

I smoked the cigarette halfway, then realized I didn't feel like having any more. I put it out and when it was good and cold, cupped it in my hand and carried it back up the stairs. I dropped it in the outside garbage can and walked along the path to the small wooded area at the back of the property and sat on the concrete bench. It felt nice and cool through my thin skirt. A dove cooed from one of the trees but I couldn't see her. Then she stopped and flapped madly, flying up past the overhanging branches and out of sight. It was quiet. There isn't much traffic on Foothill Boulevard when it's not commute time and obviously the kids were back in their classroom because I couldn't hear a sound from that direction.

Suddenly I felt as if someone was watching me. I turned around, but the pathways leading to the classrooms, the multi-purpose room, and the sanctuary were deserted. I glanced at the fence that runs along the back of the property from the sanctuary to the parking lot, but no one was there. The feeling grew stronger. I stood and turned slightly. I shoved my hands at my hips, forgetting for a minute that the skirt I was wearing didn't have pockets. My hands slid along the fabric and the force of shoving them down forced me off balance. I slammed my shin against the concrete bench.

The certainty that someone was watching didn't subside. I did a full three hundred and sixty degree turn. I was alone in the garden. Nothing but trees and shrubs and the bench. I shivered. The feeling would not leave me alone. I looked across the rose garden, out toward the street by the parking strip. A smoky, silken substance hung in the air. Not something that made me wonder whether my eyes were clouded, or a wisp of cigarette smoke had lingered, but something more substantial. It grew thicker, like the dark smoke you see when there's a forest fire, the edges turning into that brownish stuff that's impossible to see through.

It began to move up the side of the ivy-covered hill, gaining speed as if it was rushing at me. I cried out and sat down hard on the bench. My bones ached from the impact. I grabbed my arms to stop the shivering, but my legs trembled so that I wondered whether I was even capable of standing up again.

The thing was rushing at me now and I closed my eyes, certain it was vaporous enough that it would move right over and around me, but so solid that I could be wrong and it would slam against me. I knew it was Toby's ghost, but I was shaking so hard, I didn't have much time to consider how I'd come to that conclusion. I just knew. I had no idea what it was doing rushing at me, and why it was so distinct in the middle of the day, with a clear blue sky and warm summer weather — the least likely environment for seeing a ghost.

When it reached me, my thoughts stopped.

It hovered around me, pressing against me as if it wanted to strangle me. It created the same nausea and stabbing pain in my stomach as it had before. Bile swam up my throat and into my mouth and seeped into my head, making me feel as if my brain was a huge sponge filled with something rancid. I started coughing and couldn't stop. I coughed and gagged until my throat was raw and tasted of blood, like the inside had been scratched until the cells were pulled away.

The thing smelled of smoke, but not the faintly pleasant odor, at least to me, of cigarette or cigar smoke, but something that came from an explosion filled with chemicals. This was followed by an intense sadness for Toby, for his loneliness, his constant attempt to connect with people at the church, to interact with the rest of society, but instead he lived on the outside. His only friends were other drunk and drug-riddled and mentally ill people who couldn't really connect, but talked at and past and around each other. Sort of like everyone else, in some ways.

The thing clung to me as if it didn't want to leave, wanted to find some human touch some kindness or connection before he was able to leave the physical world behind.

Finally it dissolved into nothing. I didn't have my cell phone with me, so I had no idea how long it had been since I'd walked to the bench, how long I'd been smothered by that … that thing. I was scared it would come back for me, that it had attached itself to me and wouldn't let go. Ever.

I sat on the bench for a few minutes, breathing in clean, pure air. I rubbed my legs to stop the trembling. After a bit, my skin felt warm again, like it was a pleasant summer day.

I stood and walked along the path. The classrooms were silent. I went down the stairs, past the window near my desk, and opened the office door. I'd been gone less than fifteen minutes. That realization made me so disoriented, I sat in one of the chairs facing my desk and closed my eyes. I needed a few minutes to re-orient myself. I hoped the police would figure out soon who had killed Toby.

I HADN'T PACKED a lunch, so at noon I went out and walked three blocks to the Whole Foods market and bought a small tub of mozzarella balls with plum tomatoes and a pear and an Odwalla drink — strawberry-banana. I also bought a

Yoga magazine to read while I ate. I sat at one of the outside tables and read an article about a woman who took a year off to work with the Africa Development Corps as a teacher.

On the way back from the market, I walked in the opposite direction from the church. I turned down Cherry Way and looped around the neighborhood. As I walked, I studied the houses and wondered how many of them contained members of Central Avenue Church, how many contained people who attended other religious gathering places, and how many residents completely ignored the whole idea of a spiritual plane of existence. I recognized some of the addresses from mailing the church newsletter — 1333 Cherry, and when I turned the corner, 1700 Harwood. There were probably others with less distinctive house numbers that hadn't lodged themselves in my brain.

I turned left onto Central Avenue, which is perpendicular to the main thoroughfare, Foothill Boulevard. I walked more slowly, partially because it was really hot. The concrete burned through the soles of my sandals, and sweat puddled on the back of my neck and everywhere else you can think of. My hair was up off my skin, all secured in a giant clip with a silver and turquoise bar across it, but still the sweat grew thicker and oozed down my spine. I imagined my face was bright red, not an attractive color next to my coppery hair.

At my left was a two-story white house with pale gray trim. The front yard was shaded by an enormous oak tree, bordered on three sides by a dirt strip lined with rose bushes, all with white blossoms. An Adirondack chair sat on the lush grass under the tree. I desperately wanted to cut across and stand in the shade for a few minutes, possibly even sit in the chair. Although I could already see the church only half a block away, so I didn't really need a rest.

A small dog on the opposite side of the street started barking furiously. It yapped and harped as if it was in so much pain it had to let the entire world know how it felt. I couldn't see it, but it obviously saw, or smelled, me. It hardly took a breath as it yelped and cried. At the same time, a woman came around the side of the white house. She wore cut off blue jeans and a white smock and carried a can of Coke in her right hand. Caroline McCarthy. No wonder she'd been so quick to buzz over to the church to complain, instead of calling like everyone else. She lifted the can to her lips and took a long swallow. Her face was as red as mine felt. When she saw me, she stopped and took another sip of Coke.

"Hi." I lifted my hand and gave a small wave.

She squinted and yanked off her sunglasses. "Oh. Hi."

"Madison Keith, the administrative assistant at …"

"I know who you are." She gave me a stiff smile and took another sip of coke. "It's hot to be out walking."

"I went to Whole Foods to grab lunch and took the long way back …"

"Why can't that dog shut up?" Her voice was suddenly louder, and much higher pitched. She sounded as shrill and yelpy as the dog.

"Does he always get this wound up?" I stepped between two of the rose bushes and into her yard, inching toward the shade.

Caroline took a few steps closer to where I stood, which I took as an invitation to move completely into the shade.

"He drives me crazy."

"I can imagine."

She took another sip of Coke and pressed the can against her cheek. "It's just too much sometimes."

"What is?"

"Everything. That dog. Trying to keep the neighborhood pleasant. Cars driving too fast because they think they can cut through this area and avoid the traffic light at Foothill and Morrison. Homeless people taking this street to get to the church where it's so easy to find a soft touch for a handout. Especially that disgusting man who used to walk up and down the street every Sunday."

I was sure she meant Toby, but I didn't want to assume that, and I also didn't want to ask and sound stupid. I hoped she'd fill in the blanks.

"Thank goodness he's gone."

"You're glad he's dead?"

She put her hand on the back of her head and wiggled her ponytail. She switched her can of Coke to that hand. She scowled as the dog barked louder, his yelps getting faster as if he was upset that no one noticed his concern. "I wouldn't put it like that. But am I glad he's no longer walking down the street, stinking up the place, loitering in people's yards, pissing into the dirt around my roses? Yes."

"He did that?"

She looked at her feet. "Once. I called the cops and they took him away, but of course, they can't do anything permanent. It's a city street, anyone has the right to walk down it, even if they do it three or four times in a single day. He came right back. Like a swarm of ants."

"You're glad he's gone, even if he died? He never got a chance to get his life back on track."

She laughed. "People like that don't get their lives back on track."

It always amazed me that a fair number of people who attended Central Avenue Church sucked up Pastor Joe's sermons every week and read the Bible and had a very specific set of beliefs, yet seemed oblivious to how all of that might apply to their daily lives. I thought one of their primary hopes was that people could change — they could be redeemed or saved or see the light. "How do you know he would never get his life straightened out?"

"I just know." She stared at me and clenched her jaw. "Yes, I'm glad he's gone. He made my daughter very uncomfortable and I was terrified that he'd attack her."

"Did he threaten her?"

"He didn't have to. He stared at her. In a sexual way."

"What's that?"

"I don't think I have to describe it."

It horrified me that she was glad he was dead, even if she wouldn't connect the dots to come right out and speak the word *dead*. It was sad that she thought he was hopeless, but after my experience that morning, I was somewhat more sympathetic to her point of view than I might have been the day before. It scared me, and if that's the vibe he put off when he was alive, I could see why she was afraid, and I could almost see why she was relieved that she didn't have to think about him any more. Still, I felt really bad for having those thoughts, and Caroline didn't seem to feel bad at all.

"It was disgusting. He stared at her, he actually let his tongue hang out. He had this little smile on his lips, and it looked doubly disgusting because you could see his lips through that awful beard. They were bright red and they looked bloody poking out of all that filthy hair."

Despite the heat, I shivered. I guess she did have to describe it, and her description was quite vivid. There was a small part of me wondering if she was exaggerating. I'm not sure why. She seemed quite honest, looking me in the eye, her voice shaking just a little bit so I could tell she was genuinely upset — as upset as the dog, barking and barking. It hadn't stopped the whole time we were talking.

She tipped her head way back to drink the rest of her soda. When she was done, she pressed the can to her cheek again. "God, I wish that dog would shut *up*." She pulled the can away and crumpled it slightly. The aluminum made a crackling noise and collapsed in her hand as if it was made of paper.

"It was nice chatting with you, I'm sorry the subject wasn't a very pleasant one. But I'm going inside. It looks like I'll have to put on my headphones for a while until that woman realizes her stupid dog is going berserk again."

"I should get back to work. Thanks for a break and for sharing your shade with me."

She smiled but it was more of a grimace. She turned and walked quickly across the lawn and up her front path.

I cut through the roses and back to the sidewalk. It felt even hotter after standing on the soft, cool lawn, so I walked fast. It would mean even more sweat by the time I reached the church, but it would evaporate quickly once I got to my below-ground office.

As I neared the parking strip, I walked even faster until I was almost jogging. There was no sign of the ghost and I didn't have any strange feelings, but I started to wonder where it hung out. Did it lurk in the trees at the front of the property, or hunker down under the ivy? Or was it there, hovering over the parking strip but not making itself known except when I was nearby?

I glanced at the spot where Toby had died. If I closed my eyes, I could see his body lying there. The gravel was uneven so the exact spot was obvious. I stopped running and walked over and stood right next to where his head had been. Nothing. No violence, no aching thoughts, no nausea or smell. No sign of that thick brownish-gray stuff. Just a dove cooing from one of the redwood trees followed by the chirp of someone disabling a car alarm a few houses away.

That's what is so strange about lingering spirits. They set the agenda, they decide when they're going to reveal themselves and anyone who sees or experiences them is just the victim of their whims.

Seven

WALKING IN THE heat had dragged all the energy out of me, so I went to the restroom and splashed cold water on my face. I folded up a few paper towels, soaked them completely, and pressed them to the back of my neck. I dropped them in the trash and held my hands and wrists under the water for a minute or so.

Back at my desk, I wrote up all two of the phone messages for Pastor Joe and answered several emails about the church picnic. Most of the requests were the same — would I be sure to ask the person who was buying the beverages to add diet soda or clear soda or fruit drinks to the list. And would they also make sure to have some garden burgers for the vegetarians, or even those who just didn't eat beef since the only meat choices were hot dogs and hamburgers. And would they be sure to include mayo and dill pickles with the condiments. Last year they only had sweet relish and some people didn't like it. I wrote up a sentence or two assuring them I'd let the planning committee know about the request and pasted that into each email so responding went quite fast.

It was a little past two when Kate walked into the office. She had a grocery bag looped over one arm. She set it on my desk and pulled two berry-flavored sparkling waters out of the four pack. The bottle had a frosty sheen from being in the fridge. She handed one to me.

"It's so hot, I thought you might want something refreshing."

"Thanks."

We popped open the caps at the same time. They hissed from the carbonation.

"How's your day going?" Kate said.

I had no idea where to begin. She didn't buy into the idea of ghosts so I couldn't really start with that. There was my whole conversation with Caroline, and even though I now understood some of Caroline's discomfort, I didn't know if I could bring myself to repeat her awful words. It's so terrible and also so sad, that someone would die and instead of being mourned, people would be glad to be rid of you. What does that say about your life? Was it absolutely worthless? It made me want to cry. Although I never knew the guy, so that didn't seem fair to Caroline. There have certainly been horrid people throughout time whose deaths caused enormous relief and even happiness. I don't think I have to name them, everyone knows who they are. But there are other people who made a mess of their lives, and took others down with them, yet they still left behind a spouse or a child or a sibling or a friend, maybe several, who grieved when they died.

Sure, Toby smelled bad from lack of access to a shower. His beard was coated with oil and dead skin and there was a good chance there were lice living in there, or maybe they only live on your scalp, I really don't know. I'm sure his teeth were decayed and his breath foul. Who knew what else was wrong with his body, and that doesn't begin to touch on the damage in his mind, but once he was a baby that someone loved — maybe. And a little kid who was excited about animals and trucks and probably had a favorite cartoon.

"It wasn't that difficult a question, was it?"

I blinked and realized I'd drifted off, pursuing my thoughts. Kate smiled. "A boring day, or so much going on you don't know where to start?"

"I saw Toby's ghost. Twice."

She put her head back for a second and looked at the ceiling, then back at me. "I shouldn't have asked."

"Can I just tell you what happened?"

She smiled, but didn't make a snide comment. She sat up straight and put her hands on the arms of the chair as if she was bracing herself. For what, I don't know. Maybe for a rush of ghosts to assault her. Either that or crazy ideas from the administrative assistant. But she asked.

She picked up her drink and held it in front of her face, staring at the bubbles as they fizzed and fussed on the surface of the water. The blue sides of the bottle and the distance from my desk prevented me from seeing it, but I could see the bubbles in my own bottle, sitting right in front of me, untouched. Some of the bubbles leaped off the surface, trying helplessly to escape the bottle.

It made me wonder why human beings invented drinks with carbon dioxide forced into the liquid and why they enjoy the sensation of bubbles touching their lips and pulsing down their throats. What was wrong with plain water? I guess we like to add excitement any way we can. "Why do you refuse to believe I've seen ghosts?"

Kate continued to stare at the water bottle. I waited for her to give me an explanation of theology, or how the spiritual world worked, which did not include people failing to leave the earth when they died, or returning for further interaction.

"I don't know," she said.

The creamy sleeveless top she wore was almost the same color as her blonde hair, which looks white ninety percent of the time. The pale colors made her eyes with their brown and beige shadow and liner look even more dramatic than usual. Her skin was also pale and her lipstick a light pink color that was almost the same color as her naked lips. At least I think it was. I've never seen her without her perfectly, and expensively, made up face.

I waited for her to say more. At least she gave me an honest answer instead of something out of a theology book. Part of me wanted to hammer her with questions, but I knew if I waited, I'd probably get more of the real answer rather than steering her in a particular direction. She might surprise me.

"I suppose because I've never seen one. I've never experienced anything outside of the normal, physical world. It's hard to believe it's real. And so many people who do experience that kind of thing are a bit ..."

"Crazy?"

"Yes. And extreme."

"Am I extreme?" I know I'm not, but I wanted to hear what she would say. Not that everyone tells the truth when asked a blunt question like that, but it's always worth a shot.

"I don't think so. That's why I'm listening."

"Why can't you believe people's spirits might linger? It seems perfectly logical to me."

"I have no reason to believe it. No one I know has ever experienced anything like that. When I read stories about ghosts, it seems like people are trying too hard, that they want to believe someone is trying to communicate with them, so they misinterpret a trick of light or some other natural phenomenon."

"I wasn't trying hard at all. They just showed up."

"So you say."

The minute I said I wasn't trying too hard, I thought about how difficult it was for me that I never got to say good-bye to my parents, that I did desperately want them to get in touch with me, if that were possible. So on one level, maybe I am trying too hard. But not deliberately. I want too much and that might be the same as trying too hard. "I can't explain it either. I just know what I've seen. And felt."

"It would be easier to explain it as a hallucination."

"Why would I be hallucinating? I don't drink. I don't smoke pot or do other stuff to mess up my brain."

She shrugged. "People hallucinate for other reasons. And it can seem very real. I'm not saying it means you're crazy. Physical problems can cause hallucinations, even migraines." She took a small sip of water, set the bottle on the table, and put her hand to her throat. "So are you going to tell me about this ghost?"

I wheeled my chair forward and rested my elbows on the desk. To my left, the screen saver blinked out and the computer went dark. A small part of me thought she was leading me on. I wondered if she was asking me, trying to get me talking. Then she'd ridicule me, or maybe even tell Pastor Joe that I wouldn't stop going on about ghosts, and they really should think about getting another administrative assistant who wasn't in danger of filling the heads of church members with crazy ideas, leading the unstable ones into spiritual territory they shouldn't investigate, territory the church pretended didn't exist. "I saw it twice. Or experienced it, I should say."

"What does that mean?"

"It wasn't just visual. Although there was that. I saw a vaporous gray thing, almost like sheer fabric the first time. It came out of his body when he died. The second time it was even thicker, a brownish-gray cloud, is the best way to explain it. I was in the garden and it hovered out there at the edge of the street and then came up the hill and sort of … surrounded me."

She crossed her arms. Because her shoulders are so broad and her chest so large, and her neck a little on the short side, the movement always makes her torso look almost as wide as it is tall. I wasn't sure if the crossed arms meant she was pulling back, strengthening her disbelief. She wasn't smiling, and she didn't look disdainful, so I kept going. I probably would have any way, now that she'd opened the door.

"It made my throat burn and made me feel nauseous with violent cramps in my stomach, as if it was passing on to me whatever Toby felt when he died."

"How would you know that?"

"An impression. Or just knowing. Doesn't that ever happen to you? You just know something even if you don't have any information to back it up? Like when you know someone doesn't like you?"

As if to prove to myself my point about knowing things, I could tell she didn't buy into what I said until I got to that last part. I could almost see it click behind her brown-shaded eyelids, realizing that she absolutely had experienced that — knowing when someone didn't much like her. Sometimes that can be paranoia, but a lot of times it's the truth.

"I wonder if they've proven yet whether or not he was poisoned," Kate said.

"Do you think they'd tell us? If we called and asked?"

"No. So what else happened?"

"Not a lot, I just felt scared. Lonely."

"So you think those were his feelings?"

"I don't really know. The scared part was just me feeling scared of the spirit, wondering when it would leave me alone, afraid it will keep following me. Having it rush up the hill was the creepiest part, like it knew who I was."

"Because you were there when he died?"

"I think so."

"So you're worried it will never leave you alone?"

She uncrossed her arms, drank some water, and pushed herself out of the chair. "I should get to work."

"You don't believe me?"

"I don't know. You sound like you're telling the truth. It's not that I think you're making all this up, but it's too hard to believe. I can't stop thinking that you're imagining everything."

"Why would I imagine something so terrible?"

"Because you want attention, because you're searching for something beyond the physical world and you aren't attracted to conventional beliefs. I don't know. It could be a lot of reasons."

Part of me was angry at her for assuming what I'd experienced couldn't be true, but part of me felt a little bit naked, like she could see inside me and knew more about me than I'd wanted to say, and more about me than I wanted her to know. Telling JD about my murdered parents was enough. There was no way I wanted to get into that with Kate or Joe until I sorted things out with JD.

I'm not sure I'll ever tell the people I work for. I don't need them coming in every day, looking at me sideways, trying to figure out if I'm going to burst into tears, or show signs of mental illness because of the trauma. And it was a trauma, I know that. For a long time, years, I couldn't remember what my mom and dad looked like when they were alive. All I could see when I closed my eyes, or even tried to close my eyes, were their grayish faces and those round holes, nearly black, in the center of their foreheads, and their blank, staring eyes. That was the worst part, their eyes. Tears started gathering behind my own eyes just thinking about it.

"I didn't mean to upset you," Kate said.

"I'm not upset."

"You look like you're going to cry."

I blinked. "I'm not."

She crossed her arms again. She stared at me for a minute, then she uncrossed her arms, walked around the side of my desk, and patted my shoulder. The touch of her hand and her obvious regret that she thought she'd upset me, made a tear trickle forward, in danger of running down my cheek and making me a liar. I blinked more and clenched my teeth.

"I'm sorry. I know you believe it," she said.

"It's not a matter of believing."

"Okay. I don't want to argue with you."

"It really doesn't matter. You asked, I told you."

She removed her hand. Finally.

I don't like people feeling sorry for me, acting like I'm too sensitive or can't handle life. She thought she made me cry because I'm a silly girl who needs people to believe my stories, or whatever it is she thinks. I'm not. I know what I've seen and I know what I've felt and I don't need someone else to tell me I'm right. But the only way to make her stop thinking along the lines she was would be to tell her about my parents.

I didn't like it that their deaths had moved back to the forefront of my mind. It's not that I spend all my time, every day, longing for something I can't have. It was that way at first, but the past few years have been good. I don't dream about them very often, and I don't think about them every day, or even every week. Maybe telling JD about them had stirred up their ghosts in my mind, if you know what I mean.

AFER KATE WENT back to her office, I played Tetris on the computer for a while. That's kind of wasting the church's time when they're paying me to work, but part of working is being there to answer the phone and greet people. There aren't enough tasks to keep me busy all forty hours every week. If no one calls or comes into the office, that's not my fault. It was probably too hot for anyone to do either one. People that had jobs were in climate-controlled offices, and retired people and stay-at-home moms either had air conditioning, or were at a community pool, or trying to stay cool inside houses with the drapes closed in a futile attempt to escape the heat, drinking lots of soda and iced tea and eating popsicles.

While I played Tetris, part of my brain wandered over to the night before. I didn't want to think about my conversation with JD, so I thought about how thrilled I was when I opened the door and saw him on the front porch and how he wrapped himself around me when he stepped into the entryway. I wondered if that feeling ever goes away. It seems like it does. I know it did with my first boyfriend, but I attributed that to the fast slide downhill after he told me I was an airhead. Not exactly in those words, but mocking how I like to meditate to empty my mind.

JD is a good kisser. I only have the one comparison, but I love kissing him, so that makes him good no matter how others are. When he puts his mouth on mine, and I feel his tongue move inside me, it's like warm honey flowing through me all the way down to my toes.

Thinking about it made me wiggle my toes. I glanced at my feet, red and swollen from walking to the store, taking the long route past Caroline's, and standing in her yard. I leaned forward and unbuckled my sandals and slipped them off, but my feet didn't feel any cooler on the carpet, so I put them back on. It occurred to me that a toe ring would be a nice addition for the summer. I'd planned to get one the summer before but never got around to it. Wearing a toe ring would make me think of JD's kisses running down to my toes. I smiled and quit my game. I went to my email folder where I keep the prayer requests for the upcoming Sunday bulletin and started typing them into a new document. I could copy and paste them from the email, rather than re-typing everything, but sometimes that messes up the formatting and it's more trouble than it's worth to correct it. Besides, most of the prayer requests ramble on and I need to edit them slightly.

About thirty minutes later, Kate came back out. "I forgot to put the water in the fridge."

The plastic bag full of the two remaining bottles in the four-pack sat near the side of my desk. Because I'd been so absorbed in my game, I hadn't even noticed it was there. I stood. "I'll take it up."

"I can do it." She grabbed the handles of the bag. "Do you want me to bring you back a glass of ice and another bottle?"

"Sure."

"You're doing okay now?"

"I was fine before."

She gave me a tiny smile that didn't involve parting her lips and I knew she didn't believe me.

"After I get the water, can you help me paint a sign for the picnic?"

"Sure."

This wasn't the first time Kate had asked me to help with painting signs or creating posters announcing events. It's a blurry line between my job running the office and other administrative-like tasks, such as publicity for church gatherings and events. I'm responsible for publicity in the newsletter, special email announcements that go out, and getting notices onto community websites. Painting signs isn't technically my job, but who doesn't like to paint? I think she liked having my company, although that's been a bit hard to figure out. One minute I think she finds me more irritating than she can bear, and the next minute she's all chatty like she was when she asked about Toby's ghost. She's a prickly person. I think she's one of those people you either love or hate, because she kind of forces you to take her as she is. Although maybe everyone's like that.

Warm air rushed into the office when she went out. Painting signs in the basement area would be nice — it was cooler back there.

I opened my web browser and went to my bookmark for the *San Jose Mercury News* local news page. I clicked around, as I'd been doing every day, looking for news of Toby's death. There was a brief article the day after I found his body, but nothing since then. There wasn't even an obituary, which makes sense, because it's your family or friends who write those and send them in. I suppose it was too soon to think there would be any information about how he died. Once there was, I didn't know if it was important enough to make the newspaper. You would think, if they decided he'd been murdered, that was pretty important, even for a homeless guy.

I'd thought about calling the police station to see if I could find out what happened. I'd thought they would come back, asking questions, but if they'd talked to Pastor Joe or Kate when I wasn't around, no one mentioned it to me.

It was so unjust, as if no one really cared that a man was dead. It would be so easy to poison a homeless person. They accept food from anyone, or at least I imagine they do. I'm not sure how many people actually give them food, maybe they're more inclined to dig unfinished food out of trash bins. That thought made my stomach twist around on itself. Maybe he'd eaten something that was spoiled. Although the cop had been quite definite that it looked like poison, he didn't say food poisoning, he said poison.

I clicked open another tab and went to Google. I put in symptoms of strychnine poisoning, which I learned kills you very fast, and causes convulsions of your muscles, so I guess the cop knew what he was talking about. I browsed around a few articles. The descriptions of the pain he must have suffered were horrible. From there, I jumped off to check on whether convulsions could mean anything else. It was a disturbing thing to read about, but it was all I had and I was curious. The encounter with his ghost and the conversation with Caroline made me more conflicted about his death. It was so overwhelmingly sad, but also disturbing that maybe he hadn't been a very nice person. Or maybe he was a nice person at one point and drugs or alcohol or both, or living on the streets and watching the world ignore him, being angry at how his life had progressed — all those things had conspired to turn him into an unpleasant person.

Kate returned before I could find out anything more. She handed me the glass of water which was already slick on the outside from the ice that started melting during the time it took her to walk down the stairs. I took a sip and followed her back to her office. She picked up a large roll of white paper and carried it into the basement area.

I kicked off my sandals. The cold linoleum felt delicious on the bottoms of my feet. Once again I studied my toes and thought about a toe ring. Maybe two or three.

While Kate placed the roll of paper on the floor and began to unwrap a section about twelve feet long, I went into her office to get scissors.

"Would you not walk in my office with bare feet."

I grabbed the scissors and came back out.

"It's unsanitary." She held out her hand for the scissors.

"Not any more than people's hands touching everything."

She looked at me and waited. I handed the scissor to her and stood there uselessly while she cut the paper. I could have gone back to her office and carried out the bottles of paint she keeps on her shelves, but I wasn't going to put my sandals back on for that, the floor felt too nice — solid and soothing. The redness was already fading away from my feet and they were slightly less swollen.

Once she had the paint and pie tins and the brushes arranged nearby, she started sketching the words with a pencil: Central Avenue Church: 34th Annual Picnic. The church had actually been around for almost sixty years, but I guess they hadn't been picnicking that whole time, or if they had, they didn't count it every year.

Kate is very good at drawing block letters, probably because she's created so many signs over the ten years she's been a youth minister. Each part of the letter is symmetrical, and she narrows them in spots and swoops them out in others, like the bottom of the leg on the capital P that's wide and narrows where it connects to the round part. She draws tick marks to make sure she doesn't start out with letters that are too large so she runs out of space. It makes it fun to paint because it really looks very nice and professional when it's done. She usually decides what colors we'll use. It would be fun to make that choice myself, but it's her sign, so I never say anything.

This sign would be green, she decreed. Then she added an exclamation point after *picnic* and said that would be bright pink. Every so often, she reminds me that even though she's very serious, there is a fun side to her. It just doesn't poke its head out very often.

"Those are watermelon colors. We should paint wedges of watermelon in the corners," I said.

"Watermelon flesh is red, not pink."

"It's not red, red."

"Let's keep it simple." She handed me a brush with a foam pad. She dipped hers in the puddle of pink paint and drew a careful line down the length of the exclamation point.

I went to the other end of the sign, knelt on the hard floor, soaked my brush in green, and filled in the top hook of the C. We would meet in the middle.

"Do you think they'll find out who killed Toby?" I said.

"They don't even know whether he was murdered."

"I think the cop was pretty sure he was."

"I don't know. Maybe it was an accident."

"There's nothing in the news about him."

"People don't care that much when a homeless person dies. They don't really care much when a gang member is killed either. For the most part, they ignore all the people dying of hunger. They only pay attention when it's a death close to home, or someone youngish and full of potential that shocks them."

"The police care."

"I don't think it's high on their priority list." Done with the pink, she wiggled her brush in the jar of water, sloshing it vigorously, lifting it out every few swirls to see if the pink had come out of the foam.

"Do you think it was someone nearby, a neighbor?"

"Why speculate when you don't even know if he was murdered?"

"It could even be someone who belongs to the church."

"Someone from the church came over at six in the morning, or whatever it was, gave him some food or a drink with poison, and left him there to die? I don't think so," she said.

"Then you think his body was dumped there?"

She sat back on her heels, staring at the sign. Her face looked uncertain, as if she was second-guessing her choice of colors. "I really haven't thought about it. I don't know what happened. I'm sure the police will look into it."

"You just said he was a low priority."

"Why are you so curious?"

"I want to know what happened." Because she didn't believe my encounter with his ghost, she didn't fully grasp that I was a little scared. I didn't want that thing coming back to me, and making me feel sick and empty. Until he finished whatever business he thought he had here, he would be back. That, and I just wanted to know. Doesn't everyone want to know why someone was murdered? I think it's human nature, we don't want questions left unanswered. There are enough of those already.

"There are lots of unsolved murders," Kate said.

In my head, I said, *I know.* I shoved my brush into the paint and coated it with green. I pressed it on the paper and drew a long, hard stroke along the leg of the A in Avenue. I felt a bit lightheaded from kneeling. The unyielding floor was cutting off the flow of blood.

"Don't over-saturate it. If the paint's too thick, the sign will be stiff and it won't hang right."

It was premature of her to lecture me about the thickness of the paint. I could still smooth it around, which I did. "I can't stop wondering why the detective hasn't been by to ask you or Joe any questions."

"Can we talk about something else? You seem a little obsessed."

The church phone rang. There was no way I'd have time to set down my brush, stand up, and hurry to the office, so I didn't move. "I don't think I'm obsessed. It's normal curiosity."

"It's something you can't do anything about so you should put it out of your mind."

"Caroline said she's glad he's dead."

"That's cold."

"She explained a bit more about how he upset her daughter. He drooled and wiggled his tongue at her. It's gross. I can see why she was upset. She was scared, she thought he might be out to get her."

"Of course she did. She thinks everyone is out to get her girls."

"Really?"

"A year or two ago, before you were working here, she complained that one of the ushers leaned too close to her oldest daughter when he handed the offering plate to her. She said he was trying to touch her and that her daughter was so upset about it she couldn't sleep. She wanted Joe to tell the guy he couldn't collect the offering anymore. She was in here every day, describing it over and over again until it blew into something in her mind that the guy had grabbed her daughter's breast, right in front of the whole church."

"I thought you were friendly with her."

"I can be friendly with someone even if they're a partial mental case."

"What if he actually was trying to touch her?"

Kate shifted so she was sitting on one hip. She held her brush over the floor so it wouldn't drip on the sign, but it looked empty of paint. She glanced up at me. "He's a wonderful man, happily married. He has a daughter himself."

"So?"

"He would never look at another woman that way, much less a teenage girl."

"How do you know?"

"You're making me think all this involvement with ghosts has given you evil thoughts. That you really are getting into the occult."

I stared at her, hoping she'd realize how that sounded, but she didn't meet my eyes. "You can't assume Caroline is a nut case. She might have had a valid concern and you brushed it under the carpet," I said.

"I didn't. And you should stop thinking in those terms."

"It's naive to assume the guy was innocent."

"I'm not naive." She twisted back around, slapped her foam brush into the paint, and stroked it along the paper, curving around the three in *thirty-fourth*.

In my view, she was extremely naive. I guess that's what comes of living in the hot house of a church all your life — growing up going to religious schools, transferring into a religious college, and then spending your career in a church. You get a distorted view of the real world. And I suppose you might start to believe what you teach, that people really are different if they attend church and have religious practices. But how anyone can read the news about things that happen in churches and believe their church is immune is beyond me.

Although I didn't know a lot about Kate's personal life, I knew her entire world was saturated with organized religion. It could be that she and I are alike in that way, her growing up in the protected environment of church going, and me in the protected world of being home-schooled. Except my protected world smashed open like a raw egg falling on the floor. "What ended up happening?" I said.

"Joe told her she was imagining it. He said if she was that concerned, she should switch places in the pew so she was sitting at the end."

I laughed, but my voice sounded a little bitter, at least to me. I wondered if Caroline had felt her valid concerns were brushed aside. "Did she?"

"Yes. And that was the end of it. But she gave the guy dirty looks every single Sunday. She still does from time to time. She said it wasn't right that she had to make concessions for a pervert, and how did she know he wasn't still staring at her daughter from the back of the sanctuary. She said her worship experience had been permanently damaged."

"But even if you think she imagined that, which maybe she

didn't, it doesn't mean Toby wasn't making her daughter uncomfortable."

"Toby made *her* uncomfortable. Because he was homeless and deranged from drinking."

"How do you know that?" I could tell she was still annoyed with me for calling her naive. And for insulting one of their ushers, which I suppose wasn't fair, since I didn't even know the guy. She hadn't mentioned his name. But it was no worse than assuming Caroline was paranoid.

"I told you, she thinks everyone is after those girls. There was another time she was in here complaining that we let kids who aren't members of the church attend youth group activities. She said most of the boys were ungodly and they looked at her daughter with lustful expressions."

"That would probably be all teenaged boys. And teenaged girls," I said.

"Exactly."

"So you think she's imagining it?"

"I don't know what's in her head, except that she thinks every man on earth is staring at her daughter, and that she can somehow put a stop to it. I don't know what she's going to do when they're out of high school and she can't run around making complaints. I feel sorry for her children."

Kate and I were right next to each other now. She'd gone faster than I had, but my strokes were cleaner. The paint was more even on the letters I'd done. I wondered if she noticed. I'd finished *Avenue* and the C in *Church*. As she filled in the h,

I stood. It felt good to un-crimp my legs. It sounded like Caroline might have a dose of paranoia, or maybe just over-protectiveness, but it still didn't mean Toby wasn't taunting her daughter. It was hard to juggle the feelings of understanding why she was relieved he was gone and the sadness that someone's life ended on the street, that no one loved him, or didn't seem to, and that the only person with a distinct memory of him who had spoken up so far, was someone who was glad he was dead. I stuck my brush in the jar of water that was now dark brown. I always expect it to be more colorful, a blend of the colors. Why does every combination of more than two colors turn into a muddy brown?

We went to the restroom and washed the brushes and the jar.

"Thanks for the help," Kate said.

"No problem. I like painting."

"It's soothing, isn't it. You should go check the voice mail."

I didn't need her to tell me how to do my job, but I let it go. She always wants to tell people what they should be doing. I suppose that makes her a good leader or something like that. Authoritative. But it's annoying. I wonder all the time whether she talks to her friends and family that way. Like I said, I don't know much about her personal life. I know she's not married, never has been. I know she was born in California and lived here all her life. She's not a person who opens up and starts babbling about her history, but neither am I, so I guess that's why after more than a year of seeing each other three or four days a week, sometimes eating lunch together, we still don't know each other very well.

She's my boss, sort of, so it's not like we can be friends. Joe is actually my main boss. She and I are in some kind of limbo state.

THE CALL THAT came in while we were painting was from Detective Palmer. She wanted to make an appointment to talk to Pastor Joe and Pastor Kate about the death of the homeless man on the church property. Since she didn't mention Toby's name, I wondered if they didn't know his last name, or anything about his background. It was weird that the cops would call to make an appointment, but maybe they had come by and no one was around.

I called her back on the cell phone number she left, and she answered before it even rang on my end. After we set a time when I knew Joe would be in the office, I said, "I'm the person who found him. Madison Keith. Can I ask you a question?"

"Sure." Her voice sounded like she was anything but sure, in fact it sounded like she did not want to be asked any questions at all, but she couldn't very well refuse.

"Did you find out whether he was poisoned?"

"We don't have the final results back yet."

"When will you know?"

"In another week ... or twenty."

"Why does it take so long?"

"That's how it is."

"Well, do you think he was poisoned? He didn't die of a heart attack or a stroke, right? He wasn't hit by a car."

"That's correct."

"So it makes sense he was poisoned."

"Someone like him could have died from alcohol poisoning as easily as anything."

I switched the phone to my left ear. It clinked against my earrings "But you must have suspicions."

"We try not to speculate."

"But you do. Speculate. Right?"

"I need to hang up now."

"I'm not trying to be nosy. I'm just wondering. If you're wanting to interview the Pastors, you must think he didn't die naturally."

"I really can't discuss it."

"Okaaay."

"Thank you for making the appointments. Good-bye." She hung up without waiting for me to say good-bye. Very official of her, and she can get away with it as a detective, but it still felt rude. Even if you're a detective and I'm only a curious administrative assistant, we're all still human beings.

As soon as I hung up, I realized that I didn't need to know what her suspicions were, I had my own. And although Detective Palmer is probably more cynical than I am and has certainly seen a lot more crime than I have, my suspicions are just as valid. Although maybe she hasn't seen more crime than I have. In a smallish suburban community, how much real crime *is* there? I witnessed the worst crime of all, or at least the aftermath. Maybe she and I are even. Not to mention the bodies I've found.

Besides, my thoughts weren't idle speculation from a distance — I saw the guy die. I could see how young he was. If they knew it wasn't a stroke or heart attack, there weren't a lot of things left. He sure didn't kill himself. Or maybe he did. He could have poisoned himself, but that seemed weird, to take poison and walk around until you keeled over on the side of the street.

I popped my browser back open to the search I'd been doing earlier. I should have been working, but I couldn't concentrate. I knew I'd find a way to make up for it later.

On the page where I'd been searching to see what else besides strychnine causes convulsions, nothing jumped out at me except normal medical causes. Since no one had ever seen him have a seizure before, it seemed very possible that he'd been poisoned. It also seemed negligent for the detective to just be getting around to talking to people now, two days later.

I closed the browser and pushed my chair away from my desk. It was ten past four. I usually leave at five, but I'd sort of planned to leave a half hour early. I wanted to go look at parakeets, since I wanted to deliver on my promise to get a companion for Simon. It made sense to give up on working for the day — it's hard to get back into it for twenty minutes.

Besides, I can't be the perfect employee every single day. And I wanted to spend time thinking about why someone wanted to kill Toby.

It was clear people didn't like having him around, but what kind of person would go so far as to offer him something, pretending to help, and feed him a deadly substance? Because his ghost scared me, I'd tried to escape from it, but now I sort of wished I'd stayed in a more open frame of mind, trying to see if it gave me any thoughts or impressions or turned my mind in a certain direction. After all, he would know who caused his death. In fact, maybe he had been trying to tell me that before he died, and he wouldn't have needed to send his ghost at all, but I'd missed it.

I went back toward the restrooms. The paint was paler, with a few damp spots on the letters where we'd put it on thicker than we should have. Kate's door was open, but I didn't turn to look inside. It was completely quiet, so she must have been reading or working on some project.

On my way back I stopped in her doorway. Index cards were scattered across the entire surface of her desk. I was curious but not enough to ask. Toby was too much on my mind. "I'm leaving now. I have an errand."

"Okay. I doubt it will, but if the phone rings, I'll pick it up."

"Thanks." I hurried back across the basement and grabbed my stuff. When I reached the top of the stairs, I headed back toward the prayer garden that isn't really a garden, just that concrete bench and the pine trees. I wasn't deliberately thinking about making myself more available for Toby's ghost, in case it wanted to come back, but that was sort of simmering in the back of my mind.

Before I reached the garden, I saw the head teacher for the childcare center. She's a thin woman, about five or six years older than me. She has brown hair cut straight that hangs somewhat limply against her neck. She always wears longish flow-y jumpers with tiny flowers on them. She must have fifteen or twenty of them, because I'm always noticing different flower colors.

She was leaning against the corner of the building staring at her smart phone.

"Hi Jill. Where are the kids?"

She kept her eyes glued to the phone. "Watering their plants. Carla's got them all to herself for a few minutes so I could take my break."

"It's hot." I'd been outside less than thirty seconds and my face and neck already felt damp.

"It sure is."

"I haven't seen you in a while. How are things?" I said.

"Things are good. Isn't it awful about the poor man who died?"

"I found him."

"I heard that. I'd seen him around once or twice," she said, "and he was a little scary, but it's still sad." She hadn't stopped studying whatever was on her phone. Her hair hung over her face so I couldn't read her expression.

"That woman who lives a few doors down is really devastated," she said.

"Caroline?"

"No. Her name is Lily. She'd the one with the little Lhasa Apso? She walks him along Central Avenue every morning and cuts through the parking lot." Jill waved her arm at the large parking lot behind the education building. "She goes at the same time every day and I usually run into her when I'm getting to work. She used to leave food for him."

"No wonder he hung around here so much."

Jill nodded.

"The detective is coming to talk to Pastor Joe and Kate. I wonder if they'd want to talk to her?"

"Maybe." Jill tapped at her phone screen.

"Why did she go out of her way to feed him?"

"She's just one of those people with a good heart. And who actually does something to prove it."

"The one cop was pretty sure he was poisoned."

She looked up from her phone. "How awful."

"You don't think …?"

"No, absolutely not. She cared about him. And she got all choked up when we were talking about how he'd died."

"Do you know her last name? When the detective comes by, I should mention her."

"Manning. Lily Manning."

"Do you know her phone number or anything?"

"Why would I know that? She lives a few doors down. She has the little dog, they should be able to figure it out."

She slipped her phone into her pocket. "Better get back to the kids." She smiled. "She's a really nice lady. Although her dog is a pain in the ass. It barks all the time, even when she's standing right there, even when she's petting it. That would drive me nuts."

Her comment was amusing, since many people would think spending all day every day cooped up in a room with twenty preschoolers would drive them nuts. Everyone's breaking point is different, I suppose.

"I'm surprised none of her neighbors have shot it," Jill said.

Those were violent thoughts coming from a pre-school teacher. I guess the dog really bugged her, even if it was only for a few minutes every morning before she started her workday. It must be the same dog barking that got on Caroline's nerves. Unless there were lots of barking dogs on the street. When I hear a dog barking, I feel sorry for it, because I figure it's upset. I guess other people view it more like the sound of car alarms going off, or leaf blowers firing up — something that makes them contemplate murder.

Eight

IT WAS STILL in the low nineties on Sunday, but the minute my Beetle crested the hill, heading down Highway 92 into Half Moon Bay, racing to JD's condo, I felt the temperature drop ten degrees. JD and I try to trade off making the drive up the 280 freeway and over the hill, or the reverse, in JD's case. We have a very balanced relationship in terms of driving, paying for dinners out, and cooking. I like that things between us are even. Not that I'm keeping score, but I like being equal participants. I don't think I could be with a guy who expected me to cook for him all the time, and I'd feel a little guilty if he was always making long drives so we could see each other. And I definitely wouldn't want to be with one of those guys who just coasts and thinks a woman should be happy to have him. A guy who expects the female to do absolutely everything — cooking, driving to see him, washing and folding his clothes, fetching a refill of whatever, and turning off her TV show because he wants to watch something else, like he's some old king lounging on his throne.

The fog wasn't in, but the bay almost always has a breeze because even if you can't see the fog, it's lurking out there somewhere past the horizon, blowing cool air across the water and onto the shore. I opened my window and turned off the AC. The air smelled clean with a hint of eucalyptus. When I pulled into town, the eucalyptus faded, replaced by garlic from one of the restaurants.

One Sunday a month, JD gets off at two. Sundays are usually crazy busy, with people who live in Half Moon Bay and people heading to the coast for the day from San Francisco and Silicon Valley, all converging on the oceanside restaurants. The Distillery has the inside bar, where JD usually works, but they also have a secondary bar downstairs that opens to a patio area. When it's sunny, that place is packed out.

I got to his condo at two-fifteen. His SUV was already in its parking spot.

He opened the door before I knocked, and after we kissed for a while, he went into the kitchen. He returned with an iced latte and handed it to me. "I'm going to take a quick shower."

"Yum. Thanks." I poked the straw between my lips and took a long, slow drink. It was nice and strong, but smooth with milk, just the way I like it.

I sat in his rocking chair and reached into my bag for my

latest Yoga magazine. I flipped through the pages, not really reading anything, just looking at the poses and wondering when I would become more advanced. Probably never if I didn't take some classes instead of relying on practicing in front of DVDs at home. Every month the magazine does an in-depth look at a certain pose or series of poses. To be honest, it makes me a little envious to see the women in their expensive-looking outfits that are always beautiful colors or sometimes shockingly pure white, and their lean figures and the way their faces are so serene as they stand on one leg, or suspended into something like the firefly, or one of the impossible handstand poses. I know they have makeup artists, and hair stylists, and maybe an instructor helping them get into position and all of that, but I still compare myself more than I should. Looking at the pictures made me want to stand up, kick off my flip flops, and do some warrior poses, but that's not a great idea with a stomach full of iced latte.

After his shower and my latte were both finished, JD suggested we drive north along Highway One. He wanted to do some surfing, and I could either lounge on the beach or paddle around a bit in the shallow water on his surfboard. He was dying to teach me how to surf, and I was considering it, but so far, I hadn't made the leap to actually try it out. It's one of those things that looks like a lot of fun but is obviously harder than it looks. A lot harder. And the water is freezing. I like swimming, but I'm more of a San Diego beach swimmer than a northern California coast swimmer where your feet basically become numb after ten minutes in the water. The surfers in Half Moon Bay wear wet suits and sometimes foot booties.

"Maybe today will be the day," JD said.

"You have to let me build up to the idea."

"How long is that going to take?" He poked me in the ribs with his index finger, right in the spot that makes me gasp and sends a wiggly feeling down my legs.

"Not too long."

"For sure you're going to try it when I take you to Australia," he said.

"I didn't know you were taking me to Australia."

"Even though he's a pain in the ass, I still like to visit my brother once in a while. Besides, Australia makes up for some of his flaws."

He went into the bedroom and came out with his bag full of gear. He grabbed a sack of bottled water and chips off the table and I picked up my bag. I went first out the door. He stabbed his key in the lock and turned it.

"You never told me what the drama was with your brother," I said.

"I'll tell you in the car."

Once he gunned the Explorer out onto Highway One headed north, he flicked the dial on his iPod and selected a playlist of classic rock. Traffic was moving at a good pace, despite the blue sky with streaks of milky clouds, which meant double the number of Sunday-afternoon beach-goers.

I had to remind him again about his brother. I think he forgot, I don't think he'd decided not to talk about it, although his twin brother is a touchy subject.

"I told you he sleeps with too many women."

"Uh huh."

"Eventually it was going to bite him. The latest woman thought they had something special. A lot of them do, but mostly they just cry and call him and text him for a while. Then they recover their pride. This one was different. When she found out he was hooking up with one of his buddy's cousins, she flipped."

"What did she do?"

"Hired a moving truck and emptied his house."

"Wow. All his furniture and TV and computer and stuff?"

"Everything. Not a sock or a spoon or even a saltshaker left. He was *pissed* off. I had to listen to him go on about it for more than half an hour."

"Where was he when all that happened?"

"At this other girl's house for the weekend."

"Didn't the neighbors wonder what was going on?"

JD turned off the highway onto a dirt and gravel road. We bumped and bounced along and the jarring made his voice vibrate. "I guess not. It was one in the morning. She was fast. She had a bunch of friends, he thinks. One neighbor saw the truck, but didn't think anything of it since it was just sitting by the curb."

"She must have had it planned out."

He took his right hand off the wheel and grabbed at his ponytail as if he wanted to make sure it was still there. His face looked calm and smooth, so I guess he wasn't too stressed.

"What's he going to do?"

"Buy new stuff. At least the essentials."

"Are the cops talking to her?"

"How can he prove it? They talked to her, but she denied it, of course. They can't do much, unless they find the stuff … and that's probably long gone. Like I said, she had help."

"I can't imagine what it would feel like to have all your stuff gone. You'd feel like they took your life right out from under you."

"That's not the worst part."

"What else?"

"Since she has his computer, she got into his email and Facebook. She wrote bitchy things on his friends' walls. He had to shut down all his accounts. She was calling his cell and texting him hundreds of times a day and all night. He had to cancel everything."

I folded my arms around my ribs and rubbed my arms. Both windows were open and it was a little cold. My hoodie was in my bag, but I had on a sage green tank top and I didn't want to cover it because I was hoping to get a little tan. Not that I could get tan inside the truck, but that's why I hadn't worn anything over it when we left the condo. And not that redheads really have much hope of tanning, but I can get a little bit of color so I don't look quite so chalky.

I tried to imagine coming home to my place and finding everything gone. It was a little scary. I'm attached to my stuff. I would feel like I had no spot in the world. It was even scarier that someone could be so angry she would do something like that. Or maybe hurt. And angry. "I guess if he has no email or social network or phone, she has to leave him alone now."

"He's actually a little worried."

"How did he Skype with you if he doesn't have a computer?"

"From his buddy's house."

"Why's he worried?"

"He keeps looking over his shoulder, wondering what else she's going to do."

"Does he think she's dangerous?"

JD made another loop around the small parking area. Finally someone was leaving and we were lucky enough to be in the right position to see it first. He shrugged. He didn't look worried, but I was, and I don't even know the guy.

We unloaded our stuff. I carried the rolled-up towels and two beach chairs looped over my arm and the bag of water and chips — thick, natural chips that taste like real potatoes — I couldn't wait to bust into those. JD looped the straps of his backpack over his shoulders and carried his surfboard. I wondered how he managed his other things when he went surfing with his friends and they all had their hands full with those six-foot, glossy boards.

The path down to the sand was a gentle slope, not like some of the beach access in this area where you have to basically leap down a gully of dirt and rock like a mountain goat.

We set up our stuff. JD flopped down on his towel, leaning on one elbow, facing me, his back to the ocean. He grabbed a bottle of water and drank half of it. I slathered sunscreen all over me. After a while, he put on his wetsuit and carried his board to the edge of the water. He didn't even wince as he walked in and moved quickly out until the water was up to his thighs. I guess growing up near the ocean makes you not think about the cold, although I've spent a lot of time at the beach and I still have to adjust to it slowly, once I get past the tops of my feet. Plus he had on the wetsuit. Maybe you can't feel anything through all that rubber. I've never worn one, so I don't know.

I was glad he'd told me about his brother, but still felt like things were unfinished between us because of our short, strained conversation about my parents. Not that I had any idea what I would say about that subject. I didn't like that it had been left hanging in the air, and I wanted him to acknowledge we'd talked about it. In fact, I was kind of bothered he hadn't mentioned it when he first saw me. But of course, if he had, that would have bothered me too.

It was fun watching him surf. The problem is, he wasn't always surfing. There was a lot of sitting on the board, paddling around, looking at the waves, floating up as the swells passed under him, and only infrequently finding one he could ride, standing and skimming along on the curve all the way to shore. So I got bored.

I piled up all our stuff and took a bottle of water and headed off toward the cliffs at the north end of the beach. The sand was warm. There were no kids around since it's mostly a surfer beach, and most of the people were out in the water, floating on their boards, which meant I had a lot of space to myself. I walked closer to the water and let it lap over my feet and tried to sort out my thoughts about Toby and his ghost. Or what I assumed was his ghost.

It was strange that I hadn't actually seen a form, which I had most of the other times I'd encountered ghosts. This time, it was just that cloudy brown mass, like smoke from a fire full of things that shouldn't be burning. I wished someone else had seen it, that I wasn't alone in this. I wished I wasn't at its mercy, that it couldn't just show up and scare me, more than a little, every time it felt like it. And if Toby wanted to tell me something, about his life, or how he died, or who killed him, why didn't he speak up?

Central Avenue Church was still moving ahead with the memorial service and I was planning to attend. It seemed like the right thing to do, and if anyone who knew him from the past showed up, maybe I could find out more about him, understand what had troubled him before he died. Not that I was going just to be nosey and pry into his life, I really did want to be there for him, even if Joe thought that was ridiculous. You couldn't *be there* for someone who wasn't there. But Toby was there, Joe just wouldn't admit it. For all we know, lots of spirits might be present at their own funerals. We're so pompous about them being gone, and that it's all about support for those who are left behind, but who really knows?

WHEN THE TIDE started to go out, the surfing got less attractive. The tide is one of those things that feels like a mystery to me. Even though it's very scientific, controlled by the gravity of the moon, and so predictable they can map out the schedule months in advance, it still feels mysterious. With all its predictability, there's no explanation of why it moves in and out, why it happens on every ocean in the world, why the moon would affect it, and why it's necessary. Maybe it's not necessary, maybe it just is. Still, whenever I'm at the beach and notice it shifting in or out, I think about how supernatural it is, and lately, that makes me think that if there are magnetic forces that are so obvious as the tides, it makes perfect sense that magnetic or other chemical forces would allow the spirits of the dead to appear, to influence our feelings, and alter our entire view of reality.

It was almost five o'clock. Despite the bottled water and potato chips, I was getting hungry. We were having barbecued steak and potato salad that JD bought at the deli, so I suppose it wasn't really cooking. But I do know he can cook very well because he's made me elaborate dinners quite a few times.

As if his stomach was in the same state of thinking about a thick steak, he grabbed a somewhat mediocre wave and rode it to shore. He doesn't like to end the day on a small wave, he'd rather have something large that gives him a long, exciting ride, but that's not always possible.

He walked out of the water, his hair slicked back like an otter's fur. A chunk that had come loose from his ponytail hung in front of his ear. He tucked it back and it fell across his jaw again. He leaned his head back shook it, and lifted up his board. The minute his feet hit the dry part of the beach, they were coated in sand. It clung to the hair on his legs, and seemed to creep up higher toward his knees as if it was a living being.

On the drive back, we didn't talk much, just listened to music. I thought about steak and potato salad, and Toby's ghost. I'm not sure what JD was thinking about. Probably surfing.

The steak was so large we were able to split it — two thirds for him and a third for me. He cooked it medium rare. It's lucky that we both like it cooked the same way. It melted on my tongue as I chewed. He had a glass of red wine and I poured a chilled bottle of water into a glass. The water was silky on my throat and made the taste of the meat and the onion in the potato salad and the creamy mayonnaise taste extra delicious. I really don't get the whole idea that wine brings out the flavor in food. To me the flavor is wonderful all by itself and nothing is better than cool water to make every taste distinct.

We cleaned up the dishes and went for a walk along the trail that's near his condo complex. As we stepped onto the bark-covered path, he took my hand. His skin was warm and smooth and dry.

"They still haven't found out if Toby, that homeless man, was poisoned," I said.

"I've heard it takes a long time. Labs are backed up."

"I know. The detective is finally coming back to talk to Joe and Kate."

He squeezed my hand and for a minute, I forgot what I was going to say next. All I could think about was the pressure of his fingers, and how I was suddenly warm all over, as if his blood was flowing directly into mine. We walked for a few yards without talking. The sound of traffic on the highway was faint in the distance, but we were too far from the ocean to hear the roar of the waves.

"What would Joe or Kate know that could help?" he said.

"I don't know. But I'm glad they're not just dropping it. I forgot to tell you I saw the ghost again."

He laughed. "You say that so casually."

"I guess I'm getting used to seeing them, but it's still a shock. It was almost like smoke from a chemical fire."

"When have you seen a chemical fire?"

"I haven't, but that's what came to mind. It made me feel

nauseous, and really sad. Kind of depressed and scared at the same time."

He let go of my hand and put his arm around my shoulders. He pulled me close. I wrapped my arm around his waist. We took a few steps, cuddled up like that, but a minute later we both realized it wasn't a stable way to walk along a trail, so we let go. He took my hand again. "Where did you see it?"

"In the garden. I was sitting on that concrete bench."

"Why were you there at night?"

"It wasn't at night. It was the middle of the day. It was ninety degrees. It's not the kind of weather or time of day I associate with ghosts, and I have no idea why I think that way."

He laughed. "Fairy tales. Do you think he was trying to tell you something?"

"Not that I noticed. But maybe at some point he's going to tell me why he was apologizing when he died. Saying you're sorry is a strange thing to focus on when you're dying."

"Maybe not. And maybe he killed himself."

"People don't usually poison themselves, do they? Don't they try to do whatever is the least painful? Take pills or something. Dying of poison is awful. He looked miserable. The sounds were awful, and the convulsions." Talking about it made me feel sick again. "I can't believe anyone would willingly take rat poison or something like that."

"It's possible though."

"I can't believe that. And I don't think the cops believe it or why would they want to talk to Joe and Kate? They must have unanswered questions."

"Maybe their questions are about him killing himself. It's hard to believe someone would murder a homeless guy. You could see him dying in a fight, getting stabbed, but poison? That's extreme."

It made me sad that JD was so certain Toby killed himself. Not that it was our job to figure it out, but I thought he'd be more on the same track, wondering who hated him so much they killed him. Or why someone would be that cruel. Since no one seemed to know anything about Toby's life, he could have had all kinds of enemies. I suppose if your life has gone downhill so badly that you have no job and no place to live, you could collect quite a few enemies during that process.

As we continued walking, I thought about Toby being so alone, every aspect of his life was a secret that had died with him.

THE MORE WE talked, the more JD seemed convinced Toby probably killed himself, and that's why he'd said he was sorry. Toby took up so much of our conversation, most of our walk along the trail, that by the time we got back I wasn't in the mood to talk about death any more. I had really wanted to say something about my parents, but with all the time that had passed since I'd first told him, and all the thinking I'd done, I still had no idea what I wanted to say.

There was a sharp pain in my chest, like a knife pressed into my heart, working its way up so my throat felt partially blocked. It had been there since I told him about the murders and it wouldn't go away. It wasn't because of my parents, but because I felt something splitting JD and me apart. I don't know what I wanted him to say, how I wanted him to react, but saying *you poor kid* was not it.

It was probably better that I didn't bring it up until I figured that out, but I didn't like feeling there was this thing between us. A thing that was making me ache and making me pull away from him, waiting for something, even though I had no idea what it was. Part of me hoped he'd bring it up, but then he might blunder some more. It must be difficult to smooth things out with a person who doesn't even know exactly what she's upset about or what can be done to fix it.

Nine

TOBY'S MEMORIAL SERVICE was the following Tuesday at eleven in the morning. JD didn't go after all. We decided since he'd never even seen the guy it was kind of weird. And it wasn't like I was grieving and needed his support.

The weather had cooled slightly, down to the high seventies, which probably helped motivate more people to attend. I was shocked when I stepped through the doorway into the back of the sanctuary. It was almost a third full — at least fifty people. A warm feeling toward the members of Central Avenue Church rushed into my throat. They're an awfully kind-hearted group after all. At least most of them.

The church pianist was there. Her fingers danced across the keys, playing something soft and classical and so beautifully sweet it made my eyes tear up. I don't know much about classical music, but every time I hear it, I think I should start listening to it, that I should learn the names of the artists beyond just Mozart and Beethoven and Tchaikovsky. I should recognize who wrote which pieces of music. It's amazing how those notes, with no words, can stir up such feelings of either sadness or triumph or any other list of emotions.

The building was cool. It usually is in the summer, something about its size and the stone floor and no windows except two very narrow ones behind the altar that offer a glimpse of the redwood trees outside.

I sat near the back and let the music wash over me. There was no coffin, of course, it was a memorial service, his body long gone, probably cremated. Or maybe they were still keeping him somewhere, waiting to find out what killed him. I really had no idea. Not having that physical reminder made everything surreal. As if we were remembering someone who really didn't exist. And in some ways, maybe he didn't. The front rows on both sides of the center aisle, where the family would usually sit, were empty.

Pastor Joe had planned a service that didn't involve any eulogies. It was simple and to the point, some music, a few readings. One reading was delivered by Kate. She has a beautiful voice, firm and strong, and so clear it almost sounds as if she's singing when she speaks. As she read a poem by Emily Dickenson that made death sound friendly and kind, I could see the faces near me relax, transported to another realm. One woman who had a stiff jaw, her chin jutting forward, the muscles tense, exposed even though her silky brown hair covered the side of her face, looked as if she'd released one of those mouth guards the football players wear. Her lips parted slightly and her chin softened. Even her neck seemed to relax as she listened to the poem, the cords of tendon and muscle melting beneath her skin.

The service lasted just over thirty minutes. When the final song ended — a beautiful piece with trilling high notes at the end — the piano lapsed into silence. People stood and walked quietly down the aisles.

Outside, a man stood at the bottom of the wide concrete steps that lead up to the sanctuary. He held a cigarette pack, which he passed back and forth from one hand to the other. He was about forty years old with blonde hair and a neatly trimmed beard that was sort of a sandy non-color. He wore sixties-style sunglasses with dark gold lenses that lighten into regular glasses when you go indoors.

I'd never seen him before, which wouldn't necessarily mean anything because I certainly don't know every single person that belongs to or attends the church. But somehow, I had the feeling he wasn't a regular. The notice of the service had been in the church bulletin and there were a few flyers, one posted near the multi-purpose room and another on a post near the back parking lot, but you wouldn't have seen those unless you were walking on the church property.

He glanced at me and slapped the cigarette box back to his left palm.

I took a few steps closer and held out my hand. "Hi. I'm Madison, the administrative assistant for the church. I haven't met you before." It might have been a little false of me to say it like that, as if I assumed he was a member when I knew he was not, but I was too curious to care whether he thought I was being fake.

"Gary." He shook my hand. "The bum's brother."

"The bum?"

"Toby." He almost spit the name. He'd only given my hand a quick yank, and now he passed the cigarette box back to his right hand.

"We didn't think he had any family."

"Everyone has a family."

Not really, but I knew what he meant. At some point in time, everyone does, but not everyone keeps their family. Like mine, for example. Although I suppose you could still count my aunt and uncle as my family. And I'm sure I have some second cousins on the east coast, where my parents were from.

"Do you live around here?" I said.

"Santa Cruz."

"How did you know he died?"

"Sixth sense, I guess. I try to check on him every few months. I come up to this area, look around for him. Sometimes give him a bit of cash, although he pisses that away, so I don't know why I bother. I buy him a nice big dinner."

His attitude and the occasional dinner that he seemed to resent made me think for a half second that Toby's brother poisoned him, but I immediately rejected that thought because why would he show up at the service if that were the case?

"He was younger than you?"

"Ten years."

"You couldn't do anything to help him change his ... his circumstances?"

"I need a smoke. Is that allowed around here?"

"In the parking lot. I wouldn't mind sharing one," I said.

"One what?"

"A cigarette."

He raised his eyebrows well above the rims of his gold glasses, but didn't make a comment.

I started walking along the path, lacing my way through the people who stood about talking. They were seemingly reluctant to just get in their cars and drive home after a memorial service, not ready to get back quite so abruptly to the business of living, I suppose.

Gary followed me. When we reached the edge of the parking lot he lit his own cigarette, then handed one to me and held his lighter to the tip while I got it going.

"So it was a coincidence that you came to the area looking for him this week?"

"Sure was. It's been months, and I don't know what made me feel I had to come this week. I knew he lurked around this area, so I checked that garden and under the covered hallway." He nodded toward the education wing. "I saw that flyer they put up."

"I did that."

"Well thanks, I guess."

"Why didn't you let the pastor know you were here?"

"Don't want to get into a discussion."

"But you're discussing it with me."

"You got right in my face."

"You didn't have to tell me who you were."

He took a long drag on his cigarette. His cheeks collapsed against his teeth. He blew out the smoke in a big puff, almost as if he'd been punched in the stomach.

"Do you have any idea who might have killed him?" I said.

"Don't know for sure he was killed. But if he was, he had a way of making a pest of himself, so it could be any number of people."

"Anyone in particular? Anyone you know?"

"What are you an undercover cop or something? Posing as a secretary?"

"Administrative Assistant."

"Whatever. Are you?"

"I'm just curious."

"Curiosity killed the cat."

"Ha, ha."

"Or in this case, my brother."

"Why do you say that?" I puffed on my cigarette and tapped it against my finger to knock the ash off the tip.

"He was a pest."

"That's not the same as curiosity."

"He was a nuisance. I could see why someone might kill him."

"That's a terrible thing to say."

"Why?"

"Because he was a human being. Because he didn't deserve to die such a painful death."

"How do you know it was painful, and how do you know he didn't deserve to die?"

A group of three women passed us on their way to the parking lot. One batted away our smoke, but at least she didn't turn and give us a dirty look. They got in their cars, fired up their engines, and followed each other out of the parking lot. Before I could ask Gary why he was being so harsh toward his brother, a woman with a fluffy white dog on a purple leather leash passed by. Her dog went nuts, barking at us as if the smoke meant we were on fire and it was his job to alert the fire department. The woman tugged at his leash, trying to pull him away, but he leaped off the ground in his eagerness to get back near us, barking furiously the whole time.

It had to be the dog who lived across the street from Caroline, the dog who barked at Jill when she ran into its owner, Lily, before work every day. I'd seen her in the service, holding the dog, and I wondered how she managed to keep it quiet for an entire half hour.

Lily spoke to it in a low voice. "Come on Bonbon. Calm

down. It's okay. Calm down. Come with me." The dog ignored her.

"She sure gets excited," I said.

She gave me an apologetic look. "She's not feeling well, poor baby."

"Is that why she's going berserk?" I knew that wasn't the reason. Jill said she was always like that. And I'd heard her barking like a maniac when I stood in Caroline's yard that day.

"I think so."

Gary let out a guttural laugh, one short sound, like his own deep bark.

Lily bent down and scooped the dog into her arms. "Sorry to disturb you."

"Not a problem," I said.

Gary puffed on his cigarette and watched with a bit of a smirk folded along his lips.

Lily headed across the parking lot. Bonbon barked the entire time. I turned back to Gary. "Why would you think anyone deserves to die, especially your brother?"

"He made a mess of his life."

"Everyone who messes up their life *deserves* to die?"

"What would be the point in continuing to live when you're a drain on society, when all you do is annoy and scare people? You know what I mean."

"How would I know what you mean. You're a complete stranger."

He sucked on his cigarette, dropped it on the ground, and

stamped it out. "Good talking to you. I should get going." He reached into his pocket and pulled out his keys. "It was nice of the church to do this."

"It wasn't my idea."

"Whatever." He stepped out from under the overhang.

"Wait. Why did you say he scared people?"

"He was a scary guy."

"That's it? He was born scary or because he was homeless? Or just when he was drinking?"

"He was always drinking. He was very … intense. He stared at you like he wanted to eat you alive."

I laughed. Gary's tone was so serious, as if he literally meant eating you alive.

He stared at me. "It's not funny."

"Okay."

"He had a way of looking at you … I knew him and he scared me. I can't imagine what that look would do to someone else. But it could be he reserved that for me."

"Did anyone complain to you about him staring at them, making them uncomfortable?"

"I never talked to anyone here. You're the first one. I'm just telling you how he was. Anyway, I gotta go. Tell them thanks for the service."

"Even if someone deserves to die, it's nice to have a service?"

"Yes." He turned and walked across the parking lot.

I couldn't see the sanctuary from where I stood, although I

could hear voices floating through the garden. Not many had passed by us on their way to the parking lot, and twenty or so cars were still scattered across the blacktop. I wasn't in the mood to talk to anyone else, feeling a bit morose from the service, mostly because it was one-size-fits-all and had nothing to do with Toby. Not that it would have been possible to avoid that, since no one really knew him. No one knew him at all, and his brother popped up out of nowhere, but didn't introduce himself and obviously wasn't inclined to get involved.

It occurred to me, somewhat after the fact, that I hadn't gotten Gary's last name, and I had no idea where in Santa Cruz he lived, and maybe the detective would want to talk to him. Although maybe not. What could he really offer? If they wanted to talk to him, they must have other ways of digging out that information. At least I hoped they did. Nothing I could do about it now. I knew he drove a blue Honda, but that was it.

I was too unsettled to go back to the office, so I cut across the parking lot and out to Central Avenue, thinking I would go for a short walk — just up to the end of the street, and back on the opposite side, past Caroline's house.

The minute I turned onto Central, I saw Lily. She held a plaid pet carrier. Bonbon was inside, howling. She set the carrier on the ground and opened the passenger side door of her car. She put the carrier on the seat and closed the door so gently that it didn't latch. She opened the door again and closed it with more force.

I quickened my pace, eager to talk to her, although I had no idea about what. Just my usual excessively curious self, I guess.

"Hi."

She nodded and went around to the driver's side of the car. She opened the door and I could hear Bonbon yelping. Although this time it was more of a whining, howling sound than actual barking. I really had no idea how she put up with that constant noise. It would be like living with someone who whined and complained twenty-four-seven. Or maybe eighteen-seven, since everyone has to sleep at some point.

"Why does your dog bark so much? Is she okay?"

"Small dogs are like that. They want to communicate."

"How did you keep her quiet during the memorial service?"

She put her sunglasses on and stuck one leg into the car. "I can't chat right now, whoever you are. I have to take Bonbon to the vet."

"Her stomach?"

"She won't eat. And she's crying."

"Poor thing." She did sound awful. Even though the constant noise tore at my nerves, I felt sorry for her. There's nothing worse than seeing an animal suffer. They can't tell you what's wrong and they don't understand why they're hurting and it makes it so much worse, looking at their eyes and seeing their confusion. Although Bonbon was doing a valiant job at letting her owner, and everyone else on the block, know she was hurting. The thing about her was that she made so much noise all the time, it didn't seem all that different that she was in pain.

I looked across the street at Caroline's house and wondered if she could hear the howling. Then Lily sat down and pulled the car door closed and the howling was muffled. Lily started the car, backed out of the driveway, and headed toward the stop sign at the end of the street.

I continued down the street in the opposite direction. The detective had talked to Joe a few days ago, but nothing had really come of it. Joe said the questions were routine — how much time Toby spent on the church property, whether he ever had a confrontation with a member of the church, did he have any health problems Joe was aware of, and did Joe know anything about his background.

The answer to the last question was no, of course. Joe mentioned that Toby mostly came around on Sunday mornings, and that people had complained about him being there, and Caroline was upset about his behavior, and that there wasn't really any confrontation about it. Just her complaints to him and Kate.

When the detective left, she'd nodded at me but didn't say anything and she didn't look all that interested in what had happened to Toby. I know it's not fair to say that, because how would I know what was going on in her mind, but it was my impression. Kate was right, maybe they didn't really care how he died. Even his brother had a *good riddance* kind of attitude. But I cared.

I WALKED FARTHER than I'd planned, four blocks up, before I crossed the street to walk on the opposite side for my return route. I walked more quickly, realizing I'd been gone for quite some time between talking with Toby's brother, a few minutes listening to Bonbon howl, and then strolling around the neighborhood. I was sure Joe wouldn't mind, he's not fixated on having me chained to my desk, mostly to the phone, but still. I was supposed to be working. Attending a memorial service made me forget that fact.

The street was quiet, as most residential areas are at mid-day. The neighborhood surrounding the church is filled with homes that start at just under a million dollars and going up from there. It's hard to believe someone can live in a million-dollar home, but there are streets and streets lined with them. It's an older neighborhood, with houses built fifty to seventy years ago, interspersed with some that are only a few years old, places where the original homes were leveled and something new was built, usually something that's trying, but failing, to match the architectural flavor of the area.

Caroline's house looked deserted — all the drapes closed and no cars in the driveway. I slowed my pace, sort of wanting to talk to her, wanting to find out whether she was going to take it so far as to change churches because she hadn't gotten her way with canceling the memorial service.

Although what I really wanted to know was whether she knew of other people, besides Sandy, who were afraid of Toby. People even more upset about his lurking, unwanted presence than she was, someone willing to take it a lot further. Someone who would murder him to be rid of him. His brother said that people were afraid of him. His ghost sure scared me, so maybe Caroline wasn't off base.

As I came even with the path that led to her front door, I wondered why I was being so coy. Why not just ring the bell and ask her directly? I didn't have to hang around, looking like a loiterer, hoping to "run into" her. There was nothing to feel awkward about. She'd brought it up. It wasn't as if I was being nosey. And I wanted to know. I really needed to know. If the detective was going to take a low-key approach, someone had to push harder. If they found out who killed him, I expected the ghost would leave me alone. That was motivation enough to be more intrusive.

I walked up the front path and rang the bell. I realized that I was moving in the opposite direction from getting back to work. I also realized I had no idea what I was going to say.

The door opened. Caroline stood in a dark hallway, making it difficult to see her eyes.

"Hi." I waited for her to respond.

Instead, she leaned to the side and looked past my shoulder.

I don't know what she was looking for. Maybe she thought Joe was with me. Maybe she'd seen Toby's ghost and was afraid it had attached itself to me. Until that moment, it hadn't occurred to me that the ghost might have appeared to others. Finally I turned. The street was empty. "What are you looking for?"

"I haven't heard that evil dog. Maybe it finally croaked." Her face was expressionless despite the vicious edge to her words.

"It wasn't feeling well. I saw Lily, and she was taking her to the vet."

She grimaced. "What can I do for you?"

"I wanted to talk to you more about Toby bothering your daughter. I went to the memorial service and …"

"That service is an outrage."

"Anyway, I met his brother. He mentioned that Toby scared people and I wanted to ask you more about your daughter. Was it the drooling and stuff that got her upset, or was there something else?"

"What difference does it make? He's gone. And what does it have to do with you?"

"I feel sorry for him. Because he was homeless, and he died alone, on the street."

"You shouldn't."

I debated mentioning the ghost. Probably not a good idea, and possibly jeopardizing my job, given Joe's directive not to talk to the church members about ghosts. If she'd seen it, she would surely bring it up. "I wondered if you knew about anyone else who was afraid of him."

"I wasn't afraid of him. I thought he was disgusting."

"I thought he scared your daughter."

"He was a pervert and it offends me that the Pastors preferred his feelings, or his right to be homeless, or whatever, to my daughter's feelings."

"Are you going to change churches?"

"That's somewhat drastic. But I guess that's your generation, when you don't like something you quit. Get divorced, quit your job, drop of out college, whatever is easy."

I had no idea how she got to divorce and college so fast. Her comment was unfair, but I really didn't want to argue about that. "So did he leer at other girls?"

"Of course. They just wrote it off as alcohol. Said we should show compassion."

"That is what you believe, right?"

"There's a limit to compassion. Not when someone hurts my kid."

"Did he hurt her?"

"Looking at her like that, making her uncomfortable, making her afraid of being molested, that's hurting her."

I wasn't sure I saw her logic, but I also wasn't getting anywhere. I felt kind of defeated, like I was trying to find out something to which there was no answer, or stumbling around as if asking questions would suddenly reveal his killer and allow Toby some peace. I was so sad about his death, and even sadder that his brother didn't seem that upset, and Caroline was full on happy about it. No matter what he was like, it made me sick to think that way. And why was he sorry when he died?

"Do you want something specific?"

"I want to know if anyone else was afraid of him. I want to know if someone hated him so much, they gave him a meal with poison in it."

"Oh."

I waited, but she stared at me, as if she was waiting for me to speak, as if I'd paused mid-sentence.

After a few seconds of silence, she said, "The police will figure it out. I don't think you need to get involved."

"I don't. But I can't stop thinking about it. And I thought I'd ask." I backed to the edge of the porch. "Have a nice rest of the day."

"I will. Especially ..."

I waited. "Especially, what?"

"Nothing. I lost my train of thought." She smiled but her eyes were unfocused. Her smile lingered and finally I said good-bye. I was halfway down the walkway before I heard the door close softly behind me.

Ten

THE COFFEE SHOP where I met Cindee the day after the memorial service is a comfy place full of armchairs, sofas, a high-back discarded church pew right out of the middle ages, and lots of small tables and chairs. There's a bookcase along one wall. The shelves contain used books for patrons to read interspersed with pottery from local artists. The walls are decorated with paintings and photography, also from local artists.

The coffee shop isn't a Starbucks. Or a Peet's. I don't have anything against either of those, their coffee is decent, Peet's is really good. But they feel like roadside gift shops, with all kinds of impulse buy items cluttered around the cash register, food that tastes factory made, and a general veneer of phoniness, or maybe it's sameness. The point is, I like the independent coffee shop on Forest Street. It's called The Coffee Cafe and I'd go there every day if I had time.

I don't know why I'm so in love with coffee. Part of it's the buzz. It makes me feel a bit like an addict, almost worse than my smoking habit, because I'm trying to quit smoking, but I have no intention of giving up coffee. Ever. I love the taste, I love it hot, I love it with steamed milk, I love it with iced with milk. I love coffee ice cream and coffee-flavored candy. I love the smell of fresh coffee beans and brewing coffee. I even love the smell of the wet grounds when I put them in my compost bucket for the potted plants on my deck. I can't get my day started without coffee. My coffee maker is set on a timer and I know it's time to get up when the aroma creeps up the stairs and into my bedroom. I think even Simon knows the scent of coffee means it's morning, because he usually starts chirping around the time I hear the coffee maker blurp that it's almost finished.

A couple of times since I started working at the church, Cindee and I met for coffee after she dropped by the church office and we started a conversation that kept going. She seems to like coffee, although she's not obsessed with it like I am, drinking several cups a day. When we go there, she always comments on exceeding her caffeine intake and if we meet in the afternoon, she worries about the caffeine waking her in the middle of the night. I think she's imagining that.

I stepped through the door and took a deep breath, drinking in the smell of coffee and cool air. The space isn't overly bright, relying more on light from the two picture windows facing the street rather than lots of fluorescents.

Cindee wasn't there yet, so I grabbed a two-person sofa

and set my bag next to me. It was just after seven. I'd skipped breakfast so I could buy something from the Coffee Cafe. My stomach grumbled.

Most of the patrons were dressed for work. A few wore backpacks and jeans with the occasional tattoo or pierced nose, which could indicate either a software developer or a student. They looked the same. Or maybe that's a stereotype. After all, I'm neither, but I have a few tattoos. Usually the mom brigade comes to The Coffee Cafe later in the day, once the kiddos are in school.

I saw Cindee pass the front window before she opened the door and stepped inside, so I'd already moved my bag off the sofa.

She stopped a few feet away. "Hi." She dug into her pale pink leather purse and pulled out her wallet, the size of a Subway sandwich. "My treat. What do you want?"

"A large latte and a piece of banana bread."

"Whole milk, right?"

I nodded.

She walked to the counter. The wood soles of her sandals tapped the floor and her pink and green flowered skirt flowed out to the side, brushing the chairs as she wound her way through the tables to the back of the line.

I felt a little bad, ordering a four-dollar latte instead of a cup of black coffee, but I'd been planning my coffee and breakfast since I got out of the shower that morning, and I didn't know she was going to pay for me.

Once we were settled with our food and drinks on the low table in front of us, Cindee glanced around at the man in the adjacent armchair and the man and woman staring at their laptops at the table near one of the windows. "I hope it won't be hard to talk."

"They're too busy working. They won't be listening to our conversation."

She tucked her hair behind her ear and twisted her pearl earring. "I'm always listening to other conversations, even when I'm checking email."

"Do you have something super private you're planning to talk about?"

"No." She blew on the surface of her coffee but didn't test it with a sip. "Just always conscious of not gossiping, or making the church look bad by complaining."

"No one's listening."

I don't think she believed me, but after a bite of her croissant, she changed her focus. "What did you think of the service yesterday?"

"It was nice."

She sipped her coffee and carefully set the cup on the saucer. "It felt sad."

"Why?"

"The only people remembering him were strangers. It wasn't really about Toby at all."

"His brother was there."

"I didn't know he had a brother. What's his name?"

"Gary. I didn't get his last name. I was so surprised I didn't think about it until he was gone. All I know is that he lives in Santa Cruz."

"I wonder how he found out his brother was dead."

"He comes by from time to time to check on Toby. He saw the flyer."

"Well that's good. It was still sad. What a horrible way to end your life. All alone. I hate thinking about him dying in the street like that."

"Me too." When Cindee and I said we'd meet for coffee, I thought she'd ask me about the ghost. She hadn't seemed as antagonistic as she had the other times I'd mentioned encountering someone's spirit. She'd seemed really surprised that I'd never seen a ghost until I started working at the church. I was sure that's why she wanted to meet for coffee, to ask me more about that. But now, she wasn't saying anything and I wasn't sure how to bring it up without seeming like a guy in work boots tromping across a garden border of daffodils. "Were there any more complaints about having the service?'

"No."

"Caroline just dropped the whole thing?"

"That's not a surprise. She's a little unstable."

"Really? How?" I picked up my banana bread and took a tiny bite. I wanted it to last as long as my latte, and I hadn't even started that because it was still too hot.

Cindee leaned forward and reached for the oversized pink

ceramic coffee cup that looked like it was designed to match her purse and skirt. "I don't know if I should say. You know how Joe is about gossip. I shouldn't have brought it up."

That wasn't fair. It's so irritating when people start to tell you something and then worry they shouldn't. They should work that out before they open their mouths. It has a way of making me even more curious than I already am. What is that in me that wants to know other people's secrets, to hear about other human failures? At least I assumed it was some kind of failure. If she'd done something amazing, Cindee wouldn't label it scary, and she wouldn't be hesitant to mention it. She wouldn't be worrying about gossip. I suppose everyone has a morbid interest in others' failures. I never actually asked anyone, but I don't think I'm the only person on earth who wants to gossip or hear others' secrets, especially their secret sins. If we all weren't interested, they could never sell all those magazines and junky newspapers that highlight celebrity missteps. Even upstanding news organizations put the personal failure stories front and center. It makes us feel better about our own mistakes. Or makes us feel not so alone. Maybe that's it. When you know other people have done stupid or crazy things, when they fail or do something shameful or not very admirable, you don't feel so alone in remembering all your own flaws. And when it's something over the top, we feel superior.

But dying to know, and assuming other people would be just as curious, still didn't mean I should demand that she tell me what she was keeping to herself. That would be admitting I'm flawed and nosey and ghoulish — wanting to know the bad stuff. I suppose we all pretend we're above that. "I could see why she was afraid of Toby. After I saw his ghost again, it made more sense."

"What happened?"

"First, when he died, this silken think came out of his body and turned thick and dark. It made me feel nauseous. Then a few days later when I was in the prayer garden, I saw it again. There was something scarier about it the second time. It wasn't the same as when I've seen ghosts that are just lingering, wanting someone to know their stories. This seemed more … aggressive."

"How do you know?"

"How do I know what?"

"When you see these things, or feel them, how do you know it's not just your imagination?"

"Because it's real. I see it."

"You don't worry that you're hallucinating?"

It was a little insulting. And now two people had hinted that I might be seeing things that didn't really exist. "No."

"I would."

"Why?"

"Because I don't believe it's real. When someone dies, they're gone. They aren't breathing, their eyes are blank, they don't speak. There's no brain activity left. So how can there be … a … a *thing* still hovering around?"

"That's what I don't get about you and everyone at the church. You believe people have souls. You think they have a separate part of them that lives on after death. So it makes sense it separates away from their bodies when they die, right? So why can't it take a bit of time before it goes wherever it's going?"

"I never thought about it like that. But it's just so far beyond anything I've ever experienced."

"If you did, you wouldn't think you were imagining or hallucinating. You'd know."

"That sounds a little arrogant. As if you have an inside track."

"It's just how it is. I'm not trying to sound superior or like I have some special skill or insight. I can't help it. What am I supposed to do? It's hard not to talk about it."

She picked up her croissant and took a large bite. She chewed slowly. I don't know why it's so hard for people to grasp. They act like I'm lying or trying to get attention. I can't control what I see. If someone saw a giraffe in their front yard, I wouldn't demand to know how they knew or insist they'd imagined it. I suppose it's not exactly the same thing, since nearly everyone has seen giraffes, or at least photographs of them. The problem with ghosts is some people have seen them and some haven't. The people who haven't, like to label the ones who have as crazy or imaginative or wishful thinkers.

After a few more minutes of Cindee chewing her croissant,

I realized she wasn't going to pick up the conversational ball again. "It makes total sense to me that a person's spirit would linger. No one has any idea what makes a person an individual. Whether it's in their brain or something else. Like a soul, some other part that has its own being, and science hasn't found it yet. Anyway, I know it was Toby in some form. And I know he wanted to get my attention. He was trying to talk to me when he died and he came back to finish his thoughts."

"For what? To tell you who killed him?"

"He said he was sorry."

"For bothering Caroline's daughter? Is that what you think? He probably didn't even realize he was doing it. Especially since there's a good chance it was her reading into the situation." Thin flakes of croissant drifted down between Cindee's fingers, coming to rest on her skirt where they were almost invisible among the pink flowers and greenery, and scattering across the thick brown leather of the sofa where they looked a bit like dandruff in a man's dark, smooth hair. One piece of flakey dough clung to her lip. She kept dabbing her tongue at her bottom lip as if she could feel it there but couldn't quite find the texture to snag it and lick it off.

I desperately wanted to reach over and flick it off her lip. Watching it move as she chewed made my lips tickle and I couldn't take my eyes off it.

"Is that what you think? That he was sorry for leering at a teenage girl?" Cindee said.

"Maybe." I didn't know what he was sorry for. I didn't really know if he had been speaking to me or it was just general regret and the rambling thoughts of a man who only had a few breaths left in him.

"But he could have been saying he was sorry for messing up his life, for not being a productive citizen, for becoming an alcoholic, even for dying right in front of the church. Maybe he was ashamed of that. You're just guessing," Cindee said.

"Are you arguing with me?"

"Not at all. Just trying to figure out where your head's at."

"I thought you wanted to hear more about the ghost, now it sounds like you have no interest. It seems like you don't believe me at all."

"I go back and forth. Of course it's intriguing, of course it's glamorous and all of that, but for someone like me who's never seen one, it seems too much to accept."

I wanted to be friends with Cindee. I really did. But it's so hard sometimes. It's hard to connect with another person, to really be on the same wavelength and have similar thoughts. Not that you want every thought and feeling to be identical, but similarity is good. I don't know why it's so hard. I know she's older than I am by quite a bit, and married, and a mother. When I think of all those things, I'm not sure why I thought we could be friends. Mostly because from the first time I met her, and then when we went for a glass of wine in Half Moon Bay, it seemed as if there was a connection between us. Something as intangible as the ghost I was trying, and failing, to describe.

I picked up my latte and took a sip. It had cooled considerably and went down very smoothly. I took a few more nibbles of banana bread. It was amazing how much was gone even though I'd been taking baby bites. "It's not glamorous. It was dark and smelled like smoke from a chemical fire, and it felt bad. It scared me. I want to know who killed him and I want it to go away."

"How many times do you think you've seen it?"

"Only twice, but I'm afraid every time I get out of my car in the morning that it will be there, and when I leave work at the end of the day."

"You sound so upset." She put her hand on my forearm. The wisp of croissant was still on her lip, having moved closer to the corner where her upper and lower lips joined.

"I want it to stop."

"I thought you liked ghosts."

"It depends. In this case, I'm scared."

"Of what?"

"I don't even know. It's hard to describe. I guess that it might hurt me, or that it might hurt someone I care about. Or … I don't even know. It's just scary to see something you don't understand, that you don't know what it will do, or what it can do." Her hand rested limply on my arm, feeling like a damp fish. Between that and the dough on her lip, my flesh was crawling as if there were beetles running across my skin.

I moved my arm. "It makes me wonder what Caroline experienced with him when he was alive. Maybe he really was a creep."

"I told you Caroline is a little unbalanced."

I waited, knowing she definitely wanted to tell me, and maybe she was disappointed that I hadn't pushed her on that point a few minutes earlier.

"There was a cat that used to hang out in the church parking lot. One day during Summer Vacation Bible Camp, we were setting up a table of snacks for the kids. The cat got spooked and ran across the parking lot. A car was pulling in and hit the cat."

"How awful. Did the kids see it?"

"No. But Caroline laughed. She giggled. She put her hand over her mouth and couldn't seem to stop herself, as if it was the funniest thing."

"Maybe it was shock? Sometimes people laugh from shock."

"Yes, but this wasn't like that."

"How do you know?"

"I've seen people laugh when someone dies. It's more blank and has a hysterical quality to it. Their faces don't look amused, they look devastated. This was a genuine giggle. It was sickening."

I thought back over my few brief encounters with Caroline. She seemed normal, her conversation was coherent, and she seemed to have a good reason for her fears. But between what Kate had said about her thinking the usher was leering at her daughter and now this … her attitude toward Toby looked completely different. Although Gary said people were afraid of Toby, maybe those were the words of an estranged brother, not an accurate picture. A man that was frustrated with the burden of a brother who had no income and was one step away from some kind of disaster that might infringe on Gary's life.

It upsets me that people live on the streets. And I feel I should do something to help, yet what can I really do? To be honest, the people I've met who are homeless, who come around the church looking for help on a regular basis, can be very difficult. Sometimes they're belligerent, and if they're not, they're persistent to the point of insanity. They stand too close and stare too hard and generally break all the unspoken rules of social interaction. It's hard to be kind to them sometimes. You just want to give them money or a sandwich and have them go away. I want to help in theory, but I really don't know how. Once a person has lost their mind to whatever forces got the upper hand, it's hard to deal with them. You want to, but you can't. It makes me sick to my stomach to think what can happen to a human being.

I glanced at Cindee. The croissant crumb was finally gone from her lip. She stared at me, waiting for me to say something about Caroline's disturbed behavior. But it didn't line up with what I'd seen when I talked to Caroline. I was confused and suddenly very tired and it wasn't even eight o'clock in the morning. "I should probably get to work."

"Why didn't you say anything? Do you think I'm a bad person for gossiping about her?"

"Of course not. I can't digest it. Or something."

"Anyway, my point was, you shouldn't assume Toby was at fault there."

"I wasn't."

"I think you were."

"I don't know what I think."

She patted my arm. The first time was no big deal, but this time I felt like she was patronizing me. I know she's older, but if we're going to be friends, she can't act like she's my mother or that she needs to take care of me and tell me what I'm thinking or feeling.

I wrapped the rest of the banana bread in the napkin and stood. "I should get to work."

Cindee pressed the button on her phone. "This conversation sort of went all over the place." She laughed. "And I guess that was my fault. I really did want to hear more about your supernatural experience, even if I'm skeptical."

I didn't know whose fault it was, and it was complicated. I really wasn't sure I believed her that she wanted to hear more about the ghost. I thought that's why we decided to meet for coffee, but she sure got defensive, or offended, or something, awfully fast.

"Can we get a refill and talk some more?" she said. "It's not like the church office has strict hours."

I didn't know if she was pulling some sort of pastoral spouse rank or just trying to be nice. I decided to opt for the second viewpoint. I picked up her cup and saucer. I walked slowly, carrying both cups to the counter, ordered a refill for Cindee and another latte for me. Why not splurge, it wasn't like I got a latte every day.

When I was seated again, I tried to remember every detail of what I'd seen. Either she wanted to hear about it or she didn't. I explained the look and texture of the ghost, how I felt, and that I knew for certain that it was lingering until someone paid attention to how he died.

Cindee nodded but didn't say anything, not even a little murmuring, encouraging sound. But her eyes looked as if she was accepting what I said, as if she was very curious. I don't know how I knew that, but they did. I think she wanted me to prove it to her. I had the feeling she wanted to believe me, but all of her dogma put a big wall right down the center of her brain.

"It seems like you really believe all of that happened."

"I don't believe it. I saw it."

"I wonder why you never had these experiences before you started working here."

"I don't know."

"It's still hard to believe, since I've never seen anything like it."

"But I felt it. Why is that so hard for you to accept?"

"I've been told all my life that ghosts are figments of the imagination."

"Okay."

"We believe that when you die, your soul goes to be with the Lord. There's no lingering, there's no alternate plane of existence, no in-between space. You're either in heaven, or … you know."

I smiled. I wondered why she couldn't say the word. Maybe she didn't like what she believed. Maybe she didn't like being closed-minded and thinking there was no variation in levels of existence, and she certainly didn't seem comfortable saying she believed people went to heaven or hell. Maybe she didn't really believe in hell either. In my mind, that's a lot harder to swallow than a few ghosts whispering in my ear.

AFTER COFFEE, THE day was uneventful. I answered more than the usual number of phone calls, ordered office supplies, and typed up a personalized thank you email for someone who had made a very large donation to the church — ten thousand dollars. Pastor Joe would send the email, of course, I just gave him some basics to work with so he could put it into his own words.

I started cleaning out the cabinets behind my desk and got very caught up in it. Things had been stuffed in there that didn't belong, half-used reams of paper were stacked on top of each other, and there were all kinds of odds and ends — boxes of scotch tape, pens, thumbtacks. I didn't make all that mess, I'm usually organized, but lots of people come in to use the copy machine or return things they've borrowed from the office, and they aren't always as careful as they should be about remembering where things go.

When I left at five-thirty, Joe and Kate and everyone from the childcare center were already gone.

I climbed the stairs slowly. My palm was damp on the metal railing. My feet felt thick and stiff and I was cold despite the dry-smelling summer air. There was no breeze. The light was nearly as bright as mid-day, but the shadows cast by the sanctuary and the multi-purpose room were dark, so the rose bushes lining the path looked almost black. The sky was blue and the sound of traffic from Foothill Boulevard was muffled. The entire property suddenly felt very empty, filled with large, deserted buildings, surrounded by trees at the back, the vacant parking lot to one side and the parking strip, where my Beetle sat all alone.

I made my way slowly along the path. Up close, the roses no longer looked black, but they were still dark, with the red almost the color of dried blood. The thorns seemed to glitter as if the fading light was drawn to the sharp tips. I tried to walk faster but my feet still felt as if they were filled with lead. I knew what was coming, and I was afraid to even look at my car, much less the opposite end of the parking strip where Toby's body had been, but when I took the first step down, I felt compelled to turn in that direction.

The brownish gray thing hung there like a car had spewed

exhaust. It was a thick, solid mass blocking the trees behind it. I wrapped my fingers around the rail and moved my other foot down so I was on the second step from the top. After that, I couldn't move. The thing wasn't anywhere near my car, I could have hurried down the steps, popped open the door, and jumped inside, but what if it followed me in? I had no rational reason for thinking that it would. It hadn't followed me anywhere else, but still the thought was there.

Images and sounds of Toby lying on the ground, his voice straining to speak, his filthy beard, the black crud wedged into his broken fingernails and around his cuticles, and finally, the convulsions, filled my head. I felt like I was going to puke. I squeezed the rail harder until my hand ached and my skin felt like it was fusing with the metal. I started to cry. I looked up and down the street. It was commute hour. Surely someone in one of these magnificent homes would be coming or going, but the street was as deserted as the church property.

I knew I couldn't stand there all evening. I dragged my feet down each step, my hand squeaking on the rail, slick with sweat, but I couldn't loosen my grip.

The thing didn't move, just hung there, solid and dark and sad.

I decided that if I didn't cave into my own fears, I might be able to move closer to it. I might feel something about why Toby was sorry, why part of him was still hanging around the church, waiting for something. Waiting for me, maybe.

I set my bag and water container near the front bumper of

my bug. The gravel creaked and snapped under my feet, louder than usual because I was listening more carefully, my mind focused on what was now only a few yards away, hyper alert to the sensation of every step and each breath.

As I drew closer, I noticed the chemical smell. I tried to swallow but my throat was so tight it couldn't quite complete the action. I took a shallow breath and tried again. Then I stepped right up to the smoky thing so it was touching me. Rather I was inside it, I couldn't actually feel it touching me, but knew it was surrounding me. My eyes burned, but I vowed I wasn't going to back away.

Once I was completely enveloped by it, I could dimly see Toby's shaved head, his thick, untamed beard, and his eyes. They were dark brown, the whites pure, and there was a kindness to them, not a threatening glare or any of the salaciousness that Caroline had described.

"Why are you sorry?" I whispered.

The faint image of his face remained still, his lips didn't move, but inside my head, I heard a man's tired, strained voice. *I'm sorry my life was a waste. I hope it meant something that I saved the little dog.*

That was all. Suddenly, the thing dissolved. It happened so fast, it made me think of Cindee's accusation — *how do you know you're not imagining it?* Because it was as if nothing had ever been there and I was standing at the edge of the gravel strip cold and teary-eyed and confused on a warm, summer afternoon.

I had no idea what it meant. The first part was clear — he thought being homeless, letting his life slide down into nothing much to speak of was a waste. But who really knows how you're supposed to spend your life. Is it a waste if you don't do something important? If you simply exist, filling up a spot on the earth? Does that make you a waste? I can't believe that. You're still a human being, breathing and thinking and interacting with other people.

The bit about saving the dog made no sense. I assumed he referred to Bonbon since Jill said he hung around Lily's house, that she fed him. I'm glad he felt better for whatever he thought he'd done. And obviously he had nothing else to say to me. He was at peace, but I was not.

Eleven

THE NEXT AFTERNOON, Lily came home with an empty carrier. Bonbon had stayed overnight at the vet, throwing up for hours. They pumped her little stomach, but they still wanted to keep her under watch. Kate found out because she almost ran into Lily just outside the parking lot. Literally. Kate was turning out of the lot when Lily came flying down the street. Kate slammed on her brakes. Lily screeched into her driveway, stumbled out of her car, crying, and lifted the carrier out of the back seat. When Kate saw it was in the back seat instead of the passenger side, she knew something wasn't right. So she left her car near the edge of the street and walked over to Lily's driveway to check on her.

Kate told me all of this when she came into the office and collapsed on one of the wing chairs. Her eyes and the tip of her nose were red. "They think the dog ate some poisoned meatballs."

"How do they know?"

"From undigested food in her stomach."

I gritted my teeth to keep that image from taking shape and swelling through my brain. "Sort of like Toby."

"Did he eat meatballs?"

"Who knows. It's not like they report the status to me. But it's a good guess, don't you think?" I thought about what Toby's ghost had said to me about saving the dog. "Has Bonbon eaten bad meat before?"

"I don't know. Lily didn't mention it."

"I've heard of people giving poisoned food to animals. I don't know how anyone could be so heartless," I said.

To me, killing an animal, or trying to kill it, is as bad as killing a human being. I wondered if someone wanted to kill little Bonbon or if the poisoned meatballs were meant for another dog, or a cat. It seems that people hate cats more than dogs, hate their yowling, and their indiscriminate use of gardens as litter boxes, their fights, and their tendency to bring around dead rodents and drop them on your front porch. I didn't know if Bonbon would be interested in meat lying around in the street, spilled out of a garbage can, especially since she was so well cared for and not likely to be ravenous, and even less likely to be wandering outside alone. Someone must have put the meat in her backyard.

"What did Lily say about the possibility that someone might have tried to kill her dog? That can't be a great feeling."

"She didn't have any coherent thoughts, she just kept asking who would do such a thing."

I saved the little dog.

"I wonder if Toby ate those meatballs. If he was used to Lily leaving food out for him."

Kate straightened in the chair. She uncrossed her legs. "Definitely. We should call Detective Palmer."

We agreed that Kate would call. Since she was the one who had talked to Lily. We also agreed that it was beyond sad to think of a man so hungry he picked up a presumably cold, very possibly spoiled piece of meat and ate it for dinner, thinking that's what Lily had given him.

For a while I wondered how Toby would know he saved Bonbon. I guess once you die, you might know a lot of things, not everything, but certainly more than we know when we're alive.

DETECTIVE PALMER QUESTIONED Lily and a police officer went through her backyard. He found half a meatball under the chaise lounge where Bonbon likes to hunker down when the weather is really hot.

Kate and I sat on the back patio with Lily and watched them search the rest of the yard. I had managed to insert myself into the situation by tagging along when Kate went over to check on Bonbon, who was going to be coming home the following day. I mentioned Toby's brother to Detective Palmer and apologized for not getting his last name. She made a note of it, but didn't seem too concerned that I only had sketchy information.

Like all the homes surrounding Central Avenue Church, Lily's house had a large backyard with plenty of room for a swimming pool, although she didn't have one. There was an enormous vegetable garden with rows of tomato plants and posts held together by string that was draped with green bean vines. She also had two kinds of squash and some artichoke plants. She said the artichokes were hard to grow right and they were too tough to eat, but she kept trying. She also had green onions, a pumpkin plant, and a glass sided case that contained an herb garden. Toby often ate her tomatoes and zucchini, at her insistence, because those plants always bore far more than she could possibly eat or even give away to her neighbors or foist off on her children. You can only bake so many zucchini breads before everyone is sick of it.

Next to the case with the herb garden, they found an aluminum pie pan containing another chunk of meatball covered in thick tomato sauce. Detective Palmer, unlike her earlier insistence on waiting for scientific results, was willing to speculate. She said there was a good chance Toby had eaten at least one meatball, and possibly there had been a whole plateful. She guessed that someone meant to poison the dog and when the dog appeared to be healthy and lively, they came back and tried again. Of course, they probably didn't know the unintended results. Or maybe they did and didn't care. If you're full of enough hate to try to kill a cute little dog, no matter how annoying it can be, you might not care about killing a man you consider a nuisance, or a threat.

Obviously my thoughts kept circling around Caroline. At first I felt a stab of guilt that she came to mind. She was a caring mother, looking out for her children. But she hated that dog. And according to Cindee, she was off balance, if not completely sick in the head.

As the Detective went out through the side gate, I stood. "Thanks for the coffee."

Lily smiled.

"Sit down," Kate said. "We might as well enjoy the afternoon a bit longer. We, and especially you, spend way too much time cooped up in that basement."

"I really should get back."

"Relax."

I edged toward the side of the patio.

"Do you want to take some tomatoes?" Lily said.

"Sure."

While she went into the house to get a bag, I walked over to the tomato plants. Kate followed me. "Why are you in such a rush to get back to work?"

"I want some time alone. To think."

"Oh."

I reached down and lifted one of the stems of the tomato plant. The tomatoes were heavy, dark red, and smooth. I could smell them, even uncut. There's nothing in the world like a tomato that ripens on the vine. The ones in the grocery store taste watery sometimes. Even when they don't, they're bland. It's easy to forget what a real tomato tastes like, unless you can afford organic, which can be worth it because one really tasty tomato is better than two that taste like nothing. Still, plucking it off the vine is the best. I couldn't wait to eat them. I love to make mozzarella cheese and tomato salad. I could already picture my lunch for the rest of the week.

The bag was heavy, stuffed with ten tomatoes. I hoped I could eat them all before they spoiled, but Lily insisted I could. She reminded me they have antioxidants and it was almost better than the concept of an apple a day. She told me to come back if I wanted more.

I went out the side gate. I looped the handles of the bag over my arm and walked across the street to Caroline's. Once again, I had no idea what I was going to say to her. I probably should have told the Detective about my train of thought, but then I didn't want to be accusing someone of something so horrible if it turned out I was leaping to conclusions. Or maybe that's just an excuse, and I'm too curious and too eager to poke into things where I might not belong. I desperately wanted to know who was responsible for Toby's death.

As I waited for Caroline to answer the door, I wondered whether it would be considered murder if you intend to kill an animal but instead kill a human being. It seems like it should be, but that wasn't for me to decide. All I needed to know was whether or not I was right.

Caroline's teenaged daughter opened the door. She had long, dark hair and wore cutoff jeans that were so short the white stuff that formed the pockets hung out the bottom.

Her face was pale, free of makeup, and she looked sleepy. Her eyes were dark, her pupils almost fully dilated, and not shrinking even as she looked out into the afternoon light behind me. "Hi. Can I help you?"

"I'm the administrative assistant at Central Avenue Church." I lifted my arm with the tomato bag and pointed in the direction of the church. The bag slid down my arm so I shifted it to my hand.

"I've seen you before. What's up?"

"Is your mother here?"

"No."

"When will she be home?"

"Don't know. What do you want?"

"I wanted to tell her the little dog across the street almost died, but she's going to be okay." The minute I said that I wondered why I blurted it out. Now the girl would tell her mother and I wouldn't get to see her reaction. Besides, it sounded kind of odd, that I rushed over to tell them something that really had nothing to do with them. Maybe Joe was right that I don't always think ahead.

"God, my mom hates that dog. It barks all the time. It could drive you insane. I'd like to break its neck."

I stared at her and I think I made a gasping sound.

"Oh come on. It's like a little rat. People shouldn't be allowed to own dogs if they can't control them. It drives everyone crazy and we're supposed to put up with it because it's cute. Well what about our peace and quiet? Maybe I want to take a nap, since it's summer, and that stupid dog barks so loud I have to play my music with earplugs."

Wow. I think my mouth was falling open wider with every word she said. "You wouldn't really hurt it though, would you?"

She glared at me. Her eyes still dark, still dilated. Maybe she was high. She sure wasn't caring what I thought about her ugly, hateful attitude. She was blurting out a lot more than I ever did.

"Why?" she said.

"What's your name?"

"Why are you asking me these questions?" She pushed the door partway closed. "I need to go."

I put my hand on the edge of the door. "I guess you're the one who complained about Toby."

"Who's Toby?"

"The homeless man. The one who died."

"Oh, him. Yeah, he was gross."

"The dog was poisoned, you know."

"Well he wouldn't have gotten sick if she kept him in the house instead of letting him out where he can bark all the time and drive everyone out of their minds."

"Did you leave meatballs for him? With rat poison or something in it?"

She tugged on the edge of her shorts. "I need to go. My friend and I were IM'ing."

"The dog almost died."

"People put out bait for snails and stuff all the time. If people control their pets, they won't eat poisonous stuff."

"Toby ate some of those meatballs."

She glanced back into the hallway behind her. She looked back at me. "What are you trying to say? I don't feel well. I really need to go back to bed. And my friend … I'll tell my mom you came by." She closed the door.

I could feel that my mouth was still partially open. She knew exactly what I was saying. My hand was damp with sweat and I almost dropped the bag of tomatoes on the front porch. Luckily, I held on tight.

JD CAME FOR dinner that night. We hadn't planned it, but when I texted him to tell him what happened, he called in sick. He was sitting on my back deck when I got home from work.

I made a big salad with two of the tomatoes. I put in boiled eggs and provolone cheese and black olives and made an herbal vinaigrette to go with it, something light with just a little balsamic vinegar and thyme so it wouldn't drown the flavor of the tomatoes. I served it with wheat crackers and water. JD drank three glasses of water and didn't ask for wine.

It shouldn't bug me that he usually wants wine or beer with dinner. Maybe I'm trying too hard to find someone who thinks like me in every single way. I don't know. How do you know when it's the right person and you're truly in love? I think I love him. I sure like him a lot. I think about him all the time, and he's my favorite person to spend time with. Is that love?

We sat on the deck after dinner. I desperately wanted a cigarette, but decided to resist. It was the kind of day that made me want to contemplate life, and smoking enhances that reflective attitude, which is part of why it's so hard to quit. But JD was right next to me, feeling all warm and looking gorgeous with his dark hair and his ponytail that's grown quite a bit longer since I met him.

I also wanted a cigarette to help me think. I'd spent days trying to figure out what else I needed to tell him about my parents. The only thing I could come up with was that I wanted to tell him the whole story, from coming home that day, to finding them, to all the stuff that happened after — moving to a new house, living with people I really didn't know very well, eating different food, feeling like even more of an outsider than I already did from being home schooled and not starting school until I was fifteen. Even though it was irrational, it felt like if I had still been home schooled, I would have been there and they wouldn't have died.

JD is not the type — maybe most guys aren't — to say, *what are you thinking*. So we sat there quietly and it was nice, but I still wanted to say something. I wasn't sure how to start, which is quite strange for someone who can chatter her head off like I can. Finally I decided to wait. I already felt a little space between us and I didn't want to make it into the Grand

Canyon. Eventually I had to let him know his reaction had upset me, but I really needed to figure out why before I tried to talk about it. I hoped that wouldn't take me another twelve years to figure out.

Just as the sky started to turn navy blue, I looked across the iron fence that separates my strip of yard from the common area where there are benches and trees and a small pond. A bird was chirping like mad, hopping along the path.

I stood and squinted, as if that would help me see better, which it never does, so I don't know why I do it, but for some reason you get the idea you're intensifying your ability to see farther. "Do you see that bird?"

"I can sure hear it."

"It doesn't look like a regular wild bird."

He leaned forward.

I stepped down off the deck and crossed the yard to the gate. I unlatched it and walked out into the common area. The bird hopped around, flapping its wings. I walked closer. It was a green and yellow parakeet with a rounded head and alert eyes that made it look friendly and adorable. It looked like it wasn't fully grown. I moved closer and it hopped away. I turned and called to JD, "It's a parakeet. Go get something to hold it."

The bird jumped and fluffed its feathers. When I stopped trying to move closer, it settled down and just took small hops, like it felt compelled to move but was too tired to really make much effort.

A few minutes later JD came through the gate. He was carrying a sheet and cardboard box. He set the box on the ground and unfolded the sheet. He studied the bird for several minutes, then he stretched his arms wide, holding the edges of the sheet. He gently spread it over the ground, capturing the bird near the center. The bird started a wild flapping and chirping — not in a happy way. JD cupped it in his hand, placed it in the box, and we took it into the house.

We put a piece of foil across the top of the box and tore holes in it. After we put some of Simon's seed and a pan of water in the box, we made flyers with my cell phone number on them and taped them all over the condo complex and along a few nearby streets.

No one ever called about the bird, so a few days later I bought a cage. I didn't want to put the other bird in with Simon until I got him checked out to make sure he was healthy, but Simon and he had a fantastic gabfest once they could see each other.

I still want more birds. Some day, I'd like a house with an aviary in the center. When we were cuddling in bed, I mentioned this to JD. He said that was a great idea, so maybe he is my soul mate.

THE END

Cathryn Grant

LONELY GHOSTS

A Suburban Noir Ghost Story

Published by D2C Perspectives

One

THE FLIGHT FROM San Francisco to Sydney is fifteen hours. A lot can happen in fifteen hours. In this case, JD's twin brother became a suspect in the murder of his ex-girlfriend. The woman who had robbed him a few months earlier, stripping his house bare, was found in his garden with a single stab wound in her solar plexus, her clothes soaked with blood.

Our flight was uneventful, as they say. But it was so long I started to feel as if I lived in that silver tube, my entire life shrunk to the tiny space between me and the guy in front of me who kept his chair reclined even when he ate, which shoved my meals right up to my rib cage. Every time I went to the bathroom it was a major production involving the guy on the aisle getting out of his seat, then JD joining him in the aisle, and then me climbing over their chairs to get out. The scene was repeated when I returned.

We watched two movies, ate three meals, slept for five or

six hours and we still weren't there.

The sun came up as we got close to the bottom of the earth, and coming in over Sydney was amazing. We saw the opera house as we descended near Sydney Harbor. Mostly I saw it while JD leaned against my shoulder and ducked his head down near mine so he could get a glimpse.

It was another hour and twenty minutes before we got our baggage and went through immigration and customs and out into a gorgeous spring morning. We'd left autumn behind in the northern hemisphere for two weeks. We were planning five days with JD's twin brother, Luke, and nine days on Hamilton Island off the northeast coast where we we'd get to make a trip out to the Great Barrier Reef. I couldn't wait. Supposedly I was also going to learn to surf during this trip, something I was both excited and nervous about. Nervous, because it looks like the easiest thing in the world, standing on that board. It also looks like the easiest thing in the world to fall off that board and have it whack you on the head.

Even though I knew JD was an identical twin, I wasn't prepared to see this guy with dark brown hair, minus the ponytail JD wears, six-feet, two-inches tall, dark brown eyes, and hands that I would not be able to tell from JD's if they both stood behind a wall and stuck them through a slot. His voice was the same, and if I wasn't looking at JD I wasn't absolutely sure who was talking, at least until I got to know Luke better. Then I could tell by the things he said.

Luke wore cargo shorts, a bright yellow t-shirt, and flip

flops, although they call them thongs in Australia.

JD introduced me. Luke took my carry-on bag, hugged me with his free arm, and said, "Madison. The girl who knows everything. Very happy to meet you." Luke grabbed JD and hugged him and quickly let go. "You won't believe what happened. What a morning. I'm lucky I made it here to meet you."

"It's only nine-thirty," JD said. "What could have happened?"

"That chick, Elizabeth … the one who emptied my house? She was murdered."

"Wow," I said.

JD stopped walking.

"The cops talked to me for two hours — at four in the morning."

"They think you killed her?" JD said

"Yeah. Not that they did anything to find out who stole all my shit. They didn't think they could prove it was her, and now, they're all over me, like it's obvious it was her."

"Crap." JD moved forward so he was walking next to Luke and I was following behind.

"You got that right." Luke had a slow stride that covered a lot of ground quickly, exactly like JD's. Following behind, I couldn't stop flicking my gaze back and forth between the two of them. It was charming how much alike they looked, but I can't say why that's the case. Maybe because I've never been close to anyone who's a twin, and it seems even more remarkable when you know a person really well and there's a mirror image of them on the other side of the world. Although from the things JD had told me about Luke, the resemblance was all on the outside.

Luke has lived in Sydney for six years. He was traveling all over Asia, and when he got to Australia, he liked it so much he decided to stay. He met Elizabeth when he and his buddies were drinking at a pub in Sydney. She was their server. He flirted with her and they started seeing each other. She thought he was *the one*, and he thought she was number thirty-eight, or whatever count he's at in his serial dating. When he hooked up with a new woman, the same woman he was with now, Elizabeth and some friends of hers went to his house in the middle of the night with a truck and removed every piece of electronics and furniture, and every single one of his personal belongings, right down to the salt and pepper shakers and the packets of soy sauce from takeout restaurants that he'd collected in a drawer.

"Any idea who killed her?" JD asked.

"They think I did."

"But what do you think?"

Luke didn't answer, at least not that I could hear.

"They're just asking questions," JD said.

"You didn't hear these questions."

We'd reached his car, a tiny Hyundai that looked new, sparkling clean, and bright red, which made me imagine the woman bleeding in his yard. I could see her blood in my mind, even though I had no idea what she looked like or what the yard looked like. It was just my revved-up imagination, thinking about all that blood.

Luke loaded our stuff into the trunk. JD insisted I sit in the front, which made up for him leaving me trailing behind as we walked through the airport. He stuffed himself into the tiny back seat. Luke talked about the murder during the entire drive, which was understandable, but not the introduction to Australia that I'd expected.

"I found her when I got home last night. I went out to water the one potted plant she didn't steal from my patio, and saw her arm through the gate into the garden. I hope I never see anything like that again as long as I live."

I knew how he felt, having seen more than my share of lifeless bodies, starting with my parents when I was fifteen, and ending with the homeless man who died right in front of me a few months ago.

"She was on her back with a knife sticking out of her ribs. Her eyes were open, staring at me, accusing me of breaking her heart."

He shook his head as if he was trying to clear the memory, and then wrenched the wheel and we flew around a corner. Usually Luke rides a motorcycle, so I wasn't sure how much recent experience he had driving a car. I grabbed the handle above the door and pressed my tongue between my teeth so I wouldn't make unwelcome comments on his driving. It was especially unnerving because we were on the wrong side of the road and I was on the wrong side of the car.

"Did they accuse you of killing her?" My voice sounded as thin as tissue paper. JD put his hand on my shoulder and squeezed it slightly.

"No. But they kept me sitting there forever. They kept asking the same questions in different ways, so you know they were trying to get me to lie about some minor detail they could pounce on and build into a bigger lie."

"They don't try to *get* you to lie," JD said.

"How do you know?" Luke said.

JD didn't answer.

I was starting to see how they were different.

Luke glanced in the rearview mirror. "Madison, did JD tell you about my dream? That he started a cult?" He laughed and half turned in his seat, presumably to see JD's reaction. I closed my eyes as the car swerved to the left.

"It was a stupid dream, years ago. Why can't you stop talking about it?" JD said.

"It was like a premonition," Luke said.

"It was a *dream*."

"No one would ever follow me in a cult, but I could see them following you." He turned toward me and the car lurched again. "Can't you see that, Madison? He's quiet, deep. People are drawn to that, especially women."

"You don't seem to have any trouble attracting women," JD said.

"But they'd follow you even if you were already taken."

"Shut up. Just tell us who else the police are talking to."

"They didn't reveal that information to me," Luke said.

"So you're the only suspect?"

"It seems that way."

"That's not good," JD said.

"No shit."

I pulled my lip balm out of my bag and smeared it on my mouth. I didn't really need it, the air was moister than it was in California, but it gave me something to do. I decided to stay out of it and just listen to the two of them. I closed my eyes for a minute. It was nine-thirty in the morning which meant it was three-thirty in the afternoon the day before, so I shouldn't have been sleepy, but I was.

Thinking about life going on as normal back home, a day that I'd missed completely with our sudden jump forward in time, was a strange feeling. Back at Central Avenue Church, Pastor Joe might or might not be in his office, Pastor Kate was most likely in hers. Cindee was filling in for me while I was on vacation, which Joe had been apprehensive about. I was hired because he wanted an administrative assistant who wasn't a member of the church, someone detached from all the politics and gossip. Having his wife sitting at my desk was the exact opposite of what he intended, but she pushed hard for it, insisting it would be nice to get out of her regular routine around the house. Besides, what could happen in two weeks? Picturing her sitting at my desk was almost impossible, so I switched my focus back to Luke and JD.

Besides, I didn't want to miss one minute of Australia, despite the extreme unpleasantness of landing in the middle of a murder.

Two

LUKE LIVED IN an old farmhouse built in the early 1900s. The house is in the Hunter Valley, which is one of several regions in Australia known for producing wine. Not so great for me and my complete dislike of alcohol, but JD said Luke wanted to go wine tasting while we were there.

I would probably stay around the house and work on a crochet project I'd brought with me. I had just started on a huge project — using thin crochet cotton to make a lacy-looking spread for my bed. It was a big project, but not impossible because I'm quite good at crocheting. Before she was murdered, my mother had been teaching me to knit. After I'd been living with my Aunt for a while, I asked her to help me. She didn't know how to knit and figured crocheting was close enough. It's not the same at all, but I'm glad I know how to do it. Crocheting is very soothing and you can do it anywhere. There's something about the repetitive movements that calms your mind. I wonder if that's why people are attracted to video games. Focusing on your hands, playing over and over, numbs the frantic part of your brain. With crocheting, you have something to show for it when you're done. With a video game, all you have is a score to brag about, and who really cares about that? Maybe no one cares about your crocheted tablecloth or scarf either, but I like doing it and I like the results. It's kind of funny, people complain that kids who play video games are wasting time. Maybe they're not wasting any more time than people who crochet or pick up shells off the beach.

Driving through the countryside felt very much like driving through parts of California, with roads that wind around rolling hills, past oak and eucalyptus trees, grape vines, and wild grasses and flowers. The wineries were about five or six miles from Luke's place. Of course, Luke spoke in kilometers so I only had a vague sense of what he was referring to.

I wondered how long it had taken him to convert his thinking to kilometers. It also flitted through my mind that maybe he did kill Elizabeth, since she was found in his yard, and it wasn't like he lived in a high crime area. I didn't know him at all, so maybe he was capable of violence. It wasn't very nice to be suspicious of JD's twin, but Luke was coming across as a bit of a hot-tempered guy. Besides, who keeps going on, years after the fact, about a dream you had? He acted as if it was a vision that was set to become reality, and almost sounded as if he was accusing JD of being a crackpot or an unscrupulous televangelist. When JD first told me about the dream and how it upset him to hear his brother talk about it, I thought he was being over-sensitive. Now I could see his point.

When the house came into view, I had a pinch in my throat because it was white with blue trim and looked similar to the house I grew up in — the house where I found my parents bodies, lying quietly on their bed.

A wide porch ran around three sides of the farmhouse — a porch you could actually use, not like so many California houses where the porch is a four-foot wide strip to decorate the front of the house. There were lots of flowering shrubs cuddled up close to the porch as well as some tropical plants with big glossy leaves, and a few small palm trees. Inside, there were three decent-sized bedrooms, one with its own bathroom. The kitchen was long and narrow with an eating area large enough to hold a table that would seat about eight or ten people. There was a leaded glass window in a frame that opened from the kitchen to the living room — an outdoor window in the middle of the house.

Open fields surrounded the property and the nearest neighbor was about a quarter mile away. The house was visible to the neighbors, but I understood why they hadn't bothered to come by to check it out when Elizabeth showed up with that truck and carted away all of Luke's possessions. Not that suburban neighbors would bother to check out a truck that pulled up to a house in the middle of the night either, if they even noticed.

Luke insisted we would sleep in his room on his new bed and he would camp out in one of the other bedrooms in a sleeping bag. The only furniture he'd replaced was his bed and the kitchen table and chairs. He'd also purchased a new laptop computer and a coffee maker. For the most part he was cooking stuff in a borrowed microwave and eating with plastic utensils. He works as a handyman and also runs some kind of online business, but he was vague about what that was and I got the impression he was thinking about setting it up, he wasn't actually doing it yet.

After we dropped off our stuff, he took us out back, which was hard to distinguish from the front in some ways, with the porch wrapping around to that side. There was an area with a waist-high stone fence, the opening framed by an arched trellis. It was crammed full of shrubs and small trees and flowers and vines. Elizabeth's arm had been visible under the trellis. Luke had to push away a huge, tangled vine exploding with purple morning glories that covered part of her. To the right of the garden was a shed where Luke kept his Harley. Just beyond the garden was a large patch of dirt that looked ready for rows of vegetables, reminding me again it was spring. Despite the warm air, it was hard to get my head around that.

We traipsed back into the house and sat at the kitchen table.

"I'm going to open a bottle of wine," Luke said. "Red or white?"

"It's a little early," JD said.

Luke grinned. He looked exactly like JD. "You're on vacation."

"Ok. I guess. But remember, Madison doesn't drink."

"Why not?"

I smiled. That question made me warm to Luke a bit more. I like it when people are blunt, like me. Not just because they're like me, but because I appreciate knowing where people are coming from and I think we'd all be better off if we were able to speak our minds more truthfully. Of course, even I don't always say everything that's on my mind, and maybe life wouldn't be as interesting. Maybe it's all the secrets and hidden agendas that keep us on our toes. But I was glad he asked me directly because sometimes when people find out you don't drink, they tiptoe around like they're afraid you're an alcoholic and they don't want to offend you. It never occurs to most people that you might just not like the stuff. "I don't see the point," I said. "And it's not like it tastes that great."

"It's the nectar of the gods," Luke said.

"Not to me."

"Fair enough. But don't you want to unwind, turn off your brain sometimes?"

"Not really."

He glanced at JD. "You said she was direct."

JD grinned.

I wondered what else he'd said about me.

"What do you want to drink?" Luke opened the bottle of wine and filled two glasses that were stamped with the name of a winery. I guess he had his priorities in terms of re-stocking his kitchen.

"Water is good," I said.

"That's it?"

"Yes."

He pulled a bottle of water out of the fridge and held it up. "Do you need a glass?"

I shook my head and he handed it to me.

JD took a sip of wine. "So you don't have any idea who might have killed her?"

"How would I know that?"

"Just a guess. A suspicion," JD said. "You don't think it's strange her body was in your yard?"

"Of course it's strange. Someone wanted to make it look like it was me."

"Who would want to do that?" I said.

"You two sound like the cops. Why are you grilling me?" Luke said.

"We're not," JD slid his glass toward the center of the table, then pulled it back. "We're curious. You should be too."

"Why should I be curious? We split ages ago. She ripped me off." He laughed. "Unbelievable." He sipped his wine. He got up and went to the cupboard and pulled out a bag of cheese twists. He tore open the bag and put it in the center of the table.

I grabbed a handful but before I put any in my mouth I said, "If I found a body in my yard, especially someone I knew, I wouldn't be able to stop thinking about it and wondering what happened."

"Well I'm not you," Luke said.

"Calm down." JD took a sip of wine but made no move for the cheese twists.

I gobbled up my handful and waited a few seconds before reaching for another. "Could it be a neighbor?" I bit a cheese twist. "Or do they think she was killed somewhere else and her body was left here?"

"She was killed here. There was blood all over the ground."

"Do they know when she died?" JD said.

"They think it was Tuesday night or early Wednesday morning."

"Were you home? Did you hear anything? It's so quiet out here, I don't know how a person could be stabbed and you wouldn't hear something if you were in the house," I said.

"You sound like a cop again."

It seemed we'd been talking mostly about murder and I wondered if I should switch the subject to something that would allow me to get to know Luke better, since that was supposed to be the point of staying with him. Well, that and to see Australia. But I really was so curious, and his lack of curiosity had the weird effect of increasing mine. His attitude was a little cold and I suspected if he spoke that way to the police it was confirming their suspicion. "Even if you aren't curious, don't you want to know so you can point the police in the right direction? Get them looking for other suspects?"

"I didn't kill her. And they didn't find any of her blood on my clothes or anywhere in the house. And they won't find any DNA or anything of mine on her."

"Even if they don't find anything, they're still going to keep after you," I said. I took another handful of cheese twists. I realized it had been hours since we last ate on the plane and I wondered if Luke was going to offer us lunch or if the cheese twists were it.

"They'll give up when they don't get anywhere."

"That's wishful thinking," JD said.

"Are we going to eat lunch? I'm starving." I ate four more cheese twists.

Luke looked at the microwave clock. It was twelve-forty. "Sorry about that. I'm all screwed up because I ate a big breakfast after the cops finally left. What do you want for lunch? You really should try a meat pie."

That sounded good to me, but at that point, anything that wasn't cheese twists would have sounded good.

We went to a small shop in town and ate delicious meat and gravy in a pie crust and talked about other things besides murder. Luke told us a bit about his girlfriend Lavender who we would meet the next day. She's the one that caused all the trouble with Elizabeth. Well, not her directly, Luke is the one that caused the trouble, since Elizabeth thought he was her forever guy and then he went to his mate's house, and hooked up with Lavender. Now he'd been seeing Lavender for almost five months, which I guess was some kind of record for him.

As we left the pie shop, Luke stepped into the street. He turned and looked at me. He put one hand on my shoulder and leaned his face close to mine. It was very unnerving because close up like that, just for a second, it felt like JD's hand, JD's eyes looking at me.

"So this is the face that launched a thousand ships," he said.

My skin grew warm as he stared at me. "What?"

"That's what JD said about you."

"Oh," I said.

Luke kept staring. JD was partially behind me so I couldn't see his expression. I felt awkward but also strangely pleased that JD would say something so dramatic about me. Hard to figure out, but still, very flattering.

We went for a long walk through the countryside and ate meat pies again for dinner. They were delicious, and when we finally went to bed, I asked JD what all he'd said about me to Luke. He just smiled and said, "I told him you were wonderful." No matter how much I bugged him about it, that's all he'd say.

A thousand ships. It's so unbelievably corny but I couldn't stop thinking about it, and every so often, for the next few days, whenever I caught a glimpse of myself in the mirror, I'd give myself a tiny smile which made it look as if I had a secret.

Three

ON FRIDAY WE drove into Sydney to spend the weekend. JD had decided to save the wine tasting until later, or maybe never, since he didn't want to run off and do something without me, which was so sweet. Between that and the face that launched a thousand ships and telling Luke I was *the girl who knew everything*, I was starting to think he was more taken with me than I'd realized. Not that the feeling wasn't mutual, but it was the first time I'd seen the two of us through someone else's eyes, so maybe that was part of it.

During our two and a half days in Sydney we were staying at a charming old hotel in the historic area called The Rocks. The hotel had a small lobby instead of the big dramatic waste of space you see in modern hotels where they're trying to look grand. Really, it just comes across kind of cold and very noisy, especially in hotels where they make the lobby an overflow of the bar with groupings of chairs and people sit around drinking. And talking, loudly, voices echoing across the tile floor, up to a cavernous ceiling, and off the glass chandeliers and metal railings on the staircases.

Our room had a bed with an iron headboard and footboard, a glimpse of the harbor bridge, and an antique wardrobe that primarily held the TV, with a few drawers for our clothes. There was also an old-fashioned writing desk. It made me hope I'd run into a ghost so I could use the writing desk to record the experience in my ghost journal. Although ghostly experiences can go either way — pleasant or terrifying — so I have no idea why I'd hope for that just to write in a journal. Since we were taking a ghost tour of The Rocks that night, there was a small chance I'd see something unearthly.

The Rocks is the area in Sydney where Europeans first settled, starting with the prisoners England sent over, so you can imagine how that worked out for establishing a new society. Apparently, England first sent their criminals to America, but after America set out on its own, they switched to Australia.

Most of the buildings in the area are sandstone, which is how it got its name. Now, it's crowded with charming shops and restaurants, but it still has this dark history. It's also very touristy. The ghost tours, for example. They take place at night. They walk you through the less familiar streets while telling the stories of crimes committed in the area, as well as supposed hauntings over the years. I was anxious to see whether it would be silly or scary or a blend of both.

JD and I ate dinner alone while Luke waited around for Lavender to show up. She was taking the train in from Wollongong where she'd been visiting her mother, a practicing witch. That's how Lavender ended up with a highly unusual name. Her mother wanted her only child to grow up full of mystical powers and she did everything her witchy background told her would help with that, starting with the baby's name. Lavender is said to calm your nerves, and I guess that was supposed to be her function in life. I was very curious to meet her.

The restaurant we chose served some food that was beyond the limit of my willingness to be adventuresome, such as kangaroo. I couldn't understand how Australians could eat those adorable animals. I suppose you could say that about any animal. And if I thought about it enough, I might end up becoming a vegetarian, because although I never eat cute animals, such as deer or rabbits, you could think of a cow as sort of cute, and anyone who has read Charlotte's Web thinks of pigs as absolutely adorable. Once you've seen a real pig, you sort of lose that fuzzy romantic image of a roly-poly pink creature with perky ears and a precious little nose and curly tail, but still.

After seeing kangaroo listed on the menu, I really wasn't in the mood for meat at all, so I ordered pasta with Portobello mushrooms.

The patio where we ate was cobblestone and our table was rough wood with a candle in an old-fashioned holder with a pewter base and a glass globe. It was very romantic, eating outside, the sky turning dark blue and feeling that warm, moist spring air while back home everyone was thinking about firing up the furnace and adding an extra blanket to the bed.

When we finished our salads, JD reached across the table and took my hand.

After we sat quietly for a few minutes, feeling the warmth of each other's skin, marveling that we were in Sydney, Australia, I said, "Why did you tell Luke my face launched a thousand ships?" I wanted to pull my hand away, but I took a deep breath and left my fingers laced through his.

He looked over at the fountain in the center of the patio, burbling almost as loud as our voices.

I waited.

Finally he turned back and looked at our hands. "Luke has a big mouth. I told you he can't shut up."

"Why didn't you want me to know?"

He shrugged.

"I liked hearing it. I'm glad he has a big mouth."

"You might regret saying that. Anyway, it was a passing comment. He made it sound stupid."

"Not to me. What does it mean?"

"They say Helen of Troy was the cause of a ten-year war — she launched a thousand ships."

"I know who she is, I don't understand why you said that about me."

"Her beauty was legendary. Mythological."

He finally looked directly at me, but despite his words, I couldn't sense what he was thinking. I sort of regretted bringing it up because it made me feel exotic when I heard it and now that I was digging into it, the words were starting to sound ridiculously over the top. "I'm a lot of things, but drop-dead gorgeous is not one of them."

He smiled. "that's different. I didn't say you were drop-dead gorgeous." He stroked my fingers, probably worried that I was going to cry, or get pissed off.

"Okay, mythologically beautiful. And I like to think there's more to me than just my appearance."

"But you are. And there is more to you. There's this shimmer in your eyes that makes you look like all the secrets in the world are hidden inside you. Your hair is like fire and your skin is like marble, it's so smooth, so perfectly formed."

"I'm sure my face is now the color of my hair." I laughed, but my neck and cheeks and even my forehead were burning. I look okay, I'm not blind, but I'm not one of those females with an extreme focus on her looks, and no one has ever called me beautiful. Now I really, really regretted asking him about the thousand ships. Luckily, our food came and he let go of my hand, and my body temperature returned to semi-normal.

He sliced off a piece of steak, put it in his mouth and chewed, staring at me. Even though I was looking at my food, I could feel his eyes and my face started heating up again.

"What I was trying to say, why I made that comment to Luke, is that you stand apart from other women. There's more to you than just fixing yourself up — like a model in a magazine. You have something inside that comes through your face. And I love your hair."

JD and I had not yet said we loved each other. I wasn't even sure if I loved him, partially because I have no idea how you *can* be sure, and I don't want to be babbling something just to say the words because I'm supposed to. I have a feeling he views it the same way. But having him love my hair was unnerving because that made me realize he did love lots of things in a casual way. I wasn't sure how I felt about my hair being loved but not necessarily me. I decided to focus on mushrooms and pasta.

After that, we talked about our impressions of Australia, and then we talked about the ghost tour. We tried to decide whether we believed anyone had actually seen a ghost on the tour. I mentioned the murder and JD agreed with me that Luke should have been a little more curious. Since it's his twin brother, I didn't want to be too critical, but I still wondered if Luke's lack of curiosity meant he was hiding something. I asked a few leading questions to see if JD felt the same thing, but he didn't mention it, so I decided to keep that thought to myself.

WE MET LAVENDER and Luke in front of a historic barracks, the starting point for the ghost tour.

Lavender was a tall woman. I think I expected her to be dressed all in purple, but instead she wore black from head to toe. Literally. She wore a large black hat with a sheer, floppy brim, which gave her the look of a widow from another era. Her earrings were antique silver swords. Her shirt was a leotard and her ankle-length skirt was made of velvet. She wore black boots with pointy toes and narrow high heels. I couldn't imagine how she was going to walk through narrow alleys and across cobblestone in those tiny spikes. Her fingernails were painted dark purple, cut fairly short. She wore no make-up. She was quite beautiful, slender without being fashion-model skinny, and she had a nice smile that was almost sweet — a shocking contrast to all that black. Her hair was dark blonde and hung just past her shoulders.

I wondered if she was trying to make some kind of statement with her clothes, although what that statement might be, I had no idea. Luke hadn't mentioned whether she was also a witch or Wiccan or pagan or something along those lines. I know very little about any of those so I'm not sure whether they're all the same thing. Since he made a point of telling us her mother was a witch, I assumed Lavender was not. She was definitely different, and if she dressed like that all the time, I couldn't imagine that she had a regular job. Of course, that's not really fair, look at me — tattoos, lots of ear piercings, and I work in a church office. I guess I was being judgmental, but her clothes made me think she definitely wanted to stand out in a crowd. In the darkness of the ghost tour, she was likely to disappear in the shadows.

Luke put one arm around her waist and kissed her hard. When he pulled away, he batted the brim of her hat. "What's this?" He stepped back and looked at her whole outfit. "What's with all the black, and the boots?" He laughed.

Lavender frowned at him and tugged her hat back down over her forehead.

Their exchange made me even more curious — were her outrageous clothes for JD's and my benefit, or simply a new look?

She turned to me and gushed that she was so happy to meet me. She shook my hand and flashed that charming smile. "How do you like having a twin as a boyfriend?"

It was a strange introductory question, but it was the only immediate thing we had in common, so maybe not so strange, just unexpected and obviously not a conversation starter I'd ever encountered before. "I never thought about it, until I met Luke," I said.

"I think about it *all* the time."

"Why?"

She moved closer. She smelled like mint. She put her mouth close to my ear and half-whispered, "Don't you wonder if you can never really have him because his twin will always be the person he's most connected to?"

I'd never considered wanting *all* of JD. She made it sound like I might want to own him or that I was jealous of Luke. Maybe Luke gave off a different vibe to her, but I thought the opposite — that they weren't that close. When Luke had his bad motorcycle accident, JD didn't have any kind of premonition or heightened awareness of his brother's pain. He told me he'd never experienced any of the psychic twin connection that people talk about.

It's not very often that I don't know what to say. I didn't know why she'd asked such a personal question when she didn't even know me. I like outspoken people, but I suppose there's a line somewhere, and for whatever reason, her question gave me the creeps. I had no idea how to respond. Although maybe I'd missed something, and really the only response is always the truth. "I don't expect anything," I said.

She smiled, but this time it wasn't as genuine. I believe she thought I was lying.

Fortunately, the tour leader spoke up. He started off by flirting with one woman who was part of a group of four. He tried too hard to be spooky, which made the whole thing seem like a joke. The brochure had sounded fairly intelligent, as if there had been verified paranormal experiences around the older parts of The Rocks, but this guy wanted to get everyone laughing — a comedian who couldn't get a gig in a nightclub so he forced this job into something to suit his own needs. He wore black boots, a black leather Australian bush hat, and a black ankle-length cape that he kept tossing wildly over his shoulder. He handed out lanterns to a few people, including the woman he was flirting with and a big burly guy who was there with his son. Then he annoyed me even more by telling the burly guy he'd been selected because all the pretty ladies needed someone rugged to protect them if the ghosts became too aggressive. After that, I was ready to tell JD and Luke I didn't want to go, but in the end, I was more curious about the ghost stories than I was annoyed by his silly and degrading behavior.

The guide led us into the former barracks, called Cadman's cottage. He let us walk around, looking at old books and utensils in display cases while he explained the history of the area. It's a rocky headland and shoreline around the harbor. It was inhabited by indigenous people for thousands of years, like most places. Until people with more powerful weapons and equipment took over. The convicts and overseers began arriving in the late 1700s. There weren't any prisons because it was considered sufficient punishment to ship convicts ten or twelve thousand miles to a continent on the other side of the world. The Rocks area eventually transformed from an open-air jail into a quaint section of Sydney, but the buildings that survived for more than two hundred years all have stories of betrayal, violence, and murder.

As we walked along the dark streets and narrow alleys formed by tall stone buildings that rose up three stories on either side, JD held my hand. Lavender pressed against my other side, leaving Luke to trail behind us. She whispered to me while the guide was talking, and although I thought he was ridiculous, I still wanted to hear the ghost stories. For the first forty-five minutes I had to keep shushing her. Finally she got the message.

The most disappointing part of her clinging to my side was that I knew there was no way any reticent spirits were likely to reveal themselves while we were all bunched together. Although, why would they anyway? There have been sightings in The Rocks of a blonde-haired little girl dressed in a dirty pinafore, and lights and apparitions that no one can identify. Several people have seen a woman wearing a large hat looking out one of the windows. Most of the stories the guide told were of crimes that had been solved, and unless the ghosts were just lonely after hundreds of years, I wasn't sure why they would sidle up to me and start talking.

It's not that ghosts only appear when they have a specific mission, like other-worldly talk show guests who want to make sure the world knows their stories, but in my case, they seem to have something to say.

Still, it was a ghost tour and I wanted to see a ghost. Most of the time when I've seen lingering spirits, I've been by myself, and I wondered what it would be like if a group of people were together. Would we all see the same thing? Was this just a place where one or two people had faint supernatural experiences and it had all been blown out of proportion? To be honest, the guide was making me feel that way. He lowered his voice in an attempt to sound sinister. Several times he repeated the same phrase with an echoing tone — *and no one ever saw her again, maybe you will tonight!* Then he'd cackle. Literally. He sounded like a giant chicken. I felt he was treating us like children, mocking the spirits who might still inhabit The Rocks, and ridiculing the people who had seen lights or out-of-place shadows, or heard someone speaking. Tears filled the spaces behind my eyes. I felt so sad for what he was doing to the history of the area.

Some of the stories were quite gruesome, featuring buckets of blood running across the cobblestone, a severed head, and other brutal murders.

By the time we reached the end, two hours later, my feet ached and I was sleepy. I felt more tied to the earth, more out of touch with any unseen realm than if I'd simply sat in a bar all evening, or watched a TV documentary telling the same stories.

The minute the guide left us alone, Luke said, "Did you see anything, Madison?"

I shook my head. He didn't say anything more, which was good, because I didn't want to be an unappreciative guest. I felt like I'd finished a guided trek through the haunted house at Disneyland rather than an actual tour of the supernatural.

They all decided we would go to a pub and get better acquainted with Lavender. After leaning on me and talking as much as the guide during the first half of the tour, I thought I already knew her quite well, and I wasn't sure she and I were going to hit it off.

THE PUB FACED a street that sloped up through the oldest part of The Rocks. It had outdoor seating which overflowed with laughing, drinking Australians. Mixed among the lovely twang of their voices, I also heard European, Asian, and American flavors. The Americans sounded like plain vanilla, and it made me wonder whether the Australians were unaware of their accents. Did they know how marvelous they sounded? How their melodic words and tones and occasional quirky words lulled me into thinking they were all wonderful human beings, somehow less moody and selfish than the inhabitants covering the rest of the planet?

That was one thing that was helping me maintain an open mind about Lavender — her accent predisposed me to view her as warm and friendly, even if her weird, invasive question made her seem the opposite. Who asks someone if she thinks her boyfriend isn't really connected to her? Why would that be the first question out of her mouth to a total stranger? Unless, that's what she felt about Luke.

We hung around the fringe of the crowd, eyeing groups that looked close to finishing up. Luke and Lavender went inside to get drinks from the bar, after the usual discussion of my refusal to drink alcohol, punctuated by a *good for you*, from Lavender.

They returned carrying three huge glasses of beer and an equally large glass of carbonated water with a disk of lime rather than the usual wedge. Just as they took a first sip of their beers, a table cleared out and we all sat down. I pushed the plates smeared with mustard and horseradish to one side, piled the napkins on top, and lined up the empty beer glasses in a semi-circle around the pile.

"The servers will take care of that," Lavender said.

"Now we don't have to smell stale beer and food," I said. "And it will be quicker for the server."

"Why do you hate beer so much?" She took a long, deep swallow of her wheat-colored ale. When she set down her mug, a line of foam ran across her upper lip, making it difficult to focus because I was watching each tiny bubble pop. Eventually they would all pop and she'd have nothing but sticky residue, but I wondered why it wasn't tickling her. I licked my own lip in sympathy. "It's not just beer. I don't like any alcohol."

"Why?"

"Do you like every single thing you put in your mouth?"

"No."

"There is no why," I said. "I don't like it. That's all."

"But everyone else does. It helps you let go and unwind."

"I can relax just fine without it."

"Don't you want that buzz, or are you one of those high-on-life girls?"

"Something like that," I said.

She took another gulp of beer. This time, she licked her lip. "I wonder how many people on that tour thought they'd see a ghost? Raise your hand if you did."

JD and I both raised an index finger. We smiled at each other. After he saw us do it, Luke added a finger, although it was his pinky finger so he didn't look super committed.

"Why do they get sucked into it?" Lavender said. "Very few people are able to see ghosts, yet they keep signing up for the tour, like children thinking they'll get a surfboard from Santa, even though they peeked in Mum's closet and saw the unwrapped boxes of socks and a few video games. Seeing spirits is a gift."

"I don't know about that," JD said.

A guy with glistening blonde hair and six or seven leather straps around each wrist stopped beside our table. "G'day. What can I get you?"

"Fried olives," Luke said. "You have to try fried olives. And we'll have a basket of chips. Anything else?" He looked at us and cocked his head, not unlike a puppy wanting to know what he could fetch next.

"We'll be ready for another round by the time the olives are done," Lavender said.

The server grinned, shiny white orthodontia-perfect teeth against tanned skin.

"Hey," JD said. "Do you know the best places around here for a beginning surfer? We're staying in the Hunter Valley."

"Most of the beaches in Newcastle are good, not too intense. Who's learning to surf?"

JD put his arm around me and pulled me against him. "She is."

I smiled. "Maybe."

"You said you'd be ready when we came to Australia."

I tilted my head to see his face, but he had a tight grip

around my shoulders and all I could see was his chin, covered with dark stubble, and the tip of his ear. "If you think back, you'll remember it was your idea that I'd learn in Australia. I didn't actually agree."

"Saying nothing means you agree," Luke said.

"All right then," the server said. "You'll love it. You'll see. I'll get those olives started." He strolled over to another table, asked if they needed more beers, and then wandered into the restaurant as if he wasn't really sure he worked there.

JD let go of me and put his elbows on the table. He took a sip of beer. "Why do you think that seeing spirits is a gift?"

"It requires a sensitivity and the right skills and even beyond that, a gift. There's no other way to describe it. To make them want to reveal themselves to you."

"What skills?"

"A training in magic arts."

"I've seen a ghost," JD said. "I wasn't trained and I'm not particularly sensitive."

Luke stared into his beer mug. His gaze was so focused, I wondered whether he was thinking about ghosts, or about the murdered woman in his garden. He looked worried, which surprised me because he didn't seem like a worrying kind of guy.

Lavender combed her hair behind her ears and adjusted her hat. It was lower on her forehead so her eyes were no longer visible. It looked like a hat with the tip of a nose and a moving mouth, her lips almost as colorless as the skin of her jaw and chin, which gave her the appearance of someone quite ghostly herself. "Where do you think you saw a ghost?"

"The bar I work at is haunted. The ghost is called the Blue Lady. And I've seen her more than once. So has Madison."

Lavender smiled with a very small upturn of her lips, not showing her teeth. Although I still couldn't see her eyes, her smile looked condescending. I don't know if you can really draw that conclusion when you can't see someone's eyes, but that was my immediate impression and usually, first impressions are the most accurate. Usually, not always.

She followed her condescending smile with a small laugh. "Another tourist trap. Just like here. Foolish people looking for a thrill."

"I don't think people are foolish for hoping to see a ghost," I said.

"Don't take it personally. I didn't mean you."

Despite her superior smile and her sharp laugh, she still sounded pleasant. It was that accent. I bet if an Australian said you were fired, it would still sound warm and light-hearted.

"Madison has seen lots of ghosts," Luke said. "They flock to her."

"Really?" Lavender sipped her beer. "Is that why you're a teetotaler?"

"No."

"So you can stay alert and open?"

"Not at all. I told you, I don't like the taste." I couldn't figure out why she refused to believe anything I said. It made me not want to bother talking at all.

"Most people who think they've seen ghosts are being influenced by the power of suggestion. Your restaurant probably advertises the ghost, just like The Rocks tour. Am I right?"

Our food arrived — olives bathed in light golden batter and a huge basket of chips, which was really a basket of fries, and even though I knew they call fries chips, I was still startled to see French fries in the basket. It's like my mind didn't want to accept the different word.

"The Blue Lady was very distinct when I saw her," I said. "The entire outline of her body was visible and I watched her walk across the bluff. It was not the power of suggestion."

Luke put his hand on the back of Lavender's neck. "Why don't we talk about something else?"

"I feel very strongly about this," Lavender said.

"Then why did you agree to take the tour if you knew it was going to upset you?" Luke said.

"I wanted to meet your twin. I bet you have little flyers that show an image of your Blue Lady and you hand them out to every new customer. Am I right?"

"That doesn't mean seeing her is the power of suggestion," JD said.

"I *was* right." She laughed again. She downed the rest of her beer. She looked at me, or at least she tilted her hat in my direction. Her eyes remained hidden. "And what ghosts have you seen?"

"It's complicated," I said. "It would take the rest of the evening to explain it all." I popped another olive in my mouth. I couldn't see the point of telling her about my experiences, as if she was some self-appointed expert and I had to get her sign-off. I laughed.

"Why are you laughing?"

"Because this conversation is funny. You don't need any special gift to see a ghost."

"My mother spent my entire life teaching me how to communicate with the dead, how to heal people who had been invaded by evil forces, how to foresee the future."

Those all sounded like entirely different things to me, but I'd decided to be the polite visitor, so I kept my mouth shut. I took a sip of water and ate another olive. I crossed my legs and tugged my skirt down so my skin wasn't touching the wood chair. It was still muggy. The air felt like the sun had just gone down but it was getting close to eleven o'clock. I glanced up the street. The shops were closed. I hoped we'd get time to wander through them the next day. I wanted a souvenir or two, not necessarily something Australian. I don't usually buy key chains or t-shirts or mugs that tell me where I've been. And I didn't even want something like a stuffed kangaroo, although maybe that would be kind of fun. I like to buy things that remind me of my trip but the object doesn't have to advertise where I went.

Luke reached into his pocket and pulled out his phone. He

put it face down on the table. His other hand was still on the back of Lavender's neck. She arched her spine slightly.

"That detective left a voice mail earlier. They have more questions for me," he said. "I hope they don't make me drive back home tomorrow."

"We're taking the harbor tour," Lavender said.

"I know."

"Maybe they'll do it over the phone," JD said.

"Not sure that's their style."

"Back to the ghosts," Lavender said. "You can't just drop a bomb like that — *she's seen lots of ghosts* — and not tell me anything."

"I saw a woman who had drowned walking on the water. It was unusual because she was only visible, or at least we only saw her, through a telescope at my friend's house on the coast."

"We?"

"Yes, everyone who was staying at the house that weekend had seen her at one time or another. So I guess we all have a gift."

"Did you actually communicate with her?"

I'd mentioned that particular ghost because I thought it would be easy, thought it would disprove her insistence that a special gift was required. Now I could see she was about to trap me. She was going to call it group hallucination or something. "She let me know who she was — the nanny to these twin sisters who ..."

"Twins?" Lavender said.

"Yes. They were …"

"Interesting that you have so many twins in your life."

"Not really. Even though the ghost didn't speak directly to any of us, she … it's hard to explain. It's like she shifted my thoughts in the right direction until I came to see that the twins had murdered her."

"But she didn't speak to you. She didn't tell you who did it."

"She didn't have to."

"Then you aren't really communicating, and most likely, you imagined it."

"Five people imagined the same thing?"

"No, one person thought she saw something and told the others. And they all wanted to believe. Even people who have never seen ghosts want to believe. Why do you think the tour is so popular?"

"It wasn't like that," I said.

She smiled. It was very unnerving how the things she said made me not like her, but her smile was so friendly. It gave me a slight distrust of my instincts because I was getting a vibe that she was challenging me, that maybe she even wanted to pick a fight with me, but her face kept saying she wanted to be friends. The disconnect made me dislike her even more. That, and the hat. I didn't understand why she wouldn't take it off. It looked so over the top, the brim had to be six or seven inches wide and because it flopped over her eyes, it added to the effect that her smile wasn't communicating her true feelings.

"These girls murdered their Nanny when they were children?"

"They drowned her."

"Bad girls."

"It was a little more than that."

"I meant bad girls as in bad boys … women always like bad boys. You don't hear as much about bad girls."

"So that's why you like me," Luke said. He ducked his head under the brim of her hat and kissed her full on the lips. She let go of her beer and put her hands on the back of his head, gripping him closer.

After several seconds, she screeched, "Ow! You bit my lip." She pushed him away.

Luke grinned. "You said you like bad boys."

Lavender picked up her beer and took a sip. "Now my lip stings when I drink my beer. I said you hear about how women are attracted to bad boys, not that I am. And it doesn't mean biting someone's lip."

JD signaled the waiter and ordered more beer and bottled water with limes.

"Men are equally attracted to bad girls," Lavender said.

"Really?" I leaned back in my chair and stretched out my legs.

"Oh yes. It's just not talked about as much, because bad girls have a different connotation, don't they."

I know she was asking me to agree with her, but I decided not to give her the satisfaction because I wasn't sure where she was headed. I was glad she was no longer challenging me about the ghosts I'd seen, or making fun of people who were curious about the spirit world.

I let her comment hang there and then the beer came and the conversation went back to Luke and JD. Mostly Luke complaining about the cops and JD trying to assure him they would eventually satisfy themselves he hadn't done it and start looking for other suspects. Luke was just the easy choice for now. He didn't add that Luke was the obvious choice.

Let me say, the fried olives were amazing. Probably very unhealthy, taking something more or less nutritious like an olive and dipping it in batter and deep frying it, but I couldn't stop popping them in my mouth. I think I ate half the basket myself. Lavender didn't eat any, so that left more for me. We ordered a second basket.

Lavender was a little tiring and I hoped we'd be able to enjoy our boat ride the next day without arguing about ghosts, talking about murder, or analyzing bad boys.

Four

SYDNEY HARBOR IS probably the most recognized body of water in the world. Okay, maybe San Francisco Bay and the Golden Gate bridge, but that and the white shell-shaped Sydney Opera House are neck and neck when it comes to instant recognition. Docks at the center of the harbor house various options for tours, including speed boat rides. Luke had planned for us to visit Pinchgut Island, originally a penal colony named for a convict who subsisted on bread and water out there. It's the home of Fort Denison which was built later when the Australians realized the harbor was exposed to attack.

They offer a brief tour of the unused fort and lunch at an outdoor restaurant that occupies part of the tiny island. The most fun would be the boat ride, and really, I would have preferred to stay on the boat rather than spending time walking through an old stone building and hearing about military strategy.

My desire to avoid the subject of murder was not fulfilled. The minute we saw Luke sitting on one of the benches holding his tickets, he called out to us about Elizabeth's murder.

"I talked to the cops. They want to speak to me in person on Monday."

I glanced around, surprised that he said this quite loudly as we were a few yards away from him. Other tourists sat on the benches nearby, but they were studying brochures or sipping coffee drinks and eating breakfast sweets from the food stand on the pier, so maybe he figured no one was paying attention.

"I need to get our tickets," JD said.

"I got them." Luke stood and walked toward us. He handed a ticket to JD and one to me. "Why do they keep bugging me?"

"They found a woman's body in your yard," I said.

"So?"

"You don't see how that makes you the main suspect?" JD said. "Especially knowing what she did to you?"

"But I don't even have a knife, she took everything. And I have an alibi."

"Sort of," JD said.

"It's not my fault the bartender wasn't watching me all night long. They saw me a couple times during the evening."

"You still could have left, killed her, and come back."

"Who does that? Goes for a drink, sneaks home and stabs his ex, and goes back for more drinks?"

"Probably more guys than we realize," JD said.

"You know so many guys who killed their ex-girlfriends that you're an expert?"

The skipper of our speedboat stepped onto the entrance ramp.

"Where's Lavender?" JD said.

"She'll be here."

The people occupying the benches around us started moving into a line. Very politely. Not like in the US where everyone shoves up to be first. Of course, half the people taking the boat ride sounded like they were from the US, so maybe the laid-back Australian mood was infecting everyone and they were less intense about being first in line.

"I'm sure they'll rule you out sooner or later," JD said.

"Sooner. I'm done with this."

"There's nothing you can do about it. Just calm down. If you get too worked up, it'll make you look more suspicious."

"I can't look more suspicious. I didn't do it. They're jumping to conclusions."

"Do you have any ideas yet about who might have done it?" I said. "I'm sure that would help."

"No. that's one of the questions they keep asking. I only hooked up with her for two or three months. I don't know anything about her friends or her family."

The skipper removed the chain blocking the steps up to the ramp leading onto the boat. I glanced back toward the wide walkway that runs around the harbor. Lavender was heading toward us, obviously not worried about getting a good seat for the boat ride. Of course, she'd probably taken it quite a few times. Or she was one of those people who is never in a hurry, always comfortable being late because they know someone else will save them a spot. The kind of person who thinks the whole world will take care of them and they don't have to worry about anything. It's probably not fair to categorize her like that, but she didn't even quicken her pace when she saw the flow of people climbing up to the boat. She could see that she was late but didn't appear to care, which made the stereotype quite accurate, in my mind.

We were all on the boat, standing right next to the bow when she joined us, the last one on. She wore the same enormous black hat with the sheer brim and a black, strapless top and flowing black pants and gold flip-flops with fake jewels glued to the straps. Unlike the night before, she wore full make-up, which seemed odd for a boat ride. Even though I wouldn't dress like that in a hundred years, I felt a little dull next to her. My head came to her earlobe, my hair in a loose braid, nothing but sunscreen on my face, and a white tank top, dark green shorts, and white flip-flops. It looked as if we were attending two completely different events, or as if we'd planned to be black and white, except for my green shorts.

The boat was large enough to hold about thirty people. JD, Luke, Lavender, and I stood at the bow. I don't know if the people sitting on the bench facing forward liked us standing there, but I was too excited to care. Besides, it was allowed.

The skipper talked about safety rules and told us we could stay as long as we liked on the island since boats showed up for the return trip every half hour or so. They fired up the engines and backed away from the pier. We moved slowly at first, gliding within forty or fifty yards of the Opera House so we could get a view from the opposite side, and then they stomped on the gas and we flew across the water. Lavender had to clamp her hand on the top of her hat, and the brim flapped like a crow was trying to escape from beneath her arm but couldn't quite get airborne.

We raced across the water, light spray in our faces, the sun on our heads. Each time we crossed the wake of another boat, we got a wild ride. It made me excited to try surfing, if it was equally thrilling. JD had insisted it was, but the appeal of a speed boat is you don't have to work to have a fantastic time. Maybe the hard work makes surfing more fun, or being right in the water, feeling the movement and speed even more. Getting wet. It looked like I was going to find out soon.

We reached the island too fast. Like I said, I would have liked to spend half the day racing around the harbor rather than stopping at the tiny island. A tour guide met us and began telling us the history of the fort. It's not that I don't want to hear about history, and especially in an unfamiliar place, but it was spring. Only three days earlier we were headed toward winter, the days getting shorter and the nights getting darker — that sounds crazy because nights don't really get darker, but it feels like they do. Now, I wanted to be out in the sun all the time.

A stone staircase lead up into the building. We entered a round, windowless room. The guide explained how they made cannon balls in that room, that the thick stone walls and lack of windows kept the temperature stable, preventing the gunpowder in the cannon balls from exploding. Small cannon balls were stacked in triangular formations for effect. Next we climbed a much narrower, twisting staircase where there was no railing and we had to brace ourselves against the stone wall to make our way up. At the top was a room with large windows facing out at the mouth of the harbor, and three large cannons. The windows had round panes of glass at the center that were fit to the size of the cannon. There were more stacks of cannon balls. The guide explained that by the time Fort Dennison was complete, it was obsolete.

The guide was mercifully brief, and when he was done, we were free to wander around the entire island, into the museum, back to the rooms we'd already looked at, and outside along a grassy hill where the top of the fort was level with the ground. From there we had a panoramic view of Sydney. I stood for a while looking out at the bridge and the opera house and closing my eyes every few minutes because I couldn't believe I was on the other side of the world.

I left JD taking a hundred photographs of the view, after he'd taken quite a few of me standing in front of the view, and went back inside. I circled down the tiny staircase into the gunpowder room. It was so quiet and peaceful, buried like that in the center of that solid rock building. I tried lifting one of the cannon balls, which I'm sure I wasn't supposed to be doing. If I dropped it on my foot, I'd be in big trouble, in more ways than one. I could barely lift it, so I let it thunk back down on the stack.

I looked up and saw Luke had entered the room. "Hey," he said. "It's the first time I've seen you not glued to JD's side."

I shrugged.

"I wanted to ask you a favor."

"What's that?"

"The whole ghost thing … do you think you could get in touch with Elizabeth's ghost and find out who killed her? It's driving me nuts having the cops on my back."

I didn't think they'd been on his back, exactly. After all, he was in Sydney, basically enjoying a vacation. "It doesn't really work like that."

"Work like what?"

"I can't just send a text message to a ghost and tell her where to meet me to ID the killer."

He laughed, but he sounded anxious.

"You must have some way of getting in touch."

"That really is not how it is at all. They come to me. I don't go hunting for them."

"Really? Lavender says you can be open to them and lure them."

"Then ask her to help."

"I don't want to."

"Why not?"

He was quiet. He glanced at the doorway behind him.

No one was there. Apparently we were the only two interested in gunpowder. But it wasn't the gunpowder that drew me. It was the total absence of sound, the way the air felt more quiet than being alone in a regular room. The dirt on the floor was soft and smelled clean, even though that sounds like a total contradiction.

"JD said you'd experienced a lot of different ghosts. That you're hyper-sensitive."

"I suppose I am, but that doesn't mean I can force them to show up. If you think that's possible, that you can get a ghost to appear and answer your questions as easily as the cops can compel you to go to the police station for an interrogation, I don't understand why you don't ask Lavender to help."

He scuffed his foot in the dirt. It made him look like a teenage kid, staring down at his dust-covered sandals and toes. He tugged his shorts up, but they still hung low on his hip bones, emphasizing the teenaged boy impression.

"I don't want to feel like I owe her."

"Why would you owe her?"

"I have no idea how long we'll be together. I've had enough female trouble."

I laughed.

He grinned, realizing what he'd said. "She's the type to harbor grudges. Hold things over your head."

I understood that he obviously had a lot of drama with women, but it was funny he was telling me, as if I was some androgynous character. His excuse sounded weak. Didn't he already owe her? It wasn't like he could just walk away without leaving any damage behind. Although from what JD said, maybe that was his primary requirement in a relationship — the ability to walk away without tripping over any strings. I didn't see how you could label it a relationship if that's all he wanted. "I wish I could help, but like I said, that's really not how it works."

"How do you know?"

"It's not that I'm an expert. I've seen some ghosts. I've had them give me impressions or ideas. But I never went looking for them. They just showed up."

"You could sit by yourself in the garden where she died. I think the place is already haunted. I get weird feelings when I go into … I don't know how to explain it. There's a heavy, cold feeling that was never there before."

"Okay. But they appear when I'm not expecting it. It's out of my control."

"Can you at least try?"

He looked at me with those brown eyes that were exactly like JD's. Well, almost like JD's, there was something different, maybe a lack of focus, or maybe just that I didn't know him at all and despite the same color and the same dark, well-shaped brows and long lashes, they looked completely different in an indefinable way that proves there's something mysteriously singular about each human being.

Knowing it was a mistake, knowing I couldn't help him, knowing I was probably going to stir things up between him and Lavender, I said, "I'll think about it."

He patted my back and his fingers brushed across the bare skin of my arm, and it felt like any person giving me a friendly greeting, not at all the melting, warm feeling I get when JD touches me. Maybe I was more disturbed by the twin-ness than I'd realized, because why would I even think I'd feel the same way? It's just really unnerving when two people look so much alike that if the light is dim, and they aren't talking, you're really not sure whether you can tell them apart.

The boat ride back was a repeat of awesome. Luke and Lavender sat on the benches this time. Only JD and I stood at the bow. Since all we saw was Sydney ahead of us, and none of the others on the boat, it felt like our own private speedboat. JD kept his arm around my waist the whole time. I leaned my head against the inside of his shoulder. We sped across the water with a warm breeze in our faces and only the engines humming in our heads.

Five

SUNDAY MORNING WE met Luke and Lavender for brunch. After we ate, we walked to the shops. Imagine what the criminals who lived out the remainder of their lives in The Rocks would think of the stores displaying leather bags and boots, jewelry and expensive artwork. Open booths lined the center of one street, selling different kinds of olive oils in fancy bottles, flowers, ice cream, and just about anything else you might see at one of the art and wine festivals that occupy California towns from May to September.

We wandered into a covered mall area and spent quite a lot of time in a store overflowing with opals — everything from a single stone on a thin chain, to bracelets with strings of dark pink and blue and purple shimmering stones connected to one another with 14k gold. One that I really liked was green, almost the color of my eyes. It was set in a gold circle with a chain so thin it looked like thread. Part of me wanted it so badly, I thought about buying it for myself, but another part of me hoped JD would notice and buy it for me. It's kind of awkward to be with a guy and buy yourself a nice piece of jewelry.

JD came up to my side. "Do you like that?"

"It's beautiful."

"I didn't know you liked opals."

I had no idea how to answer that. If I said I liked them, it felt like I was asking him to buy it, but I would only want it if it was a surprise, if it was completely his idea. Already the thrill of that possibility had evaporated because we were discussing it, which made it clinical and too much like talking about whether the car needs gas. Besides, it wasn't that I'd been pining for an opal all my life. Australia is known for them, and an opal would be a great reminder of something unique about the continent, unless I could take home a pet kangaroo, but obviously that wasn't going to happen. I saw it and admired it, but that didn't mean I liked opals as one of my defining characteristics.

I was quiet for too long because he said, "Do you? Like opals?"

"I never thought about it. The colors are amazing."

I took a few steps away. JD walked over to where Luke stood watching Lavender. Her hips were pressed against the counter. The shopkeeper had placed six necklaces on a velvet-covered board. Lavender was trying on each one, surveying it in the mirror to her left. Next to the necklaces were three rings with various configurations of smaller opals, one with three tiny diamonds along one edge.

I wandered out of the shop and looked at the UGG boots and leather hats on display in front of the place next door. A few minutes later, the others joined me. No one was carrying a package, so I figured Lavender didn't get an opal either. Her mouth was turned down at the corners into an actual frown, and she stared past Luke's face into some spot I couldn't see, maybe an alternate universe.

Suddenly I felt kind of bad. I hadn't been as nice to her as I could have been. "I bet the guys are getting tired of shopping," I said. "Why don't we keep going and they can go have a beer?"

She grinned at me like a little kid who just got invited to a birthday party. "But doesn't JD want any souvenirs?"

"We'll be here for almost two more weeks, there's plenty of time."

JD nodded, maybe too eagerly, as if I'd pardoned his prison sentence.

Lavender and I wandered through three more shops. We came to a taffy store and went inside. The plastic looked like a spring floral display with pale yellow, green, blue, pink, and even white chunks of sticky, chewy goodness. Lavender and I each bought half a pound. We carried our white bags out into the concourse.

"You seem distracted," Lavender said.

I had no idea how she would know this since she'd only spent a few hours with me. "I'm not distracted."

"I think you're lying."

"No I'm not. Why would you say that?"

"I can see your throat chakra is a funny color. It's very dark, almost bloody. It should be blue."

"I don't know what you think you see, but I'm not lying. I'm loving Australia and having a great time being on vacation with JD."

"But not with Luke and me."

"It's not what I expected, having a murder in the middle of our vacation."

Today she wore a smaller black hat, one that was made of felt, which looked very uncomfortable in the warm, muggy air. She pushed it around on her head. "Maybe that's what I'm seeing. But there's something you're not saying, your chakra is extremely discolored."

"Isn't that an aura?"

"They're related."

I didn't think they were related, but I really had no idea, so I didn't say anything, probably making my throat chakra even darker. "I've always thought that was a bit of a fantasy, thinking people had colored balls hovering in different parts of their bodies."

"It's not a colored ball. It's energy and it has a slightly colored hue. Most people can't see them. The colors aren't what you see in drawings. It's not that distinct."

"Then how can you tell if mine is supposedly the wrong color?"

"Partially because it's so dark. It looks closed up. It means you aren't saying things you want to say. I think you wanted that opal and you didn't speak up and now you've blocked yourself. Or maybe you're always blocked. Do you have trouble expressing your thoughts?"

I sat on a bench and opened my bag of taffy. Although I have absolutely no trouble expressing my thoughts, it's not like I'm completely lacking in discretion.

I unwrapped a piece of watermelon taffy and popped it in my mouth. As I chewed, concentrating on trying to keep the taffy from gluing my teeth together, she reached over and touched the soft indentation right above the center of my collarbone. "It's right here," she said.

For a minute, I thought the pressure of her finger would make me choke. Chewing the taffy generated excess saliva and suddenly I desperately needed to swallow. The overload of sugar swimming around my mouth made my throat tighten and I felt the urge to cough but didn't want to spit gooey taffy all over the place. I wanted her to move her finger, but I couldn't talk. I swallowed but the candy remained a big blob in my mouth. Her finger moved with my throat. Her nail was painted ice blue, which I hadn't noticed earlier. How had I eaten brunch with her and shopped and not noticed her nails were ice blue? The first night, her nails had been purple but I couldn't remember what color they'd been on the boat ride. Did she change the color every day? What a waste of time.

Finally she moved her finger. I coughed. I could hardly breathe and a tiny wheezing sound came out of my throat. I loved my candy, but I knew I wouldn't be able to finish it. I grabbed the wax wrapper out of the bag and spit the gob of chewed taffy into it.

"Why did you do that?"

"I was choking. Don't put your finger on my throat again."

"I hardly touched you."

"That doesn't matter. It felt like I was strangling."

"Okay. I guess you don't have any trouble saying what you're thinking. So I'm not sure what I was seeing there. Unless it's that your bluntness is a smokescreen for other lies. Because I know you wanted that necklace and you didn't say a word."

I decided to ignore all of that. She seemed to be matching me one for one in saying exactly what was on her mind. "Are your chakras in good shape? Can you see your own, or do you need someone else to inspect you?"

"Everyone gets out of balance from time to time," she said.

"It's kind of hard to believe we all have colored spots glowing along our bodies."

"I thought you were into mystical things," Lavender said.

"I wouldn't say that."

"You claim you've seen ghosts."

"I'm not mystical, they came looking for me."

"Well aren't you special."

I shoved a piece of taffy in my mouth. I chewed, trying to figure out the flavor. It was a pale orange, but didn't taste quite like peach. "Why does it bother you so much that I've seen ghosts? It's not like you have some unique claim to communicating with the spirit world. I've heard that something like thirty percent of the population says they've had a supernatural encounter."

"It's wishful thinking."

"Is that hat squeezing your brain so you can't think?" I said. Harsh, I know, but no more rude than she was, calling me a liar.

"No. I just think if you really communicated with ghosts, you would have heard from Elizabeth's ghost. She was murdered, isn't that a prime set-up for a ghost to appear?"

"I really have no idea."

"Well if she hasn't, maybe I can help you get in touch with her."

"Why would I want to do that?"

"To find out who killed her."

"Why don't you get in touch and ask her? You don't need me."

Suddenly her eyes filled with tears. She shoved her bag of taffy into her enormous black canvas purse. She dug around without looking down, and finally came up with a tissue. She patted the tip of her nose and then pressed it under her lower eyelids. When she pulled it away, it was dotted with black mascara and eye liner, yet her eyes remained perfectly made up, not a single smear. "Luke doesn't believe I've spoken to ghosts, seen things from beyond the grave, had visions of the future."

"He seemed open to the possibility of ghosts."

"He doesn't believe *I've* seen them."

"Oh." This put Luke's request in a whole new light. It wasn't at all about not wanting to owe her something. Or maybe it still was, maybe he told her he didn't believe her to keep her at arm's length. Or to mess with her head. He was a hard guy to figure out.

"It hurts my feelings."

"I'm sure. But if *you* know you've seen them, what does it matter what he thinks?"

"I love him."

"Yes, but you can't force him to believe you."

"I know. But that doesn't mean it doesn't hurt."

"Right. But *you* know he's wrong. You should just be confident in yourself."

"I am. But I thought if you and I tried to get in touch with her together, if we could find out who killed her, or at least get some hints of how she was feeling, he would believe me."

"What does it have to do with me?"

"He seems to absolutely accept it as a fact that you've had supernatural experiences." Tears filled her eyes again. They dribbled over the edge of her eyelids. Now, the mascara started to run, great black rivers sliding across her cheekbones, widening as they hit the soft spots, then trickling along her jaw like rain pouring down a window and changing course when it hit an obstacle.

"You want me to prove you're legitimate or something?"

She shook her head. "Don't make it sound like I need you. It's the opposite." Her tears dried up as abruptly as they'd started. She wiped at her cheeks and got most of the make-up wiped up with the moisture of her tears, but a charcoal gray tint remained, making her look almost dead herself, between her black clothes and her grayish skin and red-streaked eyeballs. "I can make sure you do see the ghost, since you don't seem to be able to take charge and they only come to you on their own whims."

"That's ridiculous." I stood. "I wanted to look in that store. I was hoping to find a toe ring while I was here. But first, I'm really thirsty. I'm going back to the taffy store for a bottle of water."

She stood and followed me back the way we'd come. After I had my water, I walked quickly to a shop that had silver jewelry, lots of soaps and candles, and thin, drapey dresses, bright with tropical flowers, displayed near the front. Lavender straggled behind me, dragging the heels of her backless sandals on the ground like a sulky teenager.

I ran my palm across the fabric of the dresses, soft threads swept against my skin. It would be fun to buy a dress, but I had the toe ring on my mind and was only minutes away from having had enough shopping to last me three weeks.

The store smelled like almonds, which soothed my nerves

after the roller coaster ride of Lavender and her arrogance climbing up a steep incline, then suddenly plunging into neediness before shooting back up to a sharp, superior peak. Maybe the smell was soothing my throat chakra so the sharp words in my head would come out more softly.

The racks were filled with bracelets — leather bands, and silver chains with beads on them. There was a glass case filled with rings for every finger of your hand, and next to it, a smaller case with toe rings. I'd been wanting another toe ring ever since it occurred to me that when JD kissed me, I felt it all the way to my toes. It sounds lame, but I like toe rings anyway, and it seemed like a good excuse. Not that I need excuses to buy myself little gifts, but it makes it easier when I have a reason. As if I'm looking for some kind of purpose for everything I own, as if all the pieces of my life must have meaning.

The clerk's hair was dyed red, making it look like my hair on steroids. She also had a nose ring, which is not something you normally see in a woman who is forty-something, or possibly just a woman who has spent too much time enjoying the Australian sun so she looks forty-something.

"Can I try on the toe rings?"

"Sure, duck. As long as you show me which ones you try so I can sanitize them." It was actually good to hear they sanitized them.

I tried on three or four, but quickly settled on the one that first caught my eye — three silver strands wound around each other. I wondered how they did that without showing any joints. It fit perfectly on the second toe of my left foot, snug enough to stay in place, but not so tight I had to twist and squeeze it on. I could feel Lavender standing behind me, and smelled the licorice taffy that she'd filled half her bag with. I could hear her chewing, the suction sound as she tried to unstick her teeth. I knew that feeling, it almost forces you to chew with your mouth open to prevent everything from getting gummed up.

I left the ring on my toe and paid for it.

"Is that to compensate for JD not buying you an opal?"

"No. I wanted another one for a long time, and since summer is coming to Australia, I thought it would be a good souvenir. I have plenty of mugs and coasters and t-shirts."

As we walked toward the door, Lavender said, "So what do you think? About the ghost."

"I don't need your help to see ghosts."

"It sounds like you do."

I stopped and looked at her. She chewed her taffy. At the rate she was going, the bag would be empty before we met up with JD and Luke. "I think you have issues to work out with Luke, and I don't want to get dragged into the middle of it."

Her mouth opened and I could see black coating the insides of her lips and her tongue, outlining her teeth where it had temporarily stained her gums. She chewed a bit more. "Maybe we do. But now is not the right time. He's too upset about the police questioning him. He needs our help."

"It has nothing to do with me."

"He's your boyfriend's twin brother."

"I know who he is."

"Why are you so obstinate?"

"We should go find the guys," I said.

She grabbed my shirt. "Tell me why you're being like this. I thought we'd be friends."

"That's fine, but you insult me and then try to drag me into some issue with you and Luke. If Elizabeth's ghost has something to say to me, I'm sure she'll let me know. Please let go of my shirt."

She released her grip. Her hand shook slightly but she shoved it into her purse and dug around for her bag of taffy. She pulled it out and reached inside, then she removed her hand and peered into the bag. She folded the top and stuffed it back in her purse without taking another piece of candy. "Sorry if I insulted you. I just know a lot about the spirit world. I'm coming over to Luke's place Tuesday night. If you change your mind, and you two are still around, you can tell me then."

"We'll be here until Thursday."

As if she was suddenly glad of an excuse to change the subject, she said, "Where are you staying in Queensland?"

I told her about the place where we were staying on Hamilton Island. We talked about that and other interesting parts of Australia. The subject of ghosts and Luke didn't come up again.

AFTER WE GRABBED a quick lunch — meat pies again, but I didn't complain because I saw how they could become addictive — we said good-bye to Lavender and started the drive back to Luke's barren house. It felt a little strange, as if we had a chauffeur, because JD and I sat in the back seat and Luke was alone in the front, but I was glad JD didn't let the awkwardness deter him from sitting next to me. Seeing bits and pieces of Sydney was fun, but I felt like I'd hardly been with him for two days. Instead, my head was filled with Lavender and her quirky moods and her calculated attempts to control the spirit world. Every time I thought about her rigid approach and how dismissive she was toward me, I laughed inside. There must have been a smile on my lips because JD looked at me and lifted his eyebrow as if he wanted to ask me what was so funny, but he didn't say anything. Maybe he didn't really want to know, or he didn't want to hear my perspective with Luke sitting three feet in front of us.

During the drive, I fell asleep with my head against JD's shoulder, so the three hours flew by. When we arrived at Luke's, a thunderstorm was threatening. I looked at the thick, dark clouds every five minutes, hoping for a wild storm. We get thunderstorms in the Santa Clara Valley once every two years, if we're lucky, and even then, they're brief, the lightning faint, the thunder a mild boom, anxious to travel toward open space.

The house was dark. We turned on a few lights, but they didn't do much since there was still a strange, filtered daylight despite those fierce clouds.

"I'm going to the market to get something for dinner. Any requests?" Luke tossed his keys from one hand to the other, not even looking at what he was doing. He was constantly moving, tossing keys, jiggling his leg, running his fingers through his hair, cracking his knuckles.

"Snacks," JD said. "And not those cheese things. And beer. And bottled water."

"Beer is first on the list," Luke said.

After he left, we sat at the kitchen table. JD shuffled a deck of cards. "Gin Rummy or Crazy Eights?"

"Gin Rummy," I said.

"Good, because I just realized I can't remember the rules to Crazy Eights."

Lightning jittered across the sky, flashing through the room. The thunder followed immediately — the sound of an explosion and sudden rain that was light, in contrast.

JD dealt the cards. I stared out the window, waiting for more lightning. I picked up my cards but didn't look at them. Another flash ripped open the sky. "Let's go sit on the porch and watch the storm. We can play cards later." I set my cards face down on the table in a fan shape.

"Sure." JD folded his cards back into a neat little stack.

Two wicker chairs sat on the porch, completely dry because the porch outside the kitchen was about ten or twelve feet wide and the overhang reached out a foot or so beyond that. "I wonder why Elizabeth didn't take these?"

"Luke's neighbor brought them over." JD pointed to the nearest farmhouse on a small hill. "Luke mentioned we were visiting. And they knew what had happened."

"It was kind of a vicious thing to do. Emptying his house." I said.

"Not when you think what she could have done."

"I wonder what she was like."

He pressed his lips together.

I stretched out my legs, lifted my heels off the floor and pointed my toes. My new toe ring shimmered in the sharp light. "But when you think of it another way, it was clever. I have to admire her for doing something that got her message across without getting violent."

"Is that how it works? You have to commit a crime to get your message across? Wouldn't it be more dignified to walk away?" Thunder boomed and almost swallowed his last two words.

"Like you said, she could have done something worse."

"But you admire her? She committed a felony," JD said.

"I admire her unusual approach. It's a statement." The flashes across the sky and the boom of thunder punctuated everything we said. It made our conversation more dramatic than it was.

"It wasn't as if they had a relationship. They'd only been seeing each other a few weeks. And it's a crime."

"Obviously she thought they did have a relationship."

"That doesn't make it right," he said.

"I didn't say it was right, I just have a little bit of respect for her."

"I wonder who killed her?"

I needed to ask him about his brother. I was fairly sure his feelings for Luke were ambivalent enough that he wouldn't get upset, but I was nervous. Blood is thicker than water and all that. Still, I had to know what he was thinking. "Do you have a sliver of suspicion that he did it?"

"No." He stood. "I'm getting that last beer. Do you want some water?"

I nodded. He didn't sound annoyed, but I wasn't sure. His decision to get the beer right at that point seemed like it meant something, but maybe he'd been thinking about it the whole time and just didn't want to wait any more. Or maybe he saw the conversation heading into a tight curve and he wanted to fortify himself.

Of course he knows me well enough by now to realize that I wasn't going to let his quick escape for beer get me sidetracked. When I want to know something, I push until I find out. Most of the time. I desperately want to know who murdered my parents, but for whatever reason, that's one piece of knowledge I haven't pursued.

When he returned, I started in the minute he sat down. "You can see why the police are questioning him, can't you?"

"Of course. Process of elimination. They start with the

easy suspect and work their way through."

"But maybe there's a reason for that. Maybe, nine times out of ten, it is the obvious person. Her body was in his yard. She stole his whole life, or at least the physical evidence of it."

He stood and went to the edge of the porch. He stuck his arm out into the rain. Thunder crashed across the valley. He jerked his arm back as if he'd been shot. Still facing the yard, he said, "Do you think he killed her?"

"No."

He turned. "But you have doubts."

"I don't. I just wanted to know what you're thinking."

He laughed. "You're tricky."

I smiled.

"I'm worried about him. It's not like he has the kind of personality that's going to endear him to the police. And I have no idea what the laws are like here, if they can charge him based only on finding the body on his property. I wish he had some clue who would do that. Who hates him that much?" He walked over and sat down. He rested his right ankle on his left knee and grabbed it with his hand.

"Lavender offered to help us get in touch with her ghost. Can you believe that?" I said.

"Can she do that?"

"Who knows."

"If she can, wouldn't she have already done it?"

"That's what I thought."

"Maybe it's worth thinking about," he said.

"What is this, a carnival? I can't believe you can just hang dark curtains and light candles and wait for a ghost to show up because you have a lock of her hair and you're chanting some nonsense."

"Is that what she does?"

"I have no idea. That's what I imagine."

"Do you know why she's asking you? Why she hasn't already tried on her own?"

"It sounds like Luke doesn't really believe she's for real. I think she wants to use me for credibility."

He laughed. "Really?"

"You don't think I have credibility?"

"Credibility and seeing ghosts don't usually go together. After all the crap you put up with from your boss and the other people at the church, it's funny."

I laughed. I pictured Kate's face, her brow pulled down like her whole brain was trying to make sense of me, or Joe, his eyes pleading with me to stop talking about ghosts, his mouth pressed together like he was ready to fire me if I didn't shut up. I knew he wouldn't, because overall he likes me and he knows I do a good job, and I fulfill his purpose of having someone disconnected from the church managing the office. I know they just can't get the two conflicting aspects to line up in their heads — hearing me talk about ghosts while thinking I'm sane and moderately intelligent.

"Why don't you help her out?"

"She's annoying. And stupid. And she'll lower my

credibility in my own eyes."

"She's not stupid."

"She says stupid things."

"Like what?"

Why had I mentioned that? Now my hesitation would let him know I was holding out on him. My throat chakra might turn black, but I didn't want to tell him what she'd said. It *was* stupid — asking if I was afraid I couldn't possess him because more of him would always belong to his twin. Okay, that's not exactly what she said, but that was close enough, and it's what she meant.

"What stupid things does she say?"

"Stupid is the wrong word. I don't mean stupid as in not very bright, I mean as in rude. She was so condescending, acting like everyone who takes the ghost tour is naive. As if no one but her understands anything about supernatural events."

"I think you mis-read her. She wouldn't be asking for your help if she thought she knew everything."

The thunder was no longer crashing, more of a softer booming. The rain was heavier, slapping on the stepping stones that led to the porch and pattering on the roof. The sounds were soothing, along with the smell of wet earth and wild grass, but I couldn't relax and let them wash over me. For some reason I felt like a petulant child. Although I have no idea what sibling rivalry is really like, it seemed like I was getting a taste. I couldn't figure out why I felt like I was competing with her for leading status as someone familiar with ghosts. It was ridiculous, so childish I was embarrassed. She'd turned it into a game or a competition and I didn't want to play. Ghosts are ethereal, impossible to fully comprehend, and she was turning my experiences with the spirit world, good and bad, into a freak show or a paint-by-number piece of "art".

"Why are you so cold toward her?"

I wished he would slow down, stop firing questions and comments at me. I pulled my knees up toward my chin and put the arches of my feet on the edge of the chair. I wrapped my arms around my legs and rested my head on my knees.

"What's wrong?"

"It's hard to explain."

"I can't hear you with your mouth on your knees?"

I lifted my head and looked at him. "It's hard to explain."

"Can't you just be friendlier? There's already tension between Luke and me, and now the murder. Isn't that enough drama for one vacation?"

"I'm not creating drama. She is. Look at how she dresses. And I think that's for show. For us. Luke was teasing her about the hat, like she'd never worn it before."

He put his hand on my wrist and held it there. "I'm not criticizing you. But can't you step back and laugh at yourself for bitching about her clothes when you have tattoos and all those earrings? Some people might say the same thing about you."

I wanted to yank my arm away, but I knew he was right. Maybe I do want to draw attention to my appearance, maybe I'm trying to say, *I'm not like everyone else*. On the other hand, I never decided to go get a tattoo to make a statement, I just thought they looked cool and wanted some of my own. I wanted them to remind me of things. The string of ladybugs along the back of my neck make me think of how much I loved the cute little bugs when I was a child. They make me smile. Maybe it's subconscious. We all want to stand out and fit in at the same time.

Nothing I said was doing a very good job of explaining why I was upset. It was so obvious to me, but he didn't get it. I suppose he was more interested in keeping the peace than in drawing some kind of line in the sand over the ins and outs of supernatural phenomenon.

"Sure. I can be friendly. And I think I have been. But I don't want to discuss ghosts with her, and I'm not going to set up some kind of artificial environment to try to lure a ghost that I don't even know exists into solving a crime as if we're conducting a supernatural police line-up. It makes everything I've experienced seem cheap and phony."

"That's in your own head."

"Maybe."

"Why can't you just go along and help her? You don't have to do anything."

"Because she doesn't really think I'm helping her. She thinks she's going to help me. I don't need her help."

He gave my wrist a quick squeeze and let go. "Will you think about it?"

What he didn't get was that I had thought about it. He wasn't listening.

Six

IT WAS ONE-THIRTY in the morning when I woke up suddenly, as if there'd been a crash of thunder or someone shouting, but the house was silent. The rain had stopped. JD's breath was so shallow I almost wasn't sure if he was breathing. For a minute, it scared me. I didn't want something to happen to him when we'd had a fight, sort of. Not really a fight, but we were disconnected.

I took a few deep breaths. I had to think about him, about how it was for him to be with his brother with whom he'd had a less than ideal relationship, and now the murder. All through dinner and the evening, listening to the rain while he and Luke talked about nothing, I whispered to myself — *it's not about you. It's not about you.* But my self wasn't paying much attention.

JD and Luke drank quite a few beers. It didn't seem like they were drunk, but they got sillier and sillier. On the one hand, maybe it was helping them get back in touch, but on the other hand, I felt like I was standing in the living room, looking through the stained-glass window, its colored spots blocking part of the scene, and the rippled glass blurring the rest, hearing them laugh from a distance, not able to decipher their words. They didn't seem to notice I was watching them. It made me wonder if that's how it felt to be a ghost, observing but not having anyone aware of your presence.

At ten-thirty, I told them I was going to bed. I smiled and kissed JD nice and hard so he wouldn't think I was going to sleep because I was mad at him, or bored. I hadn't woken up when he came to bed.

I turned over and put my hand on his belly. It moved gently with his breath. His skin was warm and comforting, but listening to him sleep woke me up even more. My eyes were wide, staring at nothing because there were no lights on in the house and the moon was hidden by dark clouds. Luke's house is isolated enough that there were no streetlights or any visible lights from the nearby houses. At home, my room is never completely dark. Even when the blinds are closed, light seeps in so the night is kind of a charcoal gray rather than utter blackness.

I tried to force my eyelids down, but they didn't want to stay closed. My nostrils flared as if my lungs were trying to get an extra shot of oxygen, and my brain was sharp and alert, focused on a single point, but I couldn't figure out what that point was. I let my hand drift off JD's stomach and turned onto my other side. The pillow was warm, almost hot.

I raised my head and flipped the pillow over but the other side wasn't cool and soothing as I'd hoped. I tucked my hand under it and pulled it more tightly around my head.

My eyes were still so wide open it seemed as if my eyeballs were vibrating, straining to see, but I couldn't even see the shadow of my suitcase against the opposite wall. I turned onto my other side again and wiggled around trying to find a cooler spot on the pillow. There was none. JD's breath trailed across my skin, smelling surprisingly like damp earth instead of beer. I reached out my hand to touch him. His back was facing me. He'd turned when I was wriggling around.

I pushed the covers away and sat up. That wasn't his breath on my skin. He was still breathing softly, almost nothing, and with his back to me, there was no way I would have felt his breath.

"Hello? Luke?" My voice was a loud whisper. "Is someone there?"

Maybe it was the breeze from outside, and that's why it smelled like wet dirt. I tried to make out the location of the window. I usually like to sleep with a window open, but JD might have shut it because of the storm. I turned my face to the spot where I thought the window was, although I couldn't remember for sure. I felt nothing. I pushed the covers down to my feet and swung my legs over the side of the bed. I bent over and felt around on the floor for my yoga pants and t-shirt. After I'd tugged them on, I stood.

Keeping my hand on the mattress so I could find my way, I

inched toward the foot of the bed. With my leg pressed against the edge, I made my way around to JD's side. When I reached the corner of the bed near his feet, I had no idea what to do. I couldn't believe my eyes weren't able to distinguish anything. It didn't help that there was no other furniture. I thought the window would put off some kind of shimmer, but there was nothing. My hand shook and I wondered if I'd gone blind while I slept. I laughed softly. It was just dark. It was the tired old story of a girl used to living in suburbia who doesn't realize how dark the night is when there are miles of thick, black clouds and a sparse human population.

I let go of the bed and slid my feet along the floor. I don't know what I was worried about tripping over. I suppose there was a danger of slamming into the wall. Maybe our bodies are just designed to proceed cautiously in the dark, unsettled when the most significant sense we possess is shut down.

My hand bumped the wall. I felt along the wall until I found the window frame. A breath trailed across my face, the same heavy, earthen smell. "Who's there?" This time my voice was a normal tone.

"Madison?" The bed creaked. I heard JD pat the mattress. "Where are you?"

"Over here. By the window."

"Why? Are you too warm?"

"I felt something and I wanted to see if the window was open."

"I closed it when I came to bed. Rain was blowing into the room."

"It's so dark."

"Come back to bed."

"It felt like someone was in the room."

"Who would be in the room?"

"I felt someone's breath on my face."

"You're dreaming. Come back before you trip on something."

"What would I trip on?"

He laughed.

I heard him push the covers aside. The quilt brushed against the floor. I didn't think I'd ever heard a quilt falling on the floor before. Of course, I have carpet on my floor, so maybe that's why.

"If you want the window open, I'll open it. The wood is swollen and it's difficult to raise it."

"I can do it."

Suddenly I felt him next to me. He put one arm around my shoulders and another behind my legs and scooped me up into his arms. I laughed. He touched his nose to mine and kissed me. It was amazing that despite the total lack of light, we could easily find each other's mouths.

Still kissing me, he moved slowly until his shin bumped against the side of the bed. He leaned over and placed me on top of the covers. "Now stay there. Do you want the window open?"

"Actually, no. I want to see if I notice that breath again and if the window's open, I won't be able to tell."

"You were dreaming." He sat on the bed. It shifted as he swung his legs up and pulled the quilt over both of us.

"I wasn't dreaming."

"Maybe Elizabeth's ghost is trying to get in touch with you after all."

"I wonder."

"Lavender will be so disappointed." He turned on his side and pulled me toward him. He put his face in my hair and sighed. I slipped out from under his arms and sat up.

"What are you doing?"

"I can't sleep. I'm hyper awake. I've never felt so awake in my life."

"Lie down. We'll fall back to sleep together."

"What if that's what woke me? Elizabeth's spirit."

"You probably went to bed too early."

"Something woke me up very suddenly."

"What?"

"I don't know. I felt like there'd been a loud sound or something, but it was totally quiet."

"That makes no sense."

"It was an impression."

"You might have been dreaming about the thunder. It was louder than any storm I've ever heard. It impressed itself on our brains because it was so unusual."

I closed my eyes. What he said was logical, but it didn't feel true. It could be wishful thinking, all the speculation about Lavender's methods for summoning ghosts, all my bad feelings about her superior attitude, all working on my subconscious. Still, my eyes refused to close.

He pressed gently on my shoulder, trying to make me lie down again, but I couldn't. "You should force yourself to relax and close your eyes. If there's something here, she'll come to you. Isn't that how you said it normally happens?"

I laughed softly. Even though the door was closed, I didn't want to wake Luke. I slid down under the covers and turned on my side. I pressed my eyes closed but I could feel my eyeballs buzzing and humming behind my lids. The effort to keep them closed was as uncomfortable as trying to hold my breath. JD didn't realize how hard it was to force yourself to do something that's supposed to be the exact opposite of force, a gradual letting go and falling under the spell of sleep, a magical act that feels so natural most nights, but every so often turns into the most elusive thing in the world, as if you can't recall the steps to make it work. But there aren't any steps.

My eyes twitched and my lashes fluttered against my cheek. It felt like a butterfly landing on my face, brushing its wings across me as it trembled in fear from alighting so close to a human being, trusting her with its life. I brushed my hand across my cheek, but it didn't do any good. My eyes continued to shiver under my lids and I knew that keeping them closed one more minute would make them burst out of my head. I let them fly open. The room was dark and silent as before, JD's breath barely perceptible. Trying to lure me back to sleep, he'd fallen asleep. I smiled and snuggled closer to him but it didn't do any good. If I sat up, I might wake him again, but lying there, trying to relax was making me crazy. I carefully lifted his arm off my waist and rolled over as if I was practicing a stealth escape maneuver. I stopped right at the edge of the bed. It wasn't far because it was a double bed, not the queen-sized space I was used to at home.

I sat up, pushed my pillow against the wall and leaned back. I had no idea what I was going to do, but it was easier to sit and wait with my eyes open.

It's possible I drifted to sleep because suddenly I felt my whole body spring to full alert again, my eyes wide and a sensation under my skin that seemed as if I could feel my blood moving through my veins. I smelled the damp earth and something else I couldn't identify. The room was icy cold, as if water had drenched the walls and ceiling, even the bed and the blankets, and then frozen, leaving me encased in sheets of ice.

"Why'd it get so cold in here?" JD whispered. His teeth chattered lightly against each other as he spoke. "Did you open the window? It feels like someone put ice cubes in our bed."

I felt the bed shift as he sat up. I reached over and slid my arm across his back and pulled myself toward him, hoping our bodies would warm each other.

He pulled me to a sitting position. "You're freezing cold."

"So are you."

We held each other, shivering. He yanked the quilt up and wound it around us and still we shook with cold. The smell of mud became so strong it was hard to breathe. Tears ran down my face. I had no idea what time it was and after a few minutes, I felt as if I couldn't remember what it was like to have a normal body temperature. Even my thoughts seemed to freeze, and the earlier sensation of my blood running through my veins was gone, replaced by the awareness of a vast network of veins and arteries, like thin wires of ice throughout my body.

"Do you see that?" JD said. His voice was hoarse and low.

I had no idea where he was looking, but I saw nothing. I turned my head. Something white and transparent hung in the air near the window.

He pulled me closer, if that was possible, since I already felt like I couldn't tell where his icy cold skin ended and mine began. I swallowed. It tasted like my saliva had turned to blood. I had the urge to swallow again but resisted.

JD coughed. A few seconds went by. He coughed again. "My mouth tastes like blood."

"Mine too."

The white thing, without any real form, hovered in the corner. It didn't move closer or fade, just continued to transmit its icy presence.

We shivered against each other. I wondered if JD was as

scared as I was. I always expect guys to be less scared than females and I don't know why. Are they really, or do they feel they have to not let on when they're afraid? Some sort of cultural imperative that they're supposed to be strong and confident and in charge. Admitting fear will destroy everything they are. I don't know why that is. Women can run around saying *I'm scared, I'm terrified, that's scary*, and men stand silently, trying to comfort us.

"Are you scared?" I whispered.

"I'm too cold to think about anything else."

I was right, he didn't want to admit it. He couldn't admit it. I squeezed him and felt as if my bones were going to snap from the pressure. I relaxed my grip.

"Is it her?" he said.

"It must be."

"What do you think she wants?" he said.

"Shhh." Part of my brain skittered off, thinking about how we were seeing and feeling the same things and how it made me feel close to him. When I'd seen spirits before, I felt so alone. Yet even now, confirming back and forth what we were feeling, there was a sense of loneliness, as if we couldn't really help each other, couldn't stop the cold or the taste of blood.

"Is it ever going to leave?"

"Yes."

"How do you know?" he said.

"It has to. We can't go on like this forever. I feel like we'll die from the cold."

He relaxed his grip on me and pushed away the quilt.

"What are you doing?"

"I can't just sit here. That taste is making me sick."

He climbed out of bed and immediately the icy white thing moved over him. Because of some kind of light coming from it, I could now see JD. His lips were blue and he shook uncontrollably. His hands trembled and his head was jittering slightly. I tried to get out of bed, but my legs were numb and felt like they were locked in blocks of ice.

I heard a whisper, on a puff of air filled with that muddy odor. *I can't be alone. I was alone all my life. I want you, Luke. I won't be alone.*

My heart felt like a cube of ice. Did she think JD was Luke? Do ghosts mix people up? I suppose they could. But she'd been his girlfriend, even if it was only a month or two. She'd slept with him, couldn't she tell them apart? Maybe it was more difficult on the other side of the grave.

Now I was sobbing. I had no idea what to do. It looked as if she was intent on freezing him to death. I grabbed at the blankets and the quilt covering my legs, trying to push them away, trying to rub some life into my muscles. Although if I could reach the spot where he stood, I had no idea what I would do. Warm him up? That hadn't worked earlier.

I rolled to the side of the bed. There was a loud thud. I could no longer see JD in the center of the apparition. He must have collapsed, maybe passed out from the cold. With one huge effort, I shoved all the blankets off the side of the bed and rolled onto them. When I hit the floor it felt like my bones shattered into a thousand fragments. I pulled myself toward where I thought the window was. Something bumped my shoulder. I grabbed it — JD's foot, icy, colder than it felt after he'd been surfing for an hour or two. I tugged the blankets up and pulled them over his feet and lower body. Creeping further along the floor, I felt his stomach and then his chest. I reached up to his face and dragged my fingers gently across his cheeks. His eyes were closed.

The shimmering white thing had disappeared.

I gripped his shoulders and pulled myself closer. His breath caressed my forehead, warm and alive. Equally warm tears spilled down my face. I hoisted my upper body off the floor and moved on top of him. Both of us were warmer now. He lifted one arm and placed it across my back.

For quite some time we remained on the floor, tangled in the quilt and blankets and each other, half sleeping, half-crazed with lucid dreams. At least that's how it was for me. I had no idea what was going through JD's head, and it would be a while before I found out.

By the time we both woke fully and dragged our limp bodies back onto the bed, the space outside the window was filled with pale light. Heavy clouds still covered the sky, but not as dark as the previous afternoon. We slept.

I woke first. I turned on my side and looked out the window. Nothing moved. All I could see was grass and a wire fence where the property sloped down into a shallow ravine. Across from that were eucalyptus trees surrounded by long pale grass. It was the soft kind that sways with the slightest breeze, but it was utterly still. The crows and wild tropical birds I'd heard the day we first arrived were silent.

I wondered if Luke was sitting in the kitchen, waiting for us to come out, or if he was still wrapped up in his sleeping bag on the floor of the second bedroom. He was supposed to talk to the police that day, but I wasn't sure if he had a set time, or could show up when he felt like it. Arriving early, looking eager to help, seemed like a better strategy to me. Although, if you're innocent, hopefully you don't need a strategy.

Seven

AFTER DRIFTING IN and out of sleep several times, I finally leaned over the side of the bed and pulled my cell phone out of my bag. I'd never set it to Australia time because I'd turned off the network access so it didn't rack up hundreds or thousands of dollars trying to pinpoint where I was without my permission. It was five-thirty in the evening at home. Calculating the time took me far longer than it should have — six hours back, then a day forward. It was eleven-thirty Monday morning. I dropped the phone back in my bag. It had been years since I'd slept past seven-thirty or eight in the morning.

It was too warm under the quilt, but I couldn't bring myself to push it off my skin, remembering the piercing cold of the night before. Every muscle in my arms and legs ached, as if I'd been hiking steep, cliff-hugging trails for hours. On top of that, I was starving, although not quite ready to leave the cozy feeling of JD sleeping next to me and the soft, worn quilt on top. The quilt had the look of something that had been in the family for years, but Luke had bought it at a yard sale a few weeks ago — at least he could pretend he had something from his past.

In some ways, I envied his house, wiped clean of too many possessions and the weight of their memories. It's not that I'm a pack rat, or that my condo is stuffed to the beams with clutter, but I do have a lot of things that belonged to my parents and I can't seem to get rid of them. Things I don't necessarily need or use.

I have my mother's unfinished knitting projects, which I've thought about taking up someday, yet if I'm really going to adopt knitting, I'd prefer to start something fresh that's all mine. I have all their pre-digital photographs in albums, but I only keep one album on a bookcase in my living room. There are boxes of clothes and linens and pots and pans and books and all the small and large things a person gathers over forty-five years, times two. I can't bring myself to turn it all over to Goodwill or hand them off one by one in a yard sale, and so all these things fill my closets and I sometimes long for the freedom of losing everything. I know that sounds terrible, especially to a person who has lost all their possessions in a flood or fire, but I think carrying too much stuff with you, letting it collect more, as if your boxes are made of glue and new things attach themselves as you go, stifles your life and has a way of dragging you down. The idea of being a nomad, living in a motor home, or traveling around and not having a permanent address, really appeals to me.

JD flopped onto his back and flung his arm across my ribs. I pulled my arm out from under the quilt and wove my fingers between his.

"You're awake?" he said.

"Mm hmm."

"I was trying to let you sleep."

"It's eleven-thirty."

He sat up. "So what the *hell* was that?"

"Elizabeth's ghost, obviously."

He threw off the covers and got up. "I'm going to take a shower."

"I'm going to look for coffee." I pushed the covers off my side.

"Did I pass out?"

"I think so. It was scary. I don't feel as bad now, but I'm ... I don't know what they can do."

"Who?"

"Ghosts."

"What do you mean?"

"When she said she couldn't be without you. I guess she assumed you were Luke."

He laughed. "that's insane."

"Do you think she can do anything?"

"I have no idea. But you can be sure I'll leave the bedroom door open so she can find Luke."

"It's not funny," I said.

He went to his suitcase and lifted the lid. He dug around and pulled out a pair of shorts and a faded blue t-shirt. "It wasn't funny seeing that shadow or vapor or whatever it was, and it wasn't funny freezing my ass off while she blew her icy crypt persona around, but you have to admit, mixing me up with my twin is kind of funny."

"Not if she tries to take you, somehow. Do you think ghosts can kill people?"

"If they can, I don't want her taking Luke either."

"I'm not saying that."

"But you did. Besides, I'm sure she can't take someone. That's too wild to believe, even for you."

"What's that supposed to mean?"

He walked around the foot of the bed and sat next to me. "It doesn't mean anything. I'm trying to help you lighten up, not take it so seriously. We had a creepy experience. I'm sure that's the end of it."

"What are you going to say to Luke?"

He stood. He rubbed his hand across my head, then looped my hair around his wrist and tugged it gently so my head was tilted back, looking at him. "Don't be scared, okay? I don't know what I'm going to tell him."

"Don't turn it into a joke."

He kissed my lips gently. "I won't. I wonder what Lavender will have to say about it."

"Why do we have to tell her?"

"Why wouldn't we? It'll be interesting to get her perspective."

"Let's not mention it until we can talk about it more."

"Why?"

"Don't you want to think about it? Before we get all kinds of other opinions?"

"Whatever you want." He let go of my hair and went into the bathroom. A moment later, water gushed out of the shower and a few seconds after that, steam drifted into the bedroom.

When I opened the door to go looking for coffee, Luke was standing right there. "I was just gonna knock."

I hoped he hadn't heard our conversation. I really needed time to think. I wanted to sort it out between JD and me first.

"We slept late."

"No shit. I need to go talk to the cops. I left coffee on. And there's two mugs in the dish drainer."

"Thanks."

"No problem. It's fresh. Drank a whole pot myself and made another one just now."

He turned and walked down the hall, the slow stride, the same broad shoulders and slightly more prominent downward slope of the left shoulder as JD. They had the same muscular neck, like a football player's, but not quite as beefy. The color of their hair was identical and they both walked with their hands shoved in their pockets. For half a second I wanted to run after him and give him a hug, because even though my head told me it was Luke, a hint coming from some place deeper argued that it was JD. I could see why Elizabeth's spirit got them confused. Although I'm pretty sure JD wouldn't have liked hearing that. Maybe not Luke, either.

I stood there while he went out the door. I waited a few minutes longer until I heard the tires crunch on the gravel drive, followed by silence as the car moved onto the pavement. I went into the kitchen and filled one white mug with coffee. There was a loaf of bread and a jar of jam in the fridge, but I decided to wait for JD before I experimented with attempting to make toast in the oven.

I carried my coffee out to the porch. The boards were soaking wet, but I tested the seat of one of the wicker chairs and it was dry, so I sat down. As the sun quickly won out over the clouds, the humidity lingered, and the dirt and plants developed a steamy look.

After a few minutes, JD came out carrying his mug. He sat down and took a sip. It amazes me that he doesn't need to blow on his coffee to pretend he's cooling it, or wait for it to actually cool like I do. He lets it run across his tongue and down his throat and never seems to complain about scalding that tender skin.

The front door was on the opposite side of the house from where we sat, but it looked as if that entrance was rarely used since the parking area was on the kitchen side of the house. There was also a set of windowed double doors that opened from the living room onto the side section of the porch that faced the garden where Luke had discovered Elizabeth's body.

"I was thinking ..." JD said. He slurped his coffee. "I was thinking about ..." He took another slurp.

Hard as it was, I waited for him to finish his thought before I burst in with what was on my mind. He doesn't often have trouble finishing his thoughts, so the more he hesitated, the more curious I became.

"I'm worried that the cops haven't found anyone else to consider besides Luke."

I nodded. Luke hadn't seemed that concerned when he strolled out the front door. Of course, he knew whether or not he'd actually killed Elizabeth. He was the only person on earth who knew that for sure. And if he knew he hadn't done it, I suppose there wasn't anything for him to worry about. He was more angry about the inconvenience, the insult of being questioned.

"Not that they didn't comb the yard for every single strand of hair and scrap of fabric, but I wonder if we should look around. We'd see things with a different eye, don't you think?"

"Definitely with a different eye." I'm sure he meant his eye would see his brother as innocent, so he'd be looking for things to make Luke look better. I still wasn't really sure what kind of eye I had on the matter. I didn't want to think Luke was a killer, and in my heart I didn't think he was, but there was a very soft whisper of doubt. The whisper that tells you

— How well do you really know him? Not at all, really. And — *Who knows what it would take to push someone to the edge.* And — *Sometimes, things just get out of control.*

He drank the rest of his coffee in a few large gulps. Watching him make my throat burn. He set the mug on the porch. "Will you help me look?"

"I really can't believe the police would have missed anything."

"I know, but I feel like I have to do something. I can't sit here and hope for the best. And he has a big mouth, who knows what he'll say to shoot himself in the foot."

"If he didn't do anything, how can he shoot himself in the foot?"

He stood. "You don't believe him, do you? You think my brother is a killer?"

"No. I just don't see how he can shoot himself in the foot if he's innocent."

"The way you say it makes it sound like you think he's not."

"It doesn't sound like anything." I sipped some coffee. The air was getting warmer. The scent of cut grass and eucalyptus wafted across the porch. On the heels of those smells, was the odor of damp earth. As soon as I noticed it, my hands got cold and all I could feel was the terror from the night before.

I stood and took a step closer to him. I leaned my head against his chest. "I don't think your brother is a killer. I just didn't understand your point. Why you're worried about him talking to the police. It should be no big deal."

"They're gunning for him."

"I suppose."

"They are."

"What do you think we'd find?" I didn't expect him to have a suggestion, I had the feeling he wanted to search the yard because he couldn't think of anything else to do. I was happy to do it with him, even if it was a waste of time. It was better than having his mind wander off to think about the ghost we'd seen and decide to bring it up to Lavender so she could "help" us get in touch. I didn't want to ever see her again. And despite my mind telling me it was absurd, I was worried she had the potential to hurt JD.

I swallowed the rest of my coffee. JD took my mug. He bent down and picked up his with the same hand. He went to the screen door, opened it, and we went inside. We left the mugs on the counter and walked through the living room to the side porch without stopping to discuss the fact that we appeared to be starting our search right that minute.

The porch outside the living room was narrower, more like a porch you see on newer homes in Silicon Valley. This was a farmhouse that had been slightly modernized, and the wide porches on the other sides made it feel like it came from a quieter, more relaxing era. Although I'm sure that's a myth — the idea that time periods without technology and without every person having their own car, everyone sitting around on the wide porch, were somehow more relaxing. Life hasn't changed, just the tools we use.

Flowering shrubs grew along the edge of the porch, reaching almost to the roof line. They were covered with tiny buds, a hint of red or white poking out of the tip, announcing all the blossoms that would be coming soon. We walked down the three steps into the yard, which was as damp and squishy as it looked. Water pooled up over our feet.

There was nothing in the area that hinted someone had died there. It looked tranquil and full of life, as if she'd evaporated from the earth and everything grew over the spot where she'd died.

Beyond the walled-off garden was the empty strip of dirt. Directly in front of us was a large expanse of grass, longish in some spots, but cut short in others, as if Luke had attempted to mow it but didn't want to take the time to trim every blade. The yard sloped down and a barbed wire fence separated it from the next piece of property.

"We should get Lavender to help us," JD said.

"Why?"

"Maybe she'll sense something, get a hint of where to look."

"Why would she sense something we wouldn't? The ghost appeared to us."

"But Lavender seems to know how to get them to appear, rather than just waiting around."

"You don't know that. She *said* she could."

"Why are you pissed off? I thought we were trying to

figure out what's going on?"

"We are," I said. "I just don't like you bringing her up, as if my experiences, are somehow inadequate."

After that, we were quiet for several minutes, walking aimlessly around the yard, the soles of our flip-flops squeaking on the wet grass. I went back to the dirt area. A thin bamboo stake was lying on the ground. I picked it up and poked around in the dirt. It looked freshly disturbed, so I couldn't imagine there was anything interesting the cops had left behind, but I continued digging around anyway. I couldn't understand why JD was bugging me about Lavender. He didn't really grasp how she'd been with me. It was insulting, and it hurt a little bit, that he thought she had some kind of magic or some special tricks or techniques. And there was nothing to hint that she did. She was just a curious person, trying too hard to be an expert and wishing too much that she could command ghosts to appear and speak to her so she'd be … what? So she'd be valuable, or special?

It was fun poking at the mud. It made me feel like a little kid and I almost wanted to jump in it. I stabbed the bamboo into the ground, flipping pebbles out of the dirt where the rain had pushed them into little pockets of muck. JD was on the opposite side of the yard, looking down at his feet, scuffing through the grass. I had no idea what we were looking for and it was starting to feel even more pointless and foolish. I had no doubt the police had been very thorough.

I stopped and looked across the open space at the

farmhouse perched on the hill. It was so peaceful, so quiet. It was hard to imagine someone getting stabbed, although easy to imagine that no one had been around to witness it.

Elizabeth's ghost, assuming that's who it was, had been icy cold. I wondered if that meant anything. The day was moist and warm, definitely spring. A few feet in front of me, several shoots of unidentifiable plants poked their sharp heads out of the ground. They looked so green, so determined, so full of life. If Luke had killed her, wouldn't he have dug a deep hole in the garden area to bury her body? Surely the police would consider that. Maybe it had been the guys who helped Elizabeth empty his house. I couldn't see why they would kill her, but guys who helped with a project like that weren't likely to be the most admirable.

I glanced at JD again. He'd stopped walking, given up completely, and stood looking up at the line of eucalyptus trees on the hill. "Madison!" His voice was low, but urgent.

I pulled my stick out of the mud and walked toward him.

"Careful. Slow down."

"What is it?"

"Shhh."

I crept closer, looking at the trees, pale trunks and leaves the color of sage.

"There's a kangaroo out there."

I dropped my stick and tried to walk fast but cautiously to where he stood. It was tricky, not making any sudden moves, but getting there ASAP. If I got to see a wild kangaroo, it would make me feel like I was on vacation in an exotic place. Between Lavender and the murder and the ghost, the trip had turned into the furthest thing from a vacation I could think of. Every so often, I almost forgot I was in Australia.

I stood next to JD. He took my hand and we waited, gazing at the trees, hardly breathing.

"There," he whispered. He pointed toward the top of the hill.

I shifted my gaze. It's so hard to follow someone's directions when they're pointing. From their perspective, their fingertip is practically touching the object, yet it's so far away, they could be indicating an area half a mile wide. I squinted, as if that would help me zero in on the same spot he was looking at.

Something moved. I held my breath. From behind a tree so narrow I was surprised it could conceal the animal's body, a kangaroo hopped into the clearing. It was small, not one of the six-foot-tall ones you've seen on YouTube, shoving a man into a lake. It looked to be about the size of a ten-year-old child. It took a single hop and paused again. It didn't look in our direction, but I wondered if it heard us, or smelled us, or if it always proceeded with such caution. It looked around, ears stiff, twitching, determined to pick up the crunch of gravel or the sound of a human voice.

We stared for several more minutes while it waited, perhaps knowing on some level it had been seen. I could feel my cheeks squishing into a smile and I saw from the corner of my eye that JD was grinning too. What is it about unfamiliar wildlife that makes us so happy? I don't necessarily feel that way when I see a squirrel run through the church garden, or birds sitting on the electrical wires or swooping from tree to roof. They're around all the time. But when I'm hiking and I see a deer or rabbit, I get all excited. And a kangaroo was something new altogether. I didn't recall if I'd ever seen one at the zoo. During our time in Australia, we planned to visit a wildlife preserve, and I was sure I'd see so many, they'd seem as prevalent as rabbits. But watching one out and about, living its life as happily as a squirrel lives in Silicon Valley, made me feel like I was truly in a completely different place.

After several more minutes, it turned and hopped out of sight.

JD kept hold of my hand. "What were you digging around for?"

"Nothing. Just playing in the mud."

He laughed, although it sounded rote.

"What are we doing?" I said.

"I don't know. I just thought we had to give it a shot. Do you want to quit?"

"Maybe her ghost is here. You never know what might happen."

He squeezed my hand and still didn't let go. I turned back toward the garden area and tugged him after me. I picked up the bamboo stake and poked at the dirt again.

JD let go of my hand. He walked toward the house and sat

on the porch steps. I dragged my stick through the dirt and I walked around the perimeter. At the corner furthest from the house there was a wood stake I hadn't seen earlier because it was pressed so far into the ground that only an inch or so was visible, and it was caked with mud, making it difficult to see unless you were standing right on top of it. I glanced back and saw there were buried wood stakes at all four corners of the plot and along both sides.

JD was still on the steps, his arms crossed on his knees. He was bent over, pressing his head against his wrists.

"Hey!" I said.

He looked up.

"I could use a smoke. Do you mind getting …"

"Sure." He got up and opened the French door as if he couldn't wait to get away from the yard, mocking him that there was nothing to be found.

I popped out a few more pebbles. It was fun, almost like popping the bubbles in plastic wrap. Next to the fourth pebble was a seashell, the perfectly formed kind like a miniature conch shell. I dug that out and bent to pick it up. Mud stuck to my cuticles and got behind my fingernails. I wiped the shell with my thumb but only succeeded in smearing mud all over its curves and bumps. Even though it was muddy, I put it in my pocket. My first Australian shell, although it was about seventy miles from the ocean.

JD came out with two cigarettes. He lit one for each of us and then returned to his spot on the steps.

I walked back to the area where I'd found the seashell. I continued poking around to see if there were any more shells. I knew I'd be looking for them on beaches later, but it was kind of fun finding them buried in the mud. I stabbed the stick at the dirt again. As I started to pull it out, it caught on some kind of fiber. I dropped my cigarette in the mud and squished it out even though it was only half gone.

I pulled harder on the stick, thinking I'd toss it to the side, but it was still caught. Suddenly it came free. There was mud-caked hair wound around the tip and a Barbie doll head dangled off the end.

"What the hell is that?"

I hadn't noticed JD get up from his spot on the steps, hadn't been aware of him walking across the yard. He stood right behind me, looking over my shoulder. I lifted the stick so he could see.

"I wonder how long that's been there?"

I dragged the stick along the ground, but the hair just tangled further. The head bobbed along after it and I saw the back was sliced open. I bent over and yanked it off the end of the stick. Tucked inside the plastic head was a diamond ring. I pulled it out and held it up to JD.

"That's weird," he said.

"Definitely."

"What does it mean?"

"I wonder if we shouldn't have touched it? Should we call the police?"

"For what, a doll head?"

"I guess if it was buried it wouldn't have anything to do with Elizabeth."

"It's probably from some kid who lived here before," JD said.

"Except for the ring."

"Yeah."

I dropped the stick where I stood and we walked to the porch, the doll head swinging from my fingers. JD carried the ring.

"Let's ask Luke," he said. "Maybe he knows the child who buried it and it has nothing to do with Elizabeth. Or maybe it was there long before he moved in."

"Okay." The plastic face looked almost new. I was sure it hadn't been there very long.

JD AND I had been sitting at the kitchen table staring at the Barbie head for a long time when Luke pulled into the gravel parking area.

The screen door clattered shut behind him. He walked to the fridge, yanked it open, and pulled out a beer. He twisted off the cap, set it on the counter, and took a long swallow. His Adam's apple bobbed as the liquid flowed down his throat. He turned and looked at the table and its Barbie centerpiece. "What's that?"

"What did the cops ask you?" JD said.

"Same old shit."

"Like?"

"How did I think she ended up in my yard—was I angry with her—did I ever hit her—if I didn't kill her, why was she in my yard—why would someone kill her in my yard?"

"Oh." JD put his hand on his ponytail as if he was checking its position at the base of his skull.

"So what's the doll head?"

"Are they questioning anyone else yet?" JD said.

"Who knows."

JD put one finger on the end of the doll's hair and pulled it across the table.

"You gonna tell me why you have a doll head in the middle of my table or not?" Luke pulled out a chair and sat down. He wriggled the chair back, kicked off his flip-flops, and propped his heels on the edge of the table.

It was not pleasant, looking at the grayish film smeared across the bottom of his feet. I turned slightly. The ring inside the left front pocket of my jeans pressed against my hip bone. I might have imagined it, but it felt cold, as if the diamond was a tiny cube of ice. Of course, if it was, it would be melting in my pocket. But still, that's what it made me think of. "We found it buried in your garden. It had …" I slid two fingers into my pocket.

"What garden?"

JD lifted the head and swung it by its hair. He let go and it fell, bouncing across the table in my direction. He laughed, but he didn't sound amused, sort of sickened.

"That patch of dirt," I said.

JD picked up the head and bounced it on the table again.

Luke looked at him. "Quit bouncing that thing. It gives me the heebie jeebies." He looked at me. "It was full of zucchini plants and the zucchini was really tough so I figured the plants had run their course. I dug it up. There were some other things in there, but whatever they used to be, they weren't producing any more vegetables."

"This was inside the head." I put the ring on the table.

He stared at the ring. "Huh. I figured she took it along with everything else."

"You bought her a ring?" JD said.

"Hell no. that was part of the problem. I had that from a long time ago when I was all gummed up over that girl, Janine. Remember?"

JD nodded.

I waited, but finally I figured I wasn't going to hear about Janine. Maybe it didn't matter.

"I bought that ring for her. It was in my drawer for years." He drank some beer and set the bottle on the table.

"And?"

"Elizabeth found it. She assumed it was for her."

"Uh oh," I said.

Luke winked at me, then laughed. He took another swallow of beer. "I told her, *not even close*. She was pissed. So then when she found out about Lavender. Well …" He swept his arm around the room at the empty cabinets and blank walls.

"You said those words? *Not even close?*" The Barbie head was a few inches from my fingertips. I grabbed it and stuffed the ring inside. "that's harsh."

"I'd only known her four or five weeks. She was way out of line."

"Still," I said.

He laughed. "I know. It was harsh, but she asked for it."

I felt a sliver of her fury. It was logical that a woman who found a diamond ring in a drawer, even if she hadn't known the guy long, might think it was for her. He was almost cruel in his attitude. I could see why she wanted to hurt him back. And yet, hadn't that been her, standing in our room last night, whispering in that chilling breath that she'd come back for Luke, that she couldn't be without him?

Luke finished his beer. "Lavender's coming over in a few hours. Where do you want to go for dinner?"

"You tell us," JD said.

I wanted to finish the conversation, but maybe there wasn't anything else to talk about. "What about the head? Who do you think put it there?"

"Elizabeth. Obviously."

"Well, sure." I felt a bit stupid. He'd already said he thought she'd taken the ring with all his other stuff. "But why?"

"Who knows?"

"Maybe it was some kind of message," JD said.

"Oh, I'm sure it's some kind of message," I said.

Both guys laughed.

"I'm just wondering what kind of message." I looked at Luke. "Does it make sense to you?"

"I'm not going to try to make sense out of anything she did. It's nothing but a hollow head." Luke got up and went to the fridge. "Want a beer?"

JD nodded.

Luke twisted the caps off and handed a beer to JD.

"I'm not trying to be nosey," I said. "But you don't seem very curious. Shouldn't we give it to the cops? Don't you want to find out who did it so they'll leave you alone?"

"I suppose. I don't see how the doll head will change anything."

"We can just go by the police station and give them the head and tell them we found it."

"They'll probably be pissed you touched it. And then they'll want to know who the ring belongs to and just ask me more questions."

"Well we can't not tell them," I said.

He shrugged. "Can we stop talking about it? I'm fried from all the questions." He laughed and winked at me. "How come you sound like a cop when you start asking questions?"

JD smiled. He picked up the head and bounced it across the table at Luke.

Luke grabbed it and wrapped his hand around it. The mud-encrusted hair stuck out between his thumb and forefinger. "I thought Madison was going to get in touch with Elizabeth's ghost, find out who killed her, and we could set the cops on the right track."

I opened my mouth, annoyed that he refused to listen to what I'd said. "I told you ..."

"I know, I know," Luke said.

I glanced at JD to see whether his lips were twitching, anxious to blurt out what we'd experienced during the night. His face was closed, as if a sheet of plastic had been drawn across it. There was a flicker of pity as he glanced at me. He knew I was annoyed, so he wasn't going to mention the ghost. Not yet.

Luke leaned on the table. His eyes were dilated, pleading. "I could really use your help. Why do you think they sometimes appear and other times they don't?"

"I have no idea," I said.

He still held the doll head in his hand, his fist clenched around it.

"Why don't you quit hassling Madison," JD said. "Your girlfriend knows all about the spirit world. She chats up dead people all the time. Why don't you ask her?"

"Like you said, she chats them up. There's something phony about it. Madison is the real deal. You can tell just by looking at her. Those green eyes, that little Zen Mona Lisa smile."

My face got hot, although I don't think I actually blushed, because surely Luke would have commented on that.

JD reached over, scooped away my hair, and put his hand on the back of my neck. His fingers were warm and firm and the pressure of his hand eased the faint buzzing in my head that had been there since I woke up.

"Why are you with her if you think she's phony?" I said.

"Isn't it obvious? She's hot." He released the doll head as if it was too hot to keep wrapped inside his hand.

"You'd probably have more luck with love if hot wasn't your main criteria," JD said.

"Who said I want love?"

JD smirked. "Fair enough. But I don't see how you can be with someone if you don't respect the focal point of her life. She says she can communicate with spirits and she does it all the time. Has she brought it up? Have you even asked her?"

"No."

"Why not?"

"I told you, sometimes she just comes across like one of those people that's trying to dupe you."

I leaned my elbows on the table. "Do people pay her to communicate with the dead?"

"I don't think so."

"Then why …"

Before I could finish, JD interrupted me. "Why don't you ask? What would it hurt? Maybe between her and Madison they could do something to help."

I laughed. "Really? You really think that's a good idea."

"It doesn't sound like the police are planning to let up any time soon. Until they have another suspect, they're going to keep at him."

"It's their job to find other suspects," I said. There was no way I was going to do anything with Lavender regarding ghosts. And I would have thought after the night before, the brutal cold, and the desire of Elizabeth to come back for Luke, that JD would want to run as far as he could in the other direction. "We found the Barbie head, maybe that will help them."

"We have to figure out a way to do something," JD said.

I really didn't think we had to do anything, but it wasn't my brother, so I kept my mouth shut.

Eight

AFTER EATING HAM sandwiches with mayo and no lettuce and no tomato because Luke forgot to buy those, JD and I took a nap. At first I was a little nervous about sleeping in that room, but once I got under the blankets it was warm and cozy and the cotton drapes allowed a decent amount of light to filter through, making the room friendlier. As I settled down, Elizabeth's ghost started to seem like a bad dream. And since JD and I hadn't talked about it much, that added to the dream-like quality.

I thought eventually we would tell Luke, but right then, there didn't seem to be anything to gain. I worried a little that if the ghost was bent on taking him with her that not telling Luke was a betrayal, one that could threaten his life. But most of my brain didn't really believe that could happen, so it kept me from feeling as if I absolutely had to let him know. Clearly JD agreed.

As my brain sank into that surreal state where you're sort

of awake, but your thoughts are drifting to nonsense, it occurred to me I might be really naive in not believing that terrifying, ice-like apparition wasn't capable of hurting Luke. Then I fell asleep.

I dreamt I was floating near the arctic circle on a raft constructed of icicles. I drifted past glistening icebergs, so white they made my eyes burn. A few of them were transparent, and various people I knew were frozen inside, although they didn't look dead. They moved slightly, begging me to rescue them. I had no tools with me, and there was no way I could help them.

The sound of Lavender's voice, loud and authoritative, woke me from the dream. For the first half second, I was glad to hear her, relieved to escape the helplessness of seeing everyone I cared about — JD, my best friend Renee, Pastor Joe, Cindee, Kate, and even Fred, the church gardener who had been my friend for a brief time, but was now dead — immobilized in ice.

I couldn't make out what Lavender was saying, but she was certainly doing all the talking. There was hardly a pause to the flow of words coming out of her mouth.

I opened my eyes and turned toward JD's side of the bed. It was empty. I sat up. There was a pinched feeling in my heart. It's silly, I know, but for some reason, having him get up without me seemed like a betrayal — it's that feeling you get when you're staying with other people and they all get up in the morning before you and when you join them, you know you've missed out, that you're no longer part of the group. I don't know where that vulnerable feeling comes from, and I wonder if it's just me. That's the way it is with a lot of things. We're all supposed to be the same, our common humanity and all that. Every human being experiences love and hate and jealousy and hunger and happiness and longing. So it's easy to think your specific feelings are common, but who really knows unless you sit down and inspect each emotion under a microscope and compare with others. And not just one or two others, but a decent sample size.

I crept out of bed, pulled the quilt up, and slapped the pillows to smooth them out. I ran the water in the bathroom sink and splashed cold water on my cheeks and eyes, trying not to get it in my hair so I didn't go out there looking like I had sweat all along my hairline. The brush slid through my hair, so I guess I hadn't done much twisting and turning during my nap. The noises coming from my belly were loud, insistent, and probably complaining because we had Doritos with our ham sandwiches and they have a way of making me really hungry. All chips do that. I can't stop eating them, feel really full when I'm done, and two hours later, I'm starving.

I went out to the porch. Lavender and JD sat in the wicker chairs and Luke sat on the floor, leaning against a post. They were all drinking beer.

"Did you have a nice sleep?" Lavender said. She wasn't wearing a hat, for once. Her hair was woven into an elaborate and expert French braid. Her sundress was so low cut she had to tug at the straps to pull it back into place when she turned to inquire about my sleep. Then she had to pull at the hem to keep it from creeping further up her legs.

"Yes."

"Why are you two so tired?" she said. "You should be past jet lag by now."

"We didn't sleep much last night." JD stood. "You can have my chair." I settled into the chair, then wished I'd grabbed a bottle of water to settle the grumbling in my stomach. Maybe it was in sync with my brain, shouting out another topic of conversation to keep JD from telling them about the ghost. Despite being on vacation, not being at work, not cooking, having all this free time, I felt like I hadn't had a single second to really think about the ghost, and I wasn't even sure why JD and I hadn't talked about it. I suppose he hadn't brought it up because he was embarrassed that he'd been so scared. But why hadn't I? Was I afraid, or was it something else? If it was I couldn't figure out what. Maybe we were just numb.

"Sounds like it's dinner time," Luke said.

I laughed.

"There's a pub we like — Wollombi Tavern. They have great burgers and lots of sausages. Does that sound good?"

"The name alone makes it sound interesting," JD said. "I'm starving too." He swallowed the rest of his beer.

THE PUB WAS dark, even for a pub. Our table was near the side of the room, designed for clusters of people to stand around, requiring tall stools if you wanted to sit. Luckily the stools had backs, so it would comfortable for a whole meal. The wood of the table was rough and natural looking, not like pubs or bars at home where often the wood is coated with resin, creating glossy tabletops that look more like plastic than wood. Rock music played in the background, but it was low enough that it was easy to talk without having to shout and keep asking *what?* all the time.

Luke went to the bar and came back with three beers and a bottle of Pellegrino.

I'm used to being the odd girl out, not drinking alcohol, but for some reason I was more aware of it because it was happening so often. At home I might go out with friends once every few weeks, so I'm not faced with my outsider status on a daily, sometimes twice daily, basis like I was here.

All of us ordered burgers. Lavender wanted a basket of fried calamari, so we ordered that too. As we nibbled the fried stuff, we talked about movies we'd seen, TV shows we liked, and food. It's funny how much people like to talk about food. Even sitting there eating, we were talking about other pubs, and other times we'd eaten out, and where we'd had the best burger ever.

Lavender asked how we were liking Australia and we gushed on. It wasn't fake. Despite murder and a terrifying ghost, it was a fantastic place.

I loved Sydney and everyone was so nice. Even Lavender, although she annoyed me on several levels, was friendly. She seemed honestly glad to be with us.

"We saw a kangaroo this morning," JD said.

"That's not hard to do." Luke grabbed a piece of calamari and popped it into his mouth. He seemed to swallow it without chewing. He followed the calamari ring with a quick hit of beer.

"Do you see them all the time?" I said.

"There are more than twice as many kangaroos as there are people in Australia," Luke said.

"Really?"

He was smirking so I couldn't tell if he was making it up.

"Twenty-two million human beings, 58 million kangaroos."

I wondered where they all were, there must be areas where hundreds or thousands are hanging out.

Lavender asked when we were going to the wildlife preserve and we talked about our schedule for the rest of the week and our plans for the Barrier Reef.

About halfway through my burger, I had to pee. I climbed down from my chair.

"I'll go with you," Lavender said.

She slithered off her chair and tugged her dress — up in front, down at the sides.

"I can find it."

"I need to go too."

I started off toward the bar. Lavender trotted behind me. I really don't like socializing in restrooms, even though most women seem to enjoy it, comparing lip colors or gossiping about their dates while they wash their hands and comb their hair.

Sure enough, while I was smearing soap around my hands, Lavender caught my eye in the mirror. "JD said you saw her ghost."

I felt like I'd been punched in the stomach. I held my hands under the water. I adjusted the faucet so more hot water came out.

"Did you hear me?"

"I heard you," I said.

"So tell me what happened."

"It sounds like JD already did."

She laughed. "You know guys. Minimal information, unless it's about their rugby team or their job."

"We should get back to dinner."

"Don't be mad. He told us about it while you were taking your nap. Luke was talking about how he gets uncontrollable chills, that he's felt some kind of presence whenever he goes into his bedroom. Then JD told us what happened."

I reached for a paper towel and dried my hands.

"What's wrong with you?"

"Nothing."

"You're cold. Are you this way with everyone? You can be a bit of a bitch."

"Because I don't want to stand in a public bathroom and chat while two good-looking guys are waiting for us to finish dinner, that makes me a bitch?"

She ran her hands over her hair, her fingers danced across the strands of her braid, checking to see if it was securely in place. She let her arms fall to her sides. "I'm curious about the ghost. You're acting like I'm asking about your sex life."

"We're in the middle of dinner. This isn't the right time."

"But see, if we weren't eating dinner, you'd have another excuse. You don't want to tell me about it at all."

"How do you know what I'd do?"

"You have this shield around you."

It was clear she thought a sharp wound would produce the information she was looking for. She hoped I'd get defensive and words would pour out of my mouth. That probably works with some people.

"Aren't you going to answer me?"

I pulled a tiny bottle of jasmine-scented hand cream out of my purse and squeezed a drop into my palm. I spread it across my skin. "I want to finish my dinner. But you're right about one thing, I don't have anything more to say about the ghost than what JD told you."

"You didn't know he told us, did you?"

There was no point in lying. Although it made me feel as if she'd inserted the thin blade of a knife between me and JD, cutting us away from each other. She knew that would make me upset, but I refused to let her see that. Letting her see would drive the blade in deeper. "No."

"You wanted to keep it a secret. You're angry at him."

"No, I'm not."

"You're lying."

If it wasn't for the lotion smeared across my hands, I might have slapped her. "I'm going back to the table." I finished rubbing in the lotion. Before I could pull open the door, she grabbed the strap of my bag and yanked it. The leather bit into my shoulder. "Let go of me."

"Please wait. I need to tell you something."

My bag slapped against my hip as she let go of it. I settled it in place and waited, my hand still on the door handle.

"Ghosts are just like human beings. It's not like a person becomes pure and good by dying."

"I know that. Trust me."

"You have to be on your guard. They can have their own agendas."

"What's your point?"

"I think we should team up. It's not just because I want Luke to believe me."

"Then what is it?"

"Now that I know she's haunting his home, we need to have a plan."

"A plan?"

"JD said she was scary."

It hurt that he'd given her so much information. Encountering the ghost had been a private battle that he and I fought together, and now he'd invited Lavender into our bedroom, into an experience that we hadn't even talked about. It was possible she knew more about his reaction than

I did. I was a confusing mix of angry and hurt and filled with doubt about why he would rather talk to her than to me, his girlfriend, and the person who was actually there. In fact, in some ways, I felt as if I'd protected him from whatever the spirit wanted, putting myself over him, warming him up. Maybe the spirit was actually going to whisk him away and the heat of my skin and fighting my way to him despite the numbness flooding through my body had prevented that from happening. "She was very scary. But I don't understand why you think we need to team up, except for your own issues with Luke. We don't need a plan." I laughed. The idea of having a documented plan to approach a ghost was a perfect illustration of the differences between us.

"I just think two are better than one."

"Really? There were two of us — JD and I. that didn't seem to help. I hope I don't ever see her again. Only three more days, so the odds are in my favor."

"She'll be back. She wants something."

"We should get back to dinner."

"Why don't you want to help me? This is what I mean about you being cold. We're dating twin brothers. I thought we'd be friends."

"I live on the other side of the world."

"The world has shrunk to a Facebook page."

"True."

"Do you want Luke to go to prison?"

"I'm sure that won't happen."

"That's not how it's looking right now."

"They're not going to arrest him unless they have evidence, and if he didn't do it, what kind of evidence can they find?"

She moved closer. Her breath was cool and scented with mint, as if she'd just brushed her teeth. It was a surprising odor in the midst of a dinner of beef and fried foods and beer. Possibly she'd been sucking a mint while she washed her hands, swallowing it quickly before she started in with her questions and revelations. "JD said she had him confused with Luke. Do you want him to die?"

"That's a terrible thing to say. He's not going to die."

"How do you know? You said she was frightening."

"Ghosts don't kill people."

"That shows how little you really know. You don't have the background, the training that I have. You've had your few encounters, glimpses of something from beyond the grave, but you're no expert."

"I never said I was."

"You should be scared. You don't know what you're messing with."

"I really don't think ghosts kill people."

"You're wrong. Sure, it might be medically explained as an aneurism or, someone dying of a broken heart soon after their mate passes on. But more often than you'd think, it's a ghost coming back for a person they want."

The scent of mint had faded, and now the beer was more prevalent. I took a step back. "Are we going to eat dinner, or are we going to let the server clear it all away and leave JD and Luke wondering if we ditched them?"

She looped her arm around mine and pulled me close. "Sure. Let's go back. We can talk more later. Maybe while the boys drink beer and reminisce." She squeezed my arm. "Girl time."

We left the restroom and made our way past clusters of people drinking beer, standing behind others seated at tables, reaching over their heads to grab fries or wings, dribbling thin streams of beer on their arms as they leaned forward. No one seemed to mind the crowding and the mess and the noise. It was so loud I couldn't hear what Lavender was whispering in my ear.

AN HOUR LATER we were still nibbling at bits of fries and listening to JD and Luke try to one-up each other with stories of their bad teenaged behavior. I sipped an iced coffee while they lapped at their beers. Every so often, my thoughts wandered off to Lavender's promise that we'd talk later, and whether or not I'd play the gracious guest or tell her to go ghost hunting on her own.

I couldn't stop thinking about how Lavender tried to scare me into thinking JD might die. What kind of person deliberately tries to frighten someone, especially someone she supposedly wants to become friends with? Even if I lived in Australia, even if I thought we would visit his brother regularly, Lavender was not the person I'd pick for a friend.

I'm not trying to be rude or snobbish, but she was too bizarre and confusing. It seemed like someone had taken her brain and shaken it and all the pieces were in an unsorted heap. Equally off-putting, she had to be right all the time. Even if you think you're always right, it's good to tone it down once in a while.

Luke definitely won the *I'm badder than you* wrestling match. JD made an awesome push, telling stories of pranks that ranged from semi-harmless ones like putting an impressive collection of dead flies in his brother's backpack to stealing firewood from the neighbors. Luke's stories made him sound a bit more like a minor thug, and I wondered again if I was being too quick to look at his charming smile, his resemblance to JD, and his more or less good nature and assume he could never stab someone, even in a rage.

When he was twelve, Luke had helped JD steal a log here and there from their neighbor's wood pile. But once, when JD went inside, settling down to scribble out math problems while he watched MTV, Luke snuck back to the side of the decrepit two-bedroom house next door — although decrepit wasn't how he described it. He rolled up tubes of newspaper, lit the ends on fire, shoved them into the wood pile, and ran. Luckily for the neighbors, they were home, smelled the smoke, and the fire truck arrived promptly. Luke's rationale was that he and JD would be caught if the missing wood was noticed. His intervention made a few missing logs irrelevant.

I noticed JD wasn't laughing with the same abandon as

Luke. The tip of his nose was red, maybe from beer, maybe from something else, because the way he stared past me, as if he was looking into the past, made me think he hadn't realized until that moment what his brother had done.

The final story starred Luke at the age of nineteen. JD had gone off to college and Luke was working as a detailer at a Chevy dealership. One Saturday afternoon he'd pocketed the keys for a new Corvette that was in for service. Because of the dealership's haphazard method of hanging keys in a box that was left unlocked as often as it was locked, the manager was never able to narrow down who had taken the Corvette racing through the nearby foothills, hitting speeds of ninety on a two-lane straightaway, squealing tires around curves. The car wasn't damaged, but the manager knew it had been borrowed. Luke was sure the manager knew he'd done it, but couldn't prove anything, which Luke found entertaining. Knowing the manager was watching him while Luke stared back without fear, gave him more pleasure than the joy ride. He was almost giggling, he was so impressed with himself.

To me, the story of the fire was scarier than the temporary theft.

Nine

THERE WAS NO girl time after all. During the ten-minute drive back to Luke's place, Lavender slumped over in the back seat, her head on my shoulder. Her hair reeked of a sharp, floral scent. Underneath that was still the subtle scent of mint, cool and belying all the beer. She had to be popping peppermints into her mouth between every glass.

Luke helped her into the house then went out to her car to get her overnight case and sleeping bag. Her face was blank, not offering any hint as to how she felt about dragging a sleeping bag to her boyfriend's house, spreading it out on the hardwood floor while his brother and girlfriend snuggled into a comfy bed. No wonder she couldn't stop talking about contacting Elizabeth's ghost. She couldn't visit her boyfriend without being slapped in the face by the results of the rage he'd had managed to elicit.

For a long time I tried to sleep, but couldn't manage to drift even close to the edge of unconsciousness. I don't know if it was caffeine or apprehension that the minute I let my mind fall into another realm, a ghost would appear, her icy fingers reaching around my boyfriend's heart. Mixed with that fear was anger at Lavender for putting those thoughts in my head, working so hard to make sure I was frightened. I drink iced or hot coffee in the evenings fairly often, so I'm pretty sure my wakefulness was not from caffeine.

After an hour or more of lying on my back, staring at the darkness, feeling JD breathe with occasional small snorts, I got up. I dug around in my purse until my fingers bumped against my box of cigarettes and the metallic case of my lighter. Turning the stiff bedroom doorknob without giving off a squeak or clicks took quite a long time. I left the door partially open and walked past the other bedrooms, two bodies breathing silently in the last one, and through the kitchen. The linoleum was like a frozen lake on the bottoms of my feet. An empty beer bottle sat on the table, its amber glass reflecting moonlight. I grabbed it to use as an ashtray.

The night air was muggy and breathless, so only the screen door was closed. It didn't have a lock, which made me anxious, knowing we were sleeping in an unprotected house. Sure, it was in a rural area, but a woman had been murdered. Of course, the greatest danger we faced now came from beyond the grave, a threat undeterred by locks, so maybe it didn't matter.

I settled on one of the wicker chairs. When I snapped the lighter with a satisfying click, the flame shot up, thin and straight. I don't know why the clicks of lighters and locks and the sound of pot lids settling into place and all those other snug little noises are so comforting. Maybe they hint that things are working as they should, making me feel secure, when really, the world is anything but secure.

I dropped the lighter into the small bowl formed by my nightshirt as I sat cross-legged, my knees propped up high since there wasn't enough room to sit properly cross-legged. I held the beer bottle in my left hand and my cigarette in my right. The smoke slipped out through my lips and hung in the air as if it was waiting for me to tell it to leave. Slowly it faded into nothing and the space around me was empty until I let out another stream.

The smoke calmed me, as always, stopped my brain from turning over every word Lavender had said in the women's restroom, every grin and cocked eyebrow of Luke's as he told his stories, and every grimace from JD as he realized he shouldn't have started with the stories. Luke's stories had an edge like a razor blade that made you want to listen, but left you uncomfortable, knowing there was nothing to laugh about.

I was getting more and more impatient, waiting for my vacation to start. I felt a little selfish for thinking that way. After all, it wasn't Luke's fault a woman's body had been found in his yard. Or maybe it was. I felt guilty for the doubts that kept circling back through my mind. It was impossible to think he was capable of murder, but I'd met other people I never would have guessed could take a life. No one really knows what they'll do until they're in a situation themselves. Maybe Elizabeth said something to hurt him, maybe she ... but what could a woman do that would make a man so crazed he'd grab a knife and plunge it into her ribs? That can happen if a man desperately loves a woman, if he wants to possess her, and she hurts him beyond sanity. I'm not saying I excuse it or accept it, I can just see how a person would lose his mind and do something like that. The problem is, a man like that most likely has already lost part of his mind.

But Luke didn't love Elizabeth. He'd never loved her.

A small part of me wanted her ghost to return. Now that I knew what to expect from her, it might be less frightening. Besides, she was after Luke, not me. And if she realized she'd mistaken JD for Luke, maybe she wouldn't bring that icy cold from the grave trying to drag us back after her. It's not that I'm immune to fear, but my curiosity wins out over my fears. Most of the time.

The glow of my cigarette was close to the filter. I dropped it into the beer bottle. It hissed softly and went dark. I set the bottle on the floor, uncrossed my legs, and leaned my head on the back of the chair. Wicker scratched at my neck and grabbed a strand of hair. I loosened my hair and pulled it over my shoulder. I thought about moving my chair out from under the porch so I could look up at the sky, but I was so comfortable, floating along on a cloud of smoke that I decided not to make the effort.

"I didn't know you smoked." Lavender's voice was soft, and for half a second I wondered if I'd imagined her speaking to me.

She stood behind the screen door. I heard her flick the switch for the kitchen light, but only a faint puddle spilled out to the porch. I didn't turn to look, didn't want to give her an opening to join me. Not that I could stop her, if that's what she wanted.

"I could use a smoke. I haven't had one in ages."

The door creaked open. She stepped outside. The hem of her nightgown drifted across my toes as she walked past. She sat in the other chair. "Do you mind sharing?"

"There's no way to answer without being rude."

"I'll take that as a *no*?"

"I don't mind sharing, but I was enjoying the quiet."

"We didn't get to have any girl time."

I handed her a cigarette. She put it in her mouth and I clicked my lighter. As it flared around the tip of her cigarette, her face turned yellow in the reflected glow. Even the whites of her eyes had a yellow tint for the few seconds the flame was burning through thin paper and tobacco. Then it was lit and I snapped the cover closed. She took a few rapid puffs as if she was trying to fill the air with smoke. She puffed a few more times, not inhaling. The smell of smoke was too tempting, and I'd only had two of my allotted three smokes a day. I pulled out a cigarette and lit it. While I drew in the first puff, I vowed that when JD and I arrived at Hamilton Island,

I would cut down to two a day. I'd been lying to myself, telling myself for years I was going to quit, and yet I hadn't reduced my daily limit since before I started working in the church office.

I'm so judgmental when other people are hypocritical, excusing themselves, flat-out lying, painting beautiful portraits of themselves in their own minds, yet I'm doing the same thing. I admit that I love smoking. I know it's bad for me — not just bad, deadly. Out of one side of my mouth I insist I'm cutting back and I'm going to quit. But when? When is the magical day going to arrive?

It could be that I don't really want to quit. That I'll never quit. I do love it. I'm honest about that, and I can't imagine letting go of the tranquil feeling of sitting still, as if the earth has stopped rotating, stopped flying around the sun in its mad, circular path that feels like it isn't moving at all, yet when winter keeps racing at you every year, you know it really is traveling so fast your breath catches in your throat.

Most people think cigarette smoke stinks. They think tobacco is disgusting. I know I'm a pariah. I know it isn't great for my breath. Maybe I needed to take up the peppermint habit like Lavender. I know all those things, know I'm filling my bloodstream with nicotine and my lungs with carcinogens. I've seen the photographs of cancer-riddled lungs, black and crusty, like something left on the grill too long, flaking off in sheets of charcoal. But I can't see it inside my own body. And it's a habit that is so much more than just nicotine addiction.

I started smoking after my parents were murdered. In a single day, I stepped out of my childhood and into adulthood. In the morning I was a teenager, my biggest worry an essay for my English Lit class. By evening I was old and disengaged from the world. All my insides had been scooped out like a Halloween pumpkin and I was nothing but an echoing shell — it needed to be filled with something. With my Aunt and Uncle taking over, my whole life changed. I was so beyond the ability to absorb what had happened — a single bullet hole in each of their foreheads. Cops. Detectives. The medical examiner. The house I'd lived in all my life disappearing from under my feet. A therapist. My Aunt insisting I'd be better off at school with a normal routine. But after fifteen years of being home schooled and only two weeks in a public high school, regular classrooms were the farthest thing possible from a *normal* routine.

My Aunt was not happy when she discovered I'd started smoking. It took her all of ninety seconds to sniff it out in my hair. She went through my purse and fished out the pack. She stood over the pristine white plastic liner of the kitchen trash can and, one by one, snapped each stick in half. The sound they made was like a whimper, a rustling of grass. To emphasize her point, she dropped them into the can one half stick at a time, letting me hear each one tap the plastic bag. After that, I bummed cigarettes from other kids. She yelled at me, she grounded me, she tried to shame me by telling me how disappointed my mother would be. Well my mother wasn't there to be disappointed, was she?

I will quit. I just don't know when.

Lavender took another puff of her cigarette. She coughed for several seconds. Finally she half-wheezed, "You're quiet."

"Nothing much to talk about. I came out here to relax so I can sleep."

"Me too. It was fun listening to the guys bond with each other."

I shrugged.

"What did you think of those stories?" Lavender said.

"It's interesting to hear what people did when they were kids."

"Luke was bad."

"I can't argue with that."

"I guess it's part of the attraction," she said. "Like we were saying before, he has that bad boy thing going."

"I've never understood that." I tapped the ash off my cigarette into the beer bottle.

"Hand me the bottle." Lavender put her hand on the arm of my chair, her fingers rubbed against the wicker, whispering on the woven strands like they were crawling toward me.

I touched the bottle to her fingertips and she grabbed it by the neck. She tapped her cigarette hard against the mouth. Ash fell down the sides of the bottle and danced onto the chair arm. Some drifted inside the bottle.

"What don't you understand?" she said.

"I don't like that term. It sounds so … I don't know …"

"Sexy?"

"That wasn't the word I had in mind."

"Then what?"

"It sounds like something out of Hollywood."

"Americans think everything is related to Hollywood. Bad boys are so much more. They're a primal need."

"No they're not."

"They are. Women are attracted to the alpha male."

"Maybe some women."

"All women."

"You don't know what all women want."

"It's primal. Even if you don't recognize its presence, it's there. It's what makes you like JD's ponytail."

"What?"

"You're attracted to the hint of the bad boy. The ponytail is unconventional, and anything unconventional is bad. And for you, because you don't drink, you like that he drinks beer, that he's a bartender. I mean, come on, what person who avoids alcohol dates a bartender?"

I stood and went to the edge of the porch. Even though I don't normally like to scatter my cigarette droppings everywhere, I couldn't deal with that beer bottle covered with Lavender's ashes. I stepped down and knocked the ash into the gravel in front of the step. I looked up. The sky was thick with moisture, no rain, but that spongey feeling you get when you know it wants to let loose. The moon was hidden.

"Did I offend you?" She got up. Her flip-flops slapped across the wood porch. Her gown caught between her heel and her flip flop. She stopped and tugged it free before joining me on the gravel path.

I took a drag on my cigarette and willed her to go back inside the house. It didn't work.

"I did offend you. I'm sorry."

She put her hand on my arm — cold fingertips, hot moist palms pressed against my skin. I jerked my arm out of her grasp. My cigarette flipped out of my fingers and fell on the gravel. I bent to pick it up, but before I could touch it, she pressed her foot over it and squashed it.

"What the hell?" I looked up. The light from the kitchen seemed far away. The boggy clouds blotted out the stars and the thin sliver of moon, so it was impossible to see her expression.

"You're very unfriendly."

"So you grab my arm with your sweaty palms and stomp out my cigarette?"

"It was an impulse. I shouldn't have done that. Have mine." She held out her half-smoked cigarette.

"No thanks."

She put it between her lips and held out her hands to give me a lift up. The condition of her palms, at least the way the one had felt on my arm a moment earlier, made me doubt she could offer a firm enough grip to actually get me on my feet. I inched away from her and stood.

"Why are you so cagey?"

"I gave you one of my cigarettes. I've been sociable. I hardly know you and you keep attacking me or asking me questions that are way too personal."

"JD said you speak your mind, I figured you wouldn't be so private."

What else had JD said? He'd told her about the ghost and given her a run-down on my personality? It was starting to sound like he was the one who wasn't so private.

"What's your issue with me?" she said.

"I just told you."

"Are your feelings hurt because I said you don't know a lot about ghosts? Or is this about me calling JD a bad boy."

"I really, really hate that term."

"Interesting."

"How is it interesting?" I hated the way she kept prying into my head, interpreting everything I said. I had no idea what she wanted from me, and I suddenly wished this part of our trip was over. I couldn't wait to leave, and I was a little worried that JD was going to want to change our plans because of Luke being the main suspect. The only suspect.

It wasn't really fair to complain. JD paid the airfare, had paid for the hotel, our condo on Hamilton Island, and would probably end up buying most of our meals. But it was my vacation! I hadn't had a real vacation — a trip to a new place — since I went to New York with Renee when I turned twenty-five.

"The term has a sexual connotation and you don't want to talk about that," Lavender said.

"JD isn't *bad*, however you define it."

"You're pretending to be dumb."

"No I'm not! It makes it sound like women are twisted, and want guys who don't treat them well. Why are "bad boys" supposed to be exciting, but "bad girls" mean something negative? How unbalanced is that?"

"Maybe people don't talk about it as much, but men definitely like bad girls."

I suddenly realized I had a headache. A few drops of rain fell on my arms. I went back to the porch, pulled a cigarette out of the pack and snapped my lighter to life. Now I was past my quota for the day, but I didn't care. Besides, I hadn't finished the third one. I was only a half cigarette over the limit. I don't know why I didn't just say good-night and end the conversation. I guess I didn't want to completely antagonize her. For however long, she was the girlfriend of JD's twin. And she was sort of our host while we were in New South Wales, or at least a partial, temporary host.

It's not that I'm a hateful or judgmental person. I'm not completely normal either. No one is, really. What is normal? Keeping your thoughts to yourself? Or only saying things as bland as oatmeal without sugar? I suppose normal is when you have minor differences with other people. If you smoked cigarettes fifty years ago, you were somewhat normal. Now, in California, you're a social outcast. If your hair is medium length or short or long, it's normal because that's what everyone else does. If you shave your head, then you're not normal. It's when you wander too far off the path. And Lavender was definitely off the path.

Rain splattered on her nightgown, gluing it to her body like thumbtacks were being pressed all over her. Any minute her cigarette was going to fizzle out from the raindrops, falling faster and heavier.

"Don't sulk," I said.

"I'm not sulking. I'm enjoying the shower."

I took a drag on my cigarette and waited. Then I remembered why I'd gotten out of my chair to begin with — I didn't want to use the beer bottle for an ashtray now that it was covered with ashes from her pathetic aim. I took a few steps to the edge of the porch. Rain poured over her. The gown clung to her skin. Amazingly, her cigarette was still lit.

When her hair was soaked and her gown looked like she'd recently emerged from a lake, she shuffled up the steps. A stream of water flowed behind her as she walked to the chair. She poked her cigarette butt into the bottle. For a minute, I thought she was going to plant her sopping wet self on the wicker chair and make it impossible for anyone to sit there comfortably for the next twenty-four hours, but she turned back and walked to where I was standing.

"I just wanted to be friends. In spite of your bitchiness, I like you. I have no idea why, but I do. It might be your interest in dimensions beyond our own. Maybe it's just your hair. I always wanted red hair."

Each time I thought she might be making a connection, she spun it around and said something completely weird. Who likes someone because of the color of her hair? Or was she kidding, trying to make a joke that fell even flatter than her earlier attempt?

"So, Madison." She smiled. Her lips were slick with rain. Her skin was pale, almost glowing in the dim light coming from the kitchen. In that wet gown, I thought she'd be cold, but she didn't shiver and there was no hint she was trying to warm herself. "Are you a bad girl? Maybe that's why you don't recognize JD for what he is."

I wasn't immediately sure which part of her comment made me angrier — once again trying to analyze and categorize me, accusing me of I don't know what, or hinting that I didn't even know what kind of person JD was? As if he was hiding himself from me, pretending to be someone he wasn't. I took a long drag on my cigarette and blew out the smoke right in her face.

She didn't blink. "You are a bad girl."

"Will you stop it? It's boring, if nothing else."

She laughed.

"There's an attraction, a danger that's exciting, makes you feel more alive when someone breaks the rules. And you love to break the rules. Smoking when everyone knows it's bad for your health." She swept her arm out, waving her palm past my head and down the length of my body. "Too many piercings in your ears, the tattoos. Very bad. And JD is hooked on you, like a drug."

"Is that right." I took another drag on my cigarette.

"Oh, yeah. That's right. Luke doesn't have the same thing for me that JD has for you."

"Every couple is different."

"Did you make yourself all bad to get his attention?"

"This conversation is stupid."

"Too close to the bone?"

I sucked in smoke and closed my eyes, releasing my breath as slowly as I could.

"I know I'm right. The thing is, Luke isn't fascinated with me." Her voice was softer, trembling. Now, finally, she shivered. She wrapped her hands around her upper arms. "I recognize it, I know why it happens, but I can't completely define it. I don't know what you have that I don't."

"We're different. Maybe Luke isn't the right guy for you."

She smiled. "He's the right guy for me."

"How do you know?"

"How do *I* know about Luke? Or how does anyone know?"

"Both."

"You just do."

Her words made me anxious. I didn't know, not for sure. And it could be that JD isn't the right one, *the* one, or it could be that I don't leap to conclusions and make sweeping generalizations, like Lavender. Caution is a good thing. Not knowing is a good thing, taking time to understand another person.

"I just don't have that bad girl quality. I wish I could absorb some of yours."

"I'm going to bed. I'm getting sleepy, finally."

"Are you going to help me contact Elizabeth? JD said you might."

If all this stuff she said about him was true, maybe he was not the one for me. But for the first time, it occurred to me that she might be making it all up. Maybe JD hadn't said anything. Maybe he hadn't even mentioned the ghost. She might be guessing, or had encountered it herself. "I already told you, no."

"Please think about it. We need to help Luke."

"You think you can just ask her who killed her?"

"No. Not at all. The cops will figure it out, or give up. I want her to release her grip on him. Let him go."

"What grip?"

"Luke admires her for what she pulled. It was so grand, so outrageous. Absolutely over the top. Now that she's dead, she has even more mystique. And even though he acts all angry, there's a spark of excitement he can't resist. She knows. That's why she's come back for him."

Ten

THE WHOLE POINT of sitting on the porch enjoying a cigarette was to help my brain unwind so I could sleep, but when I returned to bed after my mind-bending conversation with Lavender, I was more awake than ever. Sure, I'd told her I was sleepy. And I was, my brain fuzzy and sagging from trying to follow her thoughts and get her to back off, but not sleepy as in collapsing into my pillow and finding immediate oblivion.

No matter how I tried to force my eyes closed, they popped open, eyeballs bugging out, trying to see something, anything in the complete darkness of our room. JD was quiet, no snores or grunts. He hadn't even shifted when I slipped into bed. For a moment, I feared I was sleeping beside a corpse. He's always a good sleeper, not awake in the middle of the night like I am, not shifting positions twenty-seven times a night so that he wakes with the blankets half on the floor, wound around his legs, and the pillow peeking out of its case.

I thought about getting up again, but I wasn't convinced Lavender had gone to sleep. I wasn't even sure she'd gotten into her sleeping bag. It would have been very uncomfortable, lying there with dripping hair soaking her pillow and bag. No sounds came from their bedroom or the bathroom, but I did not want to risk running into her again. I was a prisoner in a strange bedroom in an unfamiliar house in the middle of farmland on the opposite side of the globe from home.

It doesn't take much during wakeful hours after midnight for the brain to start wandering outside of its usual range. Perhaps it's the darkness, the lack of sound and sights pushing my thoughts in one direction or another during the day, which turns thought patterns in a different direction late at night. The whole universe shrinks to that small, densely packed ball of tissue and nerves and blood vessels wrapped inside its bone shell.

The mind does its thing, firing impulses and electrical charges. Soon, scenes from the past emerge as if they were happening real time. It can seem like you've returned to another version of yourself. You're ten years old. You're riding your bicycle, feeling powerful and light because you've had a few years of practice and now you're an expert on a two-wheeler, racing along the road, pavement flying past until it turns into something streaked and alive, the dirt and pebbles and rough spots erased, the long dry summer grass in the vacant field transformed into waves — an ocean of plants spilling into each other and becoming a single, endless expanse of life.

You feel, rather than see, your front tire hit a rock. The front wheel jerks to the left, taking the handlebars with it, the back wheel fishtails and you fly off. It's so fast, you don't really remember the flying, and what little you noticed is immediately erased by burning skin, aching shoulders and hips where parts of your body that seemed so solid slammed into something even harder.

Blood pours down your legs and you taste it in your mouth where you bit your tongue. Wheeling your bike home, limping, tears surprisingly sweet when you lick your lips, embarrassed to tell your parents you fell. Even though you thought you were in control, thought you knew how to ride fast and keep the bike upright, it all went wrong.

My mother was sympathetic, washing my cuts, pumping me up with words about how brave I was, how it happened to everyone. My father wasn't unsympathetic, at least I don't think he was, but he emphasized, *well, that's how you learn*. The problem was, it was an accident and I wasn't sure what I was supposed to have learned.

For the third or fourth time, I flopped onto my left side. With all the things I did not want to think about after a very long day and an endless night, my parents were at the top of the list. It's not that they come creeping in at three in the morning whenever I can't sleep, but they are frequent visitors in my memories, along with my job, any guy I happen to be seeing, or not seeing, and my future, which is so blurry I can't really make out anything on the horizon.

By the time I'm thirty-one, which isn't too far away, my parents will have been dead longer than I knew them which sort of makes me feel like I'm drifting on a boat so far from shore I can't see the tip of a tree or the crest of a wave. I'm sure that being in Australia, feeling more than a little disconnected from JD, increased my sense of isolation. It was not a good time to be remembering my childhood, remembering how badly damaged my bike was, and how my father bought me a brand new one a few days later, and it wasn't anywhere near my birthday or Christmas, and it was a fifteen-speed and way cooler than the bike I had before. I never fell off that bike, so maybe I did learn something, maybe my body learned how to be more in tune with the bike. Who knows.

Now, perhaps because I was so alert, my brain so twisted on itself, I couldn't shake the thoughts of my parents. Usually when I'm wakened at night, I start to fade back to sleep and memories or questions pop up, but then that half-dream state rushes in and thoughts glide and shift from one thing to another.

No more memories rose to the surface after the new bicycle, but questions about their deaths poked at me like steak knives. Why? Who? Those are really the only questions, and not in that order. I guess why comes first because I don't understand why that happened to me, or to them, but if I knew the answer to the second question, the first might take care of itself.

The police never thought it was a random killing. There wasn't anything worth stealing. Our electronics were definitely not state-of-the-art, and my mother didn't have any gems or pearls. Her wedding ring was a plain gold band. It circled the finger of her left hand, which was resting on her stomach when I found them. Their bodies were placed so neatly on the bed it looked like an act of love, according to the lead detective. Not that he expressed that opinion to me. He told my Aunt and eventually, after lots of pleading and repetitious questions from me, she released the only real insight they had. It didn't help, though.

I turned back to my right side. I poked my foot between JD's lower legs. I took a deep breath and let it out slowly. I put my thoughts on the muscles in my back and neck and made them relax their grip on my bones. I felt a little calmer and right that moment I decided — when I got back to California, as soon as I had a long weekend, I would visit the house where I grew up. I was going to talk to the neighbors and call the detective again and ask if they had any updates, since the case was still officially open.

Maybe the new owners of the house wouldn't let me inside. I'd never tried because I'd never been back. Sure, I'd asked my Aunt and Uncle, but they brushed me off continuously and then I grew up and stopped asking. The final time I mentioned it, when I turned twenty-one, my Aunt said it was a good idea to put the past behind me for good. Nothing healthy would come out of brooding over the house and going back to look around.

Just thinking about it made my body cold all over. My toes, even the ones pressed between JD's calf muscles, were like tiny cubes of ice. I couldn't feel my new toe ring. The cold was creeping up my legs, and I knew the ghost had returned.

Lavender's words flashed through my head like someone had pierced it with a sword — *There's a spark of excitement that he can't resist. She knows. That's why she's come back for him.*

I moved close to JD and pressed my face between his shoulder blades. I wrapped my arms around his waist, and shoved my other foot between his feet. He still didn't move, so I guess he didn't feel the iciness in my legs. Maybe it was inside me, replacing the marrow in my bones. It was crazy to think a ghost was going to take him away from me, absurd to think she'd mixed up twin brothers, but I still wanted to absorb his whole body into mine.

Something white, a glimpse of a figure appeared just past JD's shoulder. It wasn't distinct in any way, but her form was similar to a human shape, not as vaporous as she'd been the first time. It was the impression you have when you look at clouds and think there's a horse or a human head, but you aren't sure if you're wanting to see a familiar object and it's your own mind molding the clouds in that fashion.

Words, like pin pricks, entered my ears. *Luke. Come here.*

I whispered, barely able to hear my own voice. *What do you want?*

Love. I love him.

It's too late, you're dead. It was a heartless thing to say, but true. Besides, maybe she didn't hear me, she was dead. All the cold inside of my bones might be slicing through my body, coming off of her because she wasn't aware of it.

It's never too late.

Who killed you? My voice was hardly a whisper.

The room was silent. My legs warmed slightly and I wondered if she was gone, but I thought I could still see a shadowy specter in the corner.

I moved away from JD. I couldn't let her slip off to wherever she'd come from without knowing more. It doesn't mean I wasn't terrified that she might take JD, or Luke. I don't know why ghosts are so frightening. It's the unknown maybe, the fear of death, of seeing something decayed.

A hint of dark yellow threaded through the center of the figure. As I moved toward the edge of the bed, I felt a deeper chill. I hugged my arms. I shivered and my teeth rattled against each other like dice clinking in a cup. *Do you know who stabbed you?* I spoke louder this time, certain that nothing could wake JD. He hadn't moved or shifted his breathing the entire time.

The silence grew so intense it seemed as if I was the only living creature in the house, the only beating heart and breathing lungs for miles around. It seemed she didn't want to reveal her killer, which could mean it was Luke. But why would anyone come back, longing for a man who had stabbed you? Maybe Luke wasn't telling the truth. Or maybe something had changed. There were too many things I didn't know. It wasn't clear whether anyone was telling the truth.

I realized I was lying on my side, that after a long night of trying to keep my eyes closed, they were now closed on their own. Was I dreaming the whole thing? Dreaming of a ghost? There was no response to my question because maybe the whole scene was unfolding inside my head.

I opened my eyes. She was still there, not moving. The yellow had faded. She seemed transparent, yet I couldn't see anything through her. The yellow tinge shifted, growing even more pale, as if moisture was spreading through her, washing out the depth of the pigment, fading it into the smeared brush strokes of a water color painting.

Because she was fading, I was afraid to sit up, afraid that if I moved at all, she might disappear altogether. *Why are you here?*

The response was silence, thick and cold.

Do you want something from me?

She moved away from the wall. The yellow tinge faded more and the form drew closer until it almost touched the bed. The coldness in my legs raced up my spine. I shivered violently. My insides felt as if they'd all turned into icy water, the consistency of snow when it's slushy, running along the gutters. I wanted to cry but even my tears were frozen inside of me.

With a sudden burst of energy, I sat up. The spirit rushed back to the corner, hovering there fierce and unyielding. *I don't know why you're here? What do you want?*

The yellow streak darkened again, growing more solid, rounded, and shifting to the center of the figure. It pulsed like something living. When the intensity of the color increased, the coldness seeped out of my bones, leaving my body limp and exhausted, as if I'd finished swimming miles in frigid water.

I stood and slid my feet along the floor, wondering why I was trying to move closer and what I expected to get from being face-to-face, if you can call it that. My ears were poised for her voice, desperate to find out her secrets, to get some answers to my questions. But there was nothing. Only silence.

Did Luke kill you?

No.

Someone wants to frame him?

No.

Great, so it seemed she could speak the words love and no. I felt like I was in a cosmic game of twenty questions. Maybe I could find out something if I kept asking the right questions.

Why couldn't he love me when I was alive?

The words chilled me, literally and figuratively. I had no answer.

Did you put the ring in the doll head?

Yessss.

I shivered at the drawn-out sound of the *s*. I took a step closer. I stretched out my hand to touch the transparent white, reaching as close as I could to the yellow at the center. The temperature was cool, but not the iciness I expected, not the penetrating cold I'd felt in my body.

Why? I said.

It fit. There was a small laugh, like a breath with a hint of sound behind it.

I stepped closer and she disappeared. It was so fast, I wondered for a moment if there hadn't been anything there. Suddenly I was cold again. I hurried back to bed. I curled up on my right side, staring at the corner, hoping she would, and hoping she wouldn't, return.

Of course the ring fit in the doll head. It was a ridiculous answer. And she knew that, because she'd laughed. If she wanted something, wanted to communicate, why didn't she want to tell me who killed her, or anything coherent? Did she not care about justice or vengeance or whatever else it is that ghosts are concerned with?

Now my eyes closed easily, but my head spun, hearing her words over and over, mixed with Lavender's words about the ghost coming back for Luke. *It fit, it fit, it fit.* I didn't understand what that meant. It would have fit inside a coffee cup or a sock or a matchbox. It wasn't as if Luke had Barbie dolls lying around his house. She bought a Barbie doll and put the ring inside and left it in the yard. It made no sense.

AS SOON AS the sun rose, JD jumped out of bed and nudged my shoulder.

"We need to get out of here and have some time with just us. It's a perfect day. What do you think about finally getting you upright on a surfboard?"

I groaned. It felt as if I'd been asleep for twenty minutes, and maybe I had. When I first hit consciousness, I couldn't be sure if I'd dreamt about the ghost or she'd had actually returned. The memory of what she'd said, the questions I'd asked, was blurry. I thought we'd talked about the doll head and the diamond ring, but because of her vague responses, the whole exchange seemed dream-like.

"Wake up, sleepy." JD flopped down on the bed and turned my face toward him. He rubbed his nose against mine, and widened his eyes so the whites were more prominent, staring into my eyes like he thought he could deliver his energy to me.

Learning to surf had pretty much been on my list for the trip to Australia. And it made sense to do it in the New South Wales area because we wanted to devote our nine days in Queensland to the Great Barrier Reef and the serene tropical atmosphere. It was the perfect day for surfing — the weather was great. He knew we both needed a break from all the drama, but he didn't know I'd been up half the night, listening to Lavender and shivering in the presence of a ghost.

I rolled onto my back and closed my eyes. I yawned and tugged the blankets closer to my neck.

"Why are you so tired?"

"It was a long night."

"Why?"

He pushed my hair off my cheek and ran his finger along the edge of my ear, sending shivers across my shoulders and up the back of my neck. If it hadn't been for the ghost, they would have been very pleasant shivers, but right then, it reminded me too much of the chills in the night.

"I couldn't sleep."

"All night?"

I told him about smoking on the porch, Lavender, and finally, Elizabeth's ghost.

"All that activity and I missed it?"

"You didn't even move."

"So surfing is out?"

"No. I think I'll wake up in a minute or two."

"It's not something you want to do when you're exhausted."

I wriggled out from under the blankets. "I've had lots of rest this week, it was only one night. I'm fine."

"Are you sure?"

"As long as I eat a big breakfast. Does Luke know we're going?"

"I told him if the weather cleared we would do it today."

I got out of bed and pushed open the top of my suitcase.

It was starting to look like a pile of unfolded laundry from so much digging through and yanking things out. It would be great when we got to the condo and I could put things in drawers.

It had been two months or more since Elizabeth emptied Luke's house. I wondered how much longer it would be until he bought something besides a bed and a kitchen table with a few chairs. I didn't see how he could live with all the empty rooms, his few new clothing items in boxes on a closet floor. Every room except the bedroom we were staying in echoed when you walked through. With the gift of the wicker chairs, he had more furniture on the front porch than he did almost anywhere else in the house.

While I took a shower, JD went out to make coffee. I was toweling dry my hair when he returned with two mugs, smelling dark and rich, if it's possible to smell those two qualities. I sipped coffee and combed my hair, weaving it into a single braid while JD showered. When he came out, we lathered each other up with sunscreen. I hoped it would stay on during breakfast and the drive to the beach, but it's so much easier to get all the spots covered when you're inside than it is on the beach, battling the salty air and sand and the sun is already beating down on you, melting the cream as you spread it around.

Since I didn't want to be thinking about keeping my bathing suit in place, I wore my black one-piece instead of my navy-blue bikini that has gold rings at my hips to hold the front and the back together, and a gold ring in the center connecting the two halves of the top. The one piece hardly slips around at all and is definitely the suit of choice for the ocean where the waves tear at you as if they want to pull it off your body. I left my toe rings in my suitcase.

Lavender and Luke were asleep when we left. Part of me wondered if the ghost had paid a visit to Lavender also, but I didn't care enough to wake her and then have to extract myself from another weird conversation.

We stopped at a nearby cafe for breakfast. The inside was dark, with rough-hewn tables and unvarnished wood flooring, more like a pub, but the name was the Wallaby Cafe, so maybe they weren't sure if they were a pub or a cafe. I ate a waffle and two huge pieces of sausage. They weren't the thin finger-sized sausages served with breakfast at home, but the size of something you'd put in a bun with mustard and sauerkraut. The meal came with three slices of cantaloupe. The coffee was amazing. Coffee in Australia has all these strange names — flat white, long black, short black. They all were fairly obvious once I realized everything was espresso in some form or another, but it still took getting used to. I got a flat white and they designed a heart with curlicues at the tip in the foam. JD had an omelette and tomato juice with lemon.

JD drank half his glass of tomato juice. He put the glass down, leaned across the too-small table and grabbed my braid. "Hey. I wanted to tell you something."

I finished chewing a piece of sausage and gulped it down a

bit too soon. "What?"

"You said I was acting like your supernatural experiences were inadequate."

I swallowed again, even though there was no food in my mouth.

"I don't think that at all," he said.

"Then why are you so anxious to get Lavender involved?"

"Why not?"

"It's not like I'm over-sensitive, she's trying to annoy me."

"I don't disagree. But she wants to see this cleared up too. It can't hurt. The more ideas, the better, don't you think?"

"Sure." I actually was being over-sensitive, I could feel it, but I couldn't seem to stop myself from being annoyed. His apology made me feel slightly less sensitive. Slightly.

"Anyway, I didn't mean to imply you needed her help."

I smiled and cut off two more bite-sized pieces of sausage. I really was glad he wanted to clear the air, but there was more air-clearing needed — why he'd told Lavender and Luke about the ghost when I wasn't there, why he hadn't even mentioned to me that he'd told them. It made me feel betrayed. But maybe that was over-sensitive too. I wasn't sure, so I wasn't going to bring it up until I figured out a way to do it without sounding needy and whiney and petty. Until I was sure I wasn't *being* petty.

THREE HOURS LATER we were seated on rented boards, our shins bumping against each other as the waves rose and fell. We were about hip-deep in the water, staring out at the horizon. Straddling the board felt familiar and easy. Nearly every time I'd gone to the beach when JD was surfing, I sat on the board for a bit and paddled along the shore in water deep enough that my feet didn't touch bottom. Paddling out way over my head, standing up, and riding the curve of a wave was going to be another story.

JD knew I was nervous, partially because I'd been putting it off for a while with one very reasonable excuse after another. And although the excuses were logical on the surface, there were too many of them. Wanting to do something and taking action are worlds apart. You can want to participate in a triathlon, but cycling every day, training your body to run thirteen kilometers, increasing your swimming endurance and speed, all takes creating a new schedule, getting out of bed early, putting on your training clothes, eating different food. Or starting a band. You can't just sit in your room lost in your headphones, strumming your fingers across a set of guitar strings, or hitting sticks on a practice pad. It takes hours and hours, weeks, and years. Mind-numbing practice that most people don't have the stomach for. Not that either of those activities have anything to do with learning to surf, but the same idea — imagination versus physical activity, taking steps instead of talking. I want to be one of those people who does things instead of talking, but it's hard. Talking and dreaming are fun. Working is tiring and sometimes boring. I'd seen the surfers sitting on their boards, resting on the surface of the water for hours, waiting for waves, missing the right one, or hitting it at the wrong moment and getting tossed in the air, plunging into the water, starting over again and again.

Although he'd explained it before, JD went over the principles again. The first step is to learn to sense the cresting of the wave. If it's showing a line of foam when you start to paddle, you've already missed it. This isn't the leisurely paddling you do as you head out past the breaking waves, it requires hard, steady effort, using as much energy as it takes to swim in the ocean without a board. Getting to your feet is the trickiest part. There's one moment when you're moving fast enough that you can stop paddling, bring your feet under you, get a firm grip, and move into a crouch, then straighten. There would be lots and lots of falls. Hundreds.

"You'll drink more salt water than you ever imagined you could. But you really want to do this, right?"

"Yes." When I closed my eyes, I could feel myself flying along a wall of water, the board skating like it had muscles and strength and a will of its own, racing like I was on a jet ski but it was just me and the water and the board, no engine doing the work for me, no handlebars keeping me stabilized.

We laid down on the boards and paddled out. The water was cold, but not bone-chilling like it is along the northern California coast. About twenty or thirty surfers dotted the length of the shore, most of them sitting, waiting.

Once we got out far enough, we turned our boards to face the beach. It looked very far away.

"It happens fast," JD said. "When I say go, you need to start paddling. Don't turn to look at the waves, just listen to me and watch me. Okay?"

I nodded. It wasn't really that scary. The worst that could happen was not getting up to my feet, feeling the wave pass under me. Or getting halfway up and falling off. I'm a good swimmer, so I wasn't worried about that. I was a little nervous about losing my board and having to go hunting for it, but JD said it was rare that the board completely disappeared.

The sun warmed my head, drying my hair as we sat there. We didn't talk much. I wanted to be ready, and JD had told me numerous times that what he loves about surfing is that it's just you and the board and the waves. I figured that meant not chit-chatting like we were lounging by the side of a swimming pool.

"You don't want to actually ride the wave the first few times," he said. "Get the feel of paddling, of knowing how fast you have to paddle, and getting a good rhythm, keeping up with the speed of the wave."

I nodded. "Are you going to just paddle or ride it to shore?"

"I'll take it all the way. You can watch because you'll get a different sense of how it looks from out here."

I don't know how much time passed. Minutes faded into nothing with the ocean spread out around us. Suddenly JD said, "Now." He flopped onto his belly and started paddling and he had already pulled a few feet ahead of me by the time my body caught up with his voice and his movements.

After six or seven strokes, my shoulders felt tight. It seemed as if I was slowing down, although JD hadn't pulled any further ahead, so maybe it was the aching making me feel slow even though I really wasn't. After a few more strokes, he shifted to his knees, his heels raised up, toes pressed to the board. In one unbroken movement, he lowered his heels, straightened his legs and he was standing, racing along the face of the wave, as elegant as a dolphin diving through the water.

I slowed and stopped paddling, relieved that it wasn't my time yet.

We followed the same routine about ten more times, then JD said, "It's time to fish or cut bait."

I laughed. There was a hysterical tinge to my voice, although maybe only in my ears, because JD smiled. He didn't ask if I was scared or whether I'd changed my mind.

It felt familiar and safe when he said, *now*, and started paddling. Just like the other times, even though I knew this time was different. My life could change forever in the next few seconds, I'd be transformed from someone who wanted to surf to someone who actually had surfed. I might even become a surfer. I realized it was time to stop thinking about what I was doing, having all these monumental thoughts about life-changing experiences, and let my body take over. I did.

Of course, I fell off before I rose out of the crouching position. But those two or three seconds of riding along the wave, letting it carry me, my arms no longer racing to keep up, were enough. I couldn't wait to get to a full standing position.

I lost count of how many more times we tried, but finally, just when I had my first thought that I was kind of tired, and hungry, I did it. Not all the way. My knees were still bent more than JD's, but my feet were flat on the board. I was standing, riding a wave. It's a feeling I can't describe. Racing along, better than a roller coaster or a bike flying down a hill or roller blading.

When we got back to the shallow water, we dragged the boards across the beach. The fins left deep grooves in the sand so it looked like it was being prepared for planting seeds. JD dried his chest and shoulders and hair, but I collapsed on the towel, sprawled on my back, not caring that my arms flopped out away from my sides and were instantly caked with sand.

He spread out his towel and laid beside me. He put his hand on my stomach. "You're breathing hard."

I smiled. It felt good. The breathing hard and his warm hand.

A while later, I woke. JD stood over me. His shadow fell across my face. "You're turning red. We should go get something to eat, surfer girl."

I smiled and held up my hand so he could pull me up.

"I think you liked it," he said.

"I loved it."

"It fits."

"What do you mean?"

He picked up my towel, flapped it to get rid of most of the sand, and stuffed it into the bag we'd used to carry our stuff. "Surfing and you fit together. I knew you would."

"Why?"

"You like to be connected to things bigger than yourself. You and the ocean. It fits who you are."

We walked back to the car, but I was no longer thinking about surfing. JD talked about this wave and that move and on and on, but my mind was in the darkness of the bedroom, staring at the entity in the corner, telling me she put the ring in the Barbie head because it fit. I assumed she meant it was the right size, which was obvious. Maybe she meant it another way. That the doll head was somehow appropriate for the ring. Of course, I wasn't any closer to understanding her. Because what did *that* mean?

BECAUSE I'D BEEN so excited about surfing, and at the same time too tired to explain every single detail from the night before, I hadn't mentioned to JD some of the things the ghost had said, including the placement of the ring inside the Barbie head. The minute JD said *it fits*, the voice of Elizabeth's ghost echoed behind the words.

It was such an odd phrase for him to use, I wondered if

the ghost's voice had penetrated his dreams. It was possible, but more likely, it was one of those coincidences you only notice when you're looking for them. We returned the surfboards, put our stuff in Luke's car, and drove a few blocks to a Tapas place Luke had recommended. The scallops with caramelized onion were amazing, also the Spanish sausage and potatoes in garlic sauce, all of it made doubly tasty by my absolutely empty stomach. It felt as if every ounce of food I'd eaten in the past two days had been burned up with simple paddling, waiting for waves with all my nerve endings poised for action, and planting my feet and stabilizing my legs as I tried to do the simplest thing in the world — remain upright.

Despite the outrageously delicious food, my mind wasn't on the plate, or inside my mouth. The tastes rolled through me as if I was inhaling them, but my mind circled around the doll head. How on earth did it fit anything? Even though my brain had clicked on the use of the phrase, it almost made less sense. Why was a Barbie head fitting for a diamond ring? My brain ached from trying to think about it when I had nothing to grab on to. I could feel it twisting around itself but nothing emerged.

"You're quiet." JD picked up his glass and drank his sparkling water. The wedge of lemon bumped against his lip. When he put down the water, his tongue darted out and swiped the lemon juice off his upper lip.

"I feel limp, like all my muscles have everything squeezed

out of them."

He smiled. "And what else? I know you're thinking about that ghost again."

"I am."

"Tell me." He took a big bite of satay on a stick, chewing slowly, his eyes glistening at me.

"It makes no sense. The doll head. The ring. The ghost coming after you when Luke is right in the next room."

"Why are you trying to make sense of it?"

"I want her to leave me alone."

"Which one? The ghost, or Lavender?"

I laughed. "Both of them."

"We're only here for another day. Think about Hamilton Island. Just you and me."

"Time is going so fast."

He popped a meatball into his mouth. He tucked it to the side so his cheek looked like a squirrel's. "We shouldn't have planned to spend so many days at Luke's."

"I'm not complaining."

"I know. I wanted to see him for more than two days, but I always seem to forget what he's really like."

"It's okay. At least it hasn't been boring."

He laughed. "For the rest of today, I hope we can forget about dead bodies and ghosts and decapitated dolls."

"I won't. She must be trying to tell me something, about the doll head. Do you have any ideas?"

"I haven't given it as much thought as you have." He

reached over and tapped my nose.

It made me cross-eyed for a moment while I focused on his finger.

"Her head was full of diamonds?"

"That's too easy," I said.

"It might not mean anything. It could be she found a doll head in some trash can and didn't want the ring to get lost in the garden. She wanted to send Luke a message."

"But what message? Why?"

"You don't have to figure it out, you know."

"Having her mention it makes it hard to stop thinking about. If all I had was the doll head with a ring stuck inside, I wouldn't be obsessing over it."

"At least you recognize it."

"Recognize what?"

"That you're obsessed."

Strangely, I wasn't insulted, and I don't think he meant to insult me. Obsession isn't always a bad thing. In fact, isn't it the same kind of mindset if someone can't stop wondering why their neighbor places beer bottles into the recycling bin one by one, as if they're returning eggs to a nest, rather than dumping them into the container, and someone who wonders why certain cells run amuck as they pursue a cure for cancer?

Eleven

WHEN WE ARRIVED back at Luke's, she was still there. Lavender, not Elizabeth's ghost. As we started toward our bedroom, she appeared, seemingly out of nowhere. "I made your bed."

"Okay." I hurried ahead of JD, anxious to get into our room.

She called after me. "And tidied up your suitcase. Don't worry, I didn't snoop to see what kind of birth control you use or anything like that."

I put my hand on the doorknob and turned it, pushing the door hard so it banged against the wall.

"Careful," Lavender said.

JD was right behind me. He put his hand on the back of my neck, trying to soothe me, but it didn't work. Not for a second. Well, maybe for a second, I felt a brief melting toward him. On the other hand, maybe it did work, because I managed to enter the room without calling back over my shoulder that she had no right to put one finger on my stuff, and to point out that it's impossible to go through someone's suitcase and not snoop.

JD closed the door.

I dropped our towels on the sloppily made bed, not caring if I got sand in the quilt. "What do you think she was looking for?"

"Come on, Madison. She's just weird. Not sinister."

"She didn't need to come in this room. She must have been looking for something. And I'm sure it wasn't birth control pills."

He laughed. He grabbed my hair and pulled me close to him. He stood behind me and looped his arms around my waist. With his feet pressed against mine, he inched toward the window, half walking me in front of him like I was a giant doll. When we reached the window he pushed my legs against the sill and we looked out at the sky, white-streaked blue, and the line of eucalyptus trees, washed-out beige against all that bright light.

We stood at the window for quite a while, not talking, possibly hoping to see another kangaroo, but the landscape was motionless. Already, I was calmer. Almost completely calm, but that didn't mean I wasn't set on finding out what she'd been looking for in our room. As soon as JD got in the shower, I'd do a little snooping myself. I knew she hadn't come in to tidy up. When we'd passed by their room, the sleeping bags had been coiled on the floor, the zippers down so they looked like bodies ripped open by a surgeon. Or a medical examiner. Not that I've seen such things, but it's what I would imagine.

JD pulled away from me and went to his suitcase. He pulled out a clean pair of shorts and a t-shirt.

"I wonder where Luke is?" I said.

"He probably went to the store. Or maybe just took the Harley out for a spin." He tugged off his t-shirt. As he stretched his arms over his head, his triceps tightened. Looking at his arms made me want them wrapped around my waist again. It was sort of annoying that I was equally consumed with thoughts of a Barbie head.

"Are you coming in the shower with me?" He dropped his shirt on the floor.

"No."

He pouted and yanked down his swim trunks. "Are you sure?"

I smiled. "It's tempting. But I want to lie down for a few minutes."

I felt a little guilty not being completely honest. I *was* going to lie down, just not on the bed.

He put his hand on my chin and kissed me.

The minute the shower water started running, I stepped away from the window and looked around the room. I sat on the floor and lowered myself down to look under the bed. Since the house had been stripped bare, if there were odds and ends dropped, they would have been obvious before

Luke moved the new bed into the room. I still wanted to check.

A few dust bunnies drifted away from me, propelled by my breath, as if they were scared of my presence and looking for a place to hide. Up near the head of the bed was a coin. I wasn't familiar enough with Australian coins to recognize the denomination. I thought it might be two dollars, but since I really was tired both from not sleeping, and from surfing, I didn't feel like dragging myself across the floor to reach it.

I had no idea what I was looking for. Did I expect to see the ghost, hiding under the bed during daylight, or maybe the rest of the Barbie's body? But something made me look. I wriggled closer and decided I'd go for the coin after all. Those little coins are really cool, thicker than American coins, a dull gold color, and they feel special in some strange way I can't explain — heavy and solid. Maybe just because they're unfamiliar. I rolled to my stomach and wriggled under the bed, inching toward the head. I reached out and touched the coin with the tips of my fingers and pulled it toward me.

With the coin in my hand, I glanced around again from that angle. There was nothing else.

"What are you doing?"

I turned my head. JD was on his knees, peering under the bed. I hadn't heard the shower water stop, hadn't heard the door open. In fact, Lavender could have come into the room and been watching me from the other side and I wouldn't have noticed because I was so absorbed with looking for something I couldn't identify. It's like my brain stung from a small burr at the center, knowing something, aware of something, but having no idea quite yet what that might be, and so I focused on grabbing a coin just to have something solid to touch.

JD grabbed my ankle. "Need help getting out?"

"Sure."

He pulled gently and I slid along the floor, my hair, still a bit damp, squeaked on the wood, preventing me from sliding easily.

"What were you looking for?"

"I don't know."

"You don't know?"

I opened my hand so he could see the coin. "I found this." There was something dark red smeared across the face of the guy on the reverse side of the queen.

"Is that blood?" He took it out of my palm and held it up to the light.

It didn't seem like additional light would really help much, but he held it there for several seconds.

"That's not good," he said. "If it is blood."

"I know."

He stood and placed it on the windowsill. "Take your shower."

Standing under the hot running water, salt washing off my skin, sand trickling out of my hair, the blood on the coin faded to the back of my mind. I could not stop thinking about the Barbie head. Seeing a head by itself, no matter how plastic, is disturbing. The mind is automatically uncomfortable when the body isn't attached. I suppose we're programmed to see the entire body as one piece and it goes against some primal instinct when the parts are separated. I shivered and turned the knob to add more hot water.

I'd never had a Barbie doll when I was a kid. My mother wasn't big on dolls in general, but she was especially opposed to Barbie. Their career outfits didn't matter. In my mother's eyes, that made the superficiality worse. The disproportionate, idealized body — long slim legs, narrow waist and hips, larger than average breasts, big eyes, flawless skin, and that hair. All that hair. In the sixties I guess some Barbies had short hair, but not now. It's impossibly thick, hip-length, and silky. My mother didn't want me focusing on my appearance. She was all about what's inside, and not just my thoughts and feelings and how I treated people and the earth, but also what I put inside — what food I ate and books I read and TV shows I watched (only a few).

I don't have any memories of longing to own a Barbie, although when we went to the toy store, she did have to drag me away from that aisle. When I was about eight or nine, nearing the end of the Barbie-desiring age, I pointed out that Barbie might be a good role model. It would help me play-act whether I wanted to be an astronaut or a business-woman or a physician. My mother laughed.

"Not really. The doll is still all about appearances."

"Why?"

"The outfit defines her profession. You can't just dress up in a laminated suit and helmet and suddenly be an astronaut. You need to dedicate yourself to studying math."

Even as a child, I thought she was being a little extreme, but I wasn't really that interested. It was more to see if I could get her to look at it differently — I could not. There was always a certain appeal to Barbie. All those tiny shoes — high heels and cute little tennis shoes — perfectly fitted clothes, and, of course, all that glossy hair.

I squirted shampoo into my hand and worked it into my own hair. I love my hair, love the unusual color even though it comes with easily burned skin, and I love having it long. It reaches to the center of my back and it's fun to braid or twist into a bun.

I tipped my head back and let the water run over my scalp. The shampoo streamed out on its own for a bit before I helped it along with my hands.

As if the shampoo sliding down the strands of hair was cleansing my brain, an idea formed at the back of my head. Elizabeth's ghost told me it *fit* because that's what she thought about Lavender — an empty shell. The doll head had to be about Lavender. Elizabeth took everything out of the house to mess with Luke's mind, but she left the doll head with the ring buried in the mud to tell him he picked the wrong woman.

THE BARBIE HEAD was still in the kitchen drawer where Luke had put it the day before. When JD pulled open the drawer, the head rolled and thumped against the back. He went to the fridge, removed two apples from a plastic bag, and put the coin inside. He reached into the drawer and picked up the head by the ends of the hair. The mud had dried, making the hair stiff. He dropped it into the bag. As he was tying the top into a knot, Lavender appeared at the screen door.

"What are you doing?"

"We're taking this doll head we found to the police," I said.

"You should check with Luke." She opened the door and stepped inside. She wore a bikini that was more strings than patches of fabric. A fake tattoo was plastered across her belly — a skull and crossbones.

JD suppressed a little smile, but it didn't make me jealous because it was more of a smirk than a look of pleasure. "Luke has nothing to say about it."

"You're betraying your brother?"

"No. My brother didn't kill her, but he's lazy. He thinks dragging his feet about giving this to them means he won't have to answer more questions."

She reached out her hand. "I can take it for you. I know where the station is."

"Madison found it, we should take it."

Lavender kept her arm extended, her fingers so close to JD they almost touched his shirt. She lowered her arm for a moment and then reached forward, brushing her hand across the bag. "Let me see it."

"Nice tattoo," I said.

"It's not real."

I smiled.

She laughed. "Oh, you knew that. I'm trying it out, to see what kind I want to get."

"More of that bad girl-ness?" I said.

JD glanced at me.

Lavender tipped her head down and gave me one of the coyest smiles I'd ever seen. If she was trying to transform herself into that quintessential bad girl, the smile was the wrong choice. "Whatever works."

"Does it work? What happens when you turn back into yourself?"

"This is me. Just a different side of me." She cocked one hip to the left and stroked her fingers across her belly.

"You knew about the doll head."

Lavender looked down at her tattoo. "The doll head?"

"With the ring inside."

"I don't know what you're talking about."

"Yes, you do. When we said we were taking it to the police, you said we should ask Luke."

"He told me about it."

"Is that why you went through my suitcase?"

Her eyes bulged out and her lips were partially opened. I could tell she wanted to lie but hadn't thought far enough ahead in her lies to make them all line up. One or two lies are fairly easy, but fitting together a complex network of made up information can get tricky. There were her lies about seeing ghosts and her lie about why she was in our room. Her lie about smoking, fabricated in her effort to get closer to me. All that puffing and coughing, not actually inhaling, not being able to aim her ashes inside the beer bottle. She'd never smoked a cigarette in her life. And the biggest lie of all, which she hadn't yet told — that she didn't stab Elizabeth.

The thing that had been pressing inside my brain made sense, more sense than someone killing Elizabeth to get Luke in trouble. But who shows up at her boyfriend's house with a large knife? And there certainly weren't any knives in Luke's kitchen.

But she was beyond upset that Luke was so intrigued with Elizabeth's flamboyant revenge. For whatever reason, Lavender felt she didn't have all of him, and Elizabeth was getting in the way.

"Where's Luke?" JD said.

"He went for a walk." Lavender grinned, clearly relieved to have the conversation shift away from her slip-ups. She flattened her palm across her belly, covering most of the tattoo. Only the knob of one of the bones was visible.

JD reached for my hand. I put my hand in his and we walked around Lavender. He opened the door for me. "If he comes back, tell him where we went."

"Can I go with you?"

"Why?" he said.

"I'm scared to stay here alone. The ghost."

"I don't think you'll run into her," I said.

"How do you know?"

"She only appears in the room where we're sleeping. It's where she found the ring, where he laughed at her for thinking he loved her. So stay out of that room, you'll be fine."

On the drive to the police station, which we found by asking directions at the meat pie shop, I told JD about the lies, that I was almost positive she'd murdered Elizabeth. He wondered if Luke knew and was covering for her, but I thought he was right the first time — Luke didn't want to be bothered, he just wanted it to all go away so he could get back to whatever it is he does.

WHEN WE RETURNED from the police station, Lavender was sitting in one of the wicker chairs, still in her bikini, drinking beer. Part of the fake tattoo was missing. Even though the porch was in shadows, she wore sunglasses with lenses so dark they were almost black.

"Where's Luke?" JD said.

"He's taking a nap."

Her nose sounded clogged. She took a sip of beer and coughed.

"Good idea." JD kissed my ear. "I bet you're exhausted, surfer girl."

"Not really."

"Okay. Well I'm going to lay down for a few and when Luke wakes up we can figure out dinner."

He went into the house. The screen door clattered against the frame.

I pulled my cigarettes out of my purse and lit one. I didn't offer one to Lavender and she didn't ask.

"What did they say?" she whispered.

"Are you crying?"

She took a long swallow of beer. "What did the police say?"

"Nothing. They gave us snarly looks and complained because we touched the coin and the doll head, and didn't turn in the head the day we found it."

"A coin?"

"I found a coin under our bed. It looked like it might have blood on it."

"What did you tell them?"

"I told them where I found it, and where I found the head."

"Did you mention the ghost?"

"No. Detectives don't react well to that sort of information."

"I don't understand why the ghost appeared to you and not me."

"Because you expected her to haunt you?"

"I'm the one who took Luke away from her. I tried to get

in touch with her."

"Is that why you took the bloody coin into our room? Went through my suitcase looking for the doll head? You think talismans will entice ghosts to make themselves known?"

"Is that what you told them?"

I took a slow drag on my cigarette.

Lavender held the beer bottle in front of her belly and peeled off a strip of the label.

"What happened to your tattoo?"

Her nose reddened and a tear rolled down from behind her sunglasses. She wiped it away. Another followed. She lifted her glasses away from her face and wiped at her eyes, then pushed them back to the bridge of her nose. "Luke laughed at it."

That didn't surprise me.

"I think he's going to break up with me."

"Why?"

"It's what he does, right?"

I didn't want to agree, but I didn't want to be fake and reassure her. It was pretty clear Luke was hedging his bets with her, maybe hedging his bets with life in general.

"You think that too, don't you?"

"I don't know what he's going to do. He's a complicated guy."

She laughed. "I have no idea what he wants. I thought he was really into me, breaking it off with her so he could be with me. When she stole all his things he was so pissed. He kept talking about it, but the more he talked, the more I could tell he was impressed with how bold she was."

I took another drag on my cigarette and reached over the side of the porch to knock off the ashes.

Lavender started crying. "I'm a disappointment to everyone. My mother thought I would have all these amazing powers or whatever, I don't even know what she expected. But I'm just ordinary."

"No one is ordinary."

"It's very gracious of you to say so, but you can afford to because you're so interesting."

"I'm just myself."

"My mother thinks I'm dim. She told me I should become friends with you, that maybe you'd help me get in touch with my supernatural gifts, if I have any. I think she really doesn't believe I do." She leaned forward and set her beer bottle on the floor. She hugged her legs and sobbed. Her hair spilled across her shoulders and down over her the sides of her face. "Luke doesn't love me. He loves her, and she's dead!"

"I don't think he loves her. He might admire what she did, but that's not the same thing."

"Tell me about the ghost." She sat up and pushed her hair away from her face.

I stepped off the porch and extinguished my cigarette in the gravel. Lavender held out her empty beer bottle and I dropped the butt inside.

"JD told you about it."

"Not much. Just that it was cold. That she said she wanted Luke. But she didn't say anything else? Didn't let on who killed her?"

"No."

"I assume she's going to keep haunting the place until she gets what she wants."

"Most likely."

She picked at her tattoo and peeled off another piece at the top of the skull. She dropped the torn bits on the floor and started working on another section.

"Why are you hanging around if you think he's planning to break up with you? Maybe you should just end it."

"I'd never do that."

"The police are going to figure out you killed her, and then it'll be over anyway."

She continued picking at the tattoo. "Why would you think I killed her? If her ghost didn't let on. Or did you lie about that?"

"You're the liar, not me. You don't smoke and you've never seen a ghost. You thought you'd find the doll head in my suitcase, that you'd set up some little ritual with the coin stained with her blood. Luke told you he only felt her presence in the master bedroom. You were worried she'd point her finger at you if I saw her again."

She picked at the tattoo. She'd removed most of it. Her belly was red and slightly inflamed.

"All that stuff about chakras was just wishful thinking," I said. "The only thing you know about chakras is the location, so you knew right where to put that knife in her body."

"I didn't."

"She was in the yard, cutting open the doll head to put the ring inside. You took the knife and stabbed her. I can't figure out why you left the doll head."

"I didn't know it was there."

"She'd already buried it and you grabbed the knife. Or maybe she tried to kill you and you fought over it."

"So you aren't really that smart after all, you just keep guessing until you trip over the right thing."

"I never said I was smart."

"You act like it. All standoffish, better than everyone else. You have no idea how it is to feel ordinary, dull, just trying to be a nice person, and then have your boyfriend get all revved up over some other girl because she had balls." Lavender stood, shouting. "That's what he said, she had *balls*. And he got this stupid grin on his face when he said it. But then he found her body and now it's worse! He can't stop talking about her."

"So killing her didn't do you any good."

"It wasn't my fault. She attacked me with that huge knife. It was dark and she came rushing at me, I had no idea why she'd be in his yard with that knife unless it was to kill me. Or him."

"Then why didn't you call the police? Why didn't you tell Luke?"

"He wouldn't have believed me."

I NEED TO meet some new women. That was Luke's reaction to Lavender's arrest, more or less his parting comment before he hugged us good-bye at the airport.

"Maybe you need to get your head on straight, before you hook up with any more thieves or murderers," JD said.

"My head's on just fine. I don't need to spend my life talking to some dude about my childhood, or joining a group where everyone goes on about how weak they are."

JD put his arm around my waist. "Just a suggestion."

"Coming from you, suggestions sound like directives. You could start a religion. People would follow you without even looking back."

"Isn't that getting old?"

Luke laughed. He jabbed his elbow into JD's ribs. "I'll never quit." He took a step back and looked at me. "How did you know Lavender never saw a ghost or communicated with the dead?"

"Just a feeling I got because she was so angry at people who thought they could see ghosts, because she wanted my help but at the same time acted like I didn't know what I was talking about. She kept implying she had, but was never really specific," I said.

"Somehow Elizabeth knew she was kind of empty."

Hearing him say that made me feel sad for Lavender. She tried so hard not to be ordinary. Too hard. "Are you going to stay in that house?"

"Are you kidding? Knowing she's coming for me? I'm thinking of moving to Melbourne. Maybe I should come back to the US, I need half a planet between me and her."

"They say all the people in dreams are really yourself," JD said.

Luke shoved his hands in his pockets. "What?"

"You have more of a cult following than I ever will, bro. Women rob you blind. They kill for you."

Luke laughed.

"Think about it," JD said. He let go of my waist and looped the other strap of his backpack over his shoulder. "We need to get to security. Thanks for ... a ... for a ..."

"For a very interesting visit," I said.

JD put his arm back around my waist.

Luke grinned, "You'll love the reef. And the whole island thing. See ya." He turned and sauntered toward the escalator, as easily as he'd sauntered away from Lavender.

THE FLIGHT TO Hamilton Island was less than two hours. I slept through most of it, but JD woke me so I could see the island as we descended. It looked exactly like a tropical island should — dark green, full of palm trees and dense clusters of plants, edged with strips of white sand dissolving into pale blue water. It was hard to believe there was enough room for an airport.

When we walked out the door of the plane we were bathed

by warm air that smelled damp and sweet.

Except for the van that took us to our condo, the only vehicles on the island were golf carts. Our condo was a beautiful place with floor to ceiling doors that opened completely so that the side facing the water could be wall-less if you wanted. It had dark wood floors and comfy leather sofas and a king-sized bed. There were wood lounge chairs on the upper deck. Both decks looked out over the water at another island. The decks were deep enough that you could keep the doors open when it rained, which it did. A lot. There was a nice kitchen with an espresso machine, and a gas grill on the lower deck.

ON TUESDAY WE went to the Great Barrier Reef.

The day was cloudy but warm. After they fitted us with flippers and handed out stinger suits that had mittens and hoods to protect us from the deadly box jellyfish, we boarded the boat with about thirty other people. JD and I sat in the cabin area while we heard all the info about the trip out, the reef, the lunch they'd be serving, how to operate the toilets, and all the safety details. They sort of assumed we knew how to snorkel, which I thought was kind of strange since we were going out into the middle of the ocean. I suppose you wouldn't sign up for a trip unless you had some experience — it would be too terrifying. Later, they did question us about our swimming ability and medical condition. They weren't real excited to find out both of us were light smokers.

When the guides were done talking, JD and I went to the upper deck so we could get the full view of the water and the surrounding islands. After about an hour, every piece of land disappeared from view and there was nothing but gray blue ocean — swelling, moving water in every direction. The earth is so huge and we're such tiny specks. It's so easy to forget that, racing around in our cars and walking in and out of buildings. In some ways, we've shrunk the world to what we can manage. I felt like my whole head opened up with all that water and sky as far as we could see in any direction. We were nearly invisible on a tiny strip of endless ocean. For over an hour, we saw nothing but water as the boat zipped out into a spot that only the skipper with his nautical charts and instruments would be able to locate. I kept turning my head, looking in every direction, wishing I had eyes on all sides, unblinking eyes, hoping desperately to see a whale or a porpoise, but I never did.

After two hours, the boat slowed and eventually came to a full stop. Looking over the side, nothing was visible but the surface of the water. We climbed into our suits. We made our way to the back of the boat where we were told to spit in our masks and smear saliva around the lens which is apparently the guaranteed way to keep the mask from fogging up. We stuffed our feet into our flippers and one by one, jumped off the back of the boat. Once we were in the water, everyone looked the same — knobby black heads, alien-looking masks, and a bright colored foam noodle to help us float.

There's nothing like the silence of having your face in the water, your breath loud in your ears as it goes in and out of the plastic tube, staring at creatures swimming past who act like they don't notice you, until you move too close and they dart away.

Swimming off on your own wasn't allowed. If anyone meandered away, the guides chased after you like cattle herders and roped you back in. The swells were huge, pulling us like driftwood so that we had to swim hard to keep in line with the guide. It was easy to lose track of how far I'd moved until I paused to tread water and look around for the boat, bobbing with the undulating waves, frail and incapable of fighting the endless sea.

The coral reef was far below, covering the floor of the ocean like an entirely separate planet. As I stared down at the reef, its own landscape with canyons and anemones and varieties of coral, moving myself with an awkward half dog paddle, half frog-like propulsion, time dissolved. I was nothing but a body wrapped in spandex and rubber, aware of water holding me up, aware of JD's body next to me, of our minds prickling inside our heads, taking it all in. Along with a sudden intense connection with my breath, moving in and out, filling my lungs, I felt my pulse throbbing, reminding me it was constantly working, blood racing through my body. The water wasn't hot or cold, just comfy inside that suit.

I saw quite a few starfish, larger than my head, as blue as opals.

JD took my hand and pulled me a few feet to the side and pointed. A huge clam, the size of a suitcase, was nestled in the coral carpet. The shell had scalloped edges just like I'd seen in pictures of giant clams. It was so big and so familiar, but so unlike anything I'd seen in real life. I floated there studying it, wanting to burn it into my memory, one part of my brain amazed that a simple clam could consume every fiber of my attention another part just taking it in. I saw several more and each one was equally fascinating, a creature I wanted to remember forever.

Although time had faded to nothing, when the guide signaled us to return to the boat, I felt like I'd been in the water for less than ten minutes. Once we climbed back onto the boat, I realized I was starving. They told us we'd been out there for almost an hour.

We ate pasta salad and sliced turkey and salami with rolls and mustard, green salad and a casserole with shredded chicken. The food was plain, but something about all that water and damp air and floating out there miles from other human life, made both of us scarf down a plump sandwich and two helpings of pasta salad and the casserole, sipping from a huge bottle of water between bites.

There were two more chances to snorkel. On our last trip out, I saw three sea turtles the size of my coffee table. They looked right back at me as if they wondered what I was doing there, why I was staring at them. I felt like they wanted to swim along with us but I blinked and they darted off into the depths of the sea. My throat tightened and my eyes filled with tears, thinking that I was so lucky I got to see the Great Barrier Reef, something a lot of people never see in their lifetime.

During the ride back, we stayed on the upper deck again. The waves were huge and this time the boat bounced around a lot more, rising up on the swells then slamming down the other side. We gripped the railing and braced our feet hard to keep from falling. We couldn't stop grinning at each other. The spray soaked our hair and clothes, but the muggy air kept us warm.

Staring at the endless expanse of sea without any land or other boats made me think how much of human existence is petty compared to the hugeness of the world. Suddenly aware of my smallness and how insignificant things can get magnified inside my head, I decided I wouldn't tell JD that I felt betrayed when he talked to Luke and Lavender about our experience with the ghost or gave them an overview of my personality. It wasn't just the pettiness factor, I was still sorting it out in my mind why it bothered me. Everything he'd said about me had been true and absolutely flattering. And it wasn't as if we'd had some kind of definite agreement about the ghost. She haunted Luke's house, so he sort of had a right to know that he wasn't the only one who felt something unusual in that bedroom. But the reef and the endless ocean made it all seem less important.

I let my gaze relax over all that water and put it out of my head, for the time being.

WE DID EVERYTHING during those nine days — swam in each of the pools, slept late, stuffed ourselves with seafood and pasta and unusual meals like scallops with squid ink dribbled across the plate. JD barbecued steak three times. There wasn't any place to surf, but I spent enough time splashing in the waves, I hoped it would keep my body remembering the feeling so I could pick up where I left off when spring came around to the northern hemisphere. We rented a kayak at one of the beaches and spent several hours paddling around, hardly talking, just feeling the moist air and the rhythm of paddling. The water was so calm, it was more like a lake. We saw quite a few colorful fish zip past the kayak. We visited a wildlife preserve where we saw a crocodile eat breakfast and petted a lot of kangaroos and koalas.

On our last morning, I got up and made coffee like I'd done every day. I carried our cups out to the table on the deck. Our body clocks had synched with each other, so I knew JD would be awake any minute. As I sipped my coffee, a cockatoo swept down and sat on the rail. It tilted its head, staring at me. After a few minutes, it flew away in a loud rush. I looked behind me and saw JD standing in the doorway. He had the last few slices of bread in his hand. He broke them up and lined the pieces up on the table for the cockatoos as we'd done each morning. In fact, the cockatoos had eaten more of the bread than we had.

He sat next to me and picked up his cup. He took a sip. "You make excellent coffee."

"You say that every time."

He put his hand on my leg. "I was thinking."

I sipped my coffee and smiled at the cockatoo. He clacked across the table like he wanted some coffee with his bread, eyeing me with each step.

"What do you think about moving in together?" JD said.

I put down my cup, maybe a bit too hard, because the bird leaped away and hopped up on the railing. It turned and glared at me.

"You don't like that idea?" he said.

"It surprised me."

"You haven't thought about it?"

"Your job is in Half Moon Bay, mine's in Silicon Valley. How would that work?"

"People commute. Sometimes they change jobs."

I really wanted to think about the ocean and the gorgeous white birds watching me drink my coffee. "What made you bring that up now?"

"I was thinking about it after we saw the ghost that night. How you take care of me."

"Oh." I wasn't sure what to think. Shouldn't there be something about love, or looking at life the same way, or some other common ground?

"I guess you haven't thought about it."

We were silent for several minutes, maybe longer.

"I love you," JD said.

I looked at him. "I …" My voice sounded weak and I realized I'd been holding my breath.

"We can talk about it when we get home." He picked up his coffee and stood. "Do you want a refill?"

I handed him my cup. I wasn't sure if his feelings were hurt, or if it was no big deal and he just threw it out there and talking about it now or at home or in six months was all the same thing to him. Sometimes he's hard to read.

I guess I do have a secret … maybe more than one. I don't know who I am yet. And I don't really know what love is.

THE END

About The Author

Cathryn Grant is the author of Suburban Noir novels, ghost story novellas, and short fiction. Her writing has been described as "making the mundane menacing".

Cathryn's fiction has appeared in Alfred Hitchcock and Ellery Queen Mystery Magazines, and anthologized in The Best of Every Day Fiction. Her short story, "I Was Young Once" received an honorable mention in the 2007 Zoetrope All-story Short Fiction contest.

When she's not writing, Cathryn reads, and plays very high handicap golf. She lives in Northern California with her husband and two cats. Visit her website at CathrynGrant.com or sign up for her new book mailing list at CathrynGrant.com/contact.

www.ingramcontent.com/pod-product-compliance
Lightning Source LLC
Chambersburg PA
CBHW021117260626
47169CB00005B/1316